THE PRICELESS COLLECTION

Pearls & PERSUASION

A ROMANCE

by
ANGELITA GILL

Pearls & Persuasion

Copyright © by Angelita Gill

Cover Art by Kellie Dennis at Book Cover by Design

This is a work of fiction. Names, characters, places, events, or businesses are either the product of the author's imagination or used for fictitious purposes. Any resemblance to actual persons living or dead, actual events or locales is purely coincidental. All rights reserved. This book or any portion thereof may not be reproduced or used in any manner whatsoever without express written permission of the author.

To Daddy, my first hero

I love you

Pearls & PERSUASION

1

"DON'T DO THIS," Neil murmured.

In a tuxedo and on his cell phone, outside the extravagantly decorated tent, he paced back and forth on the manicured lawn. He heard the wedding coordinator frantically searching for him as he remained hidden behind the white silk curtains blowing in the evening breeze.

"Neil, it's time," said Stewart Iverson on the other line. "We can't hang on any longer. She'd understand."

"The bakery was everything to Juliet. Selling it..."

"Feels wrong?" A sigh. "On that I won't argue with you, but it's hard running the place on our own. We're too old to take care of it, and the young lady who wants to buy it is offering a more than fair price. She doesn't want to change the name, and she promised to keep Juliet's picture on the wall."

Neil's chest tightened with despair. He shouldn't have picked up, but whenever Mr. Iverson called, it was important, because he never did unless it had to do with *her*.

Jaw clenched, he closed his eyes, squelching the sadness. Of course he understood why they were doing it, but knowing Juliet's dream would be in the hands of a stranger shook something inside him. "Stewart. I can't talk now. Just don't—allow any other attorney to handle this," he requested softly.

"Of course not. We'll be in touch."

He hung up, tucked his phone in his pocket, and ran a hand through his hair. Stepping back inside, he nearly collided with Vaughn, the wedding coordinator, who grabbed him with a gasp of relief.

"Mr. Caenon! Where have you been? Well, it's irrelevant. Ready for your best man speech?"

Neil compartmentalized the melancholy emotions. There would be plenty of time to process the disheartening news Stewart just gave him, but not now. Not at Logan's wedding. "I was born ready," he grinned.

Vaughn rolled her eyes with a smile. "Yes, yes. Off you go."

He tucked a hand in his pocket and walked up to stand beside Logan and Jordana's table. As usual, they were smiling into each other's eyes, oblivious to everyone staring at them. It was clear on Logan's face and subtle nuzzling on Jordana's cheek that he was very ready for the honeymoon, which would start tonight at the estate before they flew to some private island tomorrow.

He looked from one to the other. "I'm about to go on. You guys nervous?"

"Not at all," Jordana smiled.

Logan, however, raised a brow, setting his arm behind her chair. "No comment."

Neil winked at them.

"And now for the best man. Neil, come on out!" the master of ceremonies announced.

Striding to the front and center of the dance floor, he accepted the microphone with a grin while four-hundred guests cheered and clapped. "Thank you, thank you. For those of you who don't know who I am…well, I feel sorry for you."

Laughter sprinkled throughout the crowd.

Smiling while the pain drifted to the back of his mind, he continued. "My name is Neil Caenon and I have been friends with Logan for almost twenty years. I've been with him through good times. So many good times. Like all those weekends on the lake with nothing but a radio and some rope. And the bad." He pointed at Logan. "Remember the time we were in Mexico on spring break, got a little too drunk, and you broke your right arm? When you came out the hospital, they'd put a cast on your left?" With the guests chuckling and Logan shaking his head with a smile, Neil mocked him, "What? I wasn't supposed to tell that one?! Too late now. Okay ladies and gentleman, I'd like to share a few things you folks might not know about the bride and groom…"

His best man speech had all the right elements: humor, anecdotes, but eventually it was time to get heartfelt. Something he rarely ever did.

As the chuckling died down, he cleared his throat, switching to a more sober tone. "I find it amusing they call me the best man, when it's Logan who deserves that title more than anyone. He's more than deserving of what he's found. I knew the first day he met Jordana he would never be the same. In a good way, of course. As my grandmother used to declare, 'Love must simply have its way.' Jordana, are you writing this down? *Great* quote." He heard the bride laugh at the inside joke, as correcting someone's quote at a party was how she and Logan met.

He looked at the groom. "I'm pretty sure you know how lucky you are to have found the love of a lifetime, and Jordana, you've got more than a husband sitting next to you. You have the best man *I* know. I want to thank you for giving Logan something he's wanted all his life. Your love." An awe swept through the room, and lifting his champagne glass, he smiled. "To Logan and Jordana!"

He took a small sip of champagne while the guests continued to clap and woot.

Now for a real drink while the servers went round and retrieved everyone's dinner plates.

After seizing a gin and tonic, he ventured back to the table, but before he could sit down, the bride interceded to bring him in a hug. "That speech was lovely. Neil, you outdid yourself."

He chuckled, kissed her cheek and whispered in her ear, "I Googled the whole thing."

She lightly slapped his arm. "You can't be serious for one minute, can you?"

He took her hand, set his glass on the table, and brought her to the dance floor. "Life is serious enough. Dance with me before someone else steals you away." The woman was a vision in her lace wedding dress, but it had nothing to do with the gown. She shone from within. Love gave her that. He wondered if he'd ever given a woman such a glow, but he was sure he hadn't. Squeals of ecstasy? Sighs of satisfaction? Yes, he'd given those. That was good enough for him.

"Are you having a good time?" she asked as they began dancing.

"Of course. One of the best weddings I've been to."

"You may be a little biased."

"Big time biased." He grinned and moved her into a turn.

"I've barely been able to talk to you since the rehearsal dinner. Why don't you have a date? I thought for sure you'd bring…oh, forgive me, what is the name of the curator you are seeing?"

"Brenda. We ended that weeks ago. In any case, I don't bring dates to weddings. Much more fun not to."

"I always found the opposite was true!" she laughed. "What happened? Logan never said a word about you two splitting up."

"You should know by now he stopped keeping track of my sex life years ago. Brenda and I just had our fill of each other, that's all."

"I see."

He studied her hazel eyes, seeing the disappointment. "Were you expecting a different outcome again? I told you I'm a lost cause, Jordana. Sweet of you to hope I'll find committed bliss like Logan has with you, but you know that isn't for me. I find bliss all the time. For about three to six weeks."

She laughed. "I can't help it. I love you like a brother and I want you to be happy."

"Jordana, look at me." She did, and he waited a couple seconds before asking, "Do I look unhappy?"

"Never. You weirdo." He laughed, and she shook her head, exclaiming, "You're a corporate lawyer. It doesn't make any sense that you're so light and carefree all the time."

"Not *all* the time. At the office, I'm the opposite of carefree. But I like the challenge of balancing my hard work and my easy personal life. It keeps me on my toes."

"Ever think *one* day your toes will settle down?"

"No way. I'm having too much fun." Time to drop this subject. "By the way, are you enjoying yourself or is this whole wedding circus more than you planned on?"

"More than I planned on. I can barely catch my breath! But it's been fun at the same time. I knew I was asking for trouble when I let Deidre help with the wedding. It's more extravagant than I would have ever put together. I practically had to promise her an organ to lower the guest list to *four* hundred."

"I don't envy you your new mother-in-law. She'll be a handful."

"She's just one woman. I'll handle ten of her to keep Logan."

Neil chuckled, and hugged his best friend's wife. Logan didn't know how lucky he was. Well, maybe he did know. Looking up, Neil saw his friend staring at Jordana. *The sap.* "When you get back from your honeymoon, there's something I want to talk to you about."

Jordana pulled back. "What is it? Tell me now."

"Wipe the worry from your pretty face. It's nothing dramatic." Seeing she wouldn't let up until he at least clued her in, he paused, desperate to get it off his chest. "The Iversons have decided to sell Juliet's bakery."

She softly gasped, squeezing his upper arms in sympathy. "Neil…oh no. When did you find out?"

"Right before my speech."

"I can't say I'm totally shocked," she admitted with a shrug. "Her parents are in their sixties, aren't they? You knew it was a matter of time before they passed the torch."

"I did know, but selling it feels like there will be nothing left of Juliet except a headstone."

"She's alive in those who remember her, Neil."

He softly smiled. "I know. All right. We can talk about this later. Besides, your husband is on his way. It's pathetic how he's unable to leave your side for more than sixty seconds," he muttered teasingly under his breath.

"You know you can always call me to talk about this. Let me know how it goes."

"I will. I'll be handling the legalities of the sale."

"Of course you will. How could they possibly go to someone else?" She smiled.

He kissed her cheek, then rolled his eyes and groaned in exaggeration as Logan came up behind her. "Just because you married him doesn't mean he's your *slave*, Jordana," he joked loud enough for Logan to hear.

Jordana giggled, knew his intent, and winked at him.

His best friend slid his arms around her waist possessively, grinning like a fool. "When I see that look on Neil's face, I know he's up to something."

"Me? You've got the wrong guy. I'm a saint among you sinners."

The couple laughed, and as per usual once they embraced, seemed to forget everyone else was there. While Logan took Jordana to the middle of the dance floor, Neil grabbed his drink then ventured around, surveying the crowd. An interesting mix. From Logan's uppity finance colleagues to his mother's closest thespian friends to Jordana's deluge of gorgeous gal pals.

Never thought he'd see the day Logan Savant lost in love, slow dancing under white, canopied fabrics, and antique, silver chandeliers. Deidre had spared no expense for the wedding. With Logan's money that is. Considering what she'd done to Jordana and Logan last year, Neil was surprised when Logan told him Deidre had taken on a whole new attitude and supported his relationship. And once Logan asked Jordana to marry him, well, Deidre wasted no time. She seized the opportunity to once again put herself in the spotlight by throwing this decadent wedding at a luxury estate in Napa.

Speaking of Logan's mother, if Neil didn't know any better, he would've sworn today was her big day, not his best friend's. The former soap actress wore some sparkling, heavily skirted gown with sequins on the bodice and sleeves, looking more ready for the red carpet than representing the modest mother-of-the-groom.

"She is *shameless*," drawled Casey, the bride's best guy friend, coming up beside Neil.

Neil sent the graphic designer a half-smile. "You read my mind."

Casey patted his tux. "Where's the chloroform when you need it?"

"I don't think Jordana or Logan care she's trying to steal the show." He nodded at the couple on the dance floor. "But if you need back up, come find me."

The slim 20-something laughed and slapped him on the back. "Thanks. Take a pic with me? I want to make my ex jealous."

"Now who's shameless?"

Casey mocked a look of affront. "It's revenge, Neil. He cheated on me with some flake who works at Hollister. Broke my heart."

"In that case, should I hold you close or gaze into your eyes for the photo?"

Casey grinned, taking out his cell phone. "Ha! I can see why you have so many admirers." He snapped his fingers and called, "Lucee! Come here. Take our picture. I'm sick of selfies."

Jordana's sister came scampering over with a smile. "Case, I so know what you're doing." She met Neil's eyes. "You do know he's just using your handsome face for petty revenge don't you?"

"I'm aware," Neil drawled, slinging his arm around Casey's neck. "People use me all the time."

"Your husband is next, Lucee," Casey announced with a cock of his head and a smile.

She snapped a couple photos then tossed the phone back. "Go for it. If you can find him among all those actors. I didn't even know Jordana or Logan knew that many people in the industry."

"They don't," Neil and Casey responded in sardonic unison.

Lucee laughed. "So glad Adam and I eloped. Anyway, someone dance with me! I love this song."

"I got 'ya, beautiful," Casey said, crooking his arm.

Last week when Neil and Logan met for lunch, his friend highly recommended Neil go to a justice of the peace if he ever got engaged, and remarked that planning a wedding was one of the most stressful endeavors he ever had to participate in. Of course, his friend had said it all with a smile. The man would do anything for his wife and it showed.

Good thing he himself never planned to cross the marriage line, no matter how happy he was to see others do it. So many things in life were necessary: oxygen, shelter, food, clothing, and above all, sex. A piece of paper that legally sealed and bound one to another just wasn't one of them. He regarded himself lucky. Not because he'd never been married, but that he'd never felt the need for someone to complete his life or give him purpose. His job did that in some ways, caring for his mom and sisters did it in other ways, and pleasure…oh above all pleasure gave him all kinds of purpose.

And like a magnet drawing his gaze, he fixated his stare on one woman: Ashtyn Turner. Logan's treasured executive assistant.

He'd danced with virtually every willing woman on the guest list except her. Even from this distance, she was absolutely stunning.

It'd taken considerable effort not to stare at her when she emerged in her bridesmaid's dress to take wedding photos, striking his desire like a blast from a shotgun.

He was so used to seeing her in her prim business attire, glasses, and hair back in some kind of trendy braid or bun. Tonight, she astounded him in her silver floor-length gown, with an open back, her blonde hair loose with the glasses left behind. She captivated a man in any light, any wardrobe, but shone like an angel tonight.

And tonight, just this once, like the devil *he* was, he'd demand a dance with her.

This was the first event he'd seen her without her husband Cliff.

But now, he thought as he smoothed the lapels of his jacket, there was no husband. They split up months ago. She was a private woman, and hadn't spoken one hard word about her ex. He was a big deal in architecture—with a big-ass mouth—and had made it clear his marriage was over. The guy wasn't a gentleman by Neil's standard. Though intelligent, he had no class. He also had no Ashtyn, and therefore Neil was free to flirt with her. As if anything ever stopped him before.

His heart pounded as he drew near.

The young man trying to flirt with her now was either ignoring her deflective body language, or didn't know when to give up. An actor. Tyler... something. One of the bride's sister's friends, and way out of his league.

Coming up behind him, he caught Ashtyn's gaze over the guy's shoulder, and she gave him a clear signal to interrupt.

The actor kept talking. "So the benefits of colon hydrotherapy really helped me lose a few pounds, if you know what I mean. Good for the skin too. Yeah, I try to go to the gym at least six days a week, lifting weights mostly..." he trailed off, looking over as Neil approached, who was trying not laugh out loud at the kid's expense.

Neil raised his eyebrows in feigned interest. "Great story. Keep going."

"Uh, hey. It's the best man!" Tyler cleared his throat. "Neil, right? You workout too, don't you?"

Out of the corner of his eye, Neil saw Ashtyn press her lips together to stifle a giggle. He tucked his hands in his pockets. "Sure. I play a lot of basketball."

"Which gym?"

"At the Y actually."

"Why the hell would you play basketball there? Aren't you a lawyer for some big time firm? Can't you afford a serious gym?"

He checked his ire. "The kids I coach can't afford a so-called serious gym. I've been a member of the Y for almost a decade. To be honest, I think the kind of gym you're referring to isn't nearly as fun to be a member of. A lot of douchebags running around, you know?"

Tyler started nodding, then blinked with a shake of his head, as if he wasn't sure whether Neil had just insulted him.

Oh, he definitely meant to.

Forgetting the punk, he turned to Ashtyn, who was bright red with the need to laugh. "You promised me a dance, remember?"

She quickly sobered. "I don't remember that."

He flashed her his best smile and grasped her hand. "That's okay. I do."

The zing up his arm shot straight to his chest, down to his groin. Her hand was small in his, fingers slim and soft. What would they feel like running up his torso as he rocked inside her? How hot would it be if she slid her palms over his face and into his hair while she moaned?

So caught up in his fantasy, he almost didn't notice she'd dropped his hand like a hot poker. He stopped and turned around. "Problem?"

As though crossing the line to the dance floor would be the point of no return, she stood at the edge. "Thanks for the rescue Caenon, but no thanks for a dance."

"Why not? Afraid I might move you the *right* way?" he teased.

Her look was reproachful. "Do you ever stop?"

"No." He smiled. "I can go all night."

She heaved a sigh. "You're wasting your juvenile innuendo on me. Why don't you go expend your charm on the pretty guests Jordana invited? Or one of the other two dozen women you've dance with tonight?"

So she'd paid attention, had she? Interesting. A blush revealed on her cheeks and she flinched with a look of regret, as if she knew what she'd just admitted. *Well, well.* "All I want is a dance, Ashtyn. You might even like it. Three minutes. Tops."

"No," she replied.

The lady needs more convincing, does she? "Look it's not a big deal. We're at a wedding. We'll sway side-to-side for a song and call it a day. Unless..." he mused, "you don't want to because then everyone will know I've finally won you over?"

"You can't *win* me. I'm not a carnival prize."

"Come on. I've gone around the floor with every woman in the room, as you put it. Everyone will assume I'm just going down the list. You can continue to throw eye daggers at me the whole time if you like, so no one will suspect you enjoy it." He leaned in. "You know, standing here arguing with me about it is attracting more attention than us dancing will."

Her eyes darted left, then right. "Fine," she relented.

He pulled her to him. A slow, romantic song started to play on cue. Most of the guests had their eyes and camera phones on the bride and groom anyway.

Neil brought her in, but not close, and as they started to move, his pulse thrummed, blood raced in his veins. Holding Ashtyn proved to be a new kind of contact high. Her sweet perfume drifted to his nose. Roses and jasmine. He'd never gotten this close to her before; it was heaven. Her soft hand in his, her scent drugging him. Maybe this was a mistake…

"You play basketball with a bunch of kids?"

Good. She'd initiated some conversation. Something to talk about. Something to distract him. "When I can. I'm a volunteer coach. Been doing it for six years."

"Is this a voluntary activity or court appointed?"

"Very funny." He was too fascinated with the curve of her hip, how it sloped and how his hand formed perfectly around it. If only he could guide his hands over every curve and line of her body, get to know it. A woman's feminine lines were nothing short of art in Neil's eyes, and Ashtyn's was no exception.

"This is such a beautiful wedding," she remarked in a quiet tone. "I'm very happy for Savant. Jordana is perfect for him."

"If there is such a thing," he said, coming in a little closer, catching the scent of her shampoo. A little fruity, but clean. A few wisps of her hair brushed his cheek.

"Still a cynic after that wonderful speech?" she asked.

"I meant every word, but I still don't believe everyone wins the love lottery like they did."

"I *know* everyone doesn't." She paused and moved back to meet his gaze. "You know my divorce is final, don't you? It's hardly a secret."

"Even so, it's nobody else's business except yours. And I'm sorry you had to go through it."

"That's what everyone says," she murmured in a weary tone. "They're sorry to hear I got a divorce."

"I didn't say I was sorry about that," he countered. Because, truly, he was ecstatic. "Just for all you had to go through to get it done."

She blinked. "Oh."

Maybe he shouldn't have said that. Clearing his throat, he decided to keep the convo light. "Did you get a good lawyer, by the way?"

"Alice Wickham. Logan referred me to her."

"Good call. She's one of the best."

"I think she anticipated more of a challenge. I didn't fight him for anything. Just my share of the house when we sell it. All I wanted was a clean break. A new place, a new life."

What had happened between Cliff and Ashtyn? Did he fight for this lovely woman, or did he just let her go? Was he abusive or unfaithful? All these questions and more popped up in his head, but he didn't dare ask. The only time he ever saw her ex and her together was at the occasional Savant Financial Group sponsored parties and the Christmas gala the Mallorys threw every year. By all appearances, they seemed like the standard, discontented couple. Especially in the last two years, the strain between them was obvious, at least to his keen observation. It pained him to see Ashtyn shackled to a man who treated her more like arm candy than a wife.

Cliff wasn't affectionate or doting, but that could've been because he was too busy kissing ass to notice his wife had a perfect ass of her own for him to kiss. He could also be annoying with his brash opinions, but Neil never tagged him as a bad guy. Guess he was wrong. "You should celebrate your newly single status. Don't they do divorce parties in Vegas?"

She let out a huff. "Hard to celebrate the death of a marriage. Even a bad one. It's been over for a while, though. The paperwork was just a formality."

That long, that bad, huh? A knot formed in his stomach at the acrimony in her voice, but then again, did divorced people ever sound otherwise? "Ashtyn, I know I'm not your favorite person in the world, and the last one you would want to talk to, but if you need anything, you can call me. Anytime."

She looked in his eyes, held them. No doubt she never expected him to utter a sincere offer, and didn't really take it seriously. She didn't of course, shifting her gaze away. "You know what I really need? A bat and a car I can take my frustration out on. Preferably one that looks just like Cliff's."

He chuckled. "That can be arranged."

"Can it?"

"Sure. Anything you want."

"That's a dangerous thing to say to a woman who's vulnerable."

Knowing he was pushing the limits, he brushed his mouth lightly over her ear. "You shouldn't admit vulnerability out loud. Certain men will take advantage of it."

She lifted her mouth to his ear, a smile in her voice. "Admitting vulnerability is not the same as admitting stupidity."

He chuckled. Damn, he liked her. "True."

"Are you one of those *certain* men?"

"I try not to be," he smiled. "Sometimes women are very good at disguising vulnerability, and it isn't apparent until after the fact. Then we men get accused of taking advantage of you when we had no idea you were susceptible to our seduction more than usual. We simply conclude our charms won you over and you just couldn't help yourselves. We're not as cunning as you think."

"Very perceptive. So you're the victim?"

"Victim is a bit of a stretch, but like I said, sometimes."

"I'm assuming when you say 'after the fact' you actually mean after the sex?"

"What else would I be referring to?"

She drew back with a raised brow. "From what I can tell, women have a hard time resisting you. Vulnerable or not."

He gave a one-shoulder shrug. "I've had my share of rejection, like any man. All lessons to be learned of what women like and what they don't." And what did Ashtyn Turner like in a man? Humor? If so, then he'd won her over years ago. Confidence? Again, he had that down. What exactly did she favor? Maybe she just liked jerks. Some women were into those. That was one thing he couldn't do, treat a woman badly. His father had taught him better.

She gave a sensual little shimmy, rotating her shoulders and locking her arms to keep him at a certain distance. They'd become too close for her comfort apparently. But it felt too good, too right, to let her widen the proximity. In what was no doubt a bold move, he slid his hand from her hip to her lower back, forcing intimacy, aligning their torsos together.

"What are you doing?" she asked in an almost accusatory way.

"You seem a little stiff. We're slow dancing, not square dancing."

After a few seconds, she gave in, and allowed their bodies to mesh. "Sorry. It's been a while since I've danced like this."

What a shame, because she was a perfect partner. At least for him. With her height and heels, they were nearly eye-to-eye, and the way they conformed together had him imagining pushing her up against the wall, cupping her knee, and molding his body between her thighs… Damn. Shouldn't think of such things with her hips so close to his. He'd get hard; she'd get mad. "Now you can do it as much as you want with whoever you want." She shot her eyes to his, and he realized his unintended double entendre. "Dance, that is. What did you think I meant?"

"Two minutes with you and my mind is already in the gutter."

"I have that effect on people."

"And you're proud of it, aren't you?"

He answered with a knowing half-smile.

She searched his eyes, finally saying, "You always have a fast response. As if you know what people want to hear or what they're going to say. How do you do that?"

They were on their second song. He couldn't believe she'd let him hold her this long. "Easy. As soon as I meet someone, I read them. You do it. We all do it. Intuitiveness is everything, and in my opinion, body language is the least difficult linguistic to interpret. I learned how to translate it to my benefit. And the eyes always give themselves away." As he looked into hers, he discovered that wasn't always true. Some eyes simply held a man captive.

"Can you read me?" she asked.

He knew she was going to ask that, and searched those blue depths, before traveling to her mouth and back. He lowered the volume of his voice, asking with a sensual, "Are you sure you want me to?"

Her little intake of breath proved he had some sort of sexual effect on her. "Why not? I'm curious how good you are. Don't," she stopped him before he could make a joke of that statement, "twist that. But I mean it. No filter, Caenon. I want an honest evaluation."

Okay…he could do that. Or could he? Actually, he thought staring at her, he still couldn't read her as easily as others, and realizing this frustrated him. She didn't have to know that, though. As an attempt to dodge her request, he said, "I have an unfair lead. I've known you for a long time so my assessment won't be very enlightening."

"You really don't *know* me at all."

So often, he wished he did. In fact, this was the most they'd ever spoken at once. Except for the time he looked up some legal information for her last fall. "You're right, I only know what you tell me, and what I see."

With a small lift of her chin, she asked, "And what do you see?"

As they slowly turned to the music, eyes holding, bodies aligned, he wondered just how candid he should be, if he should reveal his true thoughts and observations about her. Of course some opinions he would have to keep to himself, but he had to give her something, or else she'd never let it go.

"Your beauty is both a burden and a blessing in the finance world. You're militant at work so no one can accuse you of being Logan's right hand because of your sex appeal. However, you take your appearance seriously and play up your best features rather than hide them with dowdy clothing like most women in your field. Everyday chitchat bores you. Although you're happy for Logan and Jordana, you're treating the wedding like one of his meetings. You're too concerned with appearances. Too worried you'll get tipsy and show a different side, which is understandable. I've always sensed you're very self-aware. Enough to know you're a catch, and that divorce isn't the end of your world, just the end of the world as you knew it. You're going to be okay. And I don't think you're as bitter about it as you assume you should be. Nobody will ever know how you really feel.

You hold your emotions close and tight because…" he trailed off, realizing he was rambling. "Well, I don't know why. You're not like most women, Ashtyn." Damn. That last one slipped out.

Her lips parted. She blinked. "Wow. What else?"

He'd already said too much, and if he had her in his arms any longer, he might say something stupid.

An announcement was made for the bride and groom to cut the cake, and he took that as a sign. While guests moved around them to gather around Logan and Jordana, Neil broke from her. "I think we've danced long enough, don't you?"

She ignored his question and insisted, "What else were you going to say?"

"Does it matter?"

"I really want to know, yes."

He tucked a hand in his pocket, her willingness to talk to him more emboldening him to ask, "What are your plans after the reception?"

Instant wariness darkened her eyes. "No plans. Unless there's some secret after-party I don't know about?"

"If there was one, I'd be the host. But my duties as best man are over. I was…" He hesitated suggesting, because he already knew her answer. "I was going to invite you to come to my room. We can finish our conversation there without any interruptions." He'd meant for it to come out in a casual, off-hand manner, but of course she didn't hear it that way.

Her eyes widened, mouth dropped. "Are you kidding?"

He relaxed his stance. "I know what you're thinking—"

"There's no way I'm falling for that, Caenon. Just because we had a moment and danced for a minute doesn't mean I'm going to jump into bed with you."

He laughed, amused by her candor. "Who said anything about a bed?"

She dropped her chin. "It was completely implied."

"Or maybe when you think of me and you in a room, a bed automatically comes to mind." It certainly did for him. By the aghast look on her face, he regretted his facetious remark. "I'm joking. My invitation is entirely innocent."

She assessed him with a slow perusal. The picture of skepticism. "Really?"

"Yes. Too many consequences for one night of passion." *That's all I need with her.* One night of kissing that mouth, exploring her body, seeing what turned her on, what made her moan, and what—if anything—made her come undone. Then he wouldn't crave her anymore. He never craved after he'd gotten what he wanted.

As if she could read the turn his thoughts had taken, she slightly frowned. Whatever chance she might've actually come to his room blew away.

Camera flashes and oohs and ahhs sounded behind them while Logan and Jordana performed the tradition.

"What do you say, Ashtyn?" he asked after a moment. "Do you think we can be friends?"

"I have plenty of friends."

"So do I, but why set a limit? Besides, you know you don't have any friends like me." The way she was looking at him though told him she was actually thinking about it. That sliver of hope was all he needed. "Think about it. I'll be waiting in my room with a bottle ready to go."

Their rooms were almost across from one another's—he'd learned earlier when they checked in—so she knew where to find him. "Thanks for the dance. I'm going to get some cake." He strolled past her. He sensed her eyes on his back and hoped, more than he'd hoped for anything in a long time, she'd come to him.

I'M NOT GOING to Neil's room.

While he went one way to watch the cake cutting, Ashtyn went the other.

Did he honestly think there was a chance she'd take him up on that?

Dancing with him had proven so many things she'd imagined over the past four years. That he moved as smoothed as he spoke, that he smelled as good as he looked, and that he was as dangerous up close as he was from a safe distance.

Now she was all shook up and exposed, and she'd asked for it. This time last year, she would've never agreed to a dance. She would've used Cliff as an excuse and insisted it was inappropriate, but said excuse was now an ex-husband.

The divorce was final three months ago, and her new existence still felt surreal. Even though she and Cliff's marriage had emotionally and physically been over for years, it wasn't until the papers were signed, the assets were divided, and the house in the upscale neighborhood was listed for sale did it really hit her. That chapter in her life was closed. Permanently.

And at the same time a huge chapter opened for her boss.

When Logan had subtly hinted Jordana had been overwhelmed with wedding planning, Ashtyn didn't hesitate to offer assistance. She knew how controlling Deidre would be and seized a chance to stay busy outside of work. The bride had asked her a million times if she was sure she wanted to help, knowing Ashtyn had been in the middle of the divorce, but Ashtyn welcomed the distraction with open arms.

Her marriage ended, but that didn't mean she begrudged matrimonial bliss for anyone else.

Weaving between bodies surrounding the couple feeding each other cake, she smiled, watching as Jordana threw her head back and laughed, her fingers covered in icing. Her handsome husband swept her in for a long, loving kiss, and Jordana practically melted into him. It was almost enough to make Ashtyn believe in true love again. Almost, she thought sardonically, taking a plate of cake from a server. She dipped her middle finger in the icing and licked off the sugary confection.

She turned around, and gulped the frosting.

Neil had his gaze fixed on her from across the way.

A thrill raced down her spine, but she pulled her gaze away in a manner that should've told him she wasn't affected, though her heart pounding and the goosebumps on her arms proved otherwise.

"Ashtyn," Jordana called her over once the cutting of the cake had finished.

Ashtyn set down her plate and walked over, seeing the distress in the bride's eyes.

Grasping her hands, Jordana breathed, "Where's my veil?"

Ashtyn gave a single nod. That was their secret phrase that Jordana needed a break. "Excuse us everyone!" She pulled Jordana outside, behind the band, giving the wedding coordinator a nonverbal message they needed five minutes. It was quickly understood.

Jordana took a deep breath of the night air and smiled. "Thank you. I just need a couple minutes. I'm not used to all this. I don't know half of those people in there, but they're all talking to me at once. Some of them even wanted me to mention business to Logan. On our wedding day!"

Ashtyn shook her head and rested a hand on Jordana's shoulder. "Well, you're handling it all with amazing poise."

"I am? Looks like I'm fooling you, too." She giggled, then took Ashtyn's hand in hers. "How are you doing? Really?"

Ashtyn cocked her head, wondering where this was coming from. Wasn't she pulling off the happy bridesmaid flawlessly? "I'm good. Why do you ask?"

"You seem—melancholy at times. I hope you're not regretting helping us plan this beast in six short months. We couldn't have maintained our sanity if it wasn't for you. Logan and I wanted to elope, but his mother practically threatened suicide, as you recall."

Yes, how could she forget Deidre Savant marching in Logan's office that day? He'd asked Jordana to marry him mere weeks after she'd moved in with him, and had—in Ashtyn's mind—mistakenly told his mother about the engagement the next day. She swept in his office with a huge planner's book, demanding a wedding made for royalty, which would take no less than a year to plan. Logan defied her and said he wanted to marry Jordana the next week. Realizing how his mother would make them suffer for the rest of their lives if they didn't meet her halfway, Logan said if she could plan a wedding in six months, she could spend what she liked to make it happen. Not one day more, he'd emphasized.

In secret, Ashtyn believed Jordana did want a real wedding with friends and family, but nothing like the extravagant occasion happening today. But, in the end, Logan got to marry the woman of his dreams, Jordana got her special day with friends, family, and unfortunately, a mass of *strangers*, and Deidre got her way. The end.

"No regret whatsoever. I'm fine. No need to worry about me." Had Ashtyn not burst into tears out of nowhere last week, Jordana would've never asked about her well-being now. They had been going through the final checklist for the reception when tears flooded to Ashtyn's eyes and refused to be denied. She wasn't even sure what triggered it. It'd been a quick sob, enough to cause Jordana alarm, but then she'd felt better.

Maybe it'd happened because for months she'd had the wedding to keep her mind occupied, off her divorce, and after the occasion was over, she'd knew she'd be back to questioning her choices, doubting her judgment, and envisioning a future that, right now, had no path. With her ex, there'd always been a path. Forcing the fear of the unknown aside, she squeezed her friend's hands to emphasize her words. "I'm not melancholy. Just…lost in my own thoughts sometimes."

Jordana didn't appear fully convinced. "I know what it's like to go to a wedding when it's the last thing you want to do. The summer after Zach and I broke up, I had to go to three, knowing my own wedding would never happen. It was agony."

"Jordana, I *had* a wedding. A marriage and a home and a husband. Just because all that is gone doesn't mean I should continually be upset."

"But you didn't lose, Ashtyn. You let go. There's a distinction."

She hugged Jordana to hide the emotions threatening to surface. "I hope you didn't bring me out here because you thought I needed cheering up. I'm having nothing but a wonderful time. End of discussion okay?"

"Okay. I just wanted to check." Jordana pulled back. "I read somewhere to never be afraid to start over. It's a new chance to re-build what you truly want."

Ashtyn liked that. If only she knew what she wanted, she'd be in great shape. "You and your utterly appropriate quotes."

"I can't help it," she laughed. "But, before I let you go, I want to ask you something." A slow smile drew on her mouth. "I saw you dancing with Neil. After all this time, has he finally charmed you into liking him?"

"He's as arrogant and rude as ever, so not really."

"Cut the man some slack, will you? Beneath that cocky veneer, he's a great guy."

"You're saying that because of how he went out of his way to get you and Logan back together."

"True," she agreed, looping her arm in Ashtyn's and guiding them back inside. "That's when my adoration started, but after spending some time with him, I've come to realize he's sincere as they come. A good friend, a good lawyer—"

"A good player."

Jordana chuckled. "Touché. But I think he has a little crush on you."

"A crush?" A hot blush flooded her cheeks. "Don't be ridiculous. The only person he has a crush on is himself. If he *does* like me," she added as Jordana chuckled, "then it's because he knows he'll never have me, which makes him try harder."

"Whether you're meaning to or not, you're making it a challenge for him, and if anyone likes that kind of challenge, it's Neil. He won't quit until you two are on friendly terms."

"We're friendly," she asserted.

"You know what I think?"

Ashtyn was afraid to ask.

"I think," Jordana continued, "From the few occasions I've witnessed it, you like this little banter you and him have going on. You like it that—no matter what you say or do—he still tries to charm you."

Ashtyn's steps faltered. Oh God, was her friend right? Was she so hungry for attention…had it been so long since any man tried to snare *her* attention, that she kept up this game with Neil to get it? If that were true, how pathetic. "I think the champagne has revived that imagination of yours."

"Hm." Jordana slid a glance with a twist of her lips, but said nothing in response. Within seconds guests, the photographer, and the wedding planner swarmed toward her.

Determined to enjoy herself from now on, Ashtyn went to find at least one person who would just dance with her without causing any internal inferno, or who would talk to her without asking questions she didn't want to answer.

Later on in her suite, Ashtyn kicked off her heels and grabbed bottled water from the mini-fridge. She'd danced with several guests in the final hour of the reception. Thankfully, none of them had her pulse racing by the time they were done. All in all, she could say she had fun, and not once did she cross paths with Neil again.

She did get asked out by one of Jordana's friends while dancing, and it'd caught her off guard, but she'd graciously declined.

She was officially single now. Starting over. How liberating and tragic. But she refused to feel sorry for herself. No one gets married anticipating a divorce. She gave her marriage a real effort and it didn't work out. What was there to feel sorry for? Except the dreams and hopes that now had no place to go, bouncing around like the random bubbles on her computer's screensaver.

"Omigod, stop it," she told herself as the tears began to burn behind her eyes.

Think about something else. Something nice.

Neil came to mind.

Ugh. Weak choice! She shouldn't think about him either. Nevertheless, now that he'd entered her thoughts, he refused to leave.

The first time she met him at Logan's office, her inner feminine alarm went off loud and wild. A strictly physical reaction because of his good looks. Dark brown hair and brows, clear green eyes, and a smile that slayed with its sinful perfection. She remembered their first introduction well, when he came over to meet Logan for lunch and it was her third day on the job. He'd waltzed in like he owned the place, then reached and shook her hand, looking her directly in the eye.

Even now she recalled the electric current that shot up her arm and the heat that steamed between her thighs. He carried himself with masculine grace and wore a suit custom-tailored to his fit body. His whole appearance and mannerisms reminded her of men in the Rat Pack era, and he pulled it off flawlessly.

The man reeked of self-confidence and sex incarnate. And the gleam in his eye showed he knew it. From that day on, she forced herself to deflect his flirtation, brush off his comments, and ignore his attempts to rile her up. It was clear he didn't need another woman adoring him; he had plenty, from the receptionist to the CFO. She could only imagine the groupies at his law firm, Raimes & Watley.

It shouldn't have felt that good to be in his arms tonight, she thought, taking off her earrings. He should've repulsed her with his unashamed swagger and stream of innuendos.

No, she *wanted* him to repulse her, but he just didn't.

She rested a hip on the French doors leading to the balcony of her room, and looked out to the gardens of the grand estate below. Even though he pushed her buttons and she pushed back, she couldn't deny she admired him in a way. At least he didn't pretend to be anyone but himself. Who knew what he was like behind closed doors, but she had a feeling he didn't put up any fronts at any time.

She, on the other hand, couldn't say the same. For years, she tried to be who Cliff demanded as a wife, until one day she realized the scathing voice and pinched looks were coming from her. After she filed for divorce, she put on different faces for her friends and family so they got what they expected, too. Her friends encouraged the broken Ashtyn; her parents and brother encouraged the strong and resilient one.

But Neil had seen something else.

How?

She wanted to know. Would it be so wicked to find out? Maybe his perspective was exactly what she needed. Or…maybe she sought a legit excuse to go to his room that excluded her exasperating desire to be near him again. She swallowed the rest of the water, aware her tipsiness contributed to her decision as much as her curiosity. If he offered her a drink, she'd be sure to turn it down, because even though she wasn't drunk, the last thing she needed was more alcohol in Neil's presence.

With her shoes back on, she did a quick check in the mirror, then paused. What was she doing? She flipped a hand at her reflection. Didn't matter what she looked like, right? He said he wouldn't make any moves on her, wasn't interested in her that way whatsoever.

But he hit on every other woman in his sphere, why not her? She sighed. That shouldn't bother her at all.

But, it kind of did.

Ignoring that, she opened her door, peeking her head out. She didn't want anyone to see her waiting in front of Neil Caenon's suite. Looking left, then right, she stepped out, feeling like a teenager sneaking out to meet a boy.

Suddenly, the elevator chimed and she scrambled back inside like a scared rabbit. She kept the door open a crack to make sure the coast was clear before she went out again, and heard a feminine hiccup.

The nameless young woman knocked on a door. "Neeeeil," she sang. "It's Krista. Open up, handsome."

Ashtyn straightened, eyes wide. The woman was at *Neil's* door? She stuck her head out and looked left. She recognized the young woman in the poufy skirt and high heels as one of the wedding guests, from Ashtyn's side if she remembered correctly. By the way she wobbled on her shoes and leaned on the door, it was obvious she was beyond inebriated…and apparently, invited to his room, too.

"Neil," Krista called again.

Or, maybe she wasn't invited?

The door opened and even though Ashtyn couldn't see his face, she saw Krista's expression light up at the sight of him. She flung her arms open and fell into the doorway, presumably in his arms. As soon as Ashtyn heard his deep chuckle, she closed her door, disgusted. She should've known better. He probably assumed she wouldn't come and made sure to have a Plan B.

She wasn't angry. In fact, if there was anything to be angry about it would be at herself for even opening her door. Divine intervention stopped her from going to his room. A clear sign to avoid the trap of temptation. Even though she aimed to go over there to talk, who knows what could've happened if he actually seduced her. She was so lonely, she might've succumbed to it.

Then she'd be another notch in Caenon's belt and she'd never, ever forgive herself.

THE CHAMPAGNE CHILLED in the bucket while he paced the floor. When Neil heard the knock, his heart had stopped at the thought Ashtyn had changed her mind. Hard to believe he was that keyed up for her company, especially since he promised he wouldn't hit on her. He had every intention to keep that promise, too. Might be challenging as hell, but he could do it.

And then he heard another woman's voice from behind the door and he groaned with a sliver of annoyance and ripe disappointment.

He opened the door and Krista fell into him before he could react.

She sighed dramatically. "Aww. You caught me!" Then giggled and kicked the door closed.

He chuckled in amusement, scooping her up and setting her on a chair. Although he liked to party, he didn't take advantage of a truly intoxicated woman, even if she literally threw herself on him. "How did you know this was my room, Krista?"

"One of th-the bridesmaids is nes' door. She told me." She clumsily pointed a finger to the room to his left, grinned, and pushed up off the chair.

"Well aren't you resourceful?"

She flung her arms around him. Again. "Omigod, you're so hot. You're like..." She hiccupped. "The hottest guy I ever saw." A poor attempt was made to kiss him, but he smoothly deflected it to his cheek. What if Ashtyn came over and saw this girl in his room? "Okay, okay. Let's go back to your room." He hooked an arm around her waist to keep her upright.

"My room?" she exclaimed, slinging an arm around his shoulder. "What's wrong with this one?"

"The bed's lumpy," he lied.

"Oh, mine is *super* soft."

He smiled and shook his head, opening the door. "Good. I'm going to put you right on it."

"Ha! I bet you will, handsome."

Out in the hall, they passed by Ashtyn's door, and he prayed in those seconds to the elevator she wouldn't come out and see him. If she did, however, he'd tell her the truth, that he was helping a drunk wedding guest to her room. Nothing more.

He was able to get Krista on her bed. Even though she tried to pull him down, she gave up once he pulled the covers over her, and promptly passed out. He tucked her in and set a bottled water on her bedside table before he left.

Blowing out a breath, he ran a hand through his hair and headed back. As he passed by Ashtyn's room again, he paused, tempted to tap on her door, just in case she needed a little more encouragement.

He kept walking. No. She had to make the decision on her own.

Hopeful, he returned to his suite.

Before Ashtyn came along, Logan's office was just an average workplace. His previous executive assistant had been excellent, but once she started a family, her personal life took precedence, and with Logan's demanding— sometimes after-hours schedule—she had to make a choice. To spare him the aggravating task of interviewing multiple candidates, she sent over a recent grad who she assured him had all the qualities he required, and then some.

Enter Ashtyn Turner. Logan had been skeptical, but fifteen minutes into the interview, he'd hired her, later telling Neil he did so because he trusted his former assistant's recommendation, and that he liked Ashtyn's eloquent, intelligent answers. Logan referenced her as having Grace Kelly looks with Lauren Bacall's bite.

Neil was instantly intrigued. And the first time he laid eyes on her, he'd been wildly attracted to her in every way. The only *un*attractive thing about her was her marital status.

What made her even more fascinating was her constant projection of dislike toward him, and ever since, he'd lured her in a game of verbal tennis. Something he never ceased to look forward to every time he stopped by SFG. He considered it the best part of his visits, seeing her, wondering what tongue-lashing she was going to give him the next time.

To this day, she remained the only woman unwaveringly immune to his appeal. It used to bother the hell out of him. At first, he assumed she was cold-natured. Some women had little to no sense of humor and took themselves too seriously, but then he'd see her laugh with her colleagues, and charm Logan's bloated, self-important clients and he concluded, quite to his frustration, it was only *him* she didn't like.

Ever poised and polite, she was never outright mean or harsh, but she didn't smile at him like she did others. Never called him by his first name and did not make eye contact with her lovely blue eyes unless she was making a point. Oftentimes, he'd ponder what it would take for her to soften toward him, which would inevitably lead him to imagining what she was like in bed.

Though he sensed a bit of an untamed side, he could be imagining that just to fit his own fantasies. More often than not, women with a sharp tongue were either incredibly submissive in bed, or they laid there, silent, waiting for him to finish.

Regardless, he'd never know what end of the spectrum Ashtyn Turner stood on.

An hour later, a little after midnight, he knew she had no intention of coming.

Neil scrubbed a hand over his face with a sigh. He really, really didn't want to be alone with his thoughts. Since he'd sworn off work—and he never worked unless he was stone cold sober anyway—he had nothing to distract him except the stupid TV or the Internet. Neither of which he had interest in.

With the news Stewart Iverson had delivered just hours before threatening to darken his mood further, he grabbed the champagne bottle, deciding to go for a walk and drink alone.

"MUST BE NICE to be the boss's all-time favorite."

Ashtyn ignored the snide remark from Emmy, an executive assistant to one of the company's directors, and her sort of work frenemy. On occasion, they ate lunch together or stopped somewhere near the office for happy hour. They had a few things in common, but mostly the fact they both worked at SFG for demanding bosses. Emmy had cropped red hair and amber eyes and was a dedicated vegetarian. Also, a gossip and a backstabber. Ashtyn often felt outcast from the other assistants because they assumed she was too high on the scale to associate with.

Emmy, however, eagerly gave her friendship, since she was also outcast because of her catty behavior.

Ashtyn pushed in her top drawer and locked it, withholding a sigh. "Mr. Savant will be gone for two weeks on his honeymoon and I haven't taken a vacation in years." All true. She had enough work to keep her very busy, but Logan practically ordered her to take time off. He pointed out the only days she'd requested off were for court, and that a break was overdue. She couldn't argue with him.

Emmy, on the other hand, could. Crossing her arms, she watched over Ashtyn as she packed away a few things. "Yeah, but two whole weeks of paid vacation? No one gets that around here except for the title men. And half the time they're working from the beach anyway. My boss calls me every other hour even when he's in Tahiti."

"That's probably why he's had two heart attacks in the past seven years," Ashtyn stated popping her last Mentos mint and throwing away the wrapper. "Everyone needs to unplug at some point, Emmy."

"Hmm. What are you going to do? Fly somewhere fun?"

Unfortunately, she couldn't afford to go anywhere beyond the state of California. She'd just signed a lease for a new rental house, and spent a small fortune on the security deposit and first and last month's rent. Her checking account whined with the huge debit. Not to mention her attorney's fees she was desperately trying to whittle down. "No exotic vacation this time. My only plan is to unwind and relax." *And try to get a life going again.* "Maybe catch a movie. Go to the farmer's market. All those things I miss out on because I'm working."

Emmy made an obnoxious snoring noise. "You're so vanilla. I'd think being single again you could come up with something better than that. If I were you, I'd get a bikini and head to So Cal for the beach. But that's me."

She gave her a wry look. "You hate the sun."

"That's what umbrellas are for, dummy." Emmy cackled to cover her childish insult.

Done with her tidying, Ashtyn grabbed her purse. "Right. Well, I'll see you when I get back."

"Have fun. Don't consume too many calories while you're slacking off." She smiled frostily and elegantly crossed her arms. "You won't catch a new husband with new cellulite."

Ashtyn would rather catch a cold than a husband. She headed to the elevators, saying good-bye to a few people along the way before giving the receptionist the updated schedule. Honestly, she loved her job, but she was happy to leave it behind for a couple weeks.

True, she wouldn't be going anywhere tropical, but she *was* getting away. The timing of Logan's honeymoon couldn't be more perfect because her friends Lila and Mike had a house for Ashtyn to use at her leisure.

They lived in the small town of Briar's Edge, ninety minutes northeast of San Francisco. In the summer they went to England to be with Mike's family. For extra money, they rented it out to tourists to keep the place habited in their long term absence, with a housekeeper and a repair person nearby for cleaning and maintenance. Their place was the ideal getaway: a spacious four-bedroom, with a large back deck and a fire pit. Quiet, remote, and far enough away from home but not too far to break the bank. They had beach cruisers to ride around town with and a lemon tree to pluck from.

All she had to do was stop by her place and pick up her bags.

Lila called just as Ashtyn pulled up to her new, much smaller home. The sounds and commotion of SFO International could be heard in the background, as they were about to board the first leg of their trip to New York for a layover before jetting off to London.

"The house is ready when you are," Lila told her with a smile in her voice. "I had our housekeeper stock the fridge and pantry with some food so you don't have to worry about shopping."

Bless her friends. They'd been vital during the last, well, year of hell. "You didn't have to go through that trouble! I planned to go to the market tomorrow."

"Now you won't have to," Lila said cheerfully. "Besides, I know your idea of stocking up is a case of Coke Zero, tortilla chips, and frozen chicken tenders. Bonnie bought you a bunch of veggies, fruits, seafood and snacks for you to choose from, including your beloved grape soda. So if you don't cook yourself a decent meal it'll all go to waste."

"Oh I'm going to miss you Lila," she laughed.

"Back at you. We're so happy the house won't be sitting empty too long. It's not booked for guests until July and I hate leaving it vacant for more than a week at a time." Two years ago, their neighbor's home was broken into and so her friends preferred to keep the house filled with people more often than not. "Are you sure you're going be okay out there by yourself?"

"I can't imagine a better place than yours right now," Ashtyn told her friend earnestly. "Don't worry about me. I'm used to being alone these days." Ugh. That sounded utterly like bitterness.

Lila sighed. "I wish we could've stayed in town a little longer and helped you with your move."

"I'm fine," she assured her as she'd done with everybody. "Besides, that's what moving men are for. You guys enjoy your summer in the UK. You and I will get together for our usual spa retreat in September."

"Looking forward to it already." She paused. Mike's voice called in the background that they were boarding. "Oh, sorry hun, I gotta go. Uh, let's see. Bonnie said she would leave the key under the mat on the back deck. Mike put together some instructions on the kitchen table on how to get the TV going, what the Wi-Fi password is, and a few important numbers, but call me if you have any problems."

Ashtyn had plenty of problems; housesitting wouldn't be one of them. "Unless there's an emergency, I won't bug you."

"I can rest so much easier knowing you'll be there," Lila said. "Mike says thank you, too. I know Briar's Edge isn't a hot spot, but get out and explore, don't stay in the house all day and night. You might even find a stud at the bar and want to bring him home. Feel free to hump his brains out in any room. We've had at least three honeymooner couples there so I know the house has hosted its share of sexual mambo."

"Lila!"

She laughed. "Make yourself at home!"

After hanging up, Ashtyn finished packing a few small items. Her place didn't feel like home yet. Other than a new bed she just had delivered, a kitchen table, an old loveseat out of storage, she had no furnishings. They were still at the house she and Cliff used to share and she couldn't pick them up until Cliff got his things first. He grudgingly promised he'd be done by Sunday, and she would pick up her half on Monday. The agreement had been that she'd be completely moved out by June and the property put up for sale by July.

In the beginning of their divorce, she fought for the house on Jasmine Hill, and he fought back. They'd only been there a few years, but she couldn't let it go. Cliff wanted to sell it and split the profit, but she hated that idea initially. She'd put so much money, sweat, and definitely cried many tears in it, so she stood her ground, but her ex refused to yield, as usual.

In the end, exhausted, going broke and going nowhere in mediation, she gave up. Thinking about it now, she was glad she did. Why live in the home of a broken marriage? It would've been very expensive to maintain with only her income and even though she made a great salary, it would've been a burden. And every day she walked in, she'd remember all the bad times; the arguments, the pain, the gut-wrenching tension that hung in the air night after night, even when they stopped sleeping in the same room.

Emotion aside, it was the practical decision. Their neighborhood was popular, the house would sell eventually, and she could use the money—needed the money so she could rebuild her savings. She and Cliff were both on the deed and she'd used the inheritance from her grandmother to cover the down payment. But all she'd get out of the monumental investment was the furniture, kitchen ware, a few decorative pieces, and some money. Better than nothing.

She loaded her car and headed out of town, ready for a little R&R.

By the time she passed by the Briar's Edge welcome sign, population two-thousand, it was past nine pm, much later than she would've liked due to notorious California traffic. As she cruised through the dark downtown area at twenty miles-per-hour, she smiled at the picturesque buildings. All closed. A barber shop, a florist, a beauty salon, the local bank. Not even the gas station was open.

She still had to go a few miles out of town to get to Mike and Lila's. Because it was a little remote, there were no streetlights and she had to rely on her memory and headlights to watch for their mailbox. She slowly drove past the houses until, on her right, she saw 7196 Holcomb Way, and turned right. The driveway abutted a rocky hill and rounded to the left, giving the house a tucked-in feel, far from the noise of the street. Not that there was any noise other than buzzing insects to be concerned about.

She parked and walked around the back. Smelling the freshly cut grass, she smiled at the serenity and peace around her, couldn't wait to snuggle in a blanket and look at the stars.

Going up the back deck steps, a motion light came on. Tomorrow she'd take advantage of the hammock and start her summer reading.

She pulled up the mat for the spare key, but it wasn't there. Frowning, she checked under a potted plant and around the general area. No key. Did the housekeeper forget? Knowing the door would be locked, she tested it anyway, but no such luck.

Now what? She went around to the front door and searched for the key there as well, only to be disappointed again.

Perfect.

She didn't have Bonnie's phone number or else she'd call her. Her options at that point were to either sleep in her car or head to the local motel and call Lila in the morning. Neither choice appealed to her, but there wasn't much she could do.

Except maybe try a window before she completely gave up.

With all the windows surrounding the house, the chances one of them was open were good. It was worth a shot. The front windows proved to be locked up tight, so were the ones along the family and dining room. Still hopeful, she returned to the back deck and yanked on a couple more with the same result. Just when she was about to call it a night, she noticed the kitchen window cracked.

Elated, she pushed up on her tip toes and used the heel of her hand to see if it was truly unlocked. It moved another inch and she squealed in delight, but the window was too high for her to climb in without assistance. She grabbed one of the patio chairs and set it underneath the window. Able to reach it much better, she used all her strength to push it up. Problem solved. Except now she had to maneuver her body through the opening and crawl over the sink. Whatever. Little consequence to finally get inside.

She wriggled her head and shoulders in, her stomach digging in the sill. With her feet dangling outside, and her searching for purchase inside, she almost didn't register the booming voice coming from somewhere behind her.

"Hey!" shouted a very male, authoritative tone.

She froze.

"Get down. Right *now*," he commanded, coming closer. "This is the sheriff."

The sheriff?! "Er...uh...okay." She squeezed her eyes shut. Really? Could this really be happening? Her butt hanging out the window of a friend's home and getting caught by the law? Once her right foot touched the chair, she was able to squiggle her way out and ease down. Using one hand on the chair to keep her balance, she raised the other in surrender while the man marched toward her, gun drawn.

The blood drained from her face and her eyes widened. "I'm unarmed!"

Looking to be in his fifties, beefy, with a red beard, he glared at her. "You alone?" He glanced from the house to the yard below. "Anyone else, Jake?"

"No sir," said a voice from below.

"It's just me," she shakily told him.

He trained his gaze back on her. "Stay right there." Much to her relief, he tucked the pistol back in its holster, but then pulled out a pair of handcuffs.

Oh God, she was going to be sick. "Are you arresting me? No. This is a serious misunderstanding. I'm housesitting you see—"

"You're breaking and entering a property that doesn't belong to you. At the very least, you're trespassing."

She was shocked and insulted, but couldn't blame him for not taking her on her word. How did he even know she was here? She wanted to scream. And since when did burglars wear Michael Kors wedges when they broke in? Never, she was sure. "The Pratts live here. They just left for London and I'm here to housesit for a couple weeks."

"Sure, sure. We'll hear it all at the station. Hands behind your back."

She complied, even though she wanted to stomp her foot and cross her arms in rebellion. *This can't be happening. Wake up, wake up.* "There's no need for that. I haven't done anything wrong. They told me they'd leave the key under the mat but it's not there."

He grunted as he moved behind her and held her wrists, breathing heavily from his climb up the steps. To give him credit, he didn't handle her roughly, simply locked on the metal cuffs and took her arm to guide her down the stairs. "Now I'm sure you're being honest, but I have to verify. It's my job."

A blondish man in his thirties, also in a beige uniform, appeared from by the garage. He had the kind of all-American man good looks that disarmed a woman instantly. He raised a brow. "She's the perp?"

"Yep," said the sheriff, name tag said Ames. "She looks harmless, but they all do these days. This way, miss."

Once the deputy, nametag said J. Thornton, opened the backseat door, she carefully, but reluctantly, situated herself on the hard seat. She lifted her lashes with a look she hoped would convey her innocence.

He gave her a sympathetic smile. "Don't worry. It's not as scary as you think."

"Going to jail isn't scary? Speak for yourself."

He chuckled, made sure her feet were inside, then gently closed the door.

Her mind reeled with her current circumstances while the sheriff drove off through the empty streets to the town jail on the edge of downtown, only a few minutes from the house. No wonder they were there so fast.

Her mind racing with what to do next, she barely heard the sheriff mumbling something to her as they walked in. It looked more like an insurance office than an actual jail: gray file cabinets, two metal desks, typewriters, a water cooler, and in the back a large cage where they kept their lawbreakers. Thornton guided her to it, uncuffed her, and she took a seat on the wooden bench.

"The Pratts are friends of yours, you say?"

Rubbing her left wrist, she nodded. "I've known Lila for over ten years."

Sheriff Ames plopped down in his chair, which creaked under his weight. Squinting, he held up her license. "Ashtyn Turner. From San Francisco. Hmm. What do ya do for a livin' Ms. Turner?"

"I'm an assistant to the CEO for SFG. Er, Savant Financial Group," she told him, hoping a legit occupation would somehow put her in a favorable light. It was probably futile. The small town sheriff likely wouldn't have heard of the company.

He mused over that slice of information. "Well, can't exactly confirm employment this time of night. Except to see if you've got a warrant." He slid her a suspicious glare as if to ask "do you"?

She sighed and shook her head.

"Happen to know the Pratt's phone number?" he asked.

"Yes! I know Lila's cell phone at least." She relayed the number, but knew reaching Lila before tomorrow wouldn't happen.

"All right, I'll call her. You two might not be as good of friends as you say. Just relax, Ms. Turner. I'm going to find out." Seconds later, as predicted, he left a gruff message and dropped the receiver on the ancient phone. "Straight to voice mail. 'Fraid you're going to have to stay here until we can straighten this out."

"That could be into tomorrow! They're on flight to New York right now."

"Get comfortable then. Until someone can vouch for you, I gotta hold you. You understand." With a grunt, he pushed up from his chair and grabbed a pack of cigarettes on his desk, then trudged outside.

She slumped her shoulders and turned to plop down on the hard, worn bench behind her.

Thornton watched her, mouth twisting. "Are you cold?"

She nodded, holding her clammy arms. He walked over to a small locker, pulled out a leather jacket and handed it to her from between the bars.

"One of your criminals left this behind?" she asked, unable to check the frustration from her tone.

"It's mine."

"Oh. Thank you." Chagrined, she raised her gaze to his. "You believe me, don't you, Officer Thornton?" she asked, needing at least one person on her side in the room.

"Call me Jake. Don't worry, it'll all get cleared up. It's easy to see you're not the average burglar, we just have to play it by the book. Especially since the neighbors called. They'll want to know exactly who you are."

She slipped on the oversized leather jacket, thankful for it. "They called?"

He nodded. "They reported a suspicious car driving around the neighborhood too slow. Then said they saw someone prowling around the Pratt's place."

"I couldn't see anything! I was driving slow so I could find the house." She scrunched her nose. Who were these nosy neighbors anyway? *Oh wait. Probably the ones who got burglarized. That's why they were paying attention.* Couldn't blame them either for being alert. She couldn't blame anything but stupid old bad luck. "And I wasn't prowling," she grumbled. If only Mike and Lila were able to be reached right now, she wouldn't be in this mess.

"Is there anything I could do to speed up this process?" she asked him.

"Do you have someone else you can call? If you're charged, and I'm not saying you will be," he was quick to add at the fright in her eyes, "then a friend could bail you out."

She chewed on her bottom lip, thinking.

A friend. There were only a few numbers she knew by heart. Her ex's, who'd probably ignore her call, her cousin, who lived in Georgia, and her mother in Lake Tahoe. But she couldn't call her mother. She would only emphasize now more than ever Ashtyn needed to see a therapist, that she wasn't acting like herself, and would needlessly worry her daughter was headed down a criminal path. In fact, the more she thought about it, Ashtyn didn't want anyone in her inner circle to know about tonight's events. Her friends wouldn't judge her actions—they'd probably have a good laugh—but she didn't want anyone to know she'd been arrested, or bother any of them this late on a Friday night. As humorous as it was, she'd still gotten in trouble with the law.

The law. A lawyer.

She squeezed her eyes shut, disbelieving the first person that had popped in her mind.

Neil.

Hunching over, she pressed fingers to her temple. Really? Was that the best she could do? She couldn't call *him*. That smug attorney would laugh out loud about how Logan's executive assistant ended up in jail. Even if he agreed to help her out, he'd dangle this secret over her head for weeks, months, even years to come. Regardless, she *did* have his mobile number memorized; she'd dialed it so many times for Logan and her photographic memory would never forget it.

No. Think of someone, anyone, else.

"Hungry?" Jake walked in the cell and set down a pint of milk and an apple.

"Thanks." Her stomach roiled as she reached for the fruit. She recalled what Caenon had said at the wedding, the sincerity behind the words, the rarity of a serious tone.

I know I'm the last person you'd ask for help, but if you need anything, you can call me. Anytime.

Putting up with his inevitable teasing would be far better than calling her mom or spending one more needless minute in this holding cell. In essence, his mockery would be a small price to pay.

She brought her knees to her chest to warm her freezing legs. Even though it was Neil, he could be the answer to her little legal predicament. Or at least give her some advice. She had a feeling he wouldn't judge her or give her any lectures about being sensible. He wasn't high-handed or self-righteous. That just wasn't his way. To think of all he'd done to help Logan and Jordana proved he could be trusted, and was, if anything, a true friend. Even if he hung this over her head, she could take it. She'd dealt with a lot worse.

"Can I make a phone call?" she asked.

Jake pointed to the landline on the wall. "It'll have to be collect. Go ahead."

As she picked up the heavy black receiver of the jail landline, the dial tone hummed loud in her ear. Slowly, she punched in the numbers of

Caenon's personal cell phone number. It was almost ten o'clock, what were the chances he'd pick up? He was probably out and about in the city. It was Friday night after all. Half-hoping he wouldn't answer, half-dreading he would ignore the call, she followed the instructions, recorded her name with a cringe, and waited as the phone rang. And rang. And rang. Then, the recorded voice said she was now being connected.

A cry of relief caught in her throat.

He'd accepted her collect call.

Heart pounding, she nearly hung up when Caenon's unmistakably smooth yet questioning tone came through to her ear. "Ashtyn. My God, are you okay?" Instead of him joking about her circumstance right off the bat with sarcasm, he surprised her with this soft greeting.

The concern in his tone broke through her tightly wound strength and tugged at her heart. Her words broke as she grasped the phone with her other hand. "Yes, I'm okay. Actually, no, I'm not okay." She cleared her throat. "I'm in jail in Briar's Edge." Obviously he already knew that.

"And you called me," he drew out.

"I don't know what to do! I've never been arrested before and it's awful. Could you give me some advice? I'll pay whatever you charge. You're the only attorney I know other than my divorce attorney and I feel weird calling her about this. Unless you want to give me her number—"

"Of course I'll help you. Ashtyn for God's sake don't even mention money. I'm on my way."

"On your—you're going to come here? It's an hour and a half drive!"

"That's nothing. I'm leaving right now. What could you possibly be in there for?"

"Trespassing. Suspect in breaking and entering," she admitted in muttered shame. "It's all a misunderstanding!"

His soft chuckle should've annoyed her, but it didn't. It made her smile.

"Hang tight. I'll be there before you know it. Are they treating you okay?"

"They are. I just got a milk and an apple so I won't starve." She smiled at Jake who was pretending not to listen to her conversation.

"That sounds pretty standard. Okay, I'm getting dressed and will be on the road in six minutes."

Imagining that he probably slept naked, and might even have someone next to him in bed, she felt even guiltier. "You really don't have to come out here. Once the sheriff speaks to my friend, everything should be okay." Even though that could be hours from now.

"Regardless, I want to be there in case you need me. Never hurts to have a lawyer present."

4

SHE called *him*.

As Neil turned his car on the ramp to the highway, he still couldn't believe—out of all the people she knew—he got her phone call. He wanted to know why as much as he wanted to get to her as soon as possible.

Trespassing? Breaking and entering? No doubt that story would be nothing short of amusing.

He arrived in less than ninety minutes and pulled up to the town jailer. As soon as he walked in, he saw Ashtyn sitting in a lonely cell at the back of the room. She lifted her gaze and sprung up.

An older man ambled over to the counter. "I'm Sheriff Ames. Who are you?"

"Ms. Turner's attorney. Neil Caenon. How do you do?"

He shook his hand. "Fine. Fine. Neighbors called. We caught her at the Pratt's house climbing in a window."

"May I speak with my client privately?"

He frowned, raking Neil with his hard gaze before he grunted. "Go ahead."

Neil strode over. She wore a leather jacket three times too big; the only thing he could see were her long legs and manicured feet in summer heels. He hoped she had clothes under there. With her blonde hair up in a ponytail, and face pretty much free of makeup, she appeared a lot younger than her thirty years. More vulnerable. "Hi," he greeted in tender regard.

"Caenon." She grabbed his hand from between the bars, surprising him. "I can't thank you enough for coming all the way out here. I'm supposed to housesit for a friend while they're away…" She summarized the story, and he nodded, biting back a grin at the unfortunate series of events that got her in there. Obviously she hadn't done anything illegal and this would be a matter of someone who could corroborate her story. When she finished, she dropped his hand, as if realizing she'd held it too long. "They won't let me go until I can prove it."

"Don't worry, we'll figure this out," he told her, closing his fist to stop the tingling her touch had left behind. "Besides Mike and Lila, is there anyone else who knows you're housesitting? Anyone, that is, who's close by?"

While she thought about her answer, he became increasingly perturbed seeing her behind bars. Half-turning to the sheriff and his deputy, he clipped, "Is this really necessary? Keeping her in the cell? She clearly isn't a threat. You could've just brought her here like a human being and had her sit in a chair while the situation was managed. Does she look like your average low life?"

Sheriff Ames snickered. His chair squeaked as he leaned forward on his desk. "I used to work for the LAPD and if there's one thing I learned, it's to never underestimate the suspect. No matter how—pretty or seemingly innocent they *look*. I stopped falling for that a long time ago."

"Neil. It's okay," Ashtyn said, drawing his attention back to her. She set her hand on his shoulder.

Withholding a hard sigh, he softened his gaze. "At least you're in here by yourself."

"The housekeeper."

"What?"

"The housekeeper who takes care of the place while Mike and Lila are gone. Bonnie. She must know. Lila told me Bonnie would leave the key, so she can confirm my story."

"Perfect. Do you have her number?"

Her shoulders shifted low with a negative shake of her head.

"Know her last name?"

Another no. Undeterred, he decided this was a minor obstacle to overcome. Briar's Edge was a small town. So small, it wouldn't be a stretch at all to assume everybody knew everybody. Even if it took him all night, he was getting Ashtyn out of there. "Everything will work out. I'll be back." He walked over to the deputy. The phone rang and the sheriff picked it up, keeping an eye on Neil while he answered.

Deputy Thornton didn't seem nearly as contentious as his superior, and if Neil wasn't mistaken, also had a little attraction to Ashtyn. Not that Neil could blame him. "I'm guessing you're familiar with most folks in town?"

Thornton shrugged, hands on hips. "Sure. Ames knows everybody and their cousin, though."

Neil glanced at the older man, but hoped he wouldn't have to enlist his aid just yet. "I'm looking for a woman who the Pratts trust. Her name is Bonnie. While they're out of the country, she's their housekeeper. Know any trustworthy local ladies who clean houses? I have a feeling she doesn't live far from them."

After only a moment of musing over it, something clicked with the deputy and he snapped his fingers. "Miss B. She's only a few houses down from them. Used to run the garden center before her son took over. I wouldn't be surprised if he mowed the lawn for the Pratts while they're away too."

Neil gave a short, sharp nod. "Let's go. You can drive."

"It's almost midnight."

The last thing Neil cared about was the time of the night or a woman's restful sleep when Ashtyn was in jail for no reason. He gave Thornton a look expressing this and the man understood that Neil would go with or without him, possibly interrupting several locals' rest by knocking on every door until he found Bonnie.

Thornton grabbed his keys. "Yeah. Let's go."

Neil looked back at Ashtyn, sent her a wink, and walked out.

Thirty minutes later, they had the sassy "Miss B" in custody and were on their way back to the station. It took approximately eleven minutes for Bonnie to open the door, which Neil assumed meant she was way too old to be cleaning houses. Then Thornton told him she never answered the door—even in the middle of the night—without her hair and makeup done.

Once she emerged, he tried immediately to put her at ease with his best smile while explaining the unfortunate situation with Mike and Lila's guest. The woman threw up her hands and exclaimed how she'd be more than happy to assist. In hindsight, he could've had the housekeeper call rather than drag her out to the station, but he could just see the sheriff asserting Bonnie had to identify Ashtyn in person before he could release her.

While they rode back, she grasped her coat closed at her neck, and bumbled the entire ride about what a ninny Sheriff Ames was, blaming neither Neil nor Thornton for rousing her up at the late hour.

As soon as they came to a stop in front of the station, Bonnie bustled out of the patrol car before Neil or Thornton could, doing a fast waddle to the double doors. "Ames! You got a bird's nest for brains? I told you about the Pratt's situation!"

For the first time since he heard Ashtyn's voice over the phone, Neil started to feel at ease. While Bonnie bent over Ames's desk telling him to let the poor girl go, Neil walked toward the cell, grinning.

Ashtyn rose from her seat and looked from Neil to Bonnie, back to Neil. "Who's that?" she asked while Bonnie continued arguing with the sheriff, who was rightfully defending his actions.

"That," Neil thrust his thumb behind him, "is Bonnie. The housekeeper."

Her blue eyes widened, her expression changing completely to one of unfiltered relief. "Really? How did you find her?"

"It was surprisingly easy. I know what it's like to live in a town this size, and thank God it's small enough to make easy deductions. The deputy and I were able to find her on our first guess."

A chair scraped loudly behind them, and each looked over. The sheriff shot up and snatched his keys. "Christ on a cracker, woman! I'm not deaf! I heard you the first time. All I needed was someone to validate her story is all. Wouldn't be a good sheriff if I let people crawl into windows without question, would I?"

Bonnie shooed him Ashtyn's way. "Yes, well, she's probably frightened by our big hairy sheriff now. Good job! Now let her out." She waved wildly at Ashtyn, beaming as though she adored overriding the sheriff for perfect strangers. "Hi, dear! Lila has told me so much about you. You're prettier than your pictures! I got you goodies. You better eat them!"

Ashtyn lifted a hand. "Thank you so much, Bonnie. I owe you."

"Don't be silly." She flapped a hand. "Welcome to Briar's Edge! Now somebody give me a ride home."

Ames unlocked the cell, grumbling under his breath and shaking his head. "You're obviously free to go, Ms. Turner."

As soon as he slid open the door, she rushed out—and into Neil's arms. Whoa. Overall, this was no big deal at all. Regardless, he felt like her hero.

"Thank you," she whispered.

His heart thudded at the unexpected show of gratitude. Neil glimpsed at Thornton.

The deputy pressed his mouth in a firm line and looked away.

She pulled out of Neil's embrace and smiled, then turned her attention to Thornton. "Thank you, too. For being so kind." She took off the jacket and he took it from her with a murmur it was nothing. A flick of jealousy hit Neil. Someone was smitten.

Bonnie pulled Ashtyn in a hug with her chubby arms. "Forgive an old lady for forgetting to leave the key. I had it on my calendar you were coming tomorrow."

"It's okay," Ashtyn assured her quickly. "No harm done."

Bonnie thrust the key in her hand and closed her fingers around it. "If you need anything, I'm in the peach-colored house with the blue shutters, three doors down."

"Thank you, Bonnie."

While the sheriff and Bonnie argued their way to his car, Ashtyn and Neil walked to his.

Once they got in the car, she pulled the white scarf from her ponytail and ran her fingers through her blonde locks. They came to a four-way stop, and Neil watched her from the corner of his eye. The glow of the moonlight shone on her thighs. They looked so soft to the touch. He ached to trace his finger down her thigh and see for himself.

"Neil. It's a stop sign, not a red light."

He sharply set his gaze back to the road and hit the gas more than necessary.

"So you drove all the way out here for nothing," she said. "I should've just stuck it out instead of calling you. I'm sorry."

"Don't be. You never know how these situations can go."

She gave him directions to the house, and he already knew where he was going since he'd just been at Miss B's earlier.

"You're housesitting here for the next two weeks?" He pulled into the drive.

"More or less. I have to go back to the Bay for a few days, but then I'll be back here for about a week."

"Not a bad place to spend your time off." The picturesque house at the end of the drive looked spacious, but homey and comfortable. He envied her private getaway. "I'll walk you up. Hopefully she gave you the right key," he joked.

She groaned and climbed out, and he followed her to the back part of the house, where he saw the patio chair under a window. "Is this the scene of the crime?"

"Unfortunately yes. Imagine me, half in the window, half out, my butt in the air, with the sheriff ready to pull his gun on me. Not my finest hour," she chuckled, unlocking the door.

The thought of her ass in the air would actually be a very fine picture for him. So plump and perfect for his hands to squeeze. He checked a needful groan, tearing his gaze from her backside. It'd been too long since he got laid. Maybe he should do something about that when he got home.

SOMETHING HAD changed. The air. It seemed a little harder to breathe, even though there was more than enough space between her and Neil.

"Want some water or something?" she offered, feeling awkward as he remained in the doorway, hesitant. Amazing how the man heated the room with those eyes.

He shook his head. "No thanks. I should go. Looks like you've got everything under control. You sure you're okay? Regardless of the outcome, it's still unnerving getting arrested. Especially when you're innocent."

"Don't worry, I'm not that traumatized now. It's over." She turned and gave him a smile. "Plus as soon as you showed up, everything got better." She bit the corner of her lip, realizing what she said sounded so corny, but it was true and she wanted him to know how grateful she was.

"I knew nothing could get you down," he declared. "If you need anything, call me. I won't leave until morning."

"Morning? Where are you staying?"

"I saw a motel on my way into town."

Did he mean that run down establishment with all the broken glass in the parking lot? She flinched at the thought he'd get a room at that place because of her. "Why don't you stay here?" she asked.

He met her gaze. Did he see the uncertainty in her face? He must have, because he shook his head. "Very kind of you, but I'm good at the motel."

"Don't be ridiculous! It's the least I can do. As you can see, this house can handle the two of us. They have *three* extra rooms." She shrugged casually. Why was she nervous? Because the thought of him sleeping under the same roof as her seemed scandalous, even though it wasn't. Essentially, she was inviting pure temptation to spend the night. There wasn't another man alive as alluring as Neil Caenon. "It's up to you," she finally said. "But you're more than welcome."

"Are you sure your friends won't mind?" he asked, still giving her a way out.

If Lila saw you, she would insist on it, and probably toss me some condoms. "I'm positive. Lila is practically my sister. I can grab some of Mike's clothes if you need something to sleep in." If Neil slept in anything. She imagined a man like him, so comfortable in his own skin, would prefer to be nude in bed at all times.

He shut the door and took off his coat. "All right, I'm sold. Thanks for making this convenient. I brought an overnight bag in case it took all weekend getting you out, so no worries about rifling through Mike's clothes."

In case it took all weekend? How sweet. Why did the fact Neil had agreed to stay excite her? "I'll show you around. You can pick which room you want."

"Where are you sleeping? In the master?" he asked as he followed.

"No. Here." She tapped the door to her left then stopped to face the room directly across from it. "There's this one. And two more at the end—"

"This one is fine."

Of course he'd pick the room right across from hers. Only steps away once again, like at the estate. Except this time there'd be no horny wedding guests showing up at his door.

He turned to go in, his arm brushing hers and causing a shiver to course through her. She subconsciously rubbed her arms, watching him as he hung his jacket in the closet and started taking off his watch. Every move he made so smooth. With only a white button-down shirt and gray slacks, he was the perfect archetype of elegant, virile male.

She yanked her gaze and cleared her throat. "Towels are in the linen closet right next to the bathroom, if you want to shower." An image of him in the massive stone bathroom under the gentle spray of their rain showerhead sprung to mind. Ugh. More images of Neil naked. Seriously, what was her problem? Lack of physical contact with a man was her problem, and he was so…manly. And within reach.

"You hungry?" he asked, breaking her thoughts.

"Yes," she answered a little too enthusiastically. "You read my mind."

"Me too. I stay up late all the time so I'm used to having the fourth meal." He sent her a sexy smile, setting his watch on the dresser. "I'm guessing there's no diner or Chinese takeout open at this hour?"

"You guessed right."

"Then looks like we'll have to make something ourselves."

"Well, they certainly have the cookware to inspire a meal." Heading toward the kitchen, she vowed to keep her distance from him and stop this overreaction to his nearness. In public, it was easy to ignore her body's reaction to his, because she had a dozen things to distract her. Here? Alone with him? A different story altogether. While she strove to keep her attraction to him in check, she said, "Lila said I could help myself to anything. Looks like she's got food here for days. What are you in the mood for?"

He came up behind her, setting his hands at her waist to move her out of his way. "Nothing too complicated. Let me see."

She jerked away. "Sure. Go ahead." Her hips practically burned from the warmth his hands left.

While she made herself busy getting out some plates, he came out of the pantry with tortillas and tossed them on the counter, then he dug in the fridge and pulled out various items.

"What are you making?" she asked.

"You'll see."

"You cook?"

"When I have the time. Which isn't often. Don't you?"

"Not lately. These days it's just me, the microwave, and overpriced frozen dinners. Haven't really settled in to my new place yet. My pots and pans are still at the house." All those expensive kitchen essentials were hers, and for what? Seemed like a waste on her now. She enjoyed making meals for others, but now that it'd just be her, most of that specialty cookware would go unused. A toaster oven, coffee pot, and a pan were the only things she needed to be happy.

Maybe she should donate them to Neil, she thought wryly.

A comfortable silence settled while he prepped. Pulling out knives, a cutting board, and setting a pan on the stove, he was completely at ease in someone else's kitchen. She grabbed a magazine and took a seat on a stool. Not to read about the best five foods that promoted energy, but to watch Neil do his thing. It fascinated her, him acting domestic. Here she'd pictured a man who ate at restaurants for his breakfast, lunch, and dinner, and only used things like spatulas for foreplay.

What else about Neil would surprise her? She cocked her head, starting to smile, before she dragged her attention back to flipping the pages of the glossy magazine.

"Tell me," he said in an off-handed manner. "Why didn't you come to my room that night?"

5

Ashtyn looked up, caught off guard. Of course he had to break their relaxed atmosphere with a question guaranteed to ramp up her nerves. "You and I both know I wasn't going to."

"But *why* weren't you going to?" He started chopping the bell peppers, muscles flexing under his shirt. "I have my own assumption, but I'd like to hear it from you."

"Does it really matter at this point?"

He gave a one-shoulder shrug. "If you're afraid to tell me, then forget it."

Afraid? She straightened and crossed her arms. "You didn't invite me up there to talk, Caenon."

"That's exactly what I did. I told you I wouldn't try anything. Did you think I wouldn't be able to stop myself, Ashtyn?" He leveled his gaze on her. "You're not *that* irresistible." Then turned to wash his hands.

An urge to smile moved her lips, but she pressed them together to hide it. So he found her a *little* irresistible? "Look, I already told why I wouldn't come. Just because we had a few friendly moments didn't mean we should get *friendly* in your hotel room. Even just to talk."

He started slicing the peppers, gaze down, nimble fingers working the vegetables. "I see."

I see? Meaning? So he was going to leave her hanging with that? She waited a few seconds before probing. "You see what?"

"I see why you didn't come."

"Why didn't I?"

"You just told me," he said matter-of-factly.

"But I didn't really say anything."

"It's what you *didn't* say." He lifted his gaze for a second, cocked a half-smile, then resumed his task.

Her stomach flipped. "What didn't I say?"

"Does it matter?" he mocked her.

Oh I'm going to throttle him. Then she'd be arrested for assault, she thought. Caenon was teasing her, to get a rise out of her, and for the millionth time, she couldn't stand to let it go. "For your information, I *was* coming to your room, but when I walked out, there was someone else at your door. You apparently forgot you double-booked."

He ceasing his chopping, carefully set the knife aside, and then rested both hands on the island. "You mean to tell me you were on your way to my room when you saw Krista there first?"

"Yes. You're busted. She threw her arms around you and that was the end of that."

"You…" He closed his mouth and exhaled. "You jumped to conclusions. Nothing happened. I escorted her *out* of my room less than a minute later. And I didn't invite her over, before or after you. She found out my room number and invited herself." He picked up the knife again and resumed slicing the peppers, shaking his head.

Was it true? Why would he lie? She raised a brow. "I'm supposed to believe that?"

"Those are the facts. I walked her back to her room, went back to mine, and waited for you."

Her pulse picked up. "You did? Even though I told you I wouldn't come over?"

"I had a feeling you might change your mind. Sounds like my instincts were right." His mouth quirked.

"No. Your ego is just so gigantic you didn't want to believe a woman could turn you down," she retorted.

"If you say so."

He didn't say anything for a while and neither did she. Part of her wanted to accept his explanation, but then that would mean she'd missed out on a night with him because of her false assumptions. Well, she got a night with him now. The other more skeptical part of her mind refused to believe he stayed up and *waited* for her.

"Now that I know," he reminded her. "Why were you going to come to my room?"

Ugh. He was relentless. "If I tell you, will you drop it?"

"Yes."

She grabbed an apple and toyed with it. "You're keenly observant. You know that. But you were the first person to call me like you see me. My friends, even my parents—who I rarely see—they all look at me like I'm going to fall apart, even when they tell me I'm being strong. It's almost as if they *want* me to fall to pieces. It's exhausting. You were the first person to really get me. Which is hysterical because we barely know each other." She set down the apple. "I wanted to know how you did it."

The heat in his gaze cooled. Perhaps he thought she'd admit she wanted to come to his room for a different, more intimate reason. He arranged the tortillas on two plates, turned on the burner, then began to scoop the peppers in his hands and throw them on the pan. "I see what I see. Can't really explain how I read people. I just do."

His movements were sharper now, more precise. Was he disappointed in her answer? Seemed so, but she decided to drop it. With the discussion over, she went to the living room and sat on the loveseat.

"How do you know the Pratts?" he asked in a conversational manner.

Good. A safe change in topic. "I met Lila in college. Our dorms were across from each other. Her mom would send boxes and boxes of homemade brownies, and instead of eating all of it, we'd sell them for two bucks each. We were really popular with the potheads."

Neil chuckled.

She turned the question back on him. "I always wanted to know how you and Logan became friends. He's never said much about his younger days."

"Like you and Lila, we met in college. Freshman year. Well," he said stirring the veggies in the pan, "we pretty much hated each other's guts the first semester."

Neil and Logan enemies? "You're kidding."

He shook his head. "Nope. We both had our own circle of friends. I heard he was a spoiled rich kid from the Hills who didn't give a damn about anyone but himself, and he heard I was an obnoxious jerk who stole the girls from other guys. During fall semester, we avoided each other. At parties, at the games. It was a big campus, but we had a lot of mutual friends."

"What finally brought you two together?"

"Christmas break. The campus was deserted, but I had to stay. Didn't have enough cash to fly home, and my car was a piece of junk that wouldn't make it a hundred miles. Since I was broke and basketball was always free, I played in this park by my apartment. Logan jogged by me and asked what the hell I was doing in town. He said 'Shouldn't you be in Dallas or wherever?' Knowing full well I was from Denver."

She smiled, picturing this exchange.

He pointed at her. "I asked him, 'Should you be in Hollywood?' And he gave me a look equivalent to a middle finger and told me he lived in Los Angeles, which I knew. Anyway, I told him why I couldn't go home, and he told me he didn't want to because his parents fought like crazy. We started playing basketball, hung out for a few days, then he bought me a plane ticket home without me asking."

The story made her smile. "Really?"

"I made him come with me so he wouldn't spend the holiday alone, and we had a blast in my hometown. After that, we were pretty tight. We combined our groups of friends and had more fun than any two guys I know."

"How cute you two ended up in the same city."

He rolled his eyes. "It's not cute. It just worked out that way. He didn't like L.A. and I convinced him to give the Bay a shot."

She sat back and crossed her arms. "You and Jordana have something in common. The fact he made sure you got home for Christmas and he made sure she was in Vegas for her sister's wedding."

He smiled at her. "You're right. I never realized that." Going to a cabinet, he pulled down a glass. "Want something to drink? They left a Boudreaux here with your name on it. Literally." He held up the bottle with the sticky note affixed with her name and a smiley face.

No wine. No alcohol. Not around him. "I could use some water." She started to get up.

"Stay there. I'll bring it to you."

She froze, then sat back down. "Thanks," she said when he handed her a cold glass of water. Who knew he liked to play host? And why was he being so nice when he'd already done enough for her? Maybe he felt sorry for her, too. As he cooked, she sipped on her drink. This felt…strange. Surreal. To be here with Neil while he played chef and waited on her. Like they were a couple at home, enjoying a quiet Friday night. It'd been so long since she had one of those it didn't feel natural.

In fact, it was starting to make her edgy.

Perhaps she shouldn't have been so adamant about him staying, even though it would've been rude to make him get a room at that motel. He was by no means a stranger, but she'd never spent any time alone with him until now. The years she spent snubbing him and acting distant had dissolved very quickly, as if they were always meant to be like this. Getting along with easy conversation. Their dynamic would never be the same; she could no longer act as though he was just some conceited pill anymore.

So how should she act?

Before she mused over that question, he strode over, grinning, placing a plate in her hands. "Eat up."

Her stomach growled in anticipation at the smell and sight. He'd made quesadillas with the spinach tortillas, added crab meat, cheese, peppers and onions inside, topped with sour cream and a dollop of salsa. She took a bite. Delicious. "It's tasty. Thank you."

"You're welcome." He took a seat on the main sofa and ate his.

Okay now it was getting way too familiar and comfortable, and she didn't like it. Neil wasn't her friend. He was Logan and Jordana's. She had to draw the line somewhere and treat him…like an attorney, because that's why she'd called him in the first place.

Once finished, she took her plate to the sink, washed it, then headed straight for the hall. "I'm going to take a shower and go to bed."

"You okay?" he asked from behind her.

She squeezed her eyes shut. Why did he keep asking that? "I'm not a child, Caenon," she called.

"Don't I know it," he mumbled.

Even after her long hot shower, her nerves were still unsettled, but at least she was clean. She towel-dried her hair, combed through it, and changed into a pair of lounge pants and a scoop-neck tee. When she emerged, she saw Neil in the living room on the sofa, drinking a beer and flipping through something. She approached from behind the sofa, looking over his shoulder. "What are you doing? Snooping?"

He dropped his head back with a boyish smile. "Not really snooping when the book is left on the coffee table."

"Well, put it away."

"I will when I'm done," he stated in a formal tone. "Wait. Is this you?" he pointed.

She looked down and groaned. It was a photo of her from her sophomore year of college. "Yes. That's me."

"Those are some fierce streaks in your hair."

"I was in an at-home coloring phase," she explained sardonically.

"And you played guitar?"

"That's a prop. I was listening to a lot of Dave Matthews Band."

He laughed. "You were cute."

In a hot mess sort of way. "Not the kind of girl you went for, I'm sure."

"I went for all kinds." He flipped the page and burst out laughing. "What's this?"

She sighed, going around the sofa and sitting next to him for a better look. "Uh…Halloween, 2001. I was Mrs. Potato Head. I lost a bet."

He sent her a glance. "You gamble? Who knew you were so fun back in the day? I imagined you nose deep in your studies and attending lectures for extra credit. I like seeing this side of you." When he turned the page, his elbow brushed the side of her breast, and her breath caught. It wasn't on purpose, but even that slight contact made her nipples ache for more.

She cleared her throat. "That was over ten years ago. I'm a little different now." She stared at the photo of her smiling, enjoying her youth with her whole life ahead of her. She hadn't even met Cliff yet at that point.

Neil looked over at her, studying her for a few seconds before saying, "I don't think people completely change who they are at heart. Unless they wanted to. Or had to."

She snatched the book from his hands and shut it, not eager for another evaluation. "I graduated. Got married and became an adult. Not everyone lives their life like it's a party."

He huffed. "What's that supposed to mean?"

"I don't have to see a photo album to know how you were in college and how you are now have little distinguishes."

"I enjoy life and I'm good at it. Does that bother you?" He lifted his brows.

"No! It's just—life isn't all about fun and games, Caenon."

"Obviously I disagree." Turning his body, he placed his arm on the back of the sofa. "Do I sense jealousy, Ms. Turner?" he teased, beginning to grin.

He wanted to play, but she wasn't up for his verbal games, and certainly didn't need his body so close to hers. After setting the book back on the coffee table, she got up, knowing she was being a little too sensitive, but unable to stop herself from lashing at him. "I'm not jealous. You're being ridiculous and I'm going to bed. If you leave before I'm up tomorrow, lock the door behind you."

After shutting her bedroom door, she flopped on the bed, hugged a pillow, and sighed. What was that? Why did she let him get her worked up so easily?

Her phone notification flashed she had a missed call. When she checked it, she saw Lila had called her just fifteen minutes ago to check in on her during their layover, after receiving the sheriff's voicemail. She quickly called her back and relayed the story.

"Oh my God, I'm so, so, sorry," said her friend after Ashtyn told her what'd happened. "Bonnie is usually so on top of the things!"

"It's all right. Everything worked out." Ashtyn sighed. It'd worked out because of Neil, who she'd just been very rude to for no reason. "It was an interesting way to kick off my vacation. But the sheriff and deputy were friendly enough."

"So glad he and your lawyer pal figured it out so quickly. I would've felt terrible if you'd stay one minute longer! I'll make this up to you."

"Don't be silly. It wasn't your fault."

"Nevertheless, I feel terrible. You went to jail!"

"Lila, your town's jail isn't exactly San Quentin. Officer Thornton went out of his way to make sure I was comfortable, and I was out in less than three hours."

"Isn't Jake dreamy? Fun Briar's Edge fact for you: he's single."

"Yes, well, he was a complete professional."

"You should've invited him over for some grape soda after his shift," she teased. "Call him right now."

"No," Ashtyn emphasized. "Besides, I couldn't even if I had the nerve to. Neil's here."

"What?" Lila exclaimed with unconcealed joy. "Is that how you pay your attorney's fees?"

She let out a half-laugh, half-groan. "Stop. It was the least I could do. He was going to stay at the motel."

"This is so interesting," her friend mused. "A man you've claimed is nothing but a walking cock is the person you call to bail you out of jail—"

"He's an attorney!"

"And instead of letting this man stay at a perfectly decent motel for one brief night, you invite him to stay at the house with you—"

"It would've been rude not to."

Lila went on. "And now you're defending yourself as if you've been caught doing something wrong. Maybe you like this guy more than you thought? He's hot, isn't he? You once told me he looked a Disney prince."

"I'm done talking, Lila."

"Condoms are in my bathroom vanity. Middle drawer."

"*Good-bye*, Lila."

She heard her friend's laughter before she ended the call.

Back to her brooding. Fact was, she *was* jealous of Neil.

Some part of her hated she'd wasted those years with Cliff. All those things she sacrificed for one reason or another. After college, she considered studying abroad for the summer, but Cliff had talked her out of it, convincing her it was unnecessary, and it was one of her biggest regrets. Never again would she let a man persuade her out of a dream.

Neil seemed to do whatever he wanted, whenever, with whoever, and never had a care in the world. She envied that, and though he'd been teasing about her feelings, he was more right than he knew.

She stared at her door for ten minutes. Ten full minutes. Her conscience wouldn't let her go to sleep until she apologized for being short with him. He'd driven all this way to make sure she didn't rot in jail all weekend; he didn't deserve her bitchiness. It'd been so long since any man cooked for her, cared for her, looked at her that way, *affected* her that way, and she'd basically bitten his head off. Drawing in a deep breath, she forced herself out of her room and to his door.

She softly knocked. "Neil? Are you decent?"

After a few seconds, the door opened, and he stood there, resting one hand on the jamb.

Her mouth opened and closed. He was bare-chested, wearing nothing but pajama pants tied at his taut stomach. She forced herself to keep her eyes straight ahead, but it was already too late. By the barest lift of his brow, he knew she'd raked his whole body. Defensive, she asserted, "I...I asked if you were decent."

"This *is* decent," he told her, voice silken, gaze steady.

A flash of heat coursed through her. How dare he turn her on? Probably did it on her purpose. She straightened her posture and forced a mature tone. "I just wanted to apologize for snapping at you." Softening her voice, she added sincerely, "I'm sorry."

"It's all right," he told her. "You've snapped a lot harder."

True. She knew she really hadn't hurt his feelings. While he stood there silently, waiting to see if she had something else to add, she groped to extend the conversation. "Anyway. At least I came to your room this time."

He gave a hint of a smile. "I appreciate that."

When he started to close his door, she put a hand on it. He appeared satisfied to leave it at that, but she just couldn't. She wanted them back on familiar terms. Back to their usual rapport. "Can I ask you something?"

He paused. "Sure."

What made her think of this one moment from so long ago, she didn't know, but decided it would be the best topic to put them back on track. "When we first met, you asked me if I would've gone on a date with you had I been single? Do you remember?"

A corner of his mouth lifted, and he gave a single nod. "I do. You said 'no' with great emphasis."

She swallowed. "I *would've* said no, but..." She bit her bottom lip, disbelieving what she was about to confess. "I would've wanted to say yes." A simple admission, but a big one nonetheless.

He looked at her for so long, she assumed he didn't have a response for that until—

"Why?" he finally asked.

"Come on, Neil." She crossed her arms with a coy smile. "Smart girls don't take the handsome bad boy seriously. They go out with, and marry, the good guy next door." She rolled her eyes, thinking of Cliff. "Who can incidentally turn into the bad guy after five years of marriage."

"So what about the first bad guy once the girl is single again?" he asked, his voice deeper and huskier.

A rush came over her, caught in his penetrating gaze. "He's just as dangerous. More dangerous."

His eyes glinted; he knew she was right. "You won't be breaking any rules, you know. Admitting you want me as much as I want you."

Leave it to Neil to state what most people would leave unspoken. But he wasn't most people. He said what he pleased. It took a few seconds to find her voice. "I'd be breaking mine."

One moment he was behind the threshold, the next he was so close she could feel the heat from his face above hers. "Admitting it and imagining it…us giving in…is all we can do."

She took a quick breath. How did he do it? Scramble her reason and turn her on without touching her? Yes, he was sexy, but she'd met a thousand sexy guys. What made him this powerful? She took a step back before she did something she'd regret. The man radiated temptation like no other. But as he said, admitting they wanted each other didn't mean they'd ever do anything about it.

"Goodnight, Neil." She turned to her room.

6

USED TO GETTING up early, Neil awoke at dawn, grabbed his laptop, and headed to the backyard deck. Shuffling barefoot to the table, he took a seat and slid on his glasses. Might as well get some reading in and take advantage of the tranquility before he headed back to the Bay. He yearned to make coffee, but didn't want to disturb Ashtyn by making noise in the kitchen. She deserved to sleep in for the little adventure she had last night.

He couldn't help but feel this was a new start with her. Sure, he still seemed to get on her nerves, but the fact she'd later apologized spoke volumes. She'd never done that before.

Her small brush with the law had brought him into her life for one night. They'd established a friendship now, and would have more between them than idle banter. They had a bond, and it was even more special since no one else would ever know.

Seeing her in the photo album looking bright, girlish, and fun, he caught of glimpse of a different side of Ashtyn, and now he wanted more than a glimpse.

Last night, he'd been a second away from kissing her.

He'd caught her off guard answering the door without a shirt on. Desire and attraction had glowed in her eyes a mere second before it disappeared. No doubt she was so used to seeing him as a suit; seeing him as a man probably threw her off a little bit. In that split second, with naked desire flashing in her beautiful blues, he'd wanted to take her mouth before she could even think of denying him. But he'd killed the urge.

He didn't take from a woman. That wasn't his style.

A dog barking in the distance snapped him out of his train of thought.

He had reading to do. Better get to it.

Later on, it wasn't the sound of the sliding door that broke him out of his concentration, it was Ashtyn stepping out in running shoes, shorts, and a sports bra that had him doing a double take.

She gave a start when she spotted him. "Oh. Morning."

"Morning." He breathed deep in his nose and looked away. *Holy shit.* She didn't know it, but his dick was saying good morning as well at the sight of her bared stomach and thighs.

"I thought maybe you'd left," she said, closing the door.

"Without saying good-bye?"

"Seems like something you'd do."

He chuckled. She did make a lot of assumptions about him, didn't she? "Well, we didn't have sex so the need to duck out wasn't that strong."

She gestured toward him. "And here you are again. Shirtless."

He glanced down as if he just realized his state of half-dress, then shrugged. "I spend most of my life in a suit so I like to forgo shirts when I can." He smiled at her. "Does it make you uncomfortable?"

"No. The fact you're comfortable being shirtless around me makes me uncomfortable."

"I'll try to remember that next time," he remarked.

"You wear glasses?" she asked, coming over and sitting across from him.

"When I have a lot of reading to get through."

"I like them on you."

In that case, he'd wear them more often. "Where are your spectacles, by the way? I'm more used to seeing you in them than without."

"I only wear them at work." She hesitated. "I want to talk to you about last night."

He closed his laptop, sensing a serious discussion on the horizon. "What about last night?" The cool air had puckered her nipples through the sports bra. It was damn challenging not to trace his gaze over her breasts, imagining his mouth on them, between them, with his hands digging in her hips. He checked a needful groan, and was grateful the wooden patio table hid his bulge.

"Logan is your best friend," she began, and he stiffened, knowing where this was going. "But please don't tell him what happened. Even though it was a misunderstanding, I don't want him to know I was arrested. I'm humiliated enough on my own."

He frowned at the fact she needed confirmation of secrecy. "Frankly I'm insulted you think I'd gossip about you to Logan. Or to anyone. There's the little matter of attorney-client confidentiality. Not to mention I'd never utter a word about your private business to your employer. Even if he is a good friend of mine, it's essentially none of his business. Why did you think you had to verify my discretion?"

She seemed stunned at curt tone. "For one thing, you make a joke out of *everything* and the circumstances weren't that serious."

"Regardless of the level of seriousness, I never have and never will *joke* about private information. You obviously don't know me that well. Enjoy your run." He opened his laptop to cut off this absurd conversation. Him securing the title of junior partner at one of the top firms in the city didn't dissuade her from ascertaining his trust.

"Caenon—"

"Drop it," he clipped.

She sat for a few seconds more, then sighed before pushing to her feet.

He instantly regretted being harsh with her, but she had to know the one thing he did take seriously was his ethics. "I'm heading out soon," he told her while she walked down the deck steps. "I probably won't be here by the time you get back."

He felt her eyes on him, but he continued to stare at his laptop screen.

"Okay," she said softly before disappearing down the stairs.

Half an hour later, he took a quick shower and left. His cell phone continued to go off during the drive and he didn't check it until he walked in his houseboat. He had a text message from a colleague regarding a case, one from his sister reminding him of her visit in a few weeks, another from Denise, who just flew into town, and one from Willa, asking him if he was free tonight.

Now he had two options to purge some of his sexual frustration. Something needed to be done. Denise came to San Francisco often for her job and if she didn't already have plans, she'd give him the name and room number of her hotel and they'd play complete strangers at the bar. An amusing diversion.

Willa on the other hand loved to go dancing all night and have sex on the bathroom counter of her apartment. Another spicy alternative.

Either way, he was going out with one of them.

Anything to get his mind off Ashtyn.

However, later that evening while he was with Willa at a hot nightclub, not only was he still thinking about Ashtyn, he was disinterested in ending his evening with any sexual Olympics with Willa.

It wasn't her fault. She looked hot in a figure-hugging, aqua-blue dress with her long dark hair down and curled to perfection. While he'd skipped the alcohol so he could drive, she'd imbibed in several cranberry-vodkas and did her best to seduce him on the dance floor, swaying her hips and putting his hands all over her tight body. As for him…

Crickets. Not even the slightest pang of desire. To his shock, he was even bored.

Willa sensed it too, beginning to pout when he didn't respond with his usual body language. Hell, he thought, he couldn't even fake it. After three hours of trying, he gave up, and pulled her out of the nightclub to the valet for his car. He opened the door for her, then took over in the driver's seat.

"You okay?" she asked, crossing her legs and turning toward him.

No. Something is definitely wrong with me. "Sure. Just tired."

"Want a little pick-me-up? We could stop by my friend's place. She always has some blow."

He sent her a hard glance as they cruised through the green lights. "You know I don't do drugs. Since when do you do cocaine?"

"Oh! Hardly ever. Once in a while," she emphasized, seeing his deep disapproval.

He frowned. Nothing turned him off more than a girl getting caught up in drugs, even "once in a while." Plenty of lawyers used various narcotics to get through the day, but he had other—healthier—reprieves.

"Taking me home?" she asked, batting her long lashes.

"Yeah."

"Good." Shifting in her seat, she poked his arm. "Come on, Neil. Make me laugh. Say something funny. I hate to see you so blue."

"I'm not blue," he responded drolly.

"Fine." She bent down and dug around in her purse on the floor. "What's this?" she asked, pulling something silky and white from under the seat.

He flicked it a glance. "Looks like a scarf."

She laughed. "I know it's not *yours*."

A scent drifted to his nose, sparking a fire he'd been searching for all night. "Ashtyn."

"What?"

Her name had just fallen off his lips. He cleared the roughness from his throat. "It's Ashtyn's."

"Who's she?"

"A friend of mine. I gave her a ride home the other night."

"Oh," she mused, running her hand over the accessory. "It's expensive. I'm sure she'll want it back."

He held out his hand and she placed the scarf in it. Pure silk, a lot like what he imagined Ashtyn's skin would feel like. Tempted to bring the accessory to his nose and inhale like a perv, he flipped open his console and tossed it inside, way too eager to use it as an excuse to contact her.

Now he had something to look forward to tomorrow.

Before long, they were at Willa's apartment, and he walked her to her apartment, but had decided hours ago he wasn't going in.

She unlocked the door, then swiveled around with a seductive smile on her face, wrapping her arms around his neck. "I don't know what's wrong, but I know I can make you forget it."

"I'm sorry I wasn't that much fun tonight."

"Don't be silly." She kissed his chin with her full lips, seemingly unable to give up. "You can make it up to me inside."

He set his hands on her hips and gently pushed her away. "I can't."

She gave a pout and dropped her hands. "Well, this is a first."

"I know. It's not you, it's me."

"Oh, I can't believe you just said that!" she laughed. "But you're right. It *is* you."

"I'm distracted. I guess my head's just elsewhere." He leaned in and kissed her cheek. "The one on top of my shoulders, that is."

She giggled. "There's the Neil I recognize." Before he could dodge, she kissed him again, this time on the lips. He got no reaction out of it. The second she realized she was better off kissing a dead fish, she sighed and pulled away. "The scarf?"

Women always had good instincts. "The scarf," he admitted reluctantly.

She finally released him, sliding her palms down his chest. "My loss. Good luck with that."

He strolled back to his car, pissed off. This was no good. It was one thing for Ashtyn to star in his fantasies, but quite another to make him impotent for other women.

The question was, what the hell was he going to do about it?

THE DAY ASHTYN had been dreading arrived. Moving day.

Time to pick up her things and take one last look at the life she used to know.

As she turned on her old street, she mentally steeled herself. This didn't have to be an emotional trial. All she had to do was get her things from one place to another, and the movers would be doing most of the heavy lifting. The things inside were only belongings and the house was only shelter.

She gasped when she pulled up along the curb.

All her valuables weren't in the house anymore…

Because they were outside on the driveway. Literally.

Mouth agog, she climbed out of her car and stared at the pile that'd been stacked in front of the garage. Everything. The sofas, the dressers, tables, lamps, her clothes, and things she had in boxes were all flung over the furnishings and under the elements. Fuming, she went to the house and found it mostly barren. So Cliff took the liberty of putting her things outside as though it were a free yard sale? Did he think he was doing her a favor? Who knew how long everything had been out there?

Tears threatened. Nothing had been covered or wrapped for protection.

"Cliff, you bastard," she whispered, tears filling her eyes, before she quickly brushed them away. *No. No more crying. Get angry.* Anger was so much more motivating.

"Hey Ashtyn," a male voice said behind her.

She turned around.

It was Randy, her next door neighbor. He gave her a look of sympathy. "I saw Cliff and his buddy put your stuff out here. I, uh, assumed you'd be by for it."

"Didn't you think it was odd?" she asked.

"Yeah, but what was I gonna say to him?"

"I'm sorry," she said wearily. "It's not your fault."

Her neighbor shouldn't take any responsibility for her ex-husband's asshat decisions.

"Don't worry, I watched over it. For the most part. Made sure folks didn't stop by and…help themselves."

She sighed. "I appreciate it more than you know."

The older man shoved his hands in his jeans. "It'll be weird not seeing you around the neighborhood anymore. Life sucks, eh? Bad luck is going around the neighborhood. I just lost my job and you know Rita's medication is so damn expensive."

"You lost your job? I'm sorry to hear that." Truly she was, especially since he was in his fifties and starting the hunt for employment was always hard. "Let me know if you need a reference or anything. I'll see if my company has any openings, too."

A strange look cast over his face. "Appreciate it. I gotta get back to my wife. Take it easy." He walked back to his house.

Turning to her things, she had the urge to stomp her feet and scream like a wild woman, but she kept her composure and got busy taking inventory. The movers were an hour late, adding more angst to her awful day. But with everything outside, it only took them half an hour to get it all in the truck, then they followed her to her new rental.

It crossed her mind to call Cliff and verbally rip his ear off, but then she'd just add fuel to the fire. A fire she thought was out now that it'd been three months since the divorce was filed. Her ex *had* to stick it to her one last time, probably for dragging out the process. While she'd fought for the house, he constantly berated her for making the whole ordeal unnecessarily costly, even while he wouldn't bend her way under any circumstances.

Why start another fight? As long as nothing had been stolen.

When she started sorting through her bedroom items, she came across her jewelry box, which she thought she'd left in the safe, and thought Cliff would give to her later. Alarm raced through her knowing it'd been left outside. She opened it. Her engagement and wedding ring were in there, but not her pearls. Her heart thudded. Where were they?

They were twenty-four inches of the purest most beautiful antique set given to her by her grandmother, who gave them to her when she graduated college. They were heavy and took up most of the bottom of the jewelry case. Cliff emptied out the safe and carelessly left the box among her things outside. And now her pearls were missing. She prayed they were just misplaced, but an hour after tearing through every box and bag, she realized they were gone.

She started to cry.

Her mother told her only brats cried about "things."

At least that's what she told Ashtyn when she gave away her dolls and clothes after her parents divorced. Even her mom didn't know about the pearls Grandma Lauren had given to her. She remembered vividly sitting at her grandmother's bedside, alone, when her grandma reached under her bedspread and closed the necklace in Ashtyn's twenty-year-old hands.

Ashtyn cried, told her no, but Grandma Lauren wouldn't hear it. Insisted she take care of them. Her mother had hovered just outside the room, too busy muttering under her breath about who was going to cover the funeral expenses, if Lauren had left *anything* in her will to her and her daughter.

The pearls were all the more precious because they were the one thing her mother didn't pluck from her hands to pay for their bills.

But now they were lost. Somewhere between her marriage failing and moving in to her new place, the pearls had been forsaken.

7

NEIL SAT BACK in his office chair, fiddling with the scarf Ashtyn had left in his car. It wasn't a vital item to return like a cell phone or wallet, but he didn't like having it. It was distracting.

He raised it to his nose and inhaled. God. Smelled like her hair. Nevertheless, it was time to get rid of it.

He'd lied to her.

Told her she wasn't that irresistible, but she was. Why did he burn for her like this? What would make this go away? The answer to that was simple—take her to bed—but that solution wasn't likely. The fact she was now divorced eliminated the whole untouchable-married-woman prob. He thought he wanted her so badly before because he *couldn't* have her, but knowing she was single again didn't diminish his desire one bit, only heightened it.

He picked up the phone and called her. She answered on the fourth ring, so he assumed she'd debated before picking up. After the way he'd rudely ended their last conversation, he was surprised she answered.

"Neil. Hi."

His lips curved at the sound of her voice. "I have something of yours."

"You do? What is it?"

"A scarf. You left it in my car. White silky thing."

She sighed. "Oh. It isn't important. I'll get it from you the next time you stop by SFG."

"I might lose it by then. I'd rather drop it off. Tonight. Are you still in the Bay or are you back in Briar's Edge?"

"Still in town. I have some things to take care of before I go back." She paused. "You'd come to my place just to drop off a scarf?"

He'd go a lot farther for a lot less just to see her. His brows drew together; he detected a sadness in her voice. "Something wrong?"

"No. No, I'm fine."

Ah, the word fine. Was there any better word to describe its opposite meaning? "You're lying to me."

"Caenon, please don't analyze me over the phone. I'm just tired. Drop off the scarf on my desk. You literally work next door."

"How did the move go?" he asked, dodging her suggestion.

"You're just making small talk and you know I hate it. Why would you care how my move went?"

"Because I do," he told her, tucking her scarf in his inner pocket. "Is that all right? Logan cares about you. Jordana cares about you. Why can't I?"

No answer.

He softened his tone. "Have you eaten? I'll bring something. I know moving can suck the life out of you and the last thing you feel like doing is cooking."

"I was going to order some takeout."

"Perfect. I love takeout. I just got done reading a depo for six hours. Could use the break. Text me your address."

"All right," she sounded resigned.

Five minutes passed before her address popped up.

He practically bolted to his car.

Twenty minutes later, he arrived in Noe Valley, a neighborhood he hadn't ventured to in a long time. Ashtyn lived on a street of polished, brightly painted, classic Victorian houses lined up like dollhouses. Hers was a light blue with white trim, perched on top of the hill it sat on.

He rang the doorbell and grinned because he was looking forward to seeing her. When she answered the door, however, his smile faded.

Her eyes were a little red, her skin pale.

She gave him a weak smile, but he was no fool. Any man could see she was upset. Other than that, her hair was in a neat ponytail, her white halter blouse wrinkle-free, and red shorts ironed. Always so polished. Nothing gave her away except her eyes.

He took a step forward and she took a step back. "Ashtyn—"

"What kind of takeout do you want?" she swiftly evaded.

The level of yearning to pull her into his arms and comfort her was strong, and almost irresistible, but he shook away the urge. "Thai. Or Cantonese. I'm happy with a hoagie, too. You pick." Growing up with two sisters, and a mother who could cry at life insurance commercials, he'd become quite an expert in gauging how to treat them when emotions were high. One thing he learned was to never ask, because they would never tell. They always did so on their own accord, and so he chose not to press Ashtyn, and instead would try to cheer her up.

As long as she didn't kick him out, he was good. She sifted through a small stack of menus, and he gave himself a quick tour. It was a perfect place for a single woman starting over, not too big, a little over a thousand square feet, apricot-colored walls, shiny hardwood floors, and doors that opened to a small patio.

She handed him a menu when he returned to the kitchen. "Don't mind the mess. I'm still unpacking. How about Italian? Is that okay?"

"Sure." He looked it over, picked a meal, and she called in the order.

"I haven't set up my cable yet," she said stuffing her hands in her back pockets. "So no TV."

"Is this lack of background noise making you uncomfortable?" he asked, leaning back on her sofa.

"No. I just wasn't ready to entertain any guests."

"Shouldn't watch TV anyway. Rots the brain," he joked, trying to conjure a smile out of her, but failing. "How about we take advantage of your patio once the food comes?"

She liked that idea. While they waited for their delivery, she set out plates and napkins on the small table and lit a candle. She started to walk back in the house, then turned and blew it out. He smirked. Too romantic to have a Glade candle burning between them?

In her fridge, he didn't find much in regards to refreshments. "What's with you and grape soda? I noticed it at Lila's house, too. Starting to see a pattern here."

She grabbed forks from a drawer. "Love the stuff. It's a guilty pleasure."

"I always thought that was an oxymoron. You should never feel guilty about pleasure."

A hint of smile moved her mouth while she shook her head.

The doorbell rang and he beat her to the door and paid, then pulled out the containers of hot food on the patio table.

They ate in silence for a bit, which seemed weird to him. Whenever he ate a meal with someone, he encouraged conversation, otherwise, what was the point? But he didn't mind so much with Ashtyn, wanting to give her space.

"I know you're waiting for me to tell you why I'm upset," she said.

He raised a brow and gave a single nod. "If you *want* to tell me, that is."

"Well, you bought dinner. You're entitled to an explanation."

"This isn't quid pro quo, Ashtyn."

"I know, but I might as well tell you." She dropped her fork on her plate and sat back. "I sort of…got robbed."

"What?" he exclaimed.

"My grandfather gave my grandmother a pearl necklace when they got married and she gave them to me. Someone stole them. That's why I'm upset." She traced her fingers along her collarbone, as though imagining the necklace and missing it.

The despondency in her voice gave away her heartache, and he was sad for her. They obviously meant a great deal. "Stole them how?"

"During my move. When I got to the house all of my belongings were out on the driveway. Everything." She briefly closed her eyes. "My clothes. The furniture. Even my hair dryer. All were sitting in front of the garage like garbage. My ex-husband's idea of doing me a backhanded favor, I guess."

That son-of-a-bitch. Why couldn't he take his half and leave? Why cause his ex-wife unnecessary grief? Because he could. Some men needed petty revenge to feel like they had the last word. "So you think someone came by and stole your jewelry while everything sat out there?"

"That's one possibility."

"How much are they worth?"

"Twenty-thousand, I think. That's what I had them appraised at years ago."

His eyes widened. Hefty sum. "Are they insured?"

"Yes, but it's the sentimental value. I was closer to my grandmother than my mom. We were kindred spirits, two-of-a-kind. Those pearls gave me a lasting, palpable connection to her. Something to pass on. Now they're gone." She sighed, brushing crumbs from her shorts. "I know what she'd say. That they are just little baubles on a string. But I'm sick about it."

"Understandably so. Do you think Cliff took them to sell them off?"

"He's my first suspect of course because they were in my jewelry box, which was in the safe, and he must've taken them out when he took it, but it could've been one of the movers, too. Maybe it was a jogger who passed by. Who knows?" She paused, delicate brows drawing together. "But my wedding ring set was in the jewelry box, too. The engagement ring alone is worth a few grand. They would've gotten a sizable amount for the whole lot. Why would the thief leave them and take the necklace?"

He considered this. "Then maybe it *was* Cliff. Didn't care about the pearls, but wanted you to have your engagement and wedding ring. People think strangely after a divorce."

She shrugged. "I don't know. It's not like he's very hard-up for cash."

"Having money doesn't mean you never want more. Have you given him a piece of your mind for acting like an asshole?"

"So he can see how upset he's made me? I'm done fighting with him."

Tossing a napkin on his empty plate, he asked, "Are you going to confront him about the pearls at least? He might've done it just to get your attention. To make you reach out to him."

She raised a brow. "You sound like you know a lot about the mind of a divorced man."

"Haven't we all known one or two? You wouldn't believe the things people do to each other once the love is gone."

"I can imagine. Despite recent events, I'm grateful. Other than the house, we didn't fight much on anything. He let me have what I wanted in the house and I didn't push for spousal support."

"Why not?" he asked, crumpling his napkin.

"Because I'd rather sever all ties with my ex. My job pays well and I'll get a decent check once the house sells. I don't want Cliff's money."

He smiled. "Good for you. The pearls, however. You can't let the theft slide. I suggest you file a police report at the very least. If we find them at a pawn shop somewhere, we'll have a claim."

"I took care of that already. And what's with 'we'?" She sounded amused.

"You and I are going to try and track them down," he told her, putting together a plan as he went along. "Think about it. Two heads are better than one. We'll interview your ex and the movers. People tend to take you a little more seriously when you have an attorney at your side," he added in his most logical tone.

She met his gaze, her lips parting. "You don't need to do that."

God, yes, he did. For reasons he didn't care to ponder now, but he wasn't going to let her let the thief get away scot-free. Not without investigating. "Don't you want your pearls back?"

"Of course I do! But we don't even know if Cliff stole them. Could've been anybody. I just can't see him doing it."

Still, her ex couldn't be let off the hook yet. "Do you know if he's seeing anyone?"

"No. Why?"

He gave a one-shoulder shrug, and took a sip of water. "He could've stolen them to give to a woman. To impress her or something."

"That would be too ballsy for Cliff."

He understood her avoiding confrontation with her ex-husband, but giving the man a pass because she didn't want to fight with him or because of his lack of balls didn't fly with Neil. "You should at least try, Ashtyn. In most cases, people are burglarized by those closest to them. It's a sad statistic."

She chewed her lip, thinking. "Okay."

Another chance to play hero. He rose from his seat. "When are you heading back to Briar's Edge?"

"Day after tomorrow."

"Friday? Plenty of time. We'll start with Cliff at his office in the afternoon. I have meetings in the morning." He started to pick up his plate, but she told him she'd take care of it and followed him to the front door.

"Confronting Cliff isn't the greatest idea. He'll freak out and think we're ganging up on him," she warned.

"I see people freak out all the time. If he can't keep his cool, then he'll just embarrass himself. If we go to his house, he could ignore us or accuse you of harassment. Just watch me and follow my lead. I guarantee you we'll be in and out. My lie detector is pretty dependable."

The chances of finding the pearls were not in their favor. She knew that and so did he, but they had to do something. He opened her door. "Take a hot bath. Put some cucumbers on your eyes. Get some rest. Do whatever you ladies do to feel good," he smiled. When she quirked a brow, he added, "I grew up in a household of women, remember?"

"Ah. Right."

She still looked so damn crestfallen. The urge to caress her cheek and tell her it was going to be okay burned in him. But he didn't want to push his luck. "Also, it wouldn't hurt if you were dressed to kill. We male species are visual. Stick it to him with a little extra 'man you fucked up.' That'll make you feel good, too."

She laughed. A real genuine laugh. There was that smile he longed to see. "What exactly is your idea of dressing to kill? If it's spiked heels and a short skirt, then I'll disappoint you."

"No. Being yourself is what's sexy. Put on something that makes you feel confident. I'll text you when I'm on my way." He stepped out toward the walk.

"Caenon."

He turned.

She leaned in the doorway and rubbed the top of her foot along her calf, uncertainty in her expression.

He kept his eyes trained on her face instead of those gorgeous stems beckoning him beyond reason. "What?"

"I want to pay you," she said.

Why did she have to bring this up every time? "Not necessary."

"It is to me," she argued. "I don't feel comfortable accepting your help without paying. Especially if we're going to do this during your working hours. You already gave me a freebie last year, and with the situation in Briar's."

"That was no big deal. Wouldn't you say you and I are friends now?"

"Er. Yes."

"Then I refuse to charge you."

"Come on, Neil. No special treatment. Logan pays you."

"That's because what I do for him actually involves work. This'll be fun for me."

ASHTYN BEGAN TO SMILE when she saw Neil pull up in his white Lexus at noon. She'd been ready and waiting for him for all morning. Eager, in a way. She'd been so depressed about the loss of her pearls, and had thought she'd suffer alone, and deal with it. Not only did Neil's instant vehemence to find them lift her spirits, it endeared him to her even more.

He climbed out of his car as she walked out. She'd put on a black pencil dress. It hugged her curves and emphasized her waist with a red skinny belt. It had a low, square neckline and, because of that, she always wore a jacket with it. Not this time. She ditched it and put on a push-up bra, wore her hair down, straight, and added some red lip gloss to her mouth. She'd never go to work like this, but Neil told her to dress deadly. This was as close to it as she could get with her wardrobe.

He opened the passenger door and she climbed in, then he went round to the driver's side. His car smelled utterly masculine, like new leather and light cologne. It was enough to renew her ache all over again. He raised his brow as she met his gaze. Unable to wait for his opinion, she prompted him. "Well? Am I dressed to kill or do I just look like a vamped up Doris Day?"

"You look damn good and you know it," he told her, a half-smile tugging his mouth.

That was all she needed to hear.

Half an hour later, they pulled up to the architectural company where Cliff worked. As Neil had instructed, they walked past the reception straight to Cliff's office, much to some of the employees' wide eyes. She knocked on her ex's door and walked in.

He looked up and his brows lowered. Handsome in his own way, Cliff had wavy, reddish-brown hair, brown eyes, and fair skin due to his strong Scottish heritage from his mother's side. What really caught one's eye was his strong chin and defined, muscular gait due to attempting every extra-curricular fitness activity he could. Hiking, biking, even Pilates. Attractive as the outside package was, the inside could make a woman cringe when she failed to meet his expectations. Cliff had always made her feel as though it'd been a privilege to marry him, and in order to keep that honor, she had to be this way, look that way. It'd been exhausting, and she now thought divorce could also be considered a blessing *and* a privilege, too.

"Hi Cliff," she greeted almost too brightly.

"What are you doing here?" He continued to glare. Neil walked in behind her and Cliff bristled even more. "And you brought Caenon? What the hell is going on?"

"No need to raise your voice," Neil said in an amiable tone. "We're here on business."

His brows shot down. "I don't have time for this, Ashtyn. Why didn't you call first?"

"This required a face-to-face." She took a seat. "I just have one question."

"Make it quick."

"Did you take my pearls?"

He gave her a contemptuous stare. "Come again?"

"When you put everything I owned in the *driveway*, did you take my necklace with you? They were in the safe so I know they didn't vanish on their own."

"You're such a bitch."

"Cliff," Neil interceded. "It's a simple question. Answer it or find yourself in court again."

He snarled at Neil, keeping his narrowed eyes on him even as he responded to Ashtyn. "I didn't take them. I told you I wanted that safe so yeah, I took out the jewelry box and hid it under your clothes. Speaking of jewelry, I would like the ring I gave you. I know you're just going to pawn that off."

She shrugged, crossing her arms. "Sure. I'll trade you the ring for the pearls."

"I don't fucking have them. Even if I did, I'm not stupid. Why would I trade twenty-grand for five? I didn't steal your grandmother's pearls and I'm done talking to you."

To think she used to adore this man sitting across from her.

Neil rose. "Let's go."

She raised her gaze to his as if to ask "We're done already?"

He nodded and cupped her elbow.

As they turned for the door, Cliff blurted, "You're screwing him, aren't you?"

Ashtyn whirled around, stunned. "Excuse me?"

"You and Neil." His gaze went between the both of him, disgust in his features. "Christ, it's obvious. You probably screwing behind my back for months while we were still living together too. The way you two looked at each other just now? Plain as fucking day."

"That's not true," Ashtyn exclaimed, even though she had no reason to defend herself at this point. Cliff would believe what he wanted.

"Deny it all you want. I'm not blind. Whore," he muttered under his breath.

"Hey—" Neil started but she placed a hand on his shoulder to stop him, and he relaxed.

Swallowing, she turned for the door. "You make me sick."

Neil pressed a light hand to her lower back, giving her a 'good job' look, before opening the door. "Good seeing you, Cliff."

"Go to hell, Caenon."

Why hadn't Neil jumped in and also denied they were sleeping together? It bugged her a little that he hadn't, but then again, he probably knew nothing they said would make Cliff realize he was mistaken.

"Well, that was over fast," she said as they walked back to his car.

"He didn't take them."

"Your inner lie detector not going off?"

"Nope. Moving on. To the movers. No pun intended."

They sat in silence for a few minutes while he pulled into traffic. Ashtyn chewed on her bottom lip, the tension of her brief confrontation with Cliff still hovering in the air. She let her head fall back on the headrest. His accusation continued to ring in her head.

"About what Cliff said—" Neil started.

"What do you think he—?"

Neil gestured. "Go ahead."

"You first."

"I was just going to say don't let it get to you. I can see it did."

"What do you think he meant the way we looked at each other?"

He slid a glance, and if she didn't know better, saw a little smile on his mouth. "He was just making something up to get a rise out of you.

Three things set him off today." He ticked them off his fingers. "You look amazing, I was with you, and he was jealous."

Ashtyn blew out a breath and pressed a hand to her stomach, wondering if her ex would spread any untruths about her and Neil just to spite her.

At the moving company, she was told that since she signed off on the inventory sheet, they weren't held liable. She had the option of filing with the AMSA, American Moving and Storage Association, or the AMSA's Arbitration Program, but the moving company didn't have to comply for arbitration for items worth more than $10,000.

Exhausted, Ashtyn told Neil she wanted to let it go.

"Are you sure? There are other actions we can take," he told her, starting the car.

"No. You've done enough, really. I'm sure they didn't take them. My jewelry box was buried. They would've had to really dig to find it without me looking." She sighed, heartbroken.

"All right. Damn. I'm sorry, Ashtyn. I wasn't much help, was I?"

She turned toward him in her seat and covered his hand on the gear shift. "Are you kidding? Without you, I would've never confronted Cliff or the moving company. Now I know it was probably someone who got lucky when they saw everything outside. It'd be impossible to find out who." He glanced at her hand on his and she drew it away.

"Nothing is impossible." He gave a harsh sigh and glanced at the clock in the dash. "Do you mind if we stop by the Y? It's only a couple miles from here."

"Of course I don't mind," she smiled, happy to spend a little more time with him.

When they walked in the gymnasium, it was clear Neil was a bit of a big man on campus. Everyone was excited to see him, especially the teenage boys playing half-court. They literally stopped their game when they saw Neil.

"Mr. C!" one boy called out before bounding over with a grin, dribbling a basketball. Two others followed.

"Hey guys," Neil said with warmth in his voice. "Sorry I couldn't make it today."

"It's cool. We got your text." He shot a curious look at Ashtyn, who smiled at the young men.

"Been practicing the fade away?" Neil asked the tallest boy.

"Yup. Check it out." He dribbled, ran toward the net, and jumped up to make the basket.

"Much better," Neil nodded. "Watch your form. You're not going to have a ton of space when the defender is on you, but you'll want to keep your shoulders as squared as possible, and when you turn…" He squatted, shaping his hands as if he has a basketball in it, turned left, then right. "Keep the ball high, not low, otherwise you'll set up a steal from the defense. Like this."

The three of them nodded, but quickly switched the subject when they each checked Ashtyn out with curiosity in their young eyes.

"Who's this? Your boo?" asked the shorter one with the Lakers jersey looking her up and down.

Neil chuckled. "Guys, this is Ashtyn. Ashtyn, say hi to Trey, Mario, and Brandon."

She raised her hand and smiled. "Hi, guys."

"What's up, Miss Ashtyn?" Trey said, the tallest, giving her a chin raise.

"You a lawyer too?" Brandon asked. He was the one with the Lakers jersey.

"I work in finance."

He twisted his mouth. "You look like you read a lot of books and shit."

She laughed, despite Neil giving a chastising look for the language. "More like numbers and schedules."

"That's cool," Trey commented.

Brandon pointed to her. "Yo, Mr. C, you n' her, like, hanging out? Doesn't look like the kind of chick who plays any sports. Isn't that what you want in a girlfriend?"

Neil hung his head for a second and smiled, hands on hips. "I think I said I wanted her to be active, not necessarily a woman who plays a sport."

"You active?" Trey asked, giving a face he didn't think she might not be good enough for their Mr. C.

Funny inquisition she was under. "I run."

"A-ight. That's cool. My sister runs track," said Mario. "What do you wear when you run? A nice little sports bra and hip-huggin' shorts—?"

"Hey!" Neil swung an arm Mario's neck and rubbed his head while the youth laughed.

"I was kidding. For real!"

With a laugh, Neil released him.

"Mr. C. Do your thing quick," called Brandon, before he passed the basketball.

Neil caught the ball with one hand, dribbled, jumped up, and made a basket. They all hollered in boyish appreciation. Neil grinned. "We should go. I can't be in the gym with these shoes. I'll be back next week."

The boys gave him a couple fist bumps and went off to resume their game.

When he'd mentioned that he volunteer-coached with kids, she didn't imagine he cared if he missed one day. Clearly, he did. With his limited leisure time, she couldn't believe he took some of it to coach kids at the Y. It was kind of wonderful. *He* was kind of wonderful.

"Those boys adore you," she told him as they walked to the car.

"It's mutual. We have a lot of fun. I try to set a good example for them."

"You do? And here I thought you only liked hot babes in your personal life."

The car beeped as he unlocked it and winked at her. "I like to mix it up."

She laughed.

The drive to her house was relatively quiet while she digested these new feelings beginning to percolate for him. He was more attractive to her than ever.

When he walked her to the door, she said, "Thank you for today."

"No thanks necessary. I didn't help you get any closer to finding your pearls."

He sounded so disappointed in himself. "It's the fact you went out of your way to try that matters, Neil. I owe you for that."

Tucking his hands in his pockets, he said, "The case isn't over. If you think of anything or anyone who might've taken them, tell me."

"Other than my ex and the movers, I haven't a clue. Thank goodness my neighbor was watching over my things, or else much more could've been stolen."

"Your neighbor?"

"Randy. He told me he kept an eye on my belongings until I got there."

A thoughtful look cast on his handsome face, but then he cupped her elbow, and brushed a kiss on her cheek. "Your grandmother is not a strand of pearls. The loss of them is not the loss of her. What's truly priceless, is what she left in you."

The words and the chaste kiss touched her with such poignancy, tears gathered in her eyes. "Thank you, Neil," she whispered, one tear escaping before she could stop it.

He stepped back with a small smile, swiping her tear away with his thumb. "None of that now. I don't like to make women cry." Suddenly, he changed his tone back to his usual joking manner. "Unless it's my name, of course."

She gave a watery laugh. The tender moment broken.

8

THAT EVENING, she got a text from Neil. A giddiness hit her when she saw his name on the screen. She'd just seen him a few hours ago, what could he want? She opened the text message:

Are you busy right now?

She smiled, sat on the edge of the couch, and responded with:

Yes, but not in a fun way. Why?

He quickly sent another. *I'm on my way to pick you up. Right now?*

Yes. Right now. Wear something very casual. Nothing fancy.

The next thing she knew she was flying to the bathroom to fix her hair and put on some mascara. What were they going to do? She didn't care. Since she wasn't in a hurry to get on the road anyway, she'd decided to take him up on his offer. Whatever he had in mind. If he felt bad because they didn't recover her pearls, then she'd be sure to remind him she was okay. Sad, crushed, but okay.

After taking way too long to decide on a casual outfit, she settled on light blue cropped jeans, a white sleeveless blouse, and slip-on sneakers. She left her hair down because whenever she did, Neil's gaze seemed to linger a little longer. Half an hour later, she got his text he'd arrived.

His passenger window rolled down as she approached.

"Get in," he said with a smile.

"Where on earth are we going?" she asked, opening the door.

"It's a surprise. Relax." He looked her up and down. "This is your idea of casual wear?"

"What were you expecting?"

"Doesn't look like you can get dirty in those clothes."

"Dirty? I beg you. Tell me what's going on."

He shook his head, smiling, and turned up the radio. "Just enjoy the ride."

Eventually they entered the industrial part of town and her wonder only increased. They pulled into a salvage yard and her curiosity, and a tinge of wariness, doubled. She had no inkling why they would be here. When they parked and Neil got out, a skinny young man in a greased-stained t-shirt and Dickies pants greeted them. His name was Hopper and he smiled at her impishly. "This way."

As they came round the building, she spotted a shiny red sports car in the distance. Older model. A red Dodge Challenger to be exact. Neil grabbed a small sledgehammer sitting against a stack of tires and placed it in her hands, then gestured to the car. "Have at it."

Stunned, she blinked at him, looking from the car to Neil to Hopper, back to the car, and back to Neil. "Have at it?"

"I thought a sledgehammer would be more, uh, *effective* than a bat."

Where the heck did he get this idea? Then it dawned on her. The joke she'd made at the wedding. "Omigod, you're kidding. You remembered what I said?"

He crossed his arms with a proud grin. "My memory serves me well."

"I...I wasn't really serious about that!"

"Sure you were. And if you'll recall, I said anything could be arranged."

Dumbfounded, she stared at the vehicle, disbelieving *this* was his surprise. "Whose car is this?"

"Don't worry, it was abandoned months ago when they brought it out here. The engine's been taken out and instead of restoring it, I convinced Hopper to let me buy it from him so you could live out your little fantasy."

"It looks a lot like—"

"Your ex's? I know. That's the point. Now, get going before the sun sets."

She hesitated. She'd never beaten or broken anything in her life on purpose. Smashing a perfectly good vehicle seemed so wrong. "I can't."

"Why not? It's just a hunk of metal. A machine. How much does Cliff love his?"

More than he ever loved me.

"Start with the headlights and if you don't enjoy it, we'll go," Neil said resting against the wall.

She swung the sledgehammer up over her shoulder, paused, thinking of how obsessed Cliff was with image, status, and the perfection of both. Of her. How many times did she wonder if she'd only be perfect, then so would her marriage?

Wham! The headlight splintered into a dozen pieces at her feet.

You talk too much in public, he would say. *Every stupid opinion that comes out of your mouth reflects on me.*

She swung again. The second headlight exploded with a glorious sound of Cliff's voice with it.

How she'd missed her cousin's bachelorette party because he begged her to come to his company's retreat instead. He'd implored that he needed her by his side, to stand with him and show a united duo. In the end, he ignored her for three days to play round after round of golf with his boss.

Whack! There went the passenger side mirror.

Complaining her hair was too blonde, her breasts too small, her career too stagnant, her parents too redneck. That she should've majored in Economics instead of Business Administration.

A dent here, a kick there, every window smashed and every door trashed. It was the best workout she'd ever had.

By the time she was done, the Challenger was officially totaled. She was breathing hard, and her muscles were shaking, but she grinned the whole way back.

The way Neil smiled at her made her shake even more. In the car, he handed her a cold bottled water. "You're stronger than you look."

She unscrewed the top. "I don't think anyone else would've arranged something so destructive and therapeutic at the same time. My mom would probably commit me if she found out."

"It'll be our secret." He winked.

Another secret between her and Neil. Things were starting to get complicated.

Somewhere between the salvage yard and her house she decided to no longer deny what she wanted.

Him.

She was going to seduce Neil Caenon.

From beneath her lashes, she glanced at his profile. The sharp line of his nose, the sculpted mouth and jawline. Gorgeous. He'd always been, but male beauty, while she appreciated it, never made her want someone on that basis alone. Even his charisma and intelligence weren't enough. A man had to have *more* to entice her to this degree. And Neil had it. Jordana was right; beneath the surface was a man with real depth. A man with heart and compassion. Funny how she recognized these things in Logan immediately, and had often wondered how he and Neil could be such good friends. Now she understood.

When he pulled up to her house, he insisted on walking her to the door, and she got excited wondering if he might possibly make a move so she didn't have to.

Once she turned the lock on her door, however, he didn't. "Drive safe tonight. And stay out of trouble." He grinned, and started back toward his car.

Before she could think twice— "Neil."

He stopped, turned his profile, and slowly faced her. "That's the first time you haven't called me by my last name."

She blinked, shaking her head. "No it isn't. It can't be."

"Trust me, I've noticed." He gazed at her. "What's up?"

Words refused to come out. Perhaps because she hadn't prepared what was she going to say in advance. Then again, men responded to body language, right? Drawing in a breath, she got closer to him, sensing him tense, but didn't let that thwart her. She leaned in. He didn't move a muscle as she pressed her lips to his. His mouth was warm, still, firm.

Was he shocked? Or did a lack of response mean he didn't want her?

Just as she started to pull back, he cupped her elbows lightly, bringing her to him. "Ashtyn."

His breath fanned her lips.

She brushed her mouth over his, silently asking for him to take the lead, and he read that request instantly. Cupping her nape, he bent and gave her something unexpected—a tender kiss, but with more passion than any deep-throated one. He used his thumbs to tilt her face up and molded his mouth along hers. A perfect alignment. So perfect, she whimpered his name, hungry for more.

He dipped his tongue in, swirling with hers with expert, slow care.

Sometimes a first kiss was awkward, getting to know one another's moves and rhythm, but with Neil, she didn't have to do any of that. He read her; she read him. He seemed to realize this, a low moan coming from his throat. She didn't even know her feet were even moving until she felt the front door at her back, and his erection against her stomach.

God, yes, he wanted her and she wanted him.

They were going to spend the night together.

9

WHEN HE PULLED back, she panted, hazed with desire.

He stared at her, chest rising and falling with his controlled, deep breaths. Indecision warred in his eyes.

"Should I...not have done that?" she asked, a little confused.

"I don't know. I'm glad you did. You kiss—better than I ever imagined," he told her hoarsely.

She gave a shaky smile. "Do you want to come in?"

"Yes."

The swiftness of his response and the ache she heard in that one word told her how much he wanted to, and yet, he was hesitating.

"But?" she asked.

"Sex will change everything."

Lips still stinging from his kiss, she swallowed and nodded. They wouldn't make love tonight, but there *would* be a night. "I know."

Beginning to step back, he gave her a little smile. "I think I should go." He'd said it as if unsure.

"Okay," was all she was capable of saying.

She watched him leave, then she went inside, heart continuing to beat a tattoo against her chest.

Funny.

With a reputation like his, she thought it'd be him who would do the seducing, not the one wavering. She'd underestimated Neil's maturity, assumed he was a nondiscriminatory sex machine who wouldn't turn down a woman's invitation to bed for the world.

Sex would change everything? She was now beginning to disagree. They didn't have everything—they had a mutual, irresistible attraction and a blossoming friendship. What would change? If he thought she was looking to latch herself to a new man, then she'd have to assure him that was the last thing she hoped for.

Tomorrow, before she left, she intended to make that clear.

When she crawled on her bed later, all she could think about was Neil in it with her, undressing her, rolling her around, making commands and wearing her out. She groaned in her pillow, then turned to her back, restless.

Closing her eyes, she grazed her fingers over her mouth, over her chest, trailed a path, and parted her legs. Wet from her carnal thoughts, and too turned on to go asleep, she strummed her pussy, thinking only of Neil's body on hers when she climaxed.

THE WOMAN ON his mind? Ashtyn. Strong, sexy Ashtyn. The taste of her had permanently stained his mouth. He kept running his teeth on his bottom lip, reliving their kiss again and again.

Fuck it's hard to concentrate right now.

The woman sitting across from him? Her real name was Mandy, but he called her Lady Jaye, a cartoon character on G.I. Joe. To him, she looked and sounded just like her: the scratchy voice, pixie-cut hair, badass attitude and all. Lucky for him, Mandy found the nickname amusing. They'd known each other a long time and had an understanding. The understanding that no matter what *she* thought was best, he always had a better deal in mind for all parties involved.

At first, it was a bitch putting this deal together, but he liked the challenge.

Mandy sighed harshly, sitting back and crossing her arms. "I don't want a headline or a parade to show off our catch of the week. You know I don't care. All I want is the person responsible."

"Then give me the deal we negotiated on Tuesday and justice will prevail."

"If this were anyone else other than you, I wouldn't give the courtesy of this meeting," she teased.

"We're both benefitting from this. Let's be frank with each other. We usually are. You've got nothing on my clients and I'm helping you get the end result you require. I'm doing you a courtesy as well. One of the things I like about coming to the Department of Justice. Let me do what I do best and consider it done."

Mandy rolled her eyes and closed the file. "Do your magic. Just make sure Mr. O'Hare signs this, otherwise the fantastic deal is off like a Prom dress."

"Have I ever failed you?"

She didn't need long to answer. "No."

"Then don't tease me with empty threats. I'm ticklish." He winked at her, took the paperwork and strolled out.

Back at the firm, he knew by the look on his legal secretary's face his two o'clock appointment was already there. Ingrid handed him the sales agreement, and he gave her a nod, attempting to undo the glower on his face. He glanced behind him, and saw Paige and Stewart Iverson in the conference room with a woman he assumed was Bridget Hayes sitting across from them. Juliet's parents were nodding, and the young woman talked animatedly, gesturing with her hands.

From what he learned through basic research, she came from an upper class family with visions of becoming an entrepreneur before the age of thirty. In other words, a silver spoon brat who probably thought it would be fun to have her own bakery to run, when she didn't know shit about small business taxes or employee retention, let alone keeping it going in a flux economy.

He didn't like her already.

Drawing in a long breath, he walked in.

Paige stood, softly smiling, reaching out both hands to him. "Neil. It's been a while. Good to see you."

He leaned down and kissed her cheek. "Hello, Paige."

Stewart shook his hand. "Thanks for taking care of this."

Neither of them appeared tense or apprehensive, anxious, nor seemed to be having second thoughts. They were really going through with it, although there were no indications before today that they wouldn't. He'd hoped, at the last minute, severing their ties with the bakery their daughter had worked hard to accomplish would give them serious pause. Then again, they might've been thinking about this long before they told him.

Bridget Hayes stood with an overly bright smile. "Hi." She wore a yellow dress with a white jacket. Everything about her was bright. From her cropped, strawberry-blonde hair to her smile. Despite her very feminine appearance, she had a firm handshake and she looked him directly in the eyes.

He respected that.

"Nice to meet you," he greeted, though he didn't mean it. Eager to get everything over with, he opened the file and slid it across to Bridget as she sat down. "Here it is. Any questions, let me know."

"Paige and Stewart have told me so much about you," she said, ignoring the contract and smiling at him.

He kept his eyes on the agreement, smoothing his tie and taking a seat. "Is that so?"

"You must think I'm an honest thief stealing Juliet's bakery."

"Can't steal something you're buying."

"You know what I mean, Mr. Caenon."

He lifted his gaze to hers and unclicked his pen. "You're doing this on your own?" At her nod he asked, "Have you ever owned a business before?"

"No," she answered perkily. "I know it won't be easy, but then again, nothing has been easy the past couple years. I didn't think I'd ever do something like this but…" She paused, shifted her gaze for a moment, and then raised it again. "I was walking my bestie's dog one day while she was in Greece for two weeks, and made the mistake of letting him off the leash for too long. He bolted!" She chopped the air with her hand. "And I had to chase him for almost four blocks! I'm out of breath, panicking, and clearly the worst dog walker ever, but eventually I caught up with him." She smiled at the Iversons. "Right in front of How Sweet It Is. I went inside and fell in love with the place immediately. Paige and I got to know each other over the last few months, and when she told me they were selling it, something inside me clicked. It was, like—" she snapped her fingers, "—fate."

Like fate? Ha. Definitely a millennial. No more than twenty-six-years-old would be his guess. Almost the same age as Juliet, who had turned twenty-nine mere days after the bakery opened. Bridget sort of reminded him of her. Her affinity for fate, that is. "You bake?"

"I wouldn't consider owning a business I don't know dick about." Her eyes went wide and she covered her mouth. "Oh. So sorry."

He chuckled. "It's okay. Worse, much worse, has been said in this conference room than dick."

Her eyes twinkled as she dropped her hand. "I've been working since I was fifteen. Baking since I was ten. My friends call me the 'Cupcake Sheba.' Here." She leaned down to pick up something next to her chair and set a bright pink box on the table. "For you."

Reluctantly, he reached over and lifted the lid. Frosting thicker than a dictionary sat atop a brown cupcake. He recognized the recipe. Peanut butter chocolate.

"Juliet's number one seller," Bridget said before he could ask. "Your favorite."

He glanced at the Iversons, who were holding hands and giving him encouraging smiles. Now he got it. They were literally trying to sweeten him up for this deal. He hadn't had a peanut butter chocolate cupcake in years, afraid one bite would evoke deep emotions he preferred to keep locked away. They thought he was a saint for all he'd done for them after Juliet's death. Helping with the funeral, the memorial, cleaning out her apartment, selling it, and doing what he could to assist them with the bakery.

They thought he and their daughter had been planning to get married, but the truth was, she'd dumped him just days before her accident. The last few months of their relationship had been spent in misery. No one knew it but him. Not even her best girlfriends. They all thought he was the perfect boyfriend, but he had been nowhere near.

"Thank you," he said, his voice catching. He closed the box.

"The point is," Bridget said, startling him with her bluntness, "I'm not taking over the bakery for just *me*, Mr. Caenon. Even though I never met her, I feel a real kinship with Juliet. From the stories they've told me, I feel like she and I would've really hit it off, and regardless of the circumstances, I was going to have a connection to How Sweet It Is. I know you might not understand this spiritual shizzle, but I do."

"You don't need my approval, Bridget. The decision was the Iverson's, not mine. Therefore, whether or not I like it, this is happening."

"Neil," Paige reproached.

"No, it's okay," Bridget rushed in to assure them. "Do you have a sister?"

"Two."

She beamed a smile. "I have one. Half-sister. She's a singer in New York and I hardly ever see her. Hardly know her, really. Sometimes I feel we have nothing in common, but I'm hoping some day that'll change. I have a feeling this bakery will help me with that." She rolled her eyes. "She thinks

I'm impulsive and spoiled, but this is meant to be. Every time I walk in the bakery and see Juliet's picture, I talk to her. I think she'd approve. So her parents can retire and I can be responsible for once in my life. And if you don't like it, and clearly you don't, well you can stick it up your Brooks Brothers-wearing ass."

"Bridget!" Stewart admonished with a chuckle.

Despite wanting to resist her bubbly charm, Neil smiled. Juliet would definitely like this young woman. She had spunk, and enough quirkiness to keep her positive when she realizes how hard it'll be to stay in business in this city with a million other bakeries.

Juliet's dream wouldn't go anywhere anytime soon, not without a fight, and that was really all he needed to know. To him, it'd felt like Paige and Stewart were giving it up too easily, too dispassionately. But they had every right to. After all, it wasn't their dream; it was Juliet's. They weren't selling it to some greedy shit who wanted the valuable real estate either.

He couldn't imagine a more ideal situation.

Then why did the hurt continue to stab at his chest?

Because, he thought looking out the window, it only faded Juliet even further to the black. Pretty soon there would be nothing but memories left. Nothing for him or anyone else to hold, touch, see or hear of her life other than memories. Nothing left to help with the guilt.

"Mr. Caenon?"

Bridget's voice came from a faraway place.

Snapping out of it, he slid the sales agreement to her, and set his mouth in a grim line. "Sign here."

TO SAY ASHTYN was nervous with every step she took to Neil's office was a bit of an understatement. She couldn't believe what she was about to do, but would regret it forever if she didn't.

His legal secretary announced her arrival, and seconds later, she was directed to go on in.

His warm smile when she walked in tripled the race of her pulse. She closed the door behind her.

He looked at her curiously. "Is everything okay? I thought you were leaving today."

"I'm on my way now. Just wanted to stop by before I left." He gestured for her to sit down but she shook her head. "The reason for my visit—" God this felt weird to do in his office. The legal books and professional decorations almost as intimidating as the attorney standing in front of her in his dark gray suit, but she gathered her poise. "There's a fair near Briar's this Saturday. I can't remember the last time I went to one. I was wondering if you'd like to join me."

His dark brow lifted. "You want me to go to a fair with you?"

"Not just for the fair. You could stay the night. The weekend. With me." Earlier when she'd rehearsed, it came out sexier. She just couldn't be direct about it, but Neil was a smart man, he knew exactly what she was inferring.

"Ashtyn," he said gently. "You're on the rebound."

"Wouldn't that be ideal for you?" she half-laughed.

"But…it's you. You're not just any woman. Don't get me wrong, it's not that I'm not tempted. In fact, I've never been so tempted in my life." He continued to trace his fingertips on his fine, ornate desk as he came round to face her up close. "But," he started, and her heart sank, "I don't think it's wise for us to get involved. You should take things slow. Really think about what's good for you now. Go home and—"

A laugh of true disbelief escaped. "I can't believe I'm standing here inviting Neil Caenon to spend a no-strings-attached weekend and he's giving me a speech about what's good for me."

He flinched. "I was only—"

"Don't." She shifted her gaze up to the ceiling, then met his again. "You're more selective than I thought. You project yourself as God's gift to women, virtually boasting your sexual prowess. You flirt and you charm until you're out of breath. Is that all for show?"

He lowered his brows. "Regardless, you want to use me to pacify your loneliness."

That stung, because it was partially true. *Only the truth hurts like that.* "Isn't that what you do? Use women for pleasure and vice versa when one of you is lonely?"

"You and I are different. I *care* about you."

"Oh, so you prefer to sleep with women you *don't* care about?"

"That's a cold way to put it."

She sighed, understanding where he was coming from. Knowing the fact he cared about her stood in the way of what she wanted depressed her. "What about last night? The kiss?"

He bit down on his bottom lip, hard, then gestured helplessly. "The kiss…probably shouldn't have happened."

Well then. Mortification complete. "Oh my. I read this so wrong. I'm sorry I bothered you at work." She turned to the door, her whole body hot with embarrassment of putting herself out there to be rejected by a man she thought rejected no one.

"Ashtyn."

She paused and looked back at him.

With a stricken look, he said gruffly, "Don't leave like this."

She forced a smile his way. "Neil. I want nothing to do with relationships and you avoid them like no man I've ever met. If we were ever going to give in to this—attraction to each other, now would be the perfect time to."

With his heavenly green eyes boring into hers, he seemed to rethink his answer. She thought he would change his mind. The desire and temptation in them told her so.

He visibly swallowed, and she knew the answer hadn't changed.

"I'm sorry," he said, regret heavy in his tone.

She pressed her lips together and nodded, then walked out.

MAYBE HE should get his head checked, because he had to be *out of his mind* to say anything but "yes hell yes" to Ashtyn's offer to spend the weekend with her.

Neil ran a hand down his face, blowing out a breath, and rested his hands on his hips. Frankly he couldn't believe she'd asked, but then again, she was a confident woman who knew what she wanted, and went for it.

And if he went for it and slept with her, they both might regret it. For one thing, Logan would wildly disapprove. A long time ago, Neil swore he'd never lay a hand on Logan's executive assistant. There were plenty of single women in the Bay.

But none of them were Ashtyn.

If he needed a second reason, the biggest one, was the fact she was in a vulnerable position, and he didn't want to be the man who took advantage of that, permission or not. She hadn't been touched by a man in a long time, and her whole energy echoed to him how much she craved it. A situation like that was right up his alley. A woman with nothing on her mind but a good time.

Maybe the fact he'd been in a bad mood when she came by had clouded his decision. Bridget and the Iversons had just left and the old guilt that came with any reminder of his time with Juliet had him wishing to be left alone.

Then Ashtyn came in with her brazen proposal they spend the weekend together, and he'd said no.

No?!

With visceral desire and his conscience warring each other, he decided to get out of the office.

After clearing his last doc review, he drove down to Legal Services to pick up the file for a new pro bono case. Guaranteed to cool him off. As a corporate lawyer, there were times when he could go days or weeks without seeing a client and so he volunteered his services to those who couldn't afford a lawyer.

The cases he took on often gave him challenges his corporate job didn't. Mind-bending, sometimes heartbreaking challenges. There were days of little victories and days of absolute soul-crushing defeat. Nevertheless, taking on a case kept him fresh on his game and was a welcome detour from litigation. Being a lawyer, one had to be fluid. Once you hit a wall, you went left or right to find another way.

As if she knew he'd be coming today, Janet Ludwig approached him five seconds after he walked in the door. She handed him a file. "Got a case for you."

"Hi Janet. Good to see you, too," he drawled sardonically, casting her a half-smile, accepting the folder. He followed her back to her desk. "How have you been?" It was always straight to business with this old gal.

She snorted and flipped a hand. Janet had been working for Legal Services long enough to have secured a jaded, direct, blunt, no-nonsense demeanor. Despite this, she was invaluable in her department, working tirelessly.

Neil guessed for her to be in her early fifties. She had streaks of gray in her short black hair, crow's feet dashed at the corners of her brown eyes, and she wore the same strand of thin gold necklaces, one with a dove hanging off it. It didn't take much to disappoint her, but it took a lot to make her smile. Another challenge he never ceased to take on.

She plopped down in her chair with a groan and took out a small tin can of hand salve. "It's Thursday, and I want it to be Saturday. That's how I am. My dishwasher decided to vomit on my kitchen floor and my husband thinks he can fix it. He's been thinking he can fix *anything* now by looking up videos on the Internet. Drives me crazy. How have you been, Neil?"

He smiled, plucked a caramel candy from her little bowl, and sat down on the metal chair beside her desk and opened the file. "Can't complain." *Except my dick can.* Opening the manila folder, he looked over the document.

"You're easy on the eyes, make an ungodly amount of money for what you do, and you're halfway intelligent, so no," she clipped. "You can't complain." A little smile moved her wrinkly lips.

"Such flattery today. What's this one about?" he asked, scanning the paperwork.

"Diana and Ritchie Harris. Mother and son. They need representation," she explained while he read the paperwork.

He nodded. "I see that. Why a shelter hearing?"

"Diana is going to jail for solicitation for twenty months. It's a lost cause anyway because the house isn't suitable for a special needs child. Ritchie's confined to a wheelchair from an accident three years ago. He's eleven. Bright, headstrong, and unfortunately knows a lot about his mother's occupation."

"Where's the father?"

"Dead. She's remarried, but regardless, the social worker states the house isn't suitable, even with the stepfather there." She opened the drawer to put her hand salve back, and hit the side of it with her palm when it jammed. It loosened and she shut the drawer. "I think you're better off persuading them to get used to the idea of the state home. The case isn't a winner."

Neil immediately sympathized with the boy, but with his mother about to be incarcerated, and the house unsuitable for a wheelchair-bound boy, the state would probably win this one. "Okay. I'll see what I can do."

"I know what'll happen," she told him, already annoyed with his need to win. "He'll go to that home. Make that clear."

He didn't like to think that far ahead until all options were exhausted, but Janet was usually right when it came to predicting the outcome. "Thanks. I have time to meet with them today."

After a phone call, he drove out to Diana and Ritchie's home. They were both eager to meet him and talk. They lived in a decent neighborhood. He'd seen worse. Diana answered the door quickly. Tall, willowy, she had stringy blonde hair and hazel eyes, dressed in a pair of tight jeans and a black top. The boy, Ritchie, was right behind her in his chair.

"Hi!" she greeted. "Mr. Caenon, right?" she asked, widening the door for him.

He nodded with a small smile. "Right. Nice to meet you."

The place smelled like garlic and Pine Sol and was overall tidy. It was small however, with a narrow hallway and furnishings that looked old and hand-me-down. Diana offered him water, but he declined.

"Hey. I'm Ritchie," said the boy. He shook his hand. Ritchie had light blonde hair, his blue eyes alert, and wore a Captain America shirt. "My mom says you're going to help me."

"I'm going to try my best," Neil told him.

"Uh, want me to show you around or anything?" Diana asked.

He didn't need to. Already he could tell the social services rep had been right. The house wasn't suitable for a disabled child. "No that's okay. Do you mind if I speak to him alone for a minute?"

"Yeah, sure. I'll be in my room. Ritchie. Be nice."

Her son nodded and she went to a room at the far end of the hallway.

Neil set down his briefcase and leaned against the rickety kitchen table. "Do you know what's going on, Ritchie?"

"Yeah. My mom is going away to jail and I don't got a place to live yet."

"Do you know why your mom is going away?"

He nodded. "Guys pay her to be their girlfriend. It's against the law, I guess. I wanted her to quit, but she says it's how she can afford to take care of us."

Too mature of a topic to be discussing with an eleven-year-old, but he wasn't here to judge, he was here to work on the boy's behalf. "Where do you want to live? Besides here?"

"With my stepdad, Carl. He's cool."

"Where's Carl now?"

"At work."

Good to know. "Is your mom okay with you living with Carl?"

"Yeah."

"Why do you want to live with him?"

"I dunno." He shrugged. "I like him."

He gave the kid the face that told him that answer wouldn't suffice.

"Er..." Ritchie rocked his chair forward and backward. "He's funny. And he plays Game of War with me as long as I want. When my mom is tired, he'll take me places. He says he's gonna save up so I can join a wheelchair basketball league."

"Basketball?" Neil exclaimed with a smile.

"What? You think I can't do it?" the kid retorted in defense.

"The opposite. You look strong for your age. I think that's great. I happen to love basketball, too." The stepdad just scored major points with Neil and he didn't even know it.

Ritchie gave a skeptical look, as though a man in a suit couldn't be into basketball. "Who's your team?"

"Clippers."

"No kidding. Mine, too!"

He sat down in a metal chair so he could meet Ritchie eye-to-eye. "Can't believe how close we came last season to the championships. If our star player hadn't twisted his knee…"

"I know! I put a hole in the wall with my basketball when they announced it. I knew we didn't stand a chance against LeBron once that happened."

"It's okay. The season will be here before you know it."

"Yup." He squinted one eye, and looked up with the other. "One-hundred and forty-three days to go."

Neil chuckled. Smart kid he had here. "Who's counting?"

They talked a little more about their favorite team before he called Diana back into the room. Regardless of her poor career choices, she had a great son, who deserved a great home while she did her time. The next thing on his list would be to make sure the stepdad was what Ritchie said he was. Neil wondered if the man was worthy of such praise. Sometimes kids only saw what they needed to see.

"What do you think?" she said when they were outside on the sidewalk.

"I'll need some time to gather evidence in support of Ritchie's wish to live with Carl. I have to admit it'll be tough either way, unless Carl is a saint."

She rubbed her arms, anxiety etched in her fine lines. "He's no saint, but I don't know any parents who are. He's better than a fucking state home!"

"Unfortunately, the judge might not see it that way. I need you to prepare yourself and your son for that decision."

She threw up her hands. "So you're like, givin' up before we even get to the hearing?" she accused.

"No. I'm going to do my best. That's all I can promise."

Tears welled her eyes. "Look, Mr. Caenon. Ritchie shouldn't have to pay for my screw-ups, okay? He doesn't belong in no home that isn't his own. He's got it bad enough as it is in life."

He glanced back at the house. "He doesn't seem to think so."

She sniffed, nodding. "He's just like his dad. Able to block out how shitty his life really is."

He felt for Ritchie, and it was never wise to feel for any case, except for the passion it took to see it through.

An hour later, he returned to Raimes & Watley. Back in what he called "firm mode."

He got around the corner to the hallway that led to his office and crossed paths with one of the junior associates, Mitch.

"Hey Caenon, coming out tomorrow night?"

"For what?" He continued to walk, not bothering to pause for this conversation.

Mitch swiveled on a heel and hurried to catch up. "For Paul's birthday."

"Nope."

"Why not? We need more chick magnets."

"So you want me to take a few hours out of my valuable time to attract women to the party? Think again. Besides, what do you think it takes to attract ladies at a bar?"

"Money, looks, and clothes," he blurted.

"Wrong." He pushed his office door open. "Confidence and compliments. If you are having a good time, and you show it, women will naturally come to *you*."

"Get real, Caenon. Pretty boys just don't understand."

Neil paused and gave the red-headed associate a wry glance. "You guilting me is not going to work whatsoever."

"Do me a favor! You know how rare it is for me to get *two* hours to go out on a Friday night?"

"Uh, no, Mitch. I have no idea what that's like," he said sarcastically. "I worked no more than twenty hours a week when I was a junior associate."

"Not fair. You were a junior associate for all of five seconds before they promoted you."

"Regardless, I worked my ass off for years and had to miss out on a lot of birthdays for the sake of work. Get used to it."

Mitch frowned. "What put you in a lousy mood?"

Neil ignored the remark, stopped in his office, and sniffed. Was it his imagination or did he still smell Ashtyn's perfume? Had it lingered in his office this whole time just to torture him?

He groaned, pinching the bridge of his nose while he sat down. Why did he reject her again? What were those stupid reasons he gave?

At the time, he thought he was doing the right thing. Keeping hands off his best friend's employee. Not taking advantage of a woman, even if she asked for it. And wanting to preserve the small friendship they'd formed. Sex—although one of the best things in life—would throw it all away. It'd mess with their dynamic. No matter how hard they tried, women associated a good fuck into deep feelings. Her claim she didn't want anything but a fun weekend still left him skeptical.

How would he deal with it if she got emotional? How much would he regret going over there if she turned clingy or upset when the weekend was over? How hard would Logan punch him for hurting her when she'd been through so much already?

He stared at his window, frowning. Why risk it?

Because it was *Ashtyn Turner,* said a voice loud and clear in his head.

Ever since they met, he'd fantasized about her in every way. Been even a little obsessed just getting her to smile at him. Now, as she pointed out, was his only chance to fulfill that unending desire. He knew he'd never get another. Not with her.

Decision made. Consequences damned.

He checked his watch. If he plowed through the next two hours of work, delegated the deposition tomorrow to another associate, he could leave for Briar's by eight.

PARTY OF one.

Ashtyn didn't mind. She had the stereo playing soft rock, a fire going in the hearth, and was on her second glass of wine as she finished washing the dishes. Without shame, she sang along with the radio and refused, flat out refused, to think about Neil. Once the dishes were done, she planned to make some popcorn and put on an '80s movie, her favorite decade of cinema. On impulse, she'd stopped by several yard sales in Briar's Edge before coming to the house. One of the families had a box of DVDs with

PEARLS & PERSUASION

a dozen of her favorite '80s movies, and she'd spent a whole $6 for the lot of them.

Her ex-husband hated watching movies. His undiagnosed ADD wouldn't let him, unless he was doing something with his hands at the same time. It drove her bananas. But now she didn't have to deal with that anymore.

A knock on the patio door startled her, but when she saw the grinning Miss B behind it, she was pleased to see her. "Bonnie." She turned down the stereo, smiled, and unlocked the sliding door.

"Hi, sweetie. I was just thinking of you! Need anything?" She stepped in, handing her a large, covered glass dish, then looking right and left. "You here by yourself or is that stud boyfriend of yours here, too? Yoo hoo!" she called, apparently to summon Neil.

"That wasn't my boyfriend," Ashtyn informed her. "Just my attorney."

Bonnie's big brown eyes widened. "Is he married?"

"No."

She scrunched her nose. "Girlfriend?"

"No."

"Oh my, he's gay, isn't he? A man that pretty usually is."

Ashtyn stifled a laugh. "Nope, he's straight."

"Then why isn't he yours?" As if she thought Ashtyn didn't know what to do with the casserole, she took it from her hands, went to the island, and set it on some kitchen towels. "When he and Deputy Thornton came to the house, and he told me what happened and why you were at the jail, he seemed so worried about you. He sure didn't talk like your attorney. I mean, he certainly speaks like one, but I've never heard a lawyer show such…" She spun around with a dramatic speed. "Such adoration about his client. Anyway, you'd be a dummy not to catch him for your own."

She couldn't help but chuckle. "Neil isn't the catching kind."

"All men who aren't hitched, gay, or dead are catchable, Miss Turner. My advice? Feed him. And wear a skirt once in a while," she said, pointedly looking at Ashtyn's shorts.

Biting back a comment about it not being 1955, she walked over to the fridge. "Can I get you anything? Some tea or water?"

"No, no, don't bother yourself," Bonnie flipped a hand. "Ames and I are going out."

Ashtyn swiveled on the balls of her feet. "Oh, really, Bonnie? You and the sheriff? I never would've guessed from the way you two spoke to each other."

"Ha! That's just how we flirt, sweetie. He yanks my chain, I yank back."

"I see." A smile pulled at her mouth. Reminded Ashtyn of her and Neil.

"*Great* for foreplay. He may not be pretty like your lawyer, but he has a great big hairy chest I love to rest my head on. I think real men should have hair on their chests, don't you? And he's got large hands, a big laugh, and the best part? A big—"

Ashtyn thrust out her hands. "Too much information, Bonnie."

She laughed heartily. "His heart. I was going to say heart. Oh my, get your thoughts out of the gutter about my man! If you're smart and clever enough, you'll direct them toward the man who couldn't keep his eyes off you." She clasped her hands together. "Invite him over for a plate of my famous chicken fiesta casserole, give him a beer and a neck massage, and call me to thank me when he's eating out of your hand."

She chuckled, following Bonnie to the deck. "Thank you for the food."

"Have a good night, Ashtyn. I'll be back on Friday after you leave to clean up."

She closed the patio door, turned up the volume up on the stereo, and dragged herself back to the sink to finish cleaning up. The way to a man's heart was through his stomach, true, but she didn't want Neil's heart. It was as unavailable as hers.

Halfway through the movie *Sixteen Candles*, she hit the pause button and listened. Was that the music or did the doorbell just ring?

It rang again. Quickly wiping her hands on a towel, she made her way to the front door, stomach fluttering.

Neil?

11

The distorted figure in the beveled glass didn't appear to be the lawyer however.

She started to smile as she opened the door. "Deputy Thornton."

He wore a button-up shirt and dark jeans and his shoulders filled up the doorway nicely. "Jake, remember? How are you?"

"I'm well, thank you. What can I do for you?"

"I just wanted to come by and see how you're doing," he said with a friendly smile. "It can get horror-movie-quiet out here."

She laughed softly. "I love it."

"Good. You look great."

"I do?" She had on plain shorts and a casual, pink wrap top.

He chuckled. "You do. Have everything you need here? I know our grocer isn't big, but if you need anything there are a bunch of places I can tell you about that aren't too far."

"I'm all stocked up," she smiled. "In fact, I have too much food. Are you hungry by chance? Would you like to come in?"

His smile told her he'd hoped she would ask that, and he walked in.

Then she realized something. The deputy was interested in her. And if she had a brain, she should be interested in him too. Good-looking, thoughtful, nice, a man of the law. Too bad there was only one law man she burned for. *Yeah well, he burned you.*

Jake followed her to the kitchen and she offered him a drink. "Soda if you've got it."

"How about a piece of Miss B's famous chicken fiesta casserole?"

His smile widened. "I'd never say no to that."

She cut him a piece, set it on a plate, and handed him a soda. Maybe she should ask *him* to take her to the county fair. He would be a great substitute. And probably safer than Neil because he didn't stir incessant thoughts of sexual abandon.

"Do you come out to Briar's often?" he asked before taking a bite.

"Often? No. We never could get away on weekends very much." She flinched. "We" didn't apply to her anymore and she hadn't meant to bring up her ex.

Too late. Jake was intrigued. "We?"

"My ex-husband and I."

"Ah," he said with a knowing tone. "Divorced."

She twisted her lips and looked away, nodding.

"Me too."

She quickly met his gaze. "You too?"

He set down the fork. "Yep. It's been, oh, I don't know. Two years I guess. You?"

"Officially? Three months."

"Yikes, you're fresh. Kids?"

She shook her head. "We hadn't gotten to that point. We both work long hours and kept putting it off. You?"

"I wanted them, but she...wanted other things."

She could relate. Knowing when someone else had been through a divorce was almost like belonging to a club. People didn't mind sharing their sad stories of the process. It was different for everyone, but the wretched emotions one experienced were the same. An instant bond. "That's usually what it comes down to. Growing apart instead of together."

He took a couple more bites, then nodded. "Even though I kind of knew that before we got married, I'd hoped it would work out. That was my first mistake. So I wasn't surprised when she ended it. It was still a crappy thing to go through."

"Really? I had a blast," she joked.

He chuckled.

After he finished his plate, she picked up her glass of wine. "Would you like to join me out on the deck?"

"Sure thing."

Though she barely knew him, she was comfortable around Jake. It was nice being around a man without the sexual tension so high she couldn't breathe. While she perched on the loveseat bench, he sat on one of the plastic chairs and stretched out his long legs, staring out at the backyard. The moon hung high above the trees. "What a view."

She pulled up her knees and grabbed a blanket to cover them, wrapping her arms around her legs. "I know. I love this place."

"How long will you be here?"

"Just for the week. Then the house will be taken over by vacation renters."

"City girl, right?"

She nodded. "San Francisco. Did you grow up in Briar's Edge?"

"Nope. Originally from Reno. I wanted to go in law enforcement, but didn't want to stay there for the rest of my life. Or any big city. When I saw an opening here, I came down to check out the town and it just kind of... made me feel I found where I needed to be."

It'd been a long time since she'd felt at home somewhere. She softly smiled. "Lucky you. I didn't even pick San Francisco in that way. It was just the place where I received the most interviews. But I love it. Can't imagine leaving."

"Never?"

She thought about it for a moment, because one never should say never, but if he thought she might possibly leave the Bay for a small town, she had to be honest. "It's home. It's expensive, stressful, and now I have to share it with my ex, but it's where I want to be. Plus, I love my job and my friends. Sometimes," she added, "I think about starting over somewhere new, but I don't think that would make me happy."

"I can agree with that. My ex-wife did me a favor and left town so it's not awkward. It would be impossible to avoid each other."

The dating pool in Briar's Edge had to be very shallow due to its size. She could imagine plenty of women had their eye on him, he probably just didn't know it.

LED headlights shone on the garage door as a car approached and seconds later when the doorbell rang, she had a strange inkling of whom it could be as she walked to the foyer.

Neil, dressed the most casual she'd ever seen him in a shirt and a hoodie-lined leather jacket, gave her a wide smile. "Hi."

The butterflies erupted. "Er, hi. What are you doing here?"

"Obviously I came to see you." He glanced over her shoulder. "Can I come in?"

She stepped back and allowed him entry. Just then, Jake sauntered in from the back deck.

She could practically feel the energy in the room crackle.

"Mr. Caenon," Jake greeted in a voice that didn't give away any surprise. "How's it going?"

They shook hands. "Deputy."

"Jake stopped by to check on me," she told Neil as if he was owed an explanation.

"I would too," Neil said. "If I knew a beautiful woman was out here by herself."

Her face flamed as Jake chuckled, "It's a small town. I check on a lot of our single residents."

"Sure you do."

"Caenon," she said with a warning in her tone.

"It's okay. It's time I get going anyway," Jake said, vague disappointment in his features. "Thanks for the meal."

After sending Neil a glare, she walked Jake to the door. "Sorry about that. You don't have to go."

He turned. "I think I do." And looked past her shoulder to Neil. "I had a good time, but I know fierce competition when I see it. Plus—you're a city girl."

She laughed softly, nodding. "That I am. Have a good night, Jake."

He gave her a soft smile. "You too."

She closed the door then swiveled around and marched to the kitchen. Neil lounged against the kitchen island, arms crossed, jacket removed.

"That was extremely rude," she chastised him.

"What was?"

"You were and you know it. He was perfectly nice to you and practically bucked him with your antlers. Who do you think you are?"

"He knew what was up. Did he really come by with the excuse to check on you? Oldest policeman's trick in the book. No points for originality." He looked around as if searching for clues, giving a fleeting look to the TV with the movie on pause. "*Sixteen Candles* and wine? Were you on a date?"

Jealousy rears its ugly head. "That's not any of your business. He happens to be very nice."

"Is he?"

She crossed her arms. "Yes. We were having a relaxing time until you showed up. Why did you, by the way? My invitation expired the second I left your office this afternoon."

"I changed my mind," he told her matter-of-factly.

Ha! "I don't care. I'm no longer interested." As if he'd believe that lie.

He looked at her intently. "Is that why Jake was here? You'd already replaced me with someone else?"

"Maybe."

"Just like that? Any guy will do for this rebound weekend? He seems boring to me. He's not what you need."

"Oh he isn't? You're an expert on my needs suddenly?"

"I will be."

She threw up her hands. "Does your ego have no limits?"

"It's not my ego, it's my instincts. He won't do to you what I will."

Her stomach dropped, but she maintained her blasé demeanor. "Oh really?"

He shook his head, walking around the kitchen island. "I can guarantee he wouldn't tear your blouse open, spread your legs, and fuck you deep on this counter. I can also guarantee he wouldn't lie on the living room floor with you sitting on his face and lick you until you scream." She gasped in shock at his graphic descriptions. "And I can also guarantee he wouldn't rub your clit as he entered you from behind. He just doesn't seem like the man who could guess what you need."

Unable to form words, she groped for her wine and gulped a swallow. How dare he speak improper specifics, stirring her desire? Now she imagined all those scenarios and more, exciting her. "W-what made you change your mind?"

"I thought about all the reasons why we shouldn't sleep together. The fact you're Logan's assistant, just got divorced, and making decisions with your sex drive than your head. But you're aware of all these things too and you still asked me to spend the weekend with you, which means none of those are limiting factors in your mind, so they shouldn't be in mine. And you were right, I'm the last person to tell you what to do with your life."

He leveled his gaze, lowered his tone. "If any man should touch you, it should be someone who knows what he's doing, who cares about you, and has zero expectations of taking this beyond Sunday. Deputy Thornton looks like he wants a wife and babies real soon, by the way. Once the weekend was over, you'd have a suitor on your hands, and I know that's the last thing you're looking for."

He wasn't wrong. Jake had mentioned his ex-wife didn't want children, but that he did. By the way he said it, he really wanted to change his situation soon. Unfortunately, it was much too soon for her to imagine a new relationship, let alone ever remarrying and having a family.

"I'm what you need," Neil softly emphasized.

Would any other man except Neil say something like that? As if he had to convince her. No matter what he thought, Jake wasn't competition. She might've shared a drink and some conversation with him, flirted with him a little, but she had no intention of starting anything with the deputy. Especially not with Neil there.

Jake didn't turn her into a quivering pile of mush with his stare, or make her stomach knot hot and tight, and certainly didn't take her breath away just by walking in the room.

She whipped around to the sink, suddenly breathless at the thought of them going through with this.

"May I stay?" he asked behind her.

"Yes," she whispered, groping the kitchen towel, wiping down the already dry stainless steel sink.

When he was at her back, close but not touching, she pretended she hadn't noticed, even though she could feel his heat. Furiously, she kept wiping down the sink. Why was she nervous? She got what she wanted. Neil. Here. Telling her all the naughty things he wanted to do to her.

Like a crazy woman, she rubbed at the water ring.

He set his hands on her hips. Heart pounding, she parted her mouth, pulse thundering in her ears. He brought himself against her backside, but not aggressively so. Fingertips trailed up her arm and smoothed back the hair over her shoulder. His warm lips were on her neck and she froze, closing her eyes. When she opened them, she met Neil's in the reflection of the window.

"You..." Her voice came out barely above whisper. "You want to start this—now?"

He nuzzled the crook between her neck and shoulder. "Yes. Now." He pressed his body harder, trapping her between him and the sink. She dropped the towel. He unbuttoned her shorts and pulled down her zipper, and slowly slid his hand inside her panties.

A cry of total shock escaped before she could stop it, him finding her slick with need.

She could feel the hard, thick length of him between her cheeks. He wouldn't disappoint in size, she could already tell. God, it'd been so long since she'd had sex. It might hurt. Might hurt so good, too. A shiver coursed over her as he stroked his fingers between her folds.

"You're so wet." He moved from inside her shorts up her stomach and under her shirt as she just stood there and let him. Their gazes hadn't unlocked yet. It was a certain kind of thrill to keep a man's gaze as he explored your body. When he lightly cupped her breast, she sucked in a quick breath.

"Neil," she whispered.

Her wrap top allowed him easy access as he slipped his hand inside, fingers creeping to her breast. Surely he'd feel the race of her heart, and see how nervous she was.

He moved inside her bra. A little moan from him, a small pump of his hips, and she was crazy ready to fuck him. Right here, right now. He pinched her nipple between his index and middle finger and she gave a helpless noise, gripping the edge of the sink. If he ripped her panties off and entered her right here, she wouldn't complain. They didn't need a bed.

Darn. The condoms were in her room, though.

She turned around, but he didn't back off whatsoever, going in to kiss her before she could even comprehend what was next. His tongue parted her mouth with seductive aggression, and he hiked her leg up to his hip.

"Caenon?"

He went for her jaw, down her throat, running his hand up and down her thigh, grinding his hips on hers. "Hm?"

"It's been a long time since I've been with anyone," she told him, the last word coming out on a breath.

"You mean your ex-husband? How long?" He made his way up and kissed her long again.

She had to rack her memory for the answer. The last time she and Cliff had sex? So many moons ago. It'd been one of the major signs she had fallen out of love with her husband because even the thought of sex with him had recoiled her. "Two years. I think."

Neil's green eyes widened.

Of course someone like him couldn't imagine going two weeks let alone two years without sex. But even though her marriage had died months and months ago, not once did she seek physical intimacy with someone else. Not while she was married. She suspected Cliff had, especially at the end when he'd moved out. She hadn't even cared.

Sex used to be so important to her. She wanted it often from Cliff and at first he'd obliged, but after a year of marriage, she discovered he was less and less interested in the physical part. Whether it was a lack of attraction for her or just a lack of sex drive, she could never be sure.

Neil toyed with her bottom lip with his thumb, then trailed his mouth along her jaw. "Do you want to stop?"

Was he kidding? She shook her head and gave a breathless laugh while he continued to caress her.

He lifted his head. "What's so funny?"

"I don't know. When I envisioned you and I...well, I always assumed you would tear off my clothes and—"

"Mount you like a mare?"

She laughed. "Only you would imply you're a stud horse."

His nose grazed hers playfully. He looked her up and down, bracing his hands on either side of her. So seductive and sure of his effect on her. "You don't know how many times I've imagined this. Your mouth on mine. Your legs around me. Your hair in my hands. As much as I want to rip your clothes off and fuck you so good on this stainless steel, you deserve better. Unless..." He slid his hands around her ribcage and pulled her against him. "...that's what you want. Tell me what you want. I'm at your command."

"Oh? I can customize sex with you?" she teased.

He chuckled. "If you like."

"Neil." She toyed with the buttons on his shirt. "I want you and you want me. It's that simple. No instructions or expectations." She slanted a smile. "Not yet at least."

He gave her a slow, sexy smile and moved in to press kisses on her neck.

"Mmm. You can do that as much as you want," she told him.

He crept his hands up her thighs and around her butt. Seconds later, her shorts dropped to her feet.

She couldn't deny a part of her was a little scared, too. Not in a frightened way, but in a don't-know-what-to-expect way. Sex with Neil could be awesome. Or it could be awkward. Especially with her lack of recent experience. To cover her trepidation, she decided to pick up the pace.

"I don't need to be seduced for hours, Neil. Just—take me."

The declaration surprised him, which she liked because she knew it was a rare thing to shock Neil. A half-smile moved his mouth. "As you wish."

"Sorry about this." She gripped his shirt and tore it open, buttons flying, moving in to kiss him before he could voice his disapproval.

An urgency had been set. She shoved the shirt off his defined shoulders and down his arms and he helped her get rid of it completely. Next was his belt and pants.

They broke apart, both breathless and eager, and she took off her top, discarding it. As soon as his shoes were tossed away, he yanked her against his body. Every glorious, hard and smooth plane of it.

Their mouths met hungrily. He cupped her jaw and plunged his tongue inside. Ashtyn barely registered her feet were even moving until he had her against the fridge, the cool steel on her back a contrast to the hot male against her front. She moved him back and he bumped into the kitchen island, toppling over some of the spices.

Neil groaned, kissing her deeper, and moving her toward the living room.

Feverish, Ashtyn ran her hand down his hard torso, over his incredible abs, and along his thick shaft. He groaned against her lips, and she felt her sex clench at the thought of him inside her. "This is going to feel so good," she whispered.

Stepping back, she unhooked her bra from the front, and let it drop.

The fire that ignited in Neil's eyes exhilarated her.

With a smile, she hooked her arm around his neck and pulled him with her to the sofa. The urgency returned in full force. His tongue slid down her neck and he cupped one of her breasts, gently squeezing and teasing the nipple. She arched, holding his nape, closing her eyes. Down he went until his mouth caught a nipple, and he sucked, traced it with his tongue, then sucked some more, and made his way down. When he nuzzled his nose and mouth over her pussy with her panties still on, she cried out in need. How dare he tease her?

He chuckled as though he knew he tortured her, then sat up to pull her underwear down her legs.

Strands of his dark hair hung in his hungry eyes while he stared at her nakedness. "Beautiful."

She couldn't suppress the shiver. Cold without his heat, hot for his body. He got up, reached in his pants pocket and tossed several condoms on the floor next to the sofa. Now she didn't have to stop them to run to her room.

He began to move his boxer-briefs, and his cock sprung free, every panty-wetting inch of it.

She expected him to climb on top of her again, but instead he took her ankle and turned her to sit on the sofa, instead of lay on it. "What are you—?"

He silenced her with a long kiss, and shifted to his knees. Breaking away, he took her ankles and set her heels on the edge, exposing her, and dipping his head down.

She threaded her fingers in his hair, moaning, heart racing.

His tongue licked up her slick center and her eyes widened in shock, the pleasure electrifying every tiny nerve in her body. She cried out without shame; it felt that good. It was a little embarrassing having her knees up and legs spread wide but as Neil sucked on her clit and nuzzled her intimately, modesty died a good death.

"Oh…oh…" she panted, pressure building with sweet promise.

Neil moaned, the vibration of the sound tickled, exciting her, making her cry out for more. *So close.* He placed his hands under her butt and licked faster, whispering her to come.

Ashtyn's mouth dropped open at the frantic pulses of pleasure rocketing through her entire being. Digging her palms in the sofa, bowing her spine, she dropped her head back.

Neil's fingers gripped her ass as she began to shake, the ultimate wave of an orgasm crashing on her.

"Neil!" She screamed on and on while he continued to lick mercilessly at her tender flesh.

Chest heaving for breath, she was racked with quivers. Neil kissed each of her inner thighs before rising, heated gaze meeting hers. She grabbed his arm. "Come here." Sure, she just had the most amazing orgasm ever, but she still hadn't gotten what she craved most.

Scooting back so they were completely flat on the sofa together, she kissed him, tangling her tongue and pumping her hips, slicking his cock with her drenched center.

He groaned and broke away long enough to reach for a condom, put it on, and settled once again between her legs. She wrapped her arms around his neck, so ready to fuck she couldn't even think straight. He jutted an arm under her back and half-lifted her against him, bending his head to kiss her slow and deep. The blunt head of his dick entered her and she bit her lip.

Slowly, he pushed in more, and she gasped, clutching him.

"You're so tight," he breathed, body trembling.

"Keep going," she whimpered. She undulated her hips.

He hissed, squeezing his eyes shut. He choked out a curse, then sank deep all at once, causing them both to groan with mindless pleasure. Then he started moving inside her, stroking in and out of her in a steady rhythm until she matched with him. Hips meeting hips, chest meeting breasts.

She met his eyes, a dark blue storm of desire. God, he was gorgeous.

Their gazes were locked for so long, they'd begun to slow down, and her heart picked up speed. One more second, and she'd get lost.

Things were getting a little intense.

She pushed up and rolled to her left, sending them to the floor. Neil made sure to take the brunt of the fall, and he chuckled. Her hair dropped in her eyes and she raked it away, giving a yelp when he swung her back to her back.

"You make me so hot," he uttered.

"Mmm. Back at you, counselor." She ran her hands up and down his chest. She brought her leg up and set her calf on his shoulder. "Don't stop," she gasped.

"Oh, I won't." He ran his palm up and down her shin, driving in her with hard pumps.

When his mouth met hers, she laced her fingers in his hair, taking each plunge of his hips with a groan. He took her right hand, intertwined their fingers, and stretched her arm back. Holy shit he was *good*. A smile pulled at her mouth while he pressed feverish kisses down her jaw and neck. A throb began, winding and building through her pussy.

Neil groaned in the crook of her neck, thrusting faster. "Ashtyn…"

"Mmm. Yes!" The world went black for a second, stunning her, with an inner explosion so exquisite, she almost wept with it. But she kept the sob of bliss in check.

Neil's body tightened above hers. Breathing heavily, he groaned loud, then slowed down, and traveled his mouth back to hers, stealing the last of her oxygen.

When he rolled to his back, they were both heaving. And silent.

Wow. Whatever expectations she had were exceeded and then exceeded some more. She couldn't even remember what they were, other than the fact she suspected sex with Neil would be great, but not phenomenally great. Sometimes the hottest guy could be the lousiest in bed, as she'd learned in college. But Neil was the exception. A glorious exception.

"Water?" he asked, throat scratched.

She took a breath and exhaled. "Yeah."

He got up and walked to the kitchen. She heard cabinet doors opening and closing, and the sound of the cups being filled from the fridge.

A little cold now, she grabbed a throw blanket and wrapped it around her, sitting Indian-style while Neil came round the sofa to hand her a glass of water. She took three gulps of the cool liquid and wiped away the excess with the back of her hand.

He finished his glass and set it on the end table, watching her finish hers. When she did, he took her glass and set it next to his, then held out his hand. "Tired?"

She looked up at his cool green eyes, seeing mischief in the depths. "Actually no."

"Good. Bed time." He pulled her up and scooped her in his arms, blanket and all.

She let out a yelp of surprise at how easily he picked her up. "What are you doing?"

"Putting you to bed so you can rest up before round two."

"Round two?" She linked her fingers together behind his head. "Is there nothing you won't reference as a sport?"

"Sex *is* a sport. Now that I think about it, I should buy the domain name. Sex is a sport dot com."

She laughed. It was going to be a very fun weekend.

12

HER ALARM went off.

It was a simulation of a barking dog, because she could never sleep through that particular sound.

Tiredly, she lifted her head, and groped for her cell phone. She'd forgotten to cancel her daily wake up call, carelessly allowing it to go off every day of her vacation so far. The sun wasn't even up, for Pete's sake. She swiftly silenced it, blinking at the bright screen in the dark room. There were several messages for work on there, and even though she should forget them until at least the sun crested over the horizon, she decided to one. It would only take a second.

Neil, lying on his stomach with his arms under the pillow, turned his head. "What are you doing?"

Her eyes didn't leave her cell phone. "Sorry," she said, voice rough from sleep. "I forgot to switch off my alarm."

"No. What are you doing with it still in your hand?"

"Checking my email." In fact, she should respond to this one from Ted…

Neil snatched the phone out of her hand and held it away. "You're sick."

"Neil!" She sat up and reached for her lifeline. "Just—let me."

"Are you kidding me right now?" He smiled down at her.

Okay now, "morning" Neil, in the half-dark, his hair mussed, hanging in his eyes, and deep voice husky, had to be sexier than Rat Pack Neil. "Give it back," she said too weakly to be a real command.

He continued holding it away. "I'll make a deal with you."

"Oh?"

Shifting his body toward hers, eyes hooded, he said, "If you can respond to your emails without responding to *me*, then you can keep your phone for the rest of the weekend. Otherwise, if I hear one little sound, I'm hiding it."

That wasn't a fair deal whatsoever. He knew very well how good he was, and she'd probably make it ten seconds before groaning. However, even knowing she would lose—and really, giving up her cell phone for two days was hardly losing—she so wanted to play this game. Why not give it the old college try and see how long she could last? "Deal."

With dark sexual promise in his eyes, he handed her the phone, and she made a show of clearing her throat, holding her phone with both hands, and concentrating on her email. Unable to see him because the brightness of the display and the darkness of the room, she didn't know what he was up to until he began to press kisses on her chest.

Mmm. Nice, but she was still able to hit "reply" and begin her email.

Ted,

This is not accept—

Neil closed his mouth over her left nipple, drawing it to a hard pebble with the hot swirl of his expert tongue. An electric sensation bolted to her sex, making it clench, and she pressed her lips together.

acceptable. I set up this meetingggg

His fingers wandered down to her pussy, finding it slick.

Delete, delete delete.

meeting months ago.

Kisses were planted on her stomach, and he strummed her clit slowly, making it bloom and fill, aroused and aching.

Oh God.

With wide eyes and biting hard on her bottom lip, she furiously tried to finish her email:

Logan's schedule will not allow for it to be pshued baccckk

The tip of his middle finger rubbed around and over her clit, spreading her wetness, and she started to squirm, unable to keep her body from responding. She jerked.

Delete, delete, delete. Again.

But she couldn't finish the words. Neil chuckled as low as he nipped on her stomach, and licked his way up to her right breast, capturing the nipple and sucking harder. Her clit throbbed with increasing sensitivity, close to releasing.

Can't breathe. Helpless, she bowed her back. The phone clattered to the floor, and she fisted Neil's hair, crying out as the orgasm pulsated through her body and froze time. She sank to her back, moaning incoherently.

She could feel Neil smile against her neck. "I didn't finish my email," she admitted lazily.

"And now you definitely won't until I leave."

"Mm. A deal's a deal," she said, too weak to argue that at some point, she'd have to check her phone. Her eyes started to drift closed, but then he wrapped his arms around her middle and rolled over twice, with her landing on her back.

"Oh no you don't. We're waking up."

"Neil," she complained. "It's too early." She giggled when he tickled her ribcage, and rolled her back the other way on the king-sized bed, making her laugh more. "What do you want from me? It's only four o'clock…"

She kept her eyes closed, half-hoping he'd let her sleep, and the bed moved as he shifted away. Assuming he'd relented, she heard a rustle of plastic being torn, and she ran her tongue over her lips. He'd put on a condom.

He came back, spreading her legs with his knees, and kissing his way to her earlobe. "We'll sleep more. After this." He cupped the back of her knee, and slowly pushed his hard cock inside her.

Her mouth dropped open as he came down and kissed her, rocking in her body. Moans replaced shock, and she instantly succumbed, raking her fingers in his hair and lifting her hips to match his rhythm.

God, she loved how sexual he was. How much he desired her. That there were no limits, no inhibitions, no awkward moments. His ass clenched under her ankles with every deep push, and she ran her palm down the working muscles of his back, enjoying the masculine sound of his groans and increasingly ragged breathing.

The feeling of his chest, slick with sweat and rubbing on her breasts increased the pleasure, and she yearned for his mouth on hers. As if he read her mind, he sought her lips, teased her tongue, his hot breath on her chin while he pumped faster. "Do you know what you do to me?"

Did *he* know what he did to her?

Her answer was an incompressible cry as she undulated her hips harder, spread her legs wider, and scraped her nails up his chiseled chest. Neil craned his head back and let out a cry of his own, deep and approving, dipping his head back to lick her breasts. With each drive of his hips, he fondled her, hungrily sucking on one nipple and then the other.

She gasped, holding his waist.

Their gazes locked, and instead of carnal desire, she saw something else. Something intense and binding in his eyes, but she must be mistaken—

He crashed his mouth down to hers.

Best morning ever.

SHE WOKE UP by herself a few hours later. It was past nine o'clock; he'd let her sleep in, as requested. When she crept to the bathroom, there was no noise in the rest of the house. In fact, after she showered and got dressed, she was still alone.

It was a beautiful day.

She opened the sliding door. The sun rays shining through the pine tree branches and the young silence of the morning made her smile. She leaned on the rail, unable to stop grinning, thinking about last night, and only hours before. At first, she thought she'd be timid with Neil, but he'd made it impossible, and quite effortless to release her inner wantonness.

God, she'd missed sex. He was the perfect man to remind her never to go that long again.

Speak of the devil.

Neil strode from the side yard to the back, a paper bag in one hand. He bounded up the deck's wooden steps two at a time, smiling as he saw her. "Morning."

She smiled back. "What have you been up to since I stayed in bed like a sloth?"

"Caught up on some work. Went for a walk." He held up the bag. "Bagels?"

"You did all that before nine?"

"I'm a morning person."

With his line of work, she could understand he never slept in. "You must have the stealth of a ninja. I'm a pretty light sleeper and I didn't hear you leave the room."

He raised one shoulder. "I've had some practice sneaking out of a woman's bed."

"Ah." She pointed at him. "Right." Almost forgot she was dealing with a fling expert.

"Also," he said, "you looked too peaceful to disturb, so I was extra careful. I didn't want you to wake you up until you were completely rested. You'll need your energy."

She blushed as she followed him into the kitchen. "Oh do I?"

"What do you like?" he asked. "Raisin cinnamon? Blueberry? Onion? Get 'em while they're hot." He continued pulling out the bagels and little cups of cream cheese.

She took the cinnamon raisin one then got butter out from the fridge. They ate for a few minutes before he reached over and tossed the newspaper in front of her. "Still want to go to the fair?"

She smiled, swallowing her last bite. "Yes."

"Looks a little cheesy to me, but the town is all a-buzz about it," he said. "The lady at the bagel shop said it's the highlight of the summer. Arts and crafts. Rides. Churros. Local bands. Even live animals you can pet."

By the sarcasm in his tone, he definitely didn't want to go, but she really did. "Come on, it'll be fun. Good old-fashioned fun."

"Your idea of old-fashioned fun and my idea of old-fashioned fun are different things evidently."

"Oh? What's yours?"

"Skinny dipping in the lake. Naked Twister. Black-and-white movies with buttered popcorn and a big blanket in the back seat of a car—"

She held up a hand. "I think I get the gist. As long as there's nudity involved, you're game for anything."

"You catch on quick." He winked.

She twisted her mouth and plucked at her bagel. "If you don't want to go, that's okay."

His brows drew together. "Just like that? I thought you were really looking forward to it."

"If it's not your cup of tea, let's do something else." The last thing she wanted to do was drag a man to a place where he'd only balk and complain, like her ex-husband did.

He studied her for a moment. "Ashtyn, I was only teasing. I'm going to change into some jeans and we'll go."

THE LAST TIME NEIL went to a fair, it'd been the summer before his senior year in college. Where he ran into Juliet, the girl of his high school dreams. He couldn't hear the words county fair without thinking of her, without conjuring her smile in his mind, and remembering the vanilla perfume she wore. A fair was the last place he wanted to be, but was what Ashtyn wanted to do, and after last night, he wouldn't deny her a thing.

Sex with her was off the charts. And he'd climbed the charts many times over. She could be sensual and generous, needy and playful, and moaned like she never wanted it to end. She made a man feel like a sex idol, aiming to try new things just to see her body respond.

As they walked up the ticket booth, he slid her a glance. "What's your objective? The food? The rides? The games?"

"All of it!"

He smiled. She really looked excited.

"Well then," he said as he pulled out his wallet. "Might as well get the unlimited ride package."

She shooed his money away and dug in her back pocket. "This isn't a date. I can pay my own way."

Spending an afternoon eating high caloric fare and screaming on rides hardly qualified as a real date in his eyes, but whatever. "So we're going Dutch on this?"

"Going Dutch would still imply we're on a date. You pay for your half, I'll pay for mine."

He smirked at her firm insistence. "Sounds good." Felt a little weird. It was just a natural reaction to reach for his wallet to pay for things when going out with a woman. Didn't seem right to let her, but he didn't want to start their day with an argument over it.

The bored-looking booth attendant smacked on his gum. "What'll it be, folks?"

"Two unlimited ride wristbands," Neil told him. At Ashtyn's start of a protest, he added, "Uh, we're paying separately."

"Twenty bucks each," the man told them.

"I can't believe you're really getting an unlimited ride wristband with me," she said as the attendant slid her the plastic bracelet.

"Sure why not? Let's ride 'til we puke."

She laughed and shook her head. "You first."

As they meandered through the dusty grounds, more memories of Juliet kept clouding his mood, and every time he looked at Ashtyn, he'd see her. He rubbed the back of his neck, wishing she'd chosen anything but this. "What do you want to do first?" he asked, desperate to keep up the laid-back charade.

"Let's just walk around and see what we see." She glanced at him. "Is that okay?"

"Of course. We're in no rush."

She beamed at him and he determined to chill out and have fun with Ashtyn. They walked through the long aisle of food vendors, overwhelmed with the choices of what they might have for lunch later, then followed the path to the merchants hocking everything from cheap sunglasses to floor rugs.

It wasn't until they came to the miniature petting zoo that her interest really sparked. "Neil. They have bunnies and baby goats. And, oh look!" She clasped her hands. "A duck."

He chuckled at her enthusiasm, and loved how she called him by his first name almost exclusively now. "Go on in then."

A young girl in her early teens wearing two ponytail braids smiled at Ashtyn. "We have a llama too."

"You're kidding." Ashtyn smiled and handed the girl the $5 entry fee.

Neil leaned his elbows on the fence and watched Ashtyn carefully make her way through the animals that were basically running around her feet. The girl in braids handed her some feed and as soon as Ashtyn got on her knees, the duck waddled over to her, followed by a group of baby ducklings. She laughed as one hopped on her leg and into her hand. "Neil, look. They like me."

"I don't blame them." Leaning on the rail, he shook his head at the scene. On any given day, she was a lovely woman, but when happy, she outshined the sun. He never would've imagined a woman like her into farm animals, around all this hay and the smell of poop lingering around. What other nuances would he discover about her this weekend?

She picked up a bunny and wriggled her nose with it, then set it down to visit with the llama.

"Is it cool if I hang out for five more minutes?" she asked him later with a piglet in her arms.

Why did she always check with him if this or that was okay? Did her ex-husband make her do that? "Take your time, Ashtyn. I'm having fun watching you have fun."

She gave him a wide smile and went back in with the kids.

Afterwards, she washed her hands at the portable sink before they ventured back to the main area. "How about those rides now? I'm starting to get hungry, but there's no way I'm getting on anything *after* we eat."

"Agreed."

"Have anything you absolutely won't get on?"

"Me? Nah," he joked.

"Very funny." She stopped at a booth displaying handmade jewelry. "Oh, I love these earrings." Bending down, she stared at the pair in awe. Neil got a perfect view of her ass, and a corner of his mouth lifted. After all this fair nonsense, he couldn't wait to get her back to the house.

The young man behind the booth smiled at her flirtatiously. "Like them? They'd look nice on you. I'll give you a good deal, too."

She straightened. "Mm. Not today, but thank you."

"I'll be here all weekend. If I don't see you by Sunday night, you'll break my heart."

She gave a soft laugh and waved good-bye.

Neil frowned. Unnecessary jealousy smiled.

While they continued to walk around, he noticed the booth guy wasn't the only one checking Ashtyn out. She seemed completely oblivious to the men giving her double-takes and appreciative smiles. Wasn't it obvious she was with him? Well, he'd fix that.

He caught her hand, saying nothing.

And apparently, caught her off guard.

"What are you doing?" she asked.

He shrugged. "You keep wandering off. Now I can keep up." Man, he should've done this a long time ago, not only did it feel good, it felt right. Public affection—unless it included groping against the wall—was not his style, but he could deal with it. "Don't worry," he drawled, catching the uneasiness in her face. "It's still not a date."

ASHTYN'S HAND couldn't stop tingling now that Neil had decided to hold it. Out of all the intimate things they'd done, this had her pulse racing the fastest. Holding hands said many things to other people. That they were together, a couple, and in love, but she and Neil were none of those things.

Even so, she didn't mind giving the illusion in this small town she belonged to someone. Especially to a man as handsome and charming as Neil, who had little girls and grown women alike giggling as he walked by. He didn't seem to notice. Or maybe he was just used to that kind of attention.

"Interested in your fortune, doll?" asked a woman dressed in hippy-style clothes.

Ashtyn snapped out of her thoughts and looked at the woman. "Pardon?"

The woman gestured for her to come inside her tent. "I'm running a special on palm reading today."

Ashtyn stopped to read the woman's sign. Her name was Luna. Medium, palm, and tarot reader extraordinaire. "Oh. No, thank you."

"Your spirit guides are insisting I stop you," she said, taking Ashtyn's free hand.

Neil tugged her away. "We're not interested."

"No, it's okay," Ashtyn said. She looked at him and shrugged. "It's just for fun."

He allowed her to slip her hand from his and gestured for to go ahead. "Get the lotto numbers," he said in jest.

Ashtyn followed Luna inside the tent and took a seat. She didn't exactly believe in fortune tellers or spirit advisors, but she'd never gone to one before either and couldn't really judge. One of her good friends spoke to her spirit guru like some people spoke to their therapist, at least once a week, and insisted the man could tell her things no one else could possibly know.

Luna cracked her knuckles, then asked for Ashtyn's left palm. She spread Ashtyn's fingers wide and grumbled to herself for a moment before lifting her gaze. "Hmm. You just went through a big change in your life."

The woman was reading her for a reaction no doubt. Ashtyn decided not to confirm or deny and kept her expression blank.

Luna lifted a brow at her lack of response. "Testing me, eh? To be frank, your spirit guides were giving you many signs to make that change years ago, but you were stubborn and scared, and as a result, you suffered for longer than you should have. Your soul mate came to your life at the time he was supposed to, but—" She twisted her lips, "—you were too distracted trying to revive your dead marriage."

Ashtyn swallowed. How could the woman possibly know she had been divorced?

Luna adjusted in her seat and leaned in close to Ashtyn's palm. "I know you don't like to fail, but it wasn't a failure you see, it was a lesson, baby cakes. It's okay you took so long, because the love of your life is still waiting for you. You'll honor and cherish him that much more."

Now she was skeptical. "No. I'll never love again."

"Wrong." Narrowing her eyes, Luna traced her fingernail in the middle of Ashtyn's hand. "You'll love another, but this time," she raised a finger, "with *all* your heart. It won't be without its ups and downs, but you'll be blissfully happy nonetheless, and those trying times will only make your bond that much stronger. You and your soul mate will have a marriage that'll last through your lifetime. Aww. Isn't that nice?"

Ashtyn sat there blinking. "I'm going to marry again?"

The woman brightened. "Hell yes! He'll insist on it. You'll be scared, naturally, but your love will eat that fear and spit out. Strong bond. Yep. Oh and I see your man has the power of persuasion. You won't be able to say no."

Oh really? Hard to imagine such a serious relationship in her future. So trusting and enamored with a man that she'd consider marriage a second time. But since this was for entertainment, she decided to play along. "When will I meet this paragon?"

"You've already met him," she said drolly.

Then he must not stand out, or she didn't like him very much, cause… who the heck could it be? "My future second husband must be an acquaintance. I haven't met anyone new since my divorce."

The woman gave this some consideration, but shook her head. "He's not new. Your spirit guides say he's near you though. Yes. Very close."

Ashtyn glanced over her shoulder. The only man who'd been near her lately was Neil. Hilarious. This lady was way off her game. Still, she deserved to be compensated for her time. Ashtyn laid $20 on the table. "Thank you. That was…very interesting."

Luna suddenly stood, ignoring the cash. "Anytime. Don't waste your time like you did with your first marriage, doll. You've already made him wait. If you let him slip through your fingers, you'll only regret it."

Ashtyn sighed. "I already have plenty of regrets."

She emerged from the tent, where Neil turned to grin at her, hands on hips, grinning. Her heart jumped as she began to walk beside him.

Luna emerged, trailing after them. "Have fun you two! Invite me to the wedding if 'ya like. I'm real popular at weddings. Luna's the name!"

Ashtyn whipped a wide gaze to the fortune teller, who just smiled and gave a thumbs-up.

"Wedding? What was that about?" Neil asked.

"Nothing. She's just joking around."

She glanced at his profile.

Neil the love of her life?

Never.

NEIL NOTED ASHTYN seemed a little strange after her palm reading, so he strove to bring her back to her fun self. "Okay so we've got the usual thrill rides. Gravitron, Tilt-A-Whirl, Zipper, Bumper Cars. Where should we start?"

"The Zipper."

"Are you sure? It won't make you dizzy or sick? The last time I went on that I…" he trailed off, then cleared his throat. Another memory with Juliet. She'd screamed so loud that she was going to be sick, and he'd been scrambling to keep the change from flying out of his pocket. He thrust the memory aside. "I just remember I didn't go a second time."

"We can skip that one. If you're chicken." She elbowed him in the ribs.

"Challenge accepted!" he yelled.

A few minutes later, they got in the small cage of a ride, both gripping the bars in front of them. Neil glanced at Ashtyn. "You look nervous."

The ride started. "You know what? I am. Isn't that silly?"

How pretty she looked when excited, not silly at all. The ride cart lifted and he braced himself. She laughed for most of the ride, and held her breath for the rest of it.

Afterward, as they stumbled off, he guessed he knew what the ice in a shaker felt like.

Before he could regain his balance, she grabbed his hand and dragged him to the next one. "Tilt-A-Whirl."

He made sure to twist the wheel as much as he could to make their seat go round and round. Ashtyn threw her head back and laughed, trying to hold on, her body crashing against his side, hair whipping in his face. He liked that ride much better.

Next, they collided into each other with bumper cars, and stuck to the walls with the Gravitron.

Then they repeated the whole set again. Including the Zipper.

Neil hadn't laughed that much in one day in a long time. Because of Ashtyn—who he concluded had an inner child that'd been locked away for too long—he was beginning to like the fair again.

"What's this?" Ashtyn asked as they approached another attraction.

It was an large, shallow swimming pool, maybe three feet deep, with human-sized, clear plastic balls floating around. The carnie explained the game was a lot like a hamster toy. The person stood inside and pushed their ball around the surface of the pool, trying to knock their opponent down.

Ashtyn gasped with intrigue, but Neil didn't see how acting like a rodent could be any fun. "You really want to do that?"

"Afraid you can't hang?"

"I'll look like an idiot."

"No one knows you here. You'll still retain your cool points."

He laughed.

She bit the corner of her bottom lip, then waved a hand. "It's all right. We'll pass," she told the carnie.

There she goes again, giving in. "No, let's do it."

"You want to all of a sudden?" she asked.

"I want to because you do."

The carnie snorted. "What'll it be? Got people waitin'."

Because it wasn't part of the ride package, Neil handed the man the cash, and gestured for Ashtyn to go ahead of him.

Truth be told, it was a real blast. His side hurt from laughing so much, and even though he felt like a fool and knew Logan wouldn't do something like this in a million years, he ran inside the ball like a kid on candy, knocking Ashtyn, and getting dizzy in the process.

Afterward, she wrapped her arms around his neck and hugged him. "My side hurts from laughing so hard."

"That was more fun than I thought it would be."

When she pulled back, he kissed her, hard. He hadn't planned to, and she hadn't expected it, but he had to. Then he took her hand in his and they walked to the mouth-watering row of food vendors. Now that he'd started this ritual of holding her hand, he didn't want to stop.

For an appetizer, they got cheese curds. Then corn dogs. Fried pickles and lobster rolls. When Ashtyn brought over mini-donuts for dessert, Neil almost begged off. But really, who could turn down sugar-coated dough?

"There are three left in the bag," she pointed out, licking her fingertips while they sat at one of the picnic tables.

"I know. It should be a crime how much fair food I just consumed in one sitting."

"Thank you again for doing this. You must think I'm crazy dragging you from ride to ride, making you eat fried food."

"You're not making me do anything. I want to. Why would you say that?" he asked.

She shrugged, picking the sugar off her fingers. "Cliff hated these kinds of activities. He never let me—well I shouldn't say he didn't *let* me, he just didn't indulge me. He didn't like to do anything that didn't have a purpose or a concrete goal. His idea of a fun weekend was yoga in the park. Because yoga is good for you. Or taking a woodworking class at Home Depot so we can build our own shelves. Or watching a cooking channel so we can learn how to cook vegetarian for our vegetarian friends. Everything had to have a purpose."

"Productive, but what about fun for the sake of fun?"

"No, sir. He'd say 'What is the point?' If there wasn't a learning experience from it, then it was a waste of time and money." She sighed, resting her chin on her hand. "Sometimes I just wanted to unplug. He never understood that. We had a finite schedule, even on the weekends, and if we were behind one minute, the day was basically ruined, according to him."

What a geek. "Is he the reason you didn't go to many of SFG's charity events last year?"

"Yes and no. He said those parties were stupid and pointless and that I had no business going to them as an *assistant*."

Cliff deserved a solid punch in the face. "Well I hope you plan to have pointless fun until you're blue in the face."

She smiled. "I *have* no plan. That's my plan."

"I like it. Now. What's next for us?"

"Us? What do you mean?"

He chuckled. Did she really think he thought they were an 'us'? "I mean, have you had enough county fair for one day or is there something else we need to conquer before we go?"

She cocked her head. "You really don't like the fair, do you?"

No, he just couldn't wait to have her beneath him—or on top, he wasn't picky—again. "I had a good time, but I think I've hit my limit. Believe it or not, I'm glad you dragged me out here."

"Good," she smiled. "But you can breathe a sigh of relief because I'm maxed out."

DURING THE DRIVE, she remembered another thing she hadn't done in a long time. Knowing Neil, he would approve. Sliding a glance his way, brushing his thigh, which jumped at her touch, she moved to his crotch.

"What are you doing?" he drolled.

Saying nothing, she smiled, unbuttoning her top.

Neil slide her a glance with a knowing half-smile. "You're horny."

"You're speeding."

He uttered a curse and eased up on the accelerator.

Nuzzling his ear, she whispered, "Pull over."

Without any argument, he did so. Finding a side dirt road with a dead-end sign, he unbuckled his seat belt and dragged her over the console. She laughed and climbed in his lap, finding the reclining button to ease him back where she wanted him. Their mouths met hungrily and he pushed her top above her breasts. Instead of unhooking her bra, he shoved one cup aside and sucked on her nipple. She let out a desirous sound and arched her back, and he slid a hand from her back to her butt, cupping the curve.

"Neil," she groaned. "I want to fuck."

He lifted his hips. "Me too. God, me too. But I don't have any protection in here."

She grasped his face and kissed him, undulating her hips. "I brought one in my purse."

"Did you plan this?" he smiled lazily.

"Maybe."

While she reached over to grab her purse for the condom, he unhooked his belt and lowered his pants, exposing his big, erect cock. The sight of it urged her to remove her own shorts and panties before crawling on him again. She rolled the condom on, then, with a wicked smile, ran her hands under his shirt from his abdomen to his chest, grazing her nails along his torso. She parted her lips and met his tongue with her own, the head of his dick at her entrance.

Neil groaned and locked his right arm around her back, using his left hand to guide his cock where they both ached for it to be. She slid down, taking him in, crying out as she stretched to accommodate him. Closing her eyes, she moved her ass up and down on him while he gripped her, digging his fingers in her butt.

"Kiss me," he ordered in a raspy voice.

Eyes hooded, she bent her head and complied, dipping her tongue in and out of his mouth with the same rhythm as her hips. He groaned his pleasure and pumped to meet her, murmuring how tight and hot she felt.

Faster she rode him as he took a handful of hair and pulled her head back.

They were fogging the glass. She slammed a palm on the driver's side window, sitting up as best she could in the limited space and grinding her hips. He held her waist, gritting his teeth and crunching his abs as he came up, slowing her, capturing a nipple between his lips. But slowing her down wouldn't stop the orgasm climbing inside her.

One hand on the window, the other holding his head, she thrust and thrust, unable to stop from seeking the orgasm teasing her pussy.

"Neil," she panted. "I'm going to come."

He buried his face in her chest. "Me too. Ah, fuck."

While he came, gritting his teeth with a groan, Ashtyn got thrown through an onslaught of uncontrollable sensations that seized her mind and body. Heaving for breath, half-suffocating in the small confines of the car, she let the climax rip her in two, so powerful, she didn't have the strength to scream, only moan, whimper, and shudder while the orgasm rocked her world.

In the aftermath, neither of them moved for a couple minutes. Untangling their bodies was going to take effort, and it seemed neither of them had much of that.

She opened her eyes, tracing her fingers down the side of his face as he heatedly gaze in her eyes. Now she got it. How women so easily fell for Neil Caenon. He had the face of an angel, the deep voice of a demon, and made love like a god.

He broke away his gaze. "We should get back on the road in case the sheriff drives by and catches you in a compromising position again."

She climbed off and redressed in the passenger seat. If she was smart, she wouldn't fall for him. He'd done so much for her lately, and she'd spent the majority of her vacation solely with him. After their weekend fling was over, it was going to be weird not having him around. Not to mention she'd have to keep it a secret, which saddened her.

Now she knew why Jordana and the others adored him.

She'd never admit it to Neil, but now she completely adored him too.

Something told her there was no going back.

14

BACK AT the house, they went separate ways. She went to take a nap, and Neil went to the private office to catch up on some work. Maybe *he* had the energy to keep going, but having heart-stopping sex twice and running around a fair all afternoon wiped her.

A couple hours later, just as the sun started to set, she woke up a little hungry. She could hear Neil's voice coming from the den, apparently he was on the phone. Deciding not to bother him, she went to the kitchen to start on dinner.

Almost an hour later, she was scooping Fettuccine noodles and sauce on a plate when Neil emerged, breaking in a grin. "You know how to draw a man out of a cave."

"Works every time."

He pulled up a stool to the island. "Smells great."

She set down his plate and after a few minutes of watching him eat, she asked, "Verdict?"

A sound of approval came from his throat. "Very good. It's not Aurelio's, but it'll suffice." He winked at her.

"Who's Aurelio?"

"A restaurant in Stonestown. You've never been?" he asked. She shook her head and he gaped. "You're kidding. Well your life isn't complete until you've had one of their house specialties. They've practically adopted me I've been so often. Meatballs as big as your fist and garlic bread to kill for." He twirled the noodles around his fork. "We should go sometime."

She froze. Like on a date? Or as friends? Either way...no and no. Tempting, but making plans with him just wasn't in the cards. "Maybe, but anyway, you mentioned garlic bread. That reminds me. I knew something was missing. Want me to make some?"

He lifted his gaze and studied her for a second, then shook his head, reaching for his glass of tea. "No thanks. I'm getting full."

She relaxed. Looking to fill the silence, she asked, "How much work do you have left?"

"Why? Lonely without me?" He snaked a smile.

A little. Like she'd admit it. "No. In fact, I'd almost forgotten you were still here," she arched.

"Oh really?" he drawled. "Well, I'll try harder to be less forgettable."

She laughed. "I'm curious what your idea of trying harder looks like."

"Hm. I'm sure you are."

The heat in his eyes had her grabbing her glass and gulping down the rest of her soda. Reaching for her fork again, she twirled more noodles around it.

He pushed his plate away and wiped his hands on the napkin. "Can I ask you a personal question?"

Usually when something started with that preamble, it wasn't a question she wanted to answer readily. She paused in bringing the fork to her mouth and set the utensil down. "Go ahead."

"What happened with you and Cliff?"

She froze. "Why bring that up?"

He gave a one-shoulder shrug. "I want to know."

Ugh. She hated talking about her divorce. She'd done nothing but talk about it. With her attorney, her mother, her friends. There was nothing left to say except two things: it was over and thank God it was over. The annoyance of answering came through in her tone. "You want to know because you enjoy hearing about marriages that fall into the failed statistic?"

His brows drew together. "Is that what you think?" he asked defensively.

"Is it such a stretch to imagine you like vindication for your speeches about avoiding relationships and marriage? You know when *your* friends get a divorce, you're happier for them than sad. You even suggested I have a divorce party in Vegas—"

"That was a joke," he asserted.

"Every other sentence out of your mouth is a joke."

A look of understanding cast in his eyes. "You're right. I'm sorry. I wouldn't take me seriously either," he said so gently, it made her feel guilty for snapping at him. He picked up his plate and went to the sink.

Biting her bottom lip, she shoved her hands between her legs, staring at her last few bites of food. "Why do you care how it ended?"

He rinsed off his plate, then turned around, drying his hands with a towel. "It, your relationship…*he* was a big part of your life. And I want to know a little more about it. Your life, that is. I want to know more about you."

Now that was a sincere response to a question. She felt like a child wanting to ask why again, but she didn't. It gave her a slight drop in her stomach, so she aimed to lighten the mood since she was the one who got snippy. "Okay." She crossed her arms. "I require at least one cocktail."

Her answer amused him, easing the tension. "Name it."

"A very specific kind. A shot of tequila, three tablespoons of lime juice, a splash of water, *two*—" She held up two fingers, "—teaspoons of agave nectar, and some orange juice on ice. All the ingredients are in the fridge."

He smiled at her and gave a single nod. "As you wish." A few minutes later, he had her drink sliding across the island to her hand. "Two shots, right?"

"I said one."

"Well, two too late."

"Fine. But I refuse to drink alone."

"No problem." Untwisting a bottle of whiskey, he poured some over one cube of ice and set it down.

She swirled her drink, then took a sip, flinching. Yeowzers. Strong, but still yummy. Thinking of how to answer his original question of what happened between her and her ex, she waited a little bit, gathering her thoughts. So he wanted to know more about her life? Then why not start from the beginning? "For a long time, I asked myself why I married Cliff. You question *every* decision you've made after something as major as a divorce. Eventually, the answer was pretty clear."

His phone buzzed with a phone call, but he silenced it.

She took a big sip, swallowed, and sighed. "After my parents broke up, my mom and I lived out of our car for a few months during my seventh grade year, and we jumped from one generous, sympathetic family-friend to another, living in their basements or spare bedrooms. My brother was older, and he went to live with my dad in Florida. So it was just me and her. I thought we'd go live with Grandma Lauren, but my mother was too prideful. Eventually, we ended up in Lake Tahoe. My mom kept telling me she had a plan, and her plans were always so grand and ideal. She was going to go back to school, get a really good job, sign me up for art classes, buy a little house…"

Her throat clogged with emotion, remembering her mother's seemingly sincere pledges to turn their lives around. "But year after year, she never followed through. There was always an excuse, someone or something holding her back. It was just too hard for her to make it happen, even when she got financial help from my grandmother, she never could get on her own two feet. She took a job as a cashier since it paid the bills, and enrolled in night classes, but her plans never went beyond that."

She lifted her gaze to his, but saw nothing in them. Not even sympathy. He was just listening to a story. Comfortable with continuing, she said, "Fast forward. My mom remarried. A pharmacist. A really nice man who wanted to take care of her. I graduated high school with honors so I could get a scholarship. I aimed to get a degree in a demanding field, make money to support myself, and meet a nice guy to settle down with, away from Lake Tahoe. My junior year, I met Cliff and he…was just like me. At least, goal-wise. He had a plan, too. Once we started getting serious, he had a written timeline of how things would work out."

Neil's brows drew together. "A timeline?"

She gave a short nod. "Yep. After a year of dating, he said we'd move in together. A year after that, he said we'd get engaged. Then, depending on our careers and financial situation, we'd get married, and immediately save up for a house." With a dry laugh, she added, "I loved it! Especially since nothing stopped us. His plan fell into place flawlessly. I couldn't believe everything had worked out with virtually no hiccups. We followed it to the letter, and for that, I assumed it meant we were made for each other."

The smile stretching his mouth was sympathetic for the girl who thought so naively. His cell phone went off *again*, and again, he silenced it.

How kind of him to put all his attention on her. She squeezed the lime in her drink. "We got married. A professor of mine helped me with the job hunt, and his wife, Logan's previous assistant, was the one who referred me to Logan after she resigned. Cliff was already doing well as an architect. A couple years later, we bought the house. Way out of our original price range, but with my inheritance from my grandmother, we were able to put down a hundred grand as a down payment and make it work. But that's all we were doing. *Making* it work. Our marriage was nothing but a contract. There was no romance, no love. No affection. Three years in and we didn't even know each other that well. We'd accomplished a lot, but the most important thing—our marriage—failed miserably."

A buzz had taken effect, and she liked it. She'd told her sad tale to quite a few, but Neil didn't interject any questions in between, didn't automatically take her side or sympathize.

She appreciated that.

"I knew what was missing," she went on, saying more than she'd intended to. "And I tried so hard to bring feelings and expectations into our relationship that were never there. And I can't blame Cliff for being confused, for demanding the wife he'd insisted a long time ago he wanted. So I gave up, and he gave up. He stopped touching me and I stopped caring. We turned into complete strangers who bickered endlessly about everything because we were unhappy. Last summer, while helping Logan and Jordana with their wedding, I filed for divorce. And that was the end of that *perfect* plan." She raised her glass in a sardonic salute, then finished her cocktail.

Neil gave no comment, no snide remark. "I'm sorry, Ashtyn," he said, taking another sip of his drink, holding her gaze.

"You told me you weren't sorry I got a divorce, just that I had to go through it."

"Now I'm sorry for both." He shook his head. "Jesus. I am a jackass at times, aren't I?"

A self-deprecating Neil Caenon? That had to be a rare occurrence. "It's okay." She leaned in with a lilting smile, feeling the effects of the tequila. "You mean well. I know that now."

He raised his glass to his lips again, eyes crinkling at the corners. "Thanks for sharing. I had to make my own assumptions, and they were a lot worse than what actually happened between you two."

"Oh? What did you assume?"

"The usual marriage breakers. Infidelity, finances, farting in bed."

She laughed. The best kind of action after such a woeful story.

"Think you'll ever re-marry?" he asked.

People always had to know that, too. She was reminded of Luna the palm reader, who told her she'd go down the aisle again. "I don't know. Hard to imagine I would, but I'll never say never, much as I'd like to. I still love the idea of growing old with someone, having someone to come home to. The marriage part was nice. It was the man I was married to who wasn't."

He nodded, shifting his gaze before finishing his drink and pouring another. "I'll tell you a secret."

"A secret?" Her brows lifted.

"Yes. One only Logan and our friend Miranda know."

Intrigued to hear it, she rested her chin in her hand. Liquor was a magic potion if it got Neil Caenon to open up.

"I was close once. To getting married," he stated.

Now *that's* interesting. Her eyes widened. "When?"

"A long time ago."

She waited for him to elaborate, but he seemed content with leaving it at that. "And?"

"And that's my secret."

"You're not going to tell me more?"

Though he tried to give off a careless attitude, she could tell his admission carried some weight of emotion. "What for? It was another time, another place, and in the end, didn't happen. I wasn't—what she thought I was."

She wanted details about the girl who almost got Neil Caenon to the altar. What she was like, how long they were together, and most of all, why they didn't get hitched. Then again, the answer was standing right in front of her. He probably freaked out at the idea of chaining himself to one woman. Or maybe, she thought studying him, she broke his heart and that was why he played the field like he did?

"Why did you tell me?" she asked, cocking her head, wishing she had answers to her questions.

"You shared something very personal. I thought I ought to do the same." He pointed at her. "Don't tell anyone."

She mocked offense. "As if I would. Can I ask you one little question?"

"All right. One."

"Think you'll ever come close again? To getting married?"

He flinched. "Hell no."

The swiftness of his reply and the incredulous look on his face made her shoulders shake when she laughed. "That's what I thought."

He started to smile. "I don't think I've ever seen you tipsy."

"And it's not likely you will again. I rarely get more than a little buzzed in public."

"Why not?"

Because Cliff said his woman didn't drink. That was why. She twisted her lips, realizing her reason was because of her ex. "I just don't go out drinking that often," she told him.

"We can change that if you want to. One or two cocktails after work can be a nice finale to a hard day."

"Isn't that what lawyers love to do? Drink and talk?" she teased in a playfully sensual voice.

"You've got that right. Despite your assumptions about lawyers, we go through a lot of moral and emotional dilemmas."

"Oh I'm sure you do." The skepticism was heavy in her tone.

He cast a reproachful look. "There's a pro bono case I'm working on. I'm ninety-nine percent sure I'll lose it, and I don't lose. How do you think that makes me *feel?*"

She cocked her head, studying him, and seeing he was utterly serious. "Why would you be so sure you're not going to win?"

"Because what the boy—my client—wants, he can't get. The judge rarely does what children wish for. That's the nature of family court. I want to tell him there's a chance, but I don't lie to myself, and I don't lie to kids. My day job? I'm so damn good at it, I feel invincible when I win. So then I take on these pro bono cases, and whether I win or lose, they bring me down a notch. Always. I think they keep me from completely losing my soul." He gave dry chuckle.

"Hmm." She leaned on the island, folding her arms. "From what I know, it's very much in place."

He continued to stare, snaking a half-smile. "So," he began," There's this party coming up. Some networking thing I'm obligated to go to. It'll be boring as hell, but if I had a date, it'd make it less agonizing. What do you say?"

Not this again. She pressed her lips together, knowing she couldn't dodge this one. "I don't think that's a good idea."

"Why not?"

She straightened, avoided his gaze, and grabbed the first excuse that came to mind. "If we start hanging out, people will talk."

"Who cares?" After a second of studying her, he gave a look of realization. "Oh. You care. Embarrassed to be seen with me, is that it?"

"That's ridiculous," she scoffed.

"Then why not? It's just a cocktail party, Ashtyn."

She took offense at his patronizing tone. "How would it look? I've barely been divorced for three months and then I show up at a party with you." Imagining her and Neil walking in together, the looks and the whispers that would follow, put her on edge. "Everyone will know we've slept together," she added quickly.

"They might assume, but they won't know."

"With your reputation? They'd know, and they'd be right."

"Again, who gives a crap what other people think? Their opinions mean nothing." He pushed his chair back and crossed his arms, brows lowering, reading her until she was downright fidgeting. "Wait. It's not about *them* at all. You just don't want to associate yourself with *me*."

Oh God, she did *not* want to have this conversation. "That's not true."

"Sure it is. You're afraid people will judge you if word spreads you were on a date with me."

That was exactly what she worried about. After all those times she snickered at other women falling for Neil's charms, she'd look like a total hypocrite. "Cliff might already be spreading gossip about the two of us anyway. I just don't want people to talk about me. *You* may not care, but I do. Remember the rumor about Logan eloping with Jordana? Even though it wasn't true, it didn't stop people from gossiping about them for weeks."

"But eventually they did stop talking because all rumors die once there's something new to talk about. What? You want people to think you became a nun after your divorce?"

She rolled her eyes at his lack of understanding. "You don't get it because you're a man. Because you're Neil Caenon and no one would ever say a bad word about you. It's a badge of pride for a guy to date around, but for a woman, it's different. Cliff will have validation for what he already assumed, word will spread we're involved, and everyone will think I cheated on him with you. If I ever want to date in that town again, I can't risk it."

"You're way over-thinking this. All this because you go to a party with me? Christ sake I don't have *that* much influence on a woman's dating life."

Getting flustered, she strove make him see what a big deal it would be. "Regardless, I think it's best we keep this between us. Aren't you worried what Logan would say?"

"We're adults, Ashtyn. The second I decided to come here was the moment I stopped worrying about the consequences. Logan's opinion on us is irrelevant."

"There *is* no us," she emphasize. "Things will get complicated if we take this any further than tomorrow. I told you this was a no-strings weekend, and you agreed."

He came toward her, his gaze and voice soft as a caress. "I said that so the pressure would be off for the both of us, but now I've changed my mind."

Ashtyn searched his gaze, feeling as though she was being maneuvered into a series of proverbial corners. "Why?"

"I like you. One weekend isn't enough." He said it so matter-of-factly, but his eyes were sincere. When she didn't instantly respond to the explanation, he asked, lightly rubbing her arms, "What's so eventful about going to a networking event together?"

She didn't have an answer ready. Her life seemed full with starting over, and yet it was empty because of its new beginning. Reinventing her life as a thirty-year-old divorced woman would be different from doing so as a twenty-year-old single college girl. At this age, people tended to have strong opinions about your actions, especially when you failed at something as significant as marriage. To show up with Neil, even on a casual date, would stir more than she could handle. "It's hard to explain."

After moments of excruciating silence, Neil dropped his hands with a sigh, and took a small step away from her. "Forget it. You're absolutely right. It'd be a mistake to make this public." He looked her over, then he shrugged. "It can't go anywhere anyway. You're just getting back on your feet and I'm...me. Better as a rebound and a memory." He offered a tight smile before picking up his cell phone. "Thanks for dinner. I have to return these calls."

The air just became very cold while a hot knot formed in her throat. He strolled outside to the deck, and everything inside her wanted to stop him, and apologize. His curt way of ending the discussion didn't sit well. He had become someone special to her. Someone she very much cared about. The past week had been an unexpected adventure and all of the good parts had been because of him. Calling him a rebound placed him in such a disposable light. Like she'd just used him to make herself feel better.

Isn't that what you've done?

She bit the corner of her lip.

Okay, yes, but he knew the deal and what the end game entailed. Specifically, that after their weekend was over, they'd part ways. In the real world, away from their cozy hideaway in Briar's, they were different people. She preferred to keep a low profile in the social scene; Neil was the life of the party. Men like him basked in the attention while she shied from it. Her idea of a night out would probably bore him to tears. His brazen self-confidence could be grating, and she could only imagine what he was really like on a date. Never one to disguise his admiration for the opposite sex, he'd probably flirt with other women right in front of her.

The thought made her cringe.

Even though the sex was amazing—frankly, the best she ever had—and they got along in a way she never thought was possible, they couldn't go any further.

She stared at his back while he chatted on his phone.

Or could they?

15

AFTER RETURNING his missed calls, Neil rested his hands on the deck rail.

He didn't like this feeling of weighted disappointment concerning Ashtyn's rejections to go out with him. Sure, he knew she was using him for sex and good times this weekend—and he more than approved of it—but he thought they had a nice thing going. The kind of thing he could see being taken beyond the weekend.

Well. She'd basically shot that down with a verbal machine gun. Not that he could blame her for not wanting to get involved.

Even so, it pissed him off how attached he'd gotten. Attached enough for him to ask her out not once, but twice. Something had changed between them in the car after that carnal rendezvous. He felt a connection, a longing for something else on top of the great sex.

He should've dropped any talk of future dates when she ducked his suggestion about taking her to Aurelio's. Damn. He was so good at reading everyone else, but when it came to her, he couldn't read shit.

Whatever. Now that he knew he was nothing but a cock to Ashtyn, then he'd give her just that, end their weekend, and return to his life.

He went back inside, fully aware pride and machismo were what controlled his actions now.

The door to her room was open as he approached.

She was lying on the bed on her side, reading a magazine. Seeing him, she sat up. "Hi."

He grasped her ankle and pulled her to the edge of the bed. Her eyes widened as she stared up him.

No. Don't get lost in those baby blues again. Don't show what she's done to you. He silently cursed, suddenly realized just how attached to her he'd really become. But if there was one thing he was good at, it was *de*taching.

He grabbed his shirt from behind his neck and pulled it off, then started to unbutton his jeans.

Her lips parted, and the desire turned her eyes a smoky blue. She laid back and pulled off her shirt and bra. Goddamn, she turned him on. So ready to surrender to him. Too bad she wouldn't surrender anything else. If all he could have was her body, then he'd take it.

By God, he'd take it.

Stripped naked, he bent over and maneuvered her shorts and panties off at the same time, then spread her legs apart, exposing her, before dropping to his knees.

"Neil—"

He silenced her with his mouth on her sex.

She arched, cried out, clutching the comforter. He licked slow, alternating between flicking the tip of his tongue on and sucking on her clit. At least in this area he knew what he was doing. While she shook and cried out, he took his index finger and slid it in and out of her, moving his tongue over her wet pussy at the same time.

The woman went wild, panting, commanding him not to stop. He wouldn't. If this was what she wanted from him, she was going to get it so good, no other man would even come close. The next guy who came along wouldn't touch his skills in bed.

He'd make sure of it.

Hot jealousy speared through him unexpectedly. The thought of someone else serving her body... It drove him to destroy the emotion, then fueled him to use it so he could burn himself in her fantasies forever.

She rocked her hips toward his mouth, lightly scraping her nails through his hair. "Ah…ah…"

Knowing she was seconds away from climaxing, he stopped, leaving her quivering and whimpering. He found the condom he brought in his pants pocket and rolled it on his dick.

The aching sounds of her disappointment made him darkly smile. Not finishing her off was mean, but that was his intent because it'd make her orgasm that much more powerful. Pressing his hips against her, he sought more control, and more distance, as he hungrily crashed his mouth on hers.

Shit, he was *so hard.* Having his throbbing cock pressed against her soaked core obliterated his thoughts for a stunning second while he and Ashtyn teased one another with their tongues.

She slid down his jaw to his throat, catching his lobe between her lips. "Mm. Neil. Tell me what you like," she whispered.

He closed his eyes. *Keep focused. Don't let her turn this around.* What he liked didn't matter right now. What he wanted, he'd get very soon. Heart pounding, cock aching, he traveled down her throat, sucking and tenderly biting on her sweet, delicate skin, scraping his teeth and five o'clock shadow, leaving a trail to her chest. He captured her nipple between his lips, her moaning and writhing urging him on. Cupping his hand around her breast, he drew the peak to a hard, rosy pebble, circling his tongue around it. She loved that, so he did it some more, then moved to the other to repeat the act.

His head buzzed; his body burned. Getting desperate, he pressed fevered kisses on her chest, burying his face in her neck.

"Neil. Please…don't make me wait."

Unable to deny either of them any longer, he flattened his palms beside her hips and raised his body, locking his gaze with hers. She was beyond wet, beyond hot, and she pleaded with her shining blue eyes. *Just beautiful.*

"Do you want me?" he rasped.

"Yes," she groaned, rubbing her pussy along his cock.

"Then say it." He briefly closed his eyes from the raging need. What was he doing? But he couldn't turn back.

Her chest rose and fell with her breaths, gaze searching. She knew something was different, but instead of asking him what the hell kind of game he was playing, she obliged him. "I…I want you."

"What do you want me to do to you?" he commanded.

She visibly swallowed.

"What do you want me to do, Ashtyn?"

Her lip trembled as she exhaled. Now, apparently, she understood. "Fuck me."

Satisfied, he cupped her knee, positioned his cock just inside her tight sheath. He watched her eyes go round and heard her intake of breath as he slowly pushed in. It took so much from him to hold back when all he wanted to do was plunge hard and seek an end to this agony. He clenched his jaw at the warm tightness enveloping him inch by inch, and swallowed the groan that begged to tear from his throat.

Then he began to move.

He grit his teeth as she rocked and wriggled beneath him, milking his cock, trying to encourage him to meet her speed, but he refused. Taking her left leg and guiding it in front of and across his body, he maneuvered her hips to the side. Roving his hips in a circular motion, he pressed her knees together. She groaned in surprise in appreciation at this new position, and lifted on her elbow as he stroked his dick in and out of her.

Fuck. Yes. Just like that.

After a while, she turned on her stomach and he followed her lead, spreading her legs enough to push inside her from behind, pushing in so deep, he began to sweat from the need to come. His heavy breaths fanned her hair, and he took a handful and tugged. She turned her head to the side, biting her lower lip and squeezing her eyes shut. He could make her come now, but no, he wasn't done, even with his pulse thundering and cock aching for release.

With sweat rolling down his chest, he pulled out and turned her over, setting her ankles on his shoulders, and praying he could last just a little bit longer while her walls enclosed his cock once again. "You pussy is so good," he groaned out involuntarily. He swayed his hips forward and backward, gripping her waist, trying not to come inside her.

Stroking in and out of her, he studied her every expression, every look of pleasure and satisfaction. She dug her nails in his shoulders and begged him to go faster, but he didn't comply, tortured her with his languid pace. God, look at her. So responsive, so needy for this pleasure she'd been denied for years at a time.

Eventually, her little cries of frustration broke him, the rapture between her thighs too good to keep this insanely slow pace. To her relief, he changed to the rhythm she so keenly desired, driving his hips in deep and fast.

She met his thrusts with enthusiasm, dropping her ankles to hook around his ass.

"Do you like this?" His voice came out rough and hoarse.

She gasped. "Yes!"

With his balls tightening and his cock ready to explode, he reined in his need to let go and come inside her sweet pussy. That wasn't his purpose here.

Eyes watering, in blinding, actual pain, Neil licked the pad of his thumb and sought her clit, rubbing small circles over it. Clenching his jaw, breathing heavily through his nose—burying his moans—he kept his eyes locked with hers for a few seconds. *So sweet and sexy, but so not mine.*

And in those time-stood-still moments, Neil shut his emotions off.

She threw her head back and let out a long cry of ecstasy, bowing her back and clawing down his chest. He hissed in erotic pleasure at the scrapes. On and on she kept going, so he kept going, rocking in her until her cries lowered in volume, and her body relaxed.

She was done.

And so was he.

He pulled from her body, walked out of the room, and shut the door.

ASHTYN LAID there for a while, attempting to catch her breath, paralyzed.

Why did he leave like that? Shaking, she sat up and ran a hand through her hair as her senses came back in pieces. He didn't even orgasm with her or after her. Just got up and left.

Her cheeks burned with the post-sex flush. She'd succumbed to him. When he'd walked in her room and started undressing, she'd lost all reason, automatically baring her body to him, no words spoken.

The man had a way.

She pulled the bedsheet around her body. Why didn't he stay and hold her like he'd done before? That was truly bizarre.

And it hurt he pulled away with such cold finality.

There had to be an explanation. She flopped back in her bed, thighs sore. Everything sore. Exhausted, she fought sleep, telling herself to get up and find Neil. But she couldn't move. Hopefully, he'd come back and join her. Probably went back to the office to finish working or take a shower.

Yawning, she got under the covers. Tomorrow was their last day together. Why did her stomach sink at that thought?

Because she didn't want tomorrow to come, nor did she want them to end. Once he came back to bed, she'd be sure to let him know.

Only, when she woke up Sunday morning, Neil wasn't there. Hadn't been there all night.

Confused, she put on her robe and walked across the hall to the room. The door was ajar. She pushed it in and saw him asleep on his back.

Okay, so mystery solved. But still, what happened last night?

Maybe he just needed his own bed. Well, now it was her turn to do the seducing.

With a half-smile, she crawled on the bed, on him, pulling away the sheet, and rousing him awake.

He blinked his eyes open, grasping her hips as she straddled him.

To her delight, he grew hard instantly. "What are you…?"

"Shhhh." She smiled and removed her robe, bending down to place a soft kiss on his mouth. A flicker of emotion showed in his gaze, but just as fast as she saw it, it vanished.

Maybe this wasn't such a good idea. But then he grasped her hips and guided her along his iron cock, slicking it with the dew between her folds. She couldn't believe how wet he made her with just one touch, one kiss.

"Condom," he rasped. He reached over to the nightstand and got one.

While her heart said something about him seemed off, she was too aroused to analyze it. He finished putting on protection and she raised her hips and sank on his dick, the pleasure-pain of his engorged shaft filling her.

So deliciously big.

As she began to ride him, she moaned, raking her fingers in her hair. He palmed her butt and dug his fingers in, staring at her breasts.

She leaned back on her hands in between his legs, continuing to pump her hips. Neil closed his eyes and softly cursed, proving she was doing something right.

Having no idea why he couldn't orgasm last night, she was determined to make him do so this morning. Sitting up, she played with her breasts, pinching her nipples while he watched, enraptured. He took over the task, teasing the tips with his thumbs, but with a distant look in his eyes. He never seemed so disconnected, and she hoped to bring him back to her again.

Starting to slow down, she gasped when he gave a negative sound and gripped her hips to guide her in a hard and fast pace. The pressure building between her thighs chased away all confusion. Wanton and eager to satisfy him, she took his right hand and put his index finger in her mouth and sucked. He moaned loud, and bucked even faster beneath her, and she couldn't stop the orgasm claiming her mind and soul. Blind with lust, she cried out with the explosion within, but refused to collapse on him, much as she wanted to.

By Neil's long exhalation, he must've assumed it was over.

Did he really think she'd leave him like that?

Turning her back to his front, she grasped his stiff cock and eased on him, setting her hands flat on either side of his body. He grabbed her hips and thrust up eagerly as she bounced her ass up and down on his pelvis.

"You know how to fuck me," he growled.

When his fingers dug deep in her flesh, she dazedly smiled, knowing what was next. He thrust up again and again, then a rough groan ripped from his throat, and he held his hips off the bed while he came.

They both fell back on the mattress.

She rolled to her stomach, then her side, resting her head in her hand.

He inhaled deep and raked both hands through his hair, exhaling. "That was incredible."

Unable to suppress her grin, she continued staring at his handsome profile. Everything seemed fine now. Her heart thumped in anticipation. How exactly should she bring this up? *I was thinking you taking me to Aurelio's could be fun...?*

"What time is it?" he asked, then answered his own question by grabbing his cell phone next to the bed. "I need to shower." Swinging his legs over the side, he got up and stalked to the bathroom.

Ashtyn's smile faded.

He hadn't so much as glanced at her, had barely acknowledged she was still present when he decided he suddenly needed to shower. Where was the playful Neil who liked to fool around in bed even when she begged for more sleep?

She swallowed the hurt closing her throat, heading back to her room and starting her own shower. The hot water ran over her body and her thoughts ran amuck. Maybe this was Neil's modus operandi when it came to a fling. Once he accomplished enough satisfaction, he then got bored, and the lovable, affectionate side of him disappeared?

That question and more swam in her mind while she scrubbed her body and hair clean, bewildered. She climbed out of the shower, dried off, and put on her robe. After picking out some clothes, she went back to the bathroom to brush her teeth.

Then gasped.

She had small hickeys and marks everywhere. Her throat, side of her neck, her chest. Must've been from last night. She'd literally been ravished. Neil had left signs of his carnal lovemaking everywhere. *That animal.* Basically guaranteed she wouldn't be wearing anything with a cut lower than her neck for at least a week. Despite that, she giggled and shook her head.

She changed and headed out to the kitchen, where she found him freshly showered and in a plain light green v-neck shirt, wearing those reading glasses that made him even more achingly handsome. He'd started a pot of coffee and was reading the newspaper, but he looked ready to go, especially with his duffel bag sitting nearby.

"Are you leaving?" She flinched at the pathetic, high-pitched sound of her voice.

"Yes."

At 7 in the morning?

Stifling the disappointment, she asked, "Why so early?"

"I have things to do."

That vague, abrupt answer shot down any hope she had that they would be seeing each other after today.

He glanced at her, but she swung away, occupying herself with searching for a mug, fighting back emotions. What was wrong with her? Why was she suddenly upset?

"Ashtyn—"

"Do you want to take the coffee in a to-go mug? They've only got a thousand of them," she said burying her face in the bottom cupboard. "That way you can get on the road as soon as possible."

"Great. Thanks."

She grabbed the first one she found and headed to sink. "I'll wash it for you first."

"You don't have to do that."

Yeah, she did, because then she didn't have to face him yet. She turned on the faucet and got to cleaning the mug much longer than the already clean mug needed, then dried it until it squeaked. This charged silence was killing her, and she had to grasp some sense of control before he strolled out with not a care in the world.

Tossing the towel on the faucet to dry, she attempted a blasé tone when she turned around. "So how should we play this?"

He poured the coffee in the travel mug, expression nonchalant. "Play what?"

"You know." She crossed her arms and shrugged. "I think we should pretend like this never happened. Go back to being—whatever we were before."

"Before what?"

"Everything. Before the wedding." Yeah, *that* before.

He was halfway to raising the mug to his lips when he paused and met her eyes. "We weren't even friends then. You want to pretend you and I know *nothing* about each other now?" He raked his green gaze over her, as though to say, *I know everything. I've been inside you.*

Her heart began to beat like a loud drum. "I think that'll be easier than treading the line of friends pretending they hadn't slept together." The length of time he stared at her made her want to shout in frustration then too, but she held her own.

He shifted his attention to the newspaper. "Right, well, you wanted to keep this all a secret anyway. I'm cool with that."

"Good." The word came out strangled.

Neil took a sip of coffee, then screwed on the top. "Hope you aren't one of those women who say one thing, then do the opposite," he drolled.

"What are you talking about?"

"Happens more than often than not. Women *say* they don't want anyone to know, then gush to their friends, who tell *their* friends, and eventually it comes back to me."

A slap in the face. She stifled the urge to raise her voice. "You think sleeping with you is such an event that I won't be able to keep it to myself? That I'll just spill to my friends that I was one of the lucky ones to get laid by Neil Caenon?"

A slight lift of his brow proved he had no feelings toward her at all. "That's just been my experience. But I'm trusting you're not like that."

"I'm not." *Omigod, please just leave.* Her throat was tightening again. After all they'd done together...the delicate bond that'd formed in this brief time was crumbling on such an awkward, unexpectedly tense discussion. She strove to keep her voice from shaking with the emotion that accompanied true disappointment and confusion. "Don't worry, Neil. I had a great time, but I think I have a little more maturity than other women you've—hooked up with."

Did she hear him just say "we'll see" under his breath? Whether she did or not, it set her off like a switch. "'We'll see?' You're such an arrogant jerk."

Again, his tone did not change. He simply didn't care. "You've always said that. Am I supposed to be insulted?"

"Aren't you leaving?" she snapped.

"I want to know exactly how we're supposed to pretend we haven't fucked each other's brains out for the past three days."

"Fine. The only time we ever see each other is when you drop by SFG to meet Logan for lunch. Why don't you do what most people would do and send him a text message? Or meet him downstairs in the lobby? That way we don't have fake *anything* around anyone."

He set his hands on the counter, eyes cold as black ice. "How about you grow up? I'm not doing anything of sort. Suddenly I stop coming to his office and insist he meet me in the lobby? That's not 'going back to the way things were' at all. Savant will know something is up. And besides," he shrugged with a pinched face, "why should I change anything I do? Unless you don't think you'll be able to keep your cool around me. In that case, say so now, because I'd rather avoid any drama."

She raked a disgusted gaze over him. "Get over yourself. This weekend was nothing but sex to me, and I've already forgotten that part. I will be just as indifferent toward you as I ever was."

"Fantastic." He started pointing back and forth between them. "Sounds to me like we're back to exactly where we were."

It sure did, but instead of her being blithely annoyed or half-amused, she was upset, hurt, and mad. She remained calm, even though her hands curled into tight fists. Arguing with him any further wouldn't get him out the door.

They continued to stare each other down. Some pitiful part of her wanted to ask him why he was acting like this, but her sensible side already answered that for her.

This is who he is. The player, the heartbreaker. She knew that years ago and she knew it now. He did do things for her—to her—no one had, but that didn't change who he really was. He may *act* like a villain and do heroic things, and she'd never forget it, but that was only a side he showed when he chose. When it served him.

His brows snapped together. "Are we done now?"

She flinched at his sharp tone. "We're done." Unable to stand being in the room with him any longer, she turned around and headed to her room.

Less than a minute later, she heard the front door open and close, and caught a glimpse of his car backing out of the long driveway.

She took a deep breath, pressing a hand to her stomach to calm the quivering chaos inside.

Like it never happened.

17

AFTER NEIL had left that day, she couldn't stand to be in the house much longer. Not with every room reeking of him, and reminding her of every sexual act they'd performed in the kitchen, living room, and bedrooms. She'd spent the rest of that Sunday scrubbing every surface like a maniac, knowing full well Bonnie would be there following up on Friday to do it again. She ended up getting on the road early the next morning after a restless night of sleep, leaving five days ahead of when she planned to. When she told Lila why she wasn't staying the whole week, her friend understood.

When she got home, still furious and upset over her argument with Neil, she set her mind to getting busy. She plowed through her checklist of things to do, unpacking all the leftover boxes, arranging her furniture exactly how she wanted, washing laundry, and decorating her living room. She spent the weekend shopping for a few plants for her patio, wallpapering her bathroom, and lunching with friends she hadn't seen in weeks. Even though she knew it was very impractical, she splurged on a spa package and pampered herself from head to toe, including a hair gloss treatment, which transformed her blonde locks from dishwater dull to vibrantly shiny again.

Cliff used to berate her when he saw such self-indulgence on their credit card bill, and she'd stopped her trips to the salon because of it, convinced it was a luxury, not a need.

But, she'd thought, to hell with it. A woman had needs money could buy.

By the time she climbed in her car and drove to work that Monday morning, she felt renewed, confident, free, and anticipated getting back to her work routine. Knowing Logan would come to work early that Monday, she'd shown up at the office an hour before she knew he'd be there, sitting at her desk a few minutes after six.

The executive floor was quiet as a church and she embraced the calm before the Monday morning storm. It also gave her ample time to answer her long list of emails and catch up on a backlog of tasks without interruption.

Once people started to trickle in the executive offices, she was already ahead of her day, although that could change at a minute's notice at this company.

When Logan came through the doors, he grinned, striding in with a pep in his step. "Good morning."

She smiled at him and stood up. "Welcome back. How was the honeymoon?"

"Too short."

"You look tanned and happy."

"Both will be obliterated in less than a day in this office."

With a chuckle, she handed him a thick stack of reports. "I'm ready when you are to go over your schedule."

"Why don't you go to the market downstairs and grab some breakfast for us?"

"Sure. I'll make sure the conference room is stocked too for the back-to-back meetings as well."

"You're the best." He scanned over a couple papers. "I hope you took my advice and had some fun for those two weeks off. What did you end up doing?"

Oh nothing, Logan. Got arrested, lost $20,000 worth of pearls, smashed a car with a sledgehammer, hooked up with your best friend. A heat swept her body, followed by a rush of cold. "I did a lot of things."

He finally raised his gaze to hers, as though expecting her to elaborate. When she didn't, he prompted with, "And that included?"

"Er. Moved in to my house. Decorated. Read a book. Saw some friends." She shrugged.

He tapped her desk and headed to his office. "As long as you enjoyed yourself."

A little too much. Now it was back to reality without Neil. She'd gotten used to seeing the attorney every day and now she'd have to get used to *not* seeing him, and if and when she did, pretend nothing happened. Could she really pull that off? Didn't matter if she could, she *had* to.

"I'll go pick up some breakfast," she said, eager to move from his scrutiny, and mustering a pleasant smile.

Logan nodded distractedly and headed to his office. "Great. We'll have a meeting of our own when you get back."

She used the market-cafe's website to order the usual breakfast fare, then headed downstairs. The business was only a block from SFG. Felt strange to go back to her routine. Familiar and comfortable, but strange.

The line was long for pick-up orders, but that was normal for a Monday morning.

Seconds after standing in line, she got a tap on her shoulder and turned around to see Emmy. "You're back! You didn't even stop by my desk yet," Emmy said, and gave her a half-hug with an air kiss. She pulled back, giving her a once-over. "You look terrific. Two weeks off and you're glowing. Did you get a facial?"

"Yes. Among other things."

"Tell me all about it."

They moved forward in line, and Ashtyn bit the corner of her lip. She could just skip the first week. "I...uh, went shopping." *Went to jail, Neil bailed me out.* "Drove to Briar's Edge for the fair." *Then he took me on the living room floor.* "Spent the day at the salon." *Had the best sex of my life for three days.* "Got my hair done." *Neil. Neil. Neil.* "Those are the highlights of my two weeks off."

Emmy cocked her head. "Hm. Good for you. Let's do lunch this week. You won't believe what I heard about Rita in accounting."

"Friday's good." Though she had zero interest in hearing gossip. She glanced over Emmy's shoulder and her stomach dropped at who was about to walk in.

Neil. Geez. Had she manifested him with her thoughts?

Her stomach dropped. Too soon. Despite those internal dialogues with herself about how ready she was to face him, she wasn't. "I'll be back."

"But you're next."

"It's okay." Without looking back, she made a beeline for the women's restroom.

Coward. So much for maturity and acting as though nothing happened.

No.

She was fine. Seeing him so soon was just a little jarring. Little more than a week ago, she was riding him cowgirl-style and calling his name. A glance in the mirror showed evidence of a flush on her cheeks. There was nothing she could do about that unfortunately. *Okay. Get back out there. You can do this.* Head held high, she pulled the door open and walked back in line.

But Neil was nowhere to be seen. He was already gone.

That was close. He was probably just walking by.

With Logan's return, it was just a matter of time before Neil came strolling in to the office to have lunch with him. She'd rehearsed how she would act: poised, cool, unaffected. Just like she did before. God she hoped that was possible. Logan could never know what happened between them. He'd never look at her the same and she wouldn't be able to stand it. She loved her job.

Nothing had to change.

Everything could go back to the way it was.

NEIL HATED to lose.

It was anathema to him.

When he met up with Carl Newsom's parole officer, he thought he might have a shot in getting the judge to allow Ritchie to stay with his stepdad, even though he had a record. It was a case of domestic violence, and ever since, Carl had been on the straight and lawful. He held two jobs—both that paid squat unfortunately—and had recommendations from a couple law-abiding friends and previous employers.

And he clearly cared about his stepson more than he cared about his wife's occupation.

Neil watched them play around in the front yard for a little bit, throwing a baseball back and forth, before making his approach. Ritchie grinned and waved when he saw Neil coming down the sidewalk toward him.

Neil shook Carl's hand and could tell the man was more realistic with how things worked when it came to child services cases.

"Can you briefly go over what happened seven years ago when you were arrested?" Neil asked.

Carl, lanky, with hair down past his ears, rubbed the back of his neck, ambivalent to discuss the past he'd tried desperately to overcome. "What do you want to know exactly?"

"Exactly what happened. The report only says so much. You and your stepfather got in a fight, and you beat him severely enough to have charges brought against you."

"I was just a punk kid…"

Neil leveled his gaze with the man. "Weren't we all at some point? You should be frank with me, Mr. Newsom. I'm only trying to help Ritchie. Not here to judge you for something you've already been judged on."

"The asshole beat my mother. A lot. One day I just got sick of it and gave him a beating of his own."

"So this was in self-defense?"

"No. He didn't lay a hand on me. I was stronger than him." He stuffed the back of his hands in his jeans rear pockets and shrugged. "But she begged me to leave him alone. I told her one day, if he laid a hand on her again, I'd kill him, but she kept on staying with him, saying she loved him and all that. I just couldn't understand! Then I come home one day, and he's throwin' her around, made her nose bleed, and broke her hand. I...I lost it."

He swallowed visibly, the pain etched in his face at the memory. "She started screaming at me to stop. Even though she was bleeding all over his unconscious ass, even though her eye and hand were swollen twice as big as they should be—she called the cops on *me*. That's what happened."

"Did she explain the truth of the circumstance? That you were defending her?"

"Nope. She made it seem I'd beaten them both." He sighed harshly. "I don't think the cops believed her much. That's why I only got charged with assault on him."

Neil withheld his frown at this information. Without someone else to corroborate Carl's story that his stepdad was the abuser and he was essentially just retaliating to protect his mother, well, he wasn't a viable candidate to take care of Ritchie while Diana was locked up.

Instead of getting easier, the case turned the opposite.

"Thank you for your time," Neil said before heading back to his car.

He checked his cell phone, and a text message from Logan was waiting. *Back in town. Let's catch up. Lunch at the ramen place tomorrow?*

His next thought was of Ashtyn.

He'd just gotten a message from his friend and the first person he thought of was his friend's executive assistant. Ten days had passed since he saw her, and he'd been able to keep thoughts of her to a minimum. Only at night and only briefly, then he'd force her out.

He still ached, however. She still invaded his dreams, leading him to wake up in a sweat with his cock throbbing, blowing his whole theory that once he had sex with her that craving would be eliminated. But, it'd only gotten worse.

He *despised* her for it.

Realizing he was still sitting in his Lexus, daydreaming, he replied to Logan's text message and agreed to lunch.

Maybe he needed to make some changes, shake things up, and get out of this rut. Being around her had brought something new and different to his daily life, and without her, none of the things he used to do for diversion appealed to him. Text messages and booty calls from other women went unanswered.

He started the ignition and used the Bluetooth to call Ingrid. "I'm done for the day. Feeling restless. Forward any urgent messages, otherwise, they can wait until tomorrow. Also, make a reservation for my favorite ramen place for lunch."

"I know what happens when you're restless. Should I make an appointment for your tailor? Get tickets to a game? Or are you due for a shave and a cut?" she asked, attempting to anticipate his needs.

He chuckled. "No, Ingrid, I can take care of myself. I just need a night off."

"Understood. I'll see you in the morning."

Two hours later, he shook the hand of the Mercedes salesman.

A new car was just what he needed. Something sportier. An impulse buy, but not totally impractical, considering he'd been wanting to trade in his car for a few months now. He stared at his Lexus and remembered the hot sex he'd had with Ashtyn in it, her breast in his mouth while she grinded, moaned, and clutched his hair—

"You forgot this," said one of the dealership's employees. He handed Neil the to-go mug he'd taken with him from Ashtyn's friend's house that morning. Must've been rolling around the backseat.

For a second, he thought about telling the man to throw it away, but then took it. Maybe he should return the damn thing. It wasn't Ashtyn's, but it didn't belong to him either. The couple likely wouldn't miss it, but even so, how annoying would it be if she snapped at him for being so thoughtless not to give it back?

The salesman grinned and handed Neil the keys to his new Benz.

Black. Fast. New. He hopped in and peeled out.

The biggest question the next day wasn't whether or not he would close on this merger deal, but if he should defy Ashtyn's request to avoid one another at her office. Quarter to 1 o'clock rolled around, and he walked to SFG, the coffee mug in his hand, determined to stride into the executive offices and get this first face-to-face over with.

Besides, it'd been almost two weeks. Time had no doubt cooled the tension. After all, it wasn't as if he had to *talk* to her. Logan wouldn't think that was odd, in fact he'd probably like it if Neil left Ashtyn alone. The only thing he had to do was give her this damn to-go mug without Logan noticing. Since he was usually knee-deep in work when Neil arrived, giving it to her could be quick and painless.

Of course he wouldn't be rude to her. Or snipe. Or mean. He'd simply say "Hi," hand her the mug, and wait for Logan, who better not make him wait more than thirty goddamn seconds.

More than likely, Ashtyn knew about their lunch.

While the elevator soared to the top floor, he steeled his body and mind. Negating the fact she had an effect on him was pointless, because he was very aware of it, and didn't subscribe to self-denial.

"Neil!" greeted the perky executive receptionist. "It's been forever. How are you?"

At least there was one woman at SFG who would smile at him today. "I'm well. Good to see you," he winked at her while continuing to walk toward the double doors leading to Logan's office.

Ashtyn wasn't at her desk.

He didn't know whether to be disappointed or grateful. All that prep in his head for nothing. Other than her little espresso cup sitting on a saucer, there was not one item out of place. Not even a pen. He set the travel mug down, traced his fingers over her mouse as if he'd feel her on it, then sharply turned toward Logan's door and rapped twice with his knuckle. "Savant."

"Two minutes. I'm on the phone."

Logan's voice had a smile in it, and Neil knew he was either talking to Jordana or…talking to Jordana. He was never ready to go.

In those two minutes, Ashtyn could come back to her desk. "Take your time."

Little more than three minutes later, Logan emerged from his office, but Ashtyn hadn't returned. His friend had a smile so big, Neil was partly jealous. "I don't have to ask if you enjoyed your honeymoon. You're still on it."

Logan grinned, shaking his hand and clasping his shoulder in affection. "I promise I won't talk about the joys of love and marriage."

"Especially since you've only been married for two weeks. Talk to me in twenty years. On second thought, keep that shit to yourself."

Logan laughed. They started walking out and, feeling it would be strange for him not to, he gestured to the desk. "Where's Ashtyn?"

"Somewhere. Don't worry, you'll get her next time," Logan drolled with a shake of his head.

Little did Logan know Neil had had her, lost her, and there wouldn't be a next time.

NEIL WAS here.

When she came back to her desk, the yellow and black to-go mug stood out on her Chintaly Finnigan glass computer desk. She stared at it, confused, knowing it wasn't hers. And then it hit her. It was the container she'd given Neil that day, and she'd jerked a look to her left, then right, expecting Neil to waltz around the corner and mock her.

He didn't.

She slowly sat down on the edge of her chair, picked up the mug, and stuffed it in her purse. He didn't have to return it, but it was kind of him to.

Belatedly, she checked Logan's schedule on her monitor and saw he'd gone to lunch with him. He must've put that in without telling her, which he was wont to do, assuming she kept an eagle eye on his schedule. Returning the mug hadn't been the only reason Neil came by, obviously, and by pure chance, she hadn't been here when he did.

Well. Lucky her.

Two near-misses. The universe was on her side for once, though, unlike the morning at the café, she held no trepidation in seeing him now. In fact, she *wanted* to see him. If no other reason than to prove to herself she could act as she did before. Which is what she told herself every night when she fantasized about his body over hers, his hands caressing her breasts, his hot breath in her ear while he thrust deep and hard inside her.

Her body missed him, but she didn't miss the man. That would be absurd.

Yes, please, let him come in here and try to wind me up, she challenged the universe. Her mouth curved, thinking of him doing just that. He'd try, because he was Neil Caenon, and he'd hate it when she didn't play verbal tennis. It could be a whole new dynamic for them.

Let the games begin.

18

ALMOST TWO weeks later, however, Neil had yet to stop by Savant Financial Group again.

Ashtyn didn't know why this vexed her so much. She knew Logan and Neil had had lunch at least three times because Logan would put it in his schedule as per usual.

Putting together a quick salad for dinner at home, she asked herself the same questions over and over. Was Neil avoiding SFG because of her? Did he think she couldn't handle seeing him? Or did he regret their time together to such an extent that he didn't even want to be in the same room?

Well, how immature, no matter what the explanation. She had half a mind to call him and tell him to grow up, but no, *she* would look like the immature one.

Maybe he wanted to spare her the distress. Even though he'd scoffed at her insistence they avoid each other for a while, it seemed he'd actually relented to her suggestion.

Their affair was brief and ended sourly, but she missed him. His voice, his humor, his ability to electrify the very air around her. Even after all the fun she was having living in her new place and getting to know the single life again, she didn't realize how much she looked forward to those minutes he'd be at her desk attempting to shock her into a conversation, until it stopped happening.

What was he up to? Did he think of her? How many women had he been with since?

"Get a grip, Ashtyn," she whispered, continuing to chop veggies for her salad.

Her cell phone rang.

"Jordana Shaw" flashed on the display. Ashtyn smiled. She needed to change it to Jordana Savant one of these days. "Hi there," she answered. "I was hoping to hear from you sooner or later."

"So sorry it wasn't sooner. The minute we came into town, my to-do list tripled, then tripled again. I must've been out of my mind when I agreed to do all these things for sister, *and* finish my sixth book, *and* get the house ready. And by ready I mean painted, furnished, and decorated with more than an old picture of Logan and his fraternity on the wall."

Ashtyn laughed, holding the cell to her ear with her shoulder as she scooped the veggies into a bowl. "You've been trying to commit to decorating your cozy mansion for six months." Between her career writing children's books, planning for her wedding, and keeping up with the ever-demanding social schedule of the San Franciscan elite, Jordana really had no spare time.

"I know. I've yet to explore my inner Martha Stewart and to be honest, I'm just not that into it. I've found an interior decorator who comes highly recommended. In order to throw some of these parties, we need a more aesthetically-pleasing home."

"According to whom?"

"Deidre and any woman like her. I love how they ask 'When does the decorator start?' and 'How come it hasn't changed at all since the last time I was here?' Snide little inquiries that make me force a fist in my mouth."

She laughed heartily. "It'll all work out. It's your house, not theirs."

Jordana sighed. "I wish I didn't care, but I do. I want Logan to be happy."

"Are you joking? He's so happy I wouldn't be surprised if he painted the office with stars and rainbows."

"If he does, you have my permission to have him committed." She giggled. "Anyway, I'd love to talk more, but I have to get back to my list. We can catch up later. The reason I'm calling is because I was hoping you could give up an evening and volunteer with me this Saturday. My sister committed to it but of course has already bailed. Don't be afraid to say no. I'd completely understand."

Knowing she had plans for Saturday could be a wonderful distraction. "I'd love to."

PART OF NEIL'S job was avoiding going to court, and in corporate litigation, he was the master at settlements. The only reason he had to be in court today was for Ritchie, and the managing partner wished him luck, but pressured him to get back to finish his "real" job.

The thing about judges was, if they didn't like you, you were already losing the case. Unfortunately, he got Judge Edith Cramer. During his entire spiel of why Ritchie should remain in his stepfather's custody at home, he could already see the dissent in Judge Cramer's eyes.

When the attorney for the state put Carl on the stand and asked if he had any medical training, Carl admitted he was just a tire salesman, and didn't know anything outside of basic CPR. That pretty much sealed Ritchie's fate.

"It's understandable you want to stay home, young man," Judge Cramer said folding her hands together. "But I cannot grant that for your own safety. Your stepfather will have visitation hours to come see you, and your mother can petition for custody once she's free."

Ritchie stared blankly. "The state home?"

"Yes."

A fat tear rolled down his cheek, but his lip didn't tremble and he didn't sob. He brushed it away angrily. Both he and Diana looked at Neil like he'd screwed up big time, and he didn't blame them. Despite this, Carl came over and shook his hand. "We all knew this would happen. I know you did what you could. Thanks, anyway."

Neil just nodded, unable to muster any kind of smile or encouraging words. "I'm sorry."

Ritchie, however upset he was feeling inside, didn't lash out or blame Neil when they exited the courtroom, but his mother did.

"Some hotshot lawyer," she spat. "Here I thought a man who made the big bucks would stand up for my boy. Now he has to go to a *home!*"

Neil tucked a hand in his pocket, guilt-riddled. "They'll take care of him there. I know it's not what any of you wanted, but I warned you to be prepared for this decision. You won't have to worry about Carl taking care of him on his own for almost two years while juggling two jobs. It's a lot to ask." He softened his tone. "You're his mother. You know how hard it is to be responsible for a child who requires special attention. Carl cares about him, yes, but the house isn't equipped, and he doesn't have any medical knowledge. Whether or not you want to admit it, he's not prepared to handle it. And you don't know if one day he'll get fed up and leave Ritchie by himself."

"You don't know shit. Carl would never do that," she said, glancing back at the pair who were waiting for her.

"I know people. I know men. There's a reason women are the nurturers. As unhealthy as a career you chose, you were Ritchie's home. He just wanted to be as close to that as he could be with Carl."

Her gaze dropped, and chin quivered.

He stepped closer to her, and slipped his business card in her hand. "When you get out, and want to petition for custody, call me. Free of charge."

"Why the hell would I do that? Just because you normally get paid a thousand dollars an hour or whatever that makes you the best? You still fucking lost." More tears escaped, and he was sick to see a mother cry. She stomped away and left with her husband and son.

He sighed, and turned the other way.

POSITIVE ENERGY could absolutely be contagious.

As Ashtyn sat across from Jordana at an exclusive French restaurant, she continued to laugh at an embarrassing amount while the waiter refilled her wine glass.

They'd decided to meet for dinner to catch up and she was so glad they did. The restaurant was only a couple blocks away from the hotel, so afterward all they had to do was walk to the event where they were assigned to ask attendees to fill out a quick questionnaire.

For once, her divorce wasn't the spotlight of the conversation, as it had been with her other friends lately. She'd insisted Jordana tell her all about the epic honeymoon, what was next for her writing career, things like that. Jordana took Ashtyn's cue to avoid any solemn topics and indulged Ashtyn's every question. What a relief to have a friend who didn't analyze her every word and gesture.

An hour and a half later, the red wine and easy mood was starting to loosen Ashtyn's tongue. She wanted to talk to Jordana about what happened with Neil so badly it threatened to burst from her mouth. But what would be the point? Even though she knew her friend wouldn't admonish her for getting involved with her husband's best friend, she was still too embarrassed to admit to the affair. Regardless of their friendship, Jordana was Logan's wife.

It didn't matter anyway, she told herself as the server swept up the empty dessert plate, because she and Neil were over.

"I'm so glad you insisted on the crème brule," Jordana said. "It was beyond delicious."

Ashtyn shrugged with a wan smile. "What's the point of coming to a place like this and counting calories? Which reminds me. A co-worker of mine said I wouldn't catch a new husband with new cellulite."

"Emmy, I assume. Well, if and when you decide to put yourself out there again, just let me know. There are plenty of fish in the sea. And a lot of those fish do business with Logan."

She smiled. "I appreciate that, but I'm taking it extra slow. Besides. I thought matchmaking was Miranda's job."

"You're absolutely right. That *is* her area of expertise! Once she and her hubby come back from Greece, you should call her. That woman will kick your love life into overdrive."

Ashtyn laughed, dotting at the corners of her mouth with a napkin. "I needed this."

With a beautiful, sincere smile, Jordana said, "Me too."

They got to the event and were immediately put to work by the coordinator. The wine buzz had worn off and now she was just enjoying herself, mingling with the guests and assisting the staff with the questionnaire.

And then she saw Neil.

Just like that. One moment he wasn't there, the next she was out of breath.

Ashtyn's world tilted on its axis.

He strolled in, shook hands with a few gentleman and smiled, affecting the air around him the way fire affected trees. Women glanced over with little smiles of appreciation.

No matter how big the Bay area was, running into someone you didn't want to run into was inevitable. She set down the clipboard and turned her back so he wouldn't see her.

Was this the mixer he'd been referring to? The one he asked her to attend with him?

So this was where they were going to have their first face-to-face. Weeks ago, she might've discreetly hidden in herself in the volunteer break room for a minute, but now, she thought raising her chin, she was actually eager to see just how their interaction would go. If there was any interaction at all.

She spotted Jordana on the other side of the room in deep conversation, and knew once Neil saw her, she'd immediately tell him Ashtyn was here too.

Somehow she knew where Neil was even when she couldn't see him weaving through the crush. It was a matter of time before he saw her. Then again, he might already know she was there, the sharp observer he was when he walked in a room, without her noticing.

"Would you like to take a break?" asked the coordinator. "You seem restless."

"Oh. Yes, just a little. Would that be all right? I don't want to leave you hanging."

The nice woman smiled. "Not at all. It's only busy at the very beginning and the very end. Go ahead and take a load off."

"You're a saint. Thank you." Wishing she could partake in a cocktail, she meandered through the crowd, greeting people and taking her time, as she made her way toward Jordana's side.

"Ashtyn," Jordana called when she spotted her.

With a gracious smile, she turned around and saw Jordana standing with Neil and another man. The air hummed around her, feeling that inextricable pull toward the lawyer. She focused on Jordana as she made her way over, heart hammering wildly in her chest. The closer she got, the more her nerves screamed.

For him.

He fixed his cold gaze on her, but she pretended he didn't exist. Every step she took felt like she was moving in slow motion.

"Having fun?" Jordana smiled, oblivious to Ashtyn's tension.

"Good turnout, isn't it?" she remarked, then held out her hand to the man standing beside Neil. "Ashtyn Turner."

He smiled and shook her hand. "Brad Freeman. Pleasure."

She nodded, then passed her gaze over Neil, and folded her hands in front of her. "Hi, Neil."

"Ashtyn," Neil drawled a little sardonically. "It's been a while. How are you?"

His tone flicked a spark of anger in her, the same tone he'd used that Sunday morning. Biting the inside of her cheek, she chose to stare at the corner of his shoulder. "I'm well. Thank you."

Brad pointed his thumb toward the door. "Caenon. Saw you pull up in a black Mercedes. You traded in the Lexus?"

He rocked back on his heels, hands in pockets. "I did."

"That ride was badass. In God's name, why?"

Neil shrugged. "I was bored with it."

Hmph.

"What?" Neil asked, shooting his stare at her.

She blinked, heart skipping a beat. "I didn't say anything."

"You went 'hmph'."

She did that out loud? The three of them were looking at her curiously. Her face flamed with heat. "I'm…just not surprised you got bored."

"It was a car."

"Yes and you'd had your fun with it and then got rid of it after what? Barely a year?" she mocked.

"Thirteen months."

"I rest my case. Who does that?"

Brad opened his mouth. "Actually—"

"I do that," Neil quipped. "Last time I checked there was nothing wrong with wanting something new."

"I didn't say there was," she argued prettily.

"But you made a noise."

"No I didn't! It just must be nice to have that option."

"It *is* nice. If something no longer interests you, why keep it? Maybe *you* enjoy using something over and over, but I don't." He gave her a pointed look.

Oh, you pompous jerk. What was he implying? "You can't appreciate the value of anything if you cast it out before you get attached, can you?"

"Er," Brad murmured, looking between them. "Are we still talking about the car…?"

Neil ignored him, and his tone carried an edge. "I appreciate the value of many things. None of which are material, Ms. Turner. I enjoy new cars and I can trade them when I want, which I happen to like. It's what I've been doing for years."

You mean you've been trading women for years. Oh, how she *burned* to say it. "When I invest into something I want, I value it for more than a minute," she countered.

"Sometimes a minute is all I need to be satisfied." His gaze challenged her.

"Oh, I'm sure it's more often than *sometimes*."

Brad chuckled and Jordana's eyes went round.

Nonplussed, Neil quirked a brow. "You can go years wanting something, then once you have it, sixty seconds can be enough before you move on."

Her stomach dropped at the obvious double meaning. "That's what life is all about for you, isn't it? Chase and replace."

"You're damn straight," he quickly responded, gaze hard. "That's clever by the way. Chase and replace."

"I'm glad you think so."

"Remind me never to bring up the fact I traded in my car when you're around," he remarked dryly.

Unable to stand a second more, she grabbed a wine glass from a server's tray. "If you'll excuse me." Sweat rolled down her back, and even though she wanted to run to the nearest corner and scream, she forced herself to take calm steps. Instead of a corner, she chose to stare at a painting as if it held any interest to her.

She heard Jordana's heels slowly approaching, with her friend's eyes on her as she came to stand beside her. "What was *that?*" she asked with a hint of sardonic amusement.

"Nothing. Caenon is just so...you know." She flickered a shameful glance. "I'm sorry. I didn't mean to antagonize."

Her friend chuckled. "It was funny watching you two go back and forth. I wouldn't think you would get so fired up about a trade-in."

Had nothing to do with the car, and everything to do with her battling emotions where Neil was concerned. "I don't know why I overreacted. He likes to push my buttons and I always let him."

"You pushed *first* this time."

She sighed. "I know."

Jordana's close scrutiny had Ashtyn begging to tell the truth about her and Neil. The decision to spill the beans to her friend already unburdened some of mounting anxiety. "Jordana. I need to confess something."

19

BY THE LOOK in Jordana's eyes, she already suspected what Ashtyn could be referring to.

"After the party," Ashtyn requested. "It's kind of a long story."

"Oh boy. A bottle of wine long?"

"I think so, yes," she answered, relieved.

Jordana squeezed her arm reassuringly. "No problem. But you need to smile. Don't let him see you frazzled. It'll just give him more of the power."

An hour later, most of the party attendees were gone, and their volunteering obligation ended. Neil hadn't stayed much longer after their confrontation. She tried not to stare as he opened the door for a woman before following her out.

She felt sick. *Damn him.*

"Ready?" Jordana asked, slipping on her stylish light jacket.

"More than ready."

"I told Logan not to expect me home for a little while, so I'm all yours."

Jordana's driver took them to a wine bar down the road, loud enough where conversation could be private, but quiet enough one didn't have to talk over the noise. They ordered a bottle of Shiraz and poured generously.

Eager to get this off her chest, Ashtyn took one sip of wine, then set down the glass. "I had a fling with Neil."

No surprise showed on Jordana's face, but she did give a sympathetic look. "I thought so."

"You did?"

She sat back and crossed her legs, folding her hands together. "No matter what the situation, Neil can handle his own. Always has a ready, award-winning smile even if he can't stand the person in front of him, even when people are argumentative or difficult, he always maintains. As soon as you walked up, the whole—" She swept her hands out, "—air changed. And the way he was staring at you caught my attention. Like you'd hurt him."

"Hurt him?" Ashtyn exclaimed. "Trust me, after our weekend together, his feet practically started a fire when he left. If anyone was hurt, it was me," she added.

"Really?" Jordana's brows etched together. "You knew what he was like."

"I did, and therefore I thought I could predict him. But the night before he left, he made me believe we could go longer than the weekend. Even asked me to accompany him to the event tonight. At first I was dead-set against it, but then I changed my mind by morning. Before I could tell him, he behaved like a different man. Cold, sarcastic. Indifferent." The last word came out softer, because it hurt more to say it.

"Okay, start from the beginning. How did you and Neil even happen? I must know."

Taking a deep breath, she decided to be honest about it all. "I was supposed to sort of house-sit for my friend Lila…" She got through the whole tale of the jail incident, Neil coming to her rescue, the theft of her pearls, the car, the kiss, and their weekend in Briar's in less than one wine glass. "And you're completely allowed to judge me for getting involved with him."

Her friend shook her head. "Not my thing. This sounds like the perfect storm. He helped you out when you needed it. You are newly single, and let's be frank, he's irresistible. The chemistry has been there for years between you and him, and it finally came to a climax." Her eyes widened. "I didn't mean that the way it sounded!"

Ashtyn laughed. "Yes you did."

"I want to rip him a new one for treating you so unfeelingly, but—" she emphasized before Ashtyn could interrupt, "he wasn't cold or indifferent tonight. He was red-hot with some emotion. What emotion? Only Neil knows."

"You think so?"

"You could see it in his eyes. He feels something for you."

Now that was hard to believe. Recalling the scene in vivid detail, she didn't see anything except contempt. "It's probably resentment for getting involved with me. Regretting what happened. He knows Logan wouldn't be pleased if he found out." She gave a start, covering her hand. "Don't tell him. I know you two share everything, and I hate to put you in this position, but I don't think he has to know about this."

Jordana sighed, understanding in her hazel eyes. "I don't want to keep things from Logan, but you're my friend, Ashtyn. I'm sure there are things about *his* friends that I don't know about. Your secret is safe with me. If or when you think Logan should know, you'll be the one to tell him, not me. Besides, it's after the fact."

Gratitude poured through her. "Thank you." She squeezed Jordana's hand. "Your friendship means so much to me. I'm so glad I could finally tell someone."

Jordana gave a soft smile. "So, do you think you and he will be able to be in a room together without setting off a million sparks?"

Ashtyn's mouth twitched, and she shook her head. "I can't answer that."

"If he's angry, it's because of something else, not you. If he really regretted hooking up, then he'd probably avoid you altogether."

"Oh he's done that, too." Turning the base of her wine glass around, she hesitated asking Jordana her next question, but she had to know. "When you met Logan, you knew he was a bit of a player, didn't you?"

Jordana's smile grew, and she cocked her head. "It was pretty obvious from the get-go."

"You took a chance on him anyway. Why?"

She paused, shifting her gaze for a moment, before meeting Ashtyn's again. "Because he asked for one." After taking a sip of her wine, she added, "And I was head over heels. Even though the *last* time I took a chance on someone I got my heart broken, I couldn't take that out on Logan. It's risky every time, with every man, no matter what their past says."

Jordana's words rang true, but Ashtyn had no reason to ask such a thing. She and Neil were over. Despite Jordana's optimistic opinion that he had feelings for her, Ashtyn disagreed. A man with emotion would've called, stopped by the office, or been kind, instead of cruel.

Jordana continued to study her. "Why do you ask? Were you hoping he'd want something more?"

Ashtyn blinked away her thoughts. "No. I mean, I do care about him, but I have no illusions where he's concerned."

"Had you two talked at all before tonight?"

She shook her head. "He hasn't even come to the office to pick up Logan for lunch. For the first time in years, Logan goes to him. I know it's on purpose so Neil doesn't have to have some awkward moment with Logan standing right there. If *you* saw something in Neil, I imagine Logan would be just as perceptive. He used to tease Neil to leave me alone."

"What happened, or happens, between you and Neil is between you two. I have no doubt my husband would have a strong opinion about it, but that would be because he doesn't want Neil taking advantage of you."

She rushed to his defense. "He didn't. Honestly, it was the other way around. He turned me down the first time."

"Really?" she exclaimed.

Her cheeks heated with the admission. "When I asked him to join me in Briar's, he said no. Then he showed up later that night. The deputy sheriff I told you about had stopped by. Neil practically peed on my leg like a dog marking his territory and kicked Jake out. In the most gentlemanly way of course."

Jordana giggled. "You're kidding. Neil usually has more tact. So what now, Ash?"

Her smile faded. She licked her lips, gazing at her wine glass. "Nothing now. It's over. I promise the next time I'm in the same room with him, it won't be like tonight."

Jordana picked up her glass, smiling over the rim. "Some promises just can't be kept."

After she'd figured out how to use her fireplace, she opened her windows to let in the cool night air and grabbed a book. Her mind needed a re-route from Neil and she figured delving in a fictional homicide would do the trick.

Hours later, deep in her mystery novel, sorting out the possible suspects in her head, she jerked when the doorbell rang. Perplexed at who it could be, she glanced at the clock.

It was almost midnight.

She walked to the foyer and checked the peephole from her tip toes.

Neil.

Her heart thundered as she came down on her heels. Why would he show up without a call or a text? He could be here to give her a piece of his mind about tonight. Just had to have the last word. Hmph.

She opened the door, mouth open, ready to cut him off when she assessed Neil's appearance. Rumpled clothes, head hung, hair askew from its usually perfect style, as though he'd raked it with his hands again and again. Not once had she ever witnessed him so unkempt.

He leaned his palms on the doorframe as though to hold himself up. Finally raising his gaze to hers, she saw bloodshot eyes and a five o'clock shadow. Was he drunk?

Her snide greeting vanished. "Neil. What's wrong?"

"I need you tonight," he told her hoarsely.

"What are you—?"

"No." He raised a finger. "No questions, no fights, no angry rapport. I just need you." He sighed deep and straightened. "Can I come in?"

Tempted to tell him to go home, she found she couldn't. She'd never seen him in such an unbalanced condition and didn't have the strength to say no. Stepping back, she grew concerned as he walked past her and down her hall. The taxi he'd come in pulled away. Following him, she asked again what was wrong, but he didn't respond. That worried her. Whatever it was that got Neil down, had to be major. He turned to her bedroom.

When she entered her room, he caught her hand and pushed her up against the wall. His hands dove into her hair. He kissed her like a desperate man, then ran his hands over her body with hard strokes. He behaved as if he really did need her, and even though she was dying to ask why he chose to come to her, she knew he wouldn't answer any questions, and now that he'd touched her, the last thing she wanted to do was talk.

She let him undress her, let him take the lead, and do to her what he desired. As he fed on her mouth, she closed her eyes, losing herself once again to the unparalleled passion he conjured with his heat, scent, and body.

He swung her to the bed, plunging his tongue in her mouth, fingers seeking. She parted her legs more. When his hand cupped her slick core, she bowed her back and gasped when he slipped in two fingers.

His erection pressed into her thigh through his pants.

Why was he still dressed?

To remedy this, she groped for the buttons of his slacks and shoved the waist over his ass. He broke away from her mouth long enough to get rid of clothes, then returned to her arms. The hard planes of his body aligned with her soft ones, and she reveled in the masculinity against her breasts and between her thighs. Licking her nipple, then grazing his tongue and teeth up her chest and jaw, scraping her delicate skin, he ravished her and held her down by her wrists.

"Ashtyn..." he whispered in the crook of her neck, rubbing his cock along her wet folds. "I love how wet you are for me."

Spreading her legs wider, she thrust her hips, giving small mews of pleasure as he kissed her breasts, cupped them, alternatively sucking on each nipple. She gripped the back of his head and he dragged his mouth back to hers, pushing his hips in, groaning.

Clearly he was doing his best not to just plunge inside her, but she didn't require extensive foreplay. The weeks without his lovemaking supplied an abundance of pent-up desire that required no summoning.

She cried out as he swiftly entered her. He braced his hands next to her hips, and groaned long, pulled out, then pushed in again.

So hard, thick, and perfect he was. Every thrust forced a sound from her. A moan. A plea. Whispered words of more and yes. It felt so good, so good to have him inside her body, in her arms.

I need you, he'd said. And indeed, he was showing it.

While they kissed, licked, nipped, and clung to each other, something broke free in Ashtyn. They rolled on her bed, sweating and heaving for breath, hips meeting again and again, until both were screaming out sounds of soul-ascending ecstasy.

If this was a bad idea, then she'd regret it later with a smile.

20

ASHTYN WOKE up on her side, away from Neil, and remained like that for a while.

Most of her parts were tender. She needed a shower, a long hot one, but she didn't dare move. Part of her was surprised Neil hadn't already slipped out. But no, he was still there. She could feel his body heat on her back.

After the phenomenal sex, they'd collapsed and fallen asleep without speaking one word to another, which he probably appreciated as much as she did.

He stirred beside her, his arm brushing her back. "Ashtyn." His voice came through soft, but clear, as though he'd been awake for a while, too.

The pregnant silence in her bedroom grew.

Please don't let this be awkward. If he thought he had to say something to comfort her, she preferred he didn't. Morning-after platitudes would be the worst coming from him.

"Do you want me to leave?" he finally asked.

She inhaled a deep breath and turned around. "No."

"I missed you, Ashtyn," he told her hoarsely, looking at her.

Her heart leapt at the words. Turning her head, she met his gorgeous green eyes. "I missed you, too."

"When I saw you at the mixer, all I wanted to do was push you against the wall and kiss you."

Now that would've been scandalous. She floated her fingers under his chin with a small smile, relieved. No platitudes, just truth. "Maybe you should have."

"Instead I had to stand there, three feet in front of you, and talk and act unaffected to your presence."

"I thought you *were* unaffected."

He shook his head. "I was anything but that."

She sighed. "Me too."

He captured her hand and kissed the back of it. "Listen. This whole 'let's pretend nothing happened' deal is no good. I don't think you and I are done with each other. Do you?" He turned to his side, watching her steadily.

She twisted her mouth. While she agreed, things had to be cleared up before they started over. "I'm confused. That morning at the house, you acted like you couldn't get away from me fast enough. Neil...I...I'd changed my mind about not seeing other. I really liked spending time with you, and my reasons for keeping us a secret were shallow, a knee-jerk reaction. I honestly didn't expect you to want to see me again. But then I realized I wanted the same. I wanted to go to Aurelio's with you. I wanted to attend the mixer together. And I planned to tell you that morning, but then you were—"

"A complete asshole." He threaded his hand through his hair with a harsh sigh. "Christ, I had no idea you'd had a change of heart. I'm sorry, Ashtyn. I was doing my damnedest to be the guy who was cool with never seeing you again. You'd told me you wanted one weekend only and I tried to pretend I didn't care."

Heck of a job he did there, because she'd believed it. "Well, I'm sick of pretending."

He smiled at her. That gorgeous, slow, swoon-worthy grin that melted her. "Good to know we're on the same page. Now. Let's make this official." He climbed on her, kissing her neck, and spreading her apart with his knees.

One more thing, mister… She grasped his face to make him meet her eyes. "What about last night? That was more than you missing me."

He eased back with a slight frown. "Yeah. It was. The pro bono case I was working on."

"About the boy?"

He nodded. "I let him down. I lost."

She didn't have to know the details of course, but she didn't need to, to know what it meant to Neil. "Will he be taken care of?"

"Of course. Just not in the way he wanted, as I told you."

"Sometimes life leads you to what we feel is unfairness for now, to make it fair in the future. That's what I think. It may not be ideal, but as long as he's safe and taken care of, right? I know there are a lot of children out there who don't have anyone fighting for them. One day, when he's older, he'll understand. He might even thank you."

"Or hate my guts forever."

She cocked her head, wrapping her arms around him. "Oh Neil, you're a lawyer. You should be used to that."

"No doubt," he chuckled. "It was the first time, in a long time, I let the disappointment really get to me. Usually a little bourbon is all I need. Last night…" He kissed her chin. "I needed you, too."

"If that's what happens when you need me, then consider me on-call."

He chuckled, traveling down her jaw to her neck. "What about *your* needs?"

If she only knew what she needed and how long from this thing between her and Neil, she could set the perimeters, but she didn't feel the urge to. Not with him. They could have some fun, out in the open this time, and see where it led from there. She arched her body into his as he continued his erotic exploration. "You seem to know my needs without asking."

"If I happen to misread, don't hesitate to give me a heads up."

As he started kissing his way down her neck, she hesitated in letting him go much farther, knowing there was one more thing she had to share. "I told Jordana about us." He lifted his head, but she interrupted him, seeing the reproof in his eyes. "Don't be mad. She already knew. Our brief debate last night sort of gave it away and I had to tell her."

He lowered his head; strands of his hair tickled her chin. "Logan is going to hire a firing squad."

"She said she wouldn't tell him."

Raising his gaze, he lifted a brow. "And you believe her?"

"Have a little faith in her. I don't think she would lie to me, Neil. She said if and when I thought Logan should know, then it'd be me who'd tell him."

"Or me." He moved off her.

She understood his apprehension, but wouldn't let him spoil their morning together with it. She rolled on her side and rested her head in her palm, tracing his abs with her other hand. "He should know. If we're going to see each other, it'd be impossible to hide it from him, and I don't think we should or have to. He's my boss, not my guardian."

"I agree. I don't want to hide anything. I'll tell him."

"No, I will. After all, I was the one who started this," she said with a lilting smile.

He met her gaze, and lightly cupped the side of her face with his hand. "It doesn't matter who started it. It's a two-way street."

As much as she wanted to put the burden on his shoulders, she couldn't allow it. "Neil, I appreciate that, but he's my boss, and it should come from me. Promise you won't say anything until I do. It's important to me. Plus it'll be less awkward."

Smoothing the hair off her shoulder, he asked, "Less awkward?"

"If you tell him about us, then I'll have to come to work every day wondering what he's thinking. Or if he'll treat me any differently."

He considered what she said for a few seconds, then gave a short nod. "You're right. He'll respect you more if you're frank with him. Go ahead and tell him when you're ready. I promise even if I see him first, I won't say a word."

"Thank you." She bent down and kissed his chest.

"You can thank me by joining me in the shower and giving me full privilege of your body again."

She feigned a sigh of annoyance. "If I must."

He grinned and pushed off the bed, then snapped his fingers. "Come, slave girl."

With a soft laugh, she followed him to the large stand-in shower with the glass door. She squealed when he grabbed her to him under the gentle spray. "You like your shower way too cold!"

"How hot do you like it?" he asked, running his wet hands along her back and hips.

"Hot enough to make the room steam." She encircled her arms around his neck.

"We can do that on our own."

"Neil," she complained.

He gave her a relenting sigh and cranked up the hot water to her liking. "How's this?"

"Much better." She dropped her head back to let the warm water run down her scalp.

His erect cock pressed against her lower stomach. Combined with the heat firing in his eyes and how he squeezed her ass, they were going to get dirty before they got clean.

He slid his hands up and cupped her breasts. With their bodies slick with water, the steam clouding the air, and Neil just looking so damn sexy with his wet hair and hooded eyes, Ashtyn was suddenly feverish with passion. No man stroked her body like he did. His hands were like magic. Strong, masculine, and only a little rough on the palms.

When he sought her core, he was gentle on her clit while he sucked on her neck at the same time. She clutched his shoulders, eyelids fluttering from the spray of the water. She lifted her leg and pressed her heel to the tiled wall as he sank a finger deep inside, stroking her tight walls. Swaying her hips forward, she bit in his shoulder, the orgasm exploding within seconds.

She brushed the temporary teeth marks with her finger and apologized. Usually she wasn't so savage, but she couldn't help it.

He glanced at his shoulder and shrugged. "A mere sex kitten bite. I like it."

"Oh? Then you're going to love this." She grabbed a hand towel and threw it on the wet floor to spare her knees. Neil's dark brow drew together. Running her fingers down his torso while she sank to the floor, she held his gaze, giving him a naughty smile.

His fingertips grazed her chin. "What are you—?"

She grabbed his cock and began sucking and stroking, encouraged by his groans. It'd been so long since she'd done this to a man, she wasn't sure she really knew what to do. By the way he dropped his head back and groaned, she was doing it just fine. She tenderly cupped his balls with her other hand, looking up to see if he enjoyed that kind of thing. He raked his hands through his hair and let out a rough curse.

Running her tongue up and down his shaft, stroking it at the same time with her wet hand, she sucked faster, harder, concentrating on the tip.

"Oh my God, you're so fucking good at this," he choked out.

His cock tensed even more in her palm, and she knew he was close. Bobbing her head a little from side to side, she loved how she had Neil panting, moaning. When he declared he was about to come—she appreciated the advanced warning—she opened her mouth even more, wordlessly letting him know to keep going. Another choked-out swear word, a deep groan, and he released inside her mouth. She continued to gently suck on him, knowing he was at his greatest sensitivity, and he begged her to stop, but in a helpless way that told her he liked it. He shuddered as she drew back, and wiped the excess from her lips.

He looked down at her in awe. "You swallow, too? Damn. You're amazing."

She chuckled, rising to stand and rinse off. "Oh the things men say after good head." It amused her he appeared somewhat dazed and sleepy-eyed. She pumped a few squirts of shampoo in her hand and began massaging it in his hair. "All right, handsome. We need to stop wasting water and soap up."

"Wasting?" He bent his head a little while she continued washing his hair. "I'd say the water played a huge part in our pleasuring each other, and therefore every drop counted."

"Still, we're in a drought. We should be more responsible."

"You're adorable sometimes." He wrapped his arms around her and kissed the tip of her nose. "There was no other woman, you know."

Slowing her motions, she met his gaze.

"Since you. I haven't slept around. I thought…you might wonder."

A wash of relief poured through her. He was telling her the truth. She would've never asked, only assumed. "Good to know."

He watched with hooded eyes, keeping his hands on her waist. "Feels nice. I like you washing my hair."

And she kind of loved it. Made him look boyishly cute the way he smiled while she kneaded his scalp. She slid her hands through one more time, then she directed him to rinse off. They had some fun soaping each other down. Neil was way more playful than she was used to. Kept tickling and poking her ribs, then grabbing her for long kisses, and nibbling on her neck. Cliff would never shower with her. He hated to play around and when he did try to be silly, it was more exasperating than anything.

Afterward, Neil got dressed in the same clothes he wore the night before. He sniffed the collar of his sport coat and made a face. "Smells like reverse happy hour."

"How much did you drink last night?" she asked throwing her hair up in a ponytail.

"Enough to make me come over here instead of going home."

She smiled, hands on hips. "About that. I suppose you want a ride to your car?"

He rubbed his nape with a sheepish grin. "Actually, if you could give me a ride home, that'd be great. I took a cab from the marina to the bar."

The possibility of seeing where he lived intrigued her. "No problem."

"Are you sure? I don't want to put you out on your Sunday afternoon."

"Don't be silly. It's the least I can do for the multiple orgasms."

He chuckled. "The very least."

On the way to the marina, he insisted she roll down the windows and turn on the radio. When she flipped on her favorite station, he grinned, telling her it was his favorite also, playing the '80s, '90s, and today's hits in between. He propped his elbow on the window and pointed out various places he'd like to take her, like Opaque, the restaurant where patrons ate in complete darkness. And Straw, circus-inspired eatery to, as Neil put it, "Satisfy your appetite for fair fare." She got a kick out of that suggestion. He mentioned a couple other places she'd always wanted to go to but never could convince Cliff to take her. Funny how Neil just knew within a few weeks of knowing her what would make her happy.

While at a red light, she covertly glanced at his sharply handsome profile while he explained why he loved this one sushi place over another. Wow. She and Neil were sort of dating. Casually, yes, but dating.

She turned her attention back to the light, a smile forming on her mouth.

His cell phone rang, and he pulled it out of his pocket, gave a look, then silenced it. Could've been anybody, but, what if it was another woman? Did she care?

Her smile started to fade, questions of whether or not he planned to be with her while he fooled around with other women at the same time. By all accounts, he never went exclusive, and she had no right to ask him to. Part of her preferred not to either, because that would keep things light, but on the other hand, she couldn't stand the thought of sharing him. The thought made her queasy.

While he gave her directions to the houseboat, she tried to accept the fact she likely wouldn't be the only woman in his life. But she was sucking at accepting it. A lot.

When they pulled in the parking lot, a sickening feeling had settled in her stomach and refused to leave. Good thing she had sunglasses on. Without them, Neil would see the unease in her eyes in no time.

She found an open spot and pulled in. The sight of the million-dollar sailboats, houseboats, and yachts temporarily distracted her. "I can't believe you call this home."

"For the past five years. Sometimes I can't believe it either." He looked over at her, and she avoided meeting his gaze.

"Well, call me soon so we can check out that sushi place," she said.

"You can't just drop me off like this," he teased, grabbing the car door handle. "It'll make me feel cheap."

She softly laughed, some of the tension drifting away. "Would hate to do that to you."

"You should see the place. Not too many ladies have."

Oh really? She found that hard to believe, but if it was true, then she was even more excited to see what he called home. "Are we going to see other people while we're—seeing each other?" she blurted.

He stopped and turned, brow raised. "Is that what you want?"

"No. I don't do that." Heart pounding, she hoped her directness would make her sound more confident than commanding. "Less complicated. I don't have time for a dating carousel."

His sexy mouth half-lifted. "Don't worry, beautiful. I'm all yours until it stops being fun." He resumed his walk down the dock, glimpsing behind him with a quick grin, eyes twinkling.

She slowly smiled, relieved, so glad instead of torturing herself she just asked.

His houseboat, a two-story wood and steel structure, had every amenity a person could want. Inside, what he referred to as the salon, included two sofas with matching ottomans and an entertainment center. There was a hidden helm station that retracted in the floor when not in use—which according to Neil was all the time—and three columns separated the galley and dinette. A full kitchen hosted stainless steel appliances and beautiful spotlighting. The hall angled across the boat to the port side led to a cuddy cabin with a guest bed. The master state upstairs held a king bed and a full bath in black-and-white. Both front and back steps led to the upper deck as well. And he had more closet space on his boat than she did in her house.

When she followed him back to the kitchen, she shook her head in awe. "I've been on many boats, but nothing like this. I envy you living on the water."

"I lucked out. Got a good deal from a retired couple who I helped out with their will."

"Why a houseboat?" she asked running her fingertips across the marbled island in the center of the kitchen.

He crossed his arms and leaned a hip on it. "To be honest, I like the idea of picking up my whole house and leaving whenever I want."

"Oh I see. Even at home you refuse to be anchored down?"

He grinned. "Something like that. I'll probably never leave, but I like knowing I can."

Ah. Of course. Nothing could tie this man to a commitment. "It suits you perfectly."

The look on his face said he knew exactly what she was thinking. "Thanks."

"Think you'll ever trade sea for land?"

"I'd have to have a very good reason," he answered, as though he doubted he'd ever have one. Much like how she told Jake she'd never leave San Francisco. Another thing they had in common. The realization made her smile.

FOR ONCE, getting drunk had ended in something other than a hangover.

While Ashtyn was on the top deck, he went to his bedroom to change clothes, and then planned to make a couple of iced teas for them to sip on while they watched the sailboats.

He was beyond happy with his decision to get drunk. Losing the hearing for Ritchie, seeing the look on the boy's face when he realized he'd be going to a home after all, set off all kinds of emotions he usually had no problem rejecting. Culpability, disappointment, doubt of his skill as a lawyer, and having no one to talk to about it. Not one damn soul. Then he had to go to the mixer and run into Ashtyn.

As soon as he could, he tore out of the place and drove home, intending to get drunk there. But then discovered he was out of alcohol, and chose to take a cab to the nearest watering hole. He didn't want to bother Logan, afraid he might slip up about Ashtyn after a few drinks. Miranda was away on a trip with her husband. He had a few other friends, but it'd been late, and divesting his woes on them held no appeal.

Then Ashtyn came to mind and before he could think twice, he was using an app on his phone for a ride and typing in her address as the destination.

Thank God he did.

He didn't know what to expect in the morning, but had decided to be frank about how he'd missed her. As was his experience, the truth paid off.

He imagined her telling him to screw off and leave her alone. Better to expect the worst and hope for the best, and indeed, he got the absolute best outcome ever.

It killed him to know if he'd been kinder, more perceptive to her mood, and less self-centered, he might've sensed her change of heart that morning in Briar's, and could've spared them both two weeks of avoidable torture.

Ah well, he thought, when it came to her, his radar just didn't function so flawlessly.

Which was fine. Frustrating and bewildering, but fine. He'd get to know her even more now, and eventually, he'd read her like a book. He already anticipated her sexual needs with ease. In bed, indeed anywhere, he read her body like a composer read music. Of course, he brought a lot of experience with him, had known for a long time where to touch and how to move to drive a woman wild.

But Ashtyn was different. She didn't just moan and gasp for the sake of it, or scream and claw for show or to please him. More and more, she opened up in his arms like a flower too long neglected. Sensual, unreserved, and generous in her lovemaking.

He'd thought he'd never get the chance to experience it again, but, until further notice, he'd have her all he wanted. Earlier, he had seen the anxiousness in her eyes when she asked if they were going to see other people while they had their fun, and found himself more than happy to tell her no. Because hell no was another man going to take up time he'd earned.

After changing out of yesterday's clothes, he cleaned out his pockets from last night and found a receipt for his bill tab, and a napkin with notes on it. He vaguely remembered scrawling this to-do list while sulking at the bar. The last item was the only one he cared about at the moment:

Call every pawn shop within 10 miles of Ashtyn's old house.

Well, his drunk self had the right idea in mind. He had connections throughout the city, including some shady people who could procure him information on the down low. If someone was trying to hock a $20,000 pearl necklace, he stood a good chance in finding them once he put the word out in every corner of the Bay.

Shuffling through his mail, he froze when he came across a pink, black, and white postcard inviting him to the grand re-opening of How Sweet It Is. Today. If he hadn't grabbed his mail, he would've missed it entirely. He took it as a sign he should go.

He sighed, rested his palms on the table, and hung his head.

It was time to say good-bye, regardless if he was ready to or not.

After making the iced teas, he climbed the steps and handed Ashtyn one.

"Thanks." She smiled.

"You're welcome." He sat down in his chair, frowning.

"Something wrong?" she asked, gazing at his profile.

He kept his gaze straight, bringing the glass to his mouth. "No."

"Neil."

Well, it wasn't like he was trying to hide it. "Nothing's wrong. In fact, it's probably very right." Fuck it. He should go. Juliet would want him to. "There's something I'm obligated to make an appearance at this afternoon. Would you mind going to this thing with me?"

"What thing?"

"It's a grand re-opening of a bakery. I knew the previous owners and helped them transfer the sale. The new owner has invited me and…I think I should go. I'd rather not go alone, though." He didn't want to get in deep with the details about his past, but strangely felt much better about going with Ashtyn by his side, even if she wasn't aware how it affected him.

He met her gaze; there were questions in her eyes, but, instead of probing, she seemed to read how he didn't want to answer any. For now.

"I'd love to go with you," she said.

An hour later when they pulled up, there was a line outside the door. Pink and yellow ribbon and balloons were tied all around, blowing in the late afternoon breeze. Children were jumping up and down in line with excitement. There was music, free lemonade, and bakery associates walking around in aprons and handing out miniature samples of cupcakes while everyone waited to go in.

"Neil!" Paige saw him and grinned, walking over to hug him. "I'm so happy you came."

"The turnout is amazing."

"Isn't it?" She clasped her hands. "I haven't seen it like this since…well, it's been a long time." She shifted her gaze to Ashtyn, smiled, and held out her hand. "Hello. I'm Paige."

"Ashtyn. Pleasure to meet you. Are you the new owner?"

"Former owner. The bakery is now in Bridget's hands." She looked between the two of them, and by the delight in her eyes, she assumed Ashtyn was the new lady in his life. There was also a bit of sadness too, as if she was remembering when he was with her daughter. "She'll be delighted to see you came. Come on in and say hello."

"I really just wanted to stop by—" he started.

"You can't leave without taking a little something." Paige ignored him and grasped Ashtyn's hand, knowing he'd have to follow them.

They walked past the line and in to the boutique where Bridget was behind the counter, grinning, laughing, and handing over boxes of cupcakes. When she spotted Neil, she smiled, told one of her employees to take over, then swept around to the front.

Keeping his eyes off the framed photo hanging to his left, gave her a sincere smile, and shook her hand. "Congratulations."

"Thank you so much!"

The place was alive again. Even with Paige and Stewart's hard work, it didn't thrive like this. Maybe because their hearts weren't into it for any reason other than they couldn't let Juliet's dream die with her.

Bridget beamed at them both. "Would you guys like some lemonade? I have all kinds. Orange lemonade. Lime lemonade. Strawberry…?" Bridget prompted.

Ashtyn stepped up next to Neil. "I'd love to try the lime."

She clapped her hands, grinning. "Wait here."

Neil cleared his throat, uncomfortable, remembering before this place was even painted. When he and Juliet had walked in this barren space and discussed her vision.

"I can smell the frosting and cake already," she said. *"Can't you?"*

"All I smell is major overhead," he told her.

She groaned and rolled her eyes. "You can try to be happy for me."

"I am happy for you. Can we go now?"

Sighing heavily, she strode past him. "I'm already gone."

He was sorry. He was so damn sorry.

One of the patrons came up beside him, gazing up at the wall. "In loving memory of Juliet…Mom. Did you see this? Who was Juliet?"

The young woman's mother came up beside her with two boxes in her hands. "The original owner, sweetheart. She passed away some years ago."

"Oh no, how awful. She was gorgeous."

Unable to keep avoiding it, Neil turned around and looked at the picture of Juliet. The one he'd been avoiding ever since they walked in. Surprisingly, looking at her didn't kill him like it used to. Her smile was so bright while she held up a cupcake in her hands. So beautiful, and too young to go.

Ashtyn's hand twined in his.

"Did you know her?" she asked.

He broke his gaze and glanced at Ashtyn. "Yes."

Someday he'd tell her how *well* he knew Juliet. In fact, he didn't dread that conversation as much as he thought he would. Not very many people knew all the details about his last, real relationship, but he thought Ashtyn ought to know. He felt safe telling her.

Which was, to him, a dangerous feeling.

21

ASHTYN DIDN'T like secrets, especially from someone who she'd been working for this long. Now that she and Neil decided to keep going with their hot fling, it was time his friend—her boss—knew about it.

She walked to Logan's office, knocked, and when he told her to come in, she closed the door behind her and took a seat. "Logan, I think there's something you should know."

He raised his gaze, set down his pen, and gave her his total attention. He was courteous like that. "What is it?"

"Neil and I are seeing each other."

No immediate reaction. He sat back. "I'm...surprised. I didn't know there was an attraction. From you, at least. Neil never attempted to hide his."

Her cheeks heated. "Well, I'm single now and he's...Neil." What else could she say to explain them?

He chuckled. "I don't have to warn you about him."

She smiled, crossing her legs and resting her hands on her knee. "Not necessary. We're just—casual." There. Good word for it. "If it makes you uncomfortable at all, please tell me."

"Uncomfortable? Hardly. If anything, I think you're way too good for Neil, and you can tell him I said that. However, he doesn't work here so there's hardly a conflict of interest. I appreciate you being so forthcoming about this." He rested his elbow on the arm of his chair, rubbing his mouth. "Now that I think about it, Neil has been acting like there's something on his mind the past week. I'm guessing you wanted to be the one to tell me."

It took her a week to finally do it. "I made him promise not to say anything until I did."

A brow raised. "You made him promise and he kept it?"

"Only because it was important to me to come to you first."

He nodded. "I see."

She cleared her throat. Being honest about her and Neil wasn't the only thing she wanted to do. "I was also arrested while you were gone."

"You were what?" His brows shot up.

She flipped a hand. "It was all a misunderstanding. I was crawling in my friend's window because the maid didn't leave the spare key, and I got caught by the sheriff. I called Neil and he had me out faster than I could blink."

While Logan listened, vastly amused, she told him about the situation at the Briar's Edge jail, adding more lightness to the story to lessen his concern.

"And you called Neil?" Was Logan's only question after she finished.

She let out a little laugh at the incredulousness in his tone. "Yes."

He mulled over that for a moment, then said, "Well. I'm glad he came through for you."

She felt a blush creeping up her neck and cheeks, and was eager to change the subject. "Above all, I love my job, Logan. I love this company and working for you. My relationship with Neil won't affect my performance here. I'll never let my personal life interfere with my professional one."

"You never did before. Hell, I didn't even know you were unhappily married until you requested time off to meet with your divorce lawyer." He paused, leaned in and folded his hands together. "Ashtyn, I hope you know how valuable you are to the company and to me. Your honesty about this is appreciated. Thank you."

With that off her shoulders, she could breathe again. "You're welcome."

"There is something else I'd like to discuss with you," he started in a manner that had her nerves rankled all over again. "Something that's been on my mind for a while. I was just too selfish to consider it until recently."

Okay…? She attempted to keep the confusion from her expression.

"Where do you see yourself in five, ten years?" he asked.

"Running Savant Financial so you can retire early," she quipped lightly, then froze with a small gasp. She never made jokes at work.

However, to her relief, Logan thought it was amusing. "Neil is already an influence on you, I can see."

"I'm sorry, that was silly joke to a serious question. I suppose I'm a little nervous after telling you about Neil."

"Ashtyn, it's all right. Jokes are not a crime." He sat back, studying her with a glint in his eye. "Now for the real answer?"

She hadn't thought of it lately with so much of her personal life in upheaval. In fact, she was grateful for her job more than ever. The one steady thing that hadn't changed. "I see myself right here. Right outside your door," she smiled. It was the truth.

Her answer pleased him. More and more her boss smiled like that, and she knew it was because he was madly in love, and less and less of a work tyrant. She liked this balance he'd found. Finally, he began with, "I've come to realize you're more than an executive assistant. You have done more than my previous assistants have ever done and you know more about the P&L reports than the COO sometimes. You've worked hard to create divisional program communications, collaborate with the HRBPs, and keep up with our charitable contributions and obligations. Besides being the ruler of my schedule, you complete ad-hoc requests out of nonsensical data reports, and you never, ever break a sweat."

Touched by his deep praise, she smiled. "It's my job."

"No. Many of those things are not. It's only because of your intelligence and acumen that you find these things and take them on. Are you satisfied being my executive assistant?"

"Yes." She didn't have to think about that one. "SFG is my home, Logan."

"I'm beginning to wonder if you've outgrown your position." He idly rubbed his chin, watching her. "And I don't want to hold you back."

"I'm not looking to be set free," she assured him. "With everything else turned upside down in my life, my job as your assistant is always right side up."

"You don't have ambitions to move up in the company?"

She considered his question for a minute. Where would she go? What would make her as happy as she was now? "Right now? No. Truth is, Logan, this is where I want to be. If you see me somewhere else where I can do better for SFG, then I'd consider it. Otherwise, I'm where I need to be for the time being."

He softly smiled, then stood up, holding out his hand.

She rose and clasped his hand.

"So just a bonus then?" he asked.

"A bonus?" she exclaimed. "It's not even Christmas. The finance department will frown on it."

He laughed. "Ashtyn, I'm the CEO and President. I do have a say."

"Even so…"

"Your divorce attorney didn't come cheap. Neither did moving. I need my assistant worry-free from her financial woes."

She leveled her gaze, dropping her hand. "I'm *not* woeful. I'm just fine."

"I know you are. Are you really turning down a bonus?"

"If it's out of pity and favoritism, yes."

He sighed, smiling, then rifled through some papers on his desk and handed her an invitation. "The charity event this Saturday. Jordana and I were going to attend, but I'd like you to go to represent the company."

"Me?"

"Yes. Take Neil with you. He loves those things."

A smile curved her mouth thinking of the last networking event they both attended. And how the night ended for the both of them. "All right. I'd be happy to go."

"I'll reimburse you for the time. Ten percent of your salary."

Again with the bonus. "Logan."

"I'm sorry, but I have to take this call," he said as his cell phone buzzed, dismissing her, and she started to head back to her desk. "And Ashtyn?"

She turned around.

"I once told Jordana 'Don't argue. You won't win.' Got it?"

Overwhelmed, she sighed, and gave a single nod, throat closing. An unexpected bonus just when she needed it the most? There were no words for her gratitude. "Thank you, Logan."

WHEN LOGAN TEXTED him to meet for drinks after work—a command, not a request—Neil knew exactly what it was about. He put it off as long as he could, then walked to Tied Up, a popular, upscale joint close to the financial district where businessmen drank and strategized.

Logan was there first, leaning an elbow on the bar, sans suit jacket, drink in hand. From what Neil could discern from the body language, his friend wasn't angry.

Good sign. The tension in Neil loosened.

He strolled toward him and moved the stool out of the way. Both preferred to stand when they went to bars. "I know what this is about, and I know what you're going to say."

Logan's mouth moved in wry consternation. "Do you?"

"Ashtyn told you about us." He paused, searching his friend's gaze. "I wanted to tell you immediately. I had no intention of hiding this." He gestured to the bartender and ordered a gin and tonic.

"I believe you, but how long have you been chasing my assistant?"

He flinched. "I haven't been chasing her. It just happened a few weeks ago."

"So all this started while I was on my honeymoon?"

"More or less. Trust me, I fought it as long as I could."

"I doubt it," Logan uttered in that tone that said a lecture would soon follow. "Neil. Why Ashtyn? I made it clear a long time ago she was off-limits. Not just because she's my employee, but also because she's like family to me. Of all the available tail in the Bay, why did you have to go for her?"

"She's not *available tail*," he said in a warning tone.

His friend blanched. "That's not what I meant."

"Look, there were many reasons why I kept my distance, and one of them was you. I knew you'd be pissed, but I'm not the wolf about to eat Red Riding Hood here. It's different with Ashtyn. I'm letting *her* decide how this plays out."

"Oh really?" Logan sipped his liquor.

He nodded, grabbing his drink and thanking the bartender. "That's right."

"And how long will you be able to keep that up?"

"We'll see. I rather like it. Giving the woman all the control."

Logan made a noise in the back of throat of total disbelief.

Neil ignored that. "If you're worried I'll hurt her and she'll show up to work in tears, then you don't know her as well as you think you do."

"I'm not worried whatsoever about how she handles her private business. I know she'll never be anything but amazing at her job. It's what it'll be like when things end between you two, because they will."

Neil swallowed his liquor, clenched his jaw, and set down his glass a little too hard. "What do you want from me, Savant?"

A pause. "I don't know. In a way, it feels as though you two have been inevitable. Every time you were in a room together, I could cut the sexual tension with a machete. Once her divorce was final, it was probably a matter of time. Here I always thought you annoyed her. Now I see it was probably the attraction to you that was annoying."

"I think it was a little of both." He smiled, moving his shoulders. "Plus I came to her rescue once or twice. That helped, I'm sure."

This wasn't as contentious as Neil thought it would be. Then again, he always expected the worst, even from his closest friend.

"You know what I find most interesting?" Logan asked. "That she made you promise not to tell me, and you kept it."

"What's so interesting about that?" he drawled.

"Unless it's your mother or sisters, you never do what a woman tells you to. And you tend not to keep promises when they ask you to."

"That's because other women want me to promise the moon. Ashtyn only made me promise to let her tell you first and I agreed. Simple as that."

Logan pursed his lips. "Huh."

"Savant. Listen." He rested his forearm on the bar. "I'm crazy about her. I'm not even seeing anybody else while she and I are together, and I don't plan to."

"Now that's new." Logan leaned back on both elbows. "Think it'll get serious?"

"What? Hell no. We're just enjoying each other's company."

"I think I echoed those *exact* words regarding Jordana not too long ago," he said sardonically.

"Oh no, you don't. Don't compare. The ink on Ashtyn's divorce papers just dried, and I wouldn't know what a relationship looked like if it slapped me in the face."

"Wouldn't be the first time you got slapped."

"Ah, the best days of my youth."

They both chuckled.

"Fine," Logan sighed in his drink. "As long as she knows what she's getting into."

"Hey. I'm not that bad. We've both been very clear about where we stand."

"I highly recommend you keep it that way. Don't ever assume." Logan straightened as an acquaintance walked up to shake his hand and say hello.

They exchanged pleasantries for a minute while Neil blew out a breath of relief.

Now that that was over with, he foresaw nothing but smooth sailing for him and Ashtyn. They could go together wherever whenever, and actually look at each other when he stopped by SFG.

Logan said good-bye to the man who'd interrupted, then turned to Neil, eyes narrowing. "Curious. Are you falling for her?"

The liquor traveled down Neil's throat, coating the brief catch in his throat. Now the man was talking crazy. "Falling? Pfft. It's only been a few weeks."

"Didn't take me long to fall for Jordana, if you'll recall."

"Oh, I think I knew that even before you did. I don't know where this thing between me and Ashtyn is going, but I don't see it going *that* far. That game isn't for this player. I've been there, done that."

A pregnant pause hung in the air. Neil already knew what—moreover, *who*, Logan was going to mention next.

Logan cleared his throat. "You and Juliet were a long time ago. I know she wouldn't want you damning relationships for the rest of your life because of her."

"It's not *because* of her."

"Then why haven't you given love a chance ever since?"

"Because I choose not to," Neil shot back. "I know what love feels like. Ashtyn and I care about each other, but it isn't love." *A whole lot of lust though.*

Logan frowned. "You put Juliet on a pedestal so high no other woman can compete. That's not fair. To you or any girlfriend."

Some part of him knew Logan was right, but talking about Juliet was off limits. It conjured pain. "Appreciate the psych eval, but I don't need it. Especially from you."

"Just giving you food for thought. You know, I never bring up Juliet. Neither does Miranda. But when I think it's interfering with your future, I can't help it."

"Savant. For the love of God, drop it."

"Now you know how it feels when your best friend tells you something you don't want to hear," he said, not-so-subtly hinted at those times Neil had an opinion about Logan and Jordana's relationship. "Anyway, Ashtyn told me about her mistaken arrest."

"Oh yeah?" he chuckled. "She must really be over it if she shared that with you."

"I thought it was pretty funny how it went down. Of course I don't hold it against her. She actually thought I would."

"Just a misunderstanding. Nosy neighbors. Small town law. It was nothing."

"Frankly, I was shocked she called *you*."

"So was I." Had she not, none of this would've happened, and for that he was grateful.

"Why do you think, out of all the people in her life, you were the one she asked to help her?" Logan asked.

"The fact that I'm a lawyer and she had my phone number memorized."

Logan's wheels were turning again. "You don't think what you've done for her proves you have real feelings for her?"

"I did those things as a friend before she and I hooked up. I don't know why you're taking this to extremes," Neil argued, irritated. "Ashtyn and I are sleeping together. It's great; it's temporary. I can't hurt her because she's not in a position to *be* hurt. She knows what I am and hasn't once asked me to change. We have chemistry and we're enjoying it until it fizzles out. Bottom line. End of story." He threw back the rest of his cocktail.

Were his feelings for her running deeper than he'd realized? He couldn't think about that right now, especially with Logan staring at him with watchful eyes. Time to change the subject. All he had to do was flip the script. "Guess who I ran into the other day?"

Logan kept his stare straight ahead. "Who?"

"Danyer Makdesi." A mutual friend of theirs from college.

The CEO shifted his eyes to Neil's and smiled. "No kidding. Been a long time since I heard from him. What's he been up to?"

"Working at his offices in Europe. Now he's making a permanent home in the Bay. You know his old man passed away a few years ago."

Logan swirled the ice in his glass, contemplative. "I remember. Big loss there for that family and the industry. He was a man to be reckoned with."

"So is Danyer from what I hear. A chip off the old block. Word is those two fought like alpha dog and younger alpha dog for years." He relaxed, now that the topic of conversation had changed. "Told him you were out here, too. Said he might swing by. The three of us should get together and catch up."

"You mean your firm could use another ace client," Logan said.

Neil raised his glass. "Old friends make the best clients."

22

AT THE CHARITY cocktail party, all Ashtyn wondered about was when Neil would arrive. Under pressure to close a deal for the firm, he'd sent her a message that he'd be there later in the evening.

Though they'd been out on quite a few dates, this would be their first event with their mutual friends and acquaintances in attendance, including a few who were personally associated with Cliff.

From her first step inside, little knots had made a home in her stomach.

Some people had come up with sympathetic gazes asking how she was holding up since the big D.

And just like that, she was back to putting on a regretful face with a regretful tone, telling them that it'd been hard, but that she was managing fine. Both were true. Why people thought they were entitled to her personal business just because she went through a publicly documented divorce, Ashtyn would never understand.

A server offered her a glass of sparkling wine and she took it with a polite smile.

Just then an arm slung around her shoulders. "Ashtyn Turner! I didn't know you'd be here!" Charlie Richmond came round to face her with his oily smile and bourbon-heavy breath, blatantly raking his gaze up and down her body. He snapped his fingers and pointed at her. "Or is it back to your maiden name now?"

"It's still Turner." For now. Easier to keep it than go through the rigors of changing it back.

"Shit, you look amazing. How long it has been?" he exclaimed.

Not long enough. She knew eventually she'd run into one of her husband's co-workers or friends, but why did it have to be one of her least favorite of them? Three words summed up Charlie: conceited, blunt, and uncouth. While he was successful, she often wondered why he seemed to gain access to parties when inviting him almost exclusively guaranteed some cringe-worthy moment. Cliff had liked him and thought Charlie's unfiltered behavior humorous. A lot of people did. Ashtyn could only conclude they viewed Charlie like an entertaining clown, and he loved the attention acting like one garnered him.

"It's been a few months at least, Charlie. How are you?" she asked, taking a discreet step back from his offensive breath.

"Me? Life is great. Just bought a speedboat."

She smiled. "Good for you."

"You should see it, it's fucking fantastic. Here." He proceeded to take out his cell phone.

Holding the screen mere inches from her face, he pointed out the bold yellow and blue boat, scrolling through thirty pictures before Ashtyn's eyes started to cross. To cease the unending slideshow, she took a sip of her sparkling wine then asked, "Have you taken it out yet?"

His eyes brightened. Oops. Wrong question to ask because now he thought she was interested in a ride.

"Of course I have! I'll take you *anytime*."

Hmm. How to decline that offer ad infinitum? "That's so kind of you, but no thanks. I'm—terrified of boats." A necessary white lie.

"What the hell is there to be scared of? I promise not to go that fast. I know chicks don't dig speed, but trust me, once the wind starts blowing through your hair—" He tugged on a lock of hers. "You'll be *begging* me to go faster."

She didn't know whether to shudder or laugh at his innuendo. In a way, this guy was an obnoxious version of Neil, but instead of charming, he was revolting. How did she ever think Neil was this bad?

"I'm sorry, but I just don't want to," she said, hoping he'd let it go at that.

He appeared offended. "Why not? Look if you're worried about Cliff, screw him. He'll get over it."

"We've been divorced three months," she said, groping for another excuse he might buy. "I'm just putting the pieces back together. I don't really have time to be—dating." She cringed inwardly. Now that was a lie. So much of her time had been with one man alone lately.

"All right so you show up looking like *this*, and you're not out on the prowl? Yeah right. Are you even wearing a bra?"

His maniacal laughter caught the attention of a few people around them, and Ashtyn briefly closed her eyes, embarrassed, inhaling for patience. *And I'm done.* "Well, good to see you, Charlie. I see someone I need to speak to."

She headed for the first familiar face she saw: Jaclyn Reilly, who stood with her best friend, Kiki Winters, and as Ashtyn approached, they pasted on their bright smiles. At least they wouldn't make sleazy comments about her breasts. Jaclyn was a widow and attended every social soiree on the calendar in search of a new husband, and Kiki, divorced twice over, prided herself on knowing everything about everybody. Despite their cattiness, they were overall friendly. If they decided someone bored them, however, they were equally cutting.

Kiki reached out and squeezed Ashtyn's forearm. "Hello dear. You look absolutely fabulous. Where did you get this dress?"

Ashtyn glanced down at her simple, blue knee-length wiggle dress. It had three-quarter sleeves and an open back. "A boutique store in Santa Clara, I think."

"Which one?"

"I'm not sure. I've had it a while."

"Well, it's adorable," Kiki gushed. "Isn't it, Jaclyn?" She gave a look to her closest friend as though to say "Jump in the conversation anytime."

Jaclyn cocked her head, earrings sparkling. "I was just thinking about you last week. Be honest. How are you holding up with the divorce final?"

She withheld a sigh. "I'm doing well. Thank you for asking."

"I saw Cliff the other day."

Ashtyn moved her gaze from one to the other. She could almost see them holding their breaths at this offering of information. Were they expecting her to go on a rant about her ex-husband? Damn his existence? Is that what ex-wives were expected to do?

Kiki spoke to fill the silence. "Don't worry yourself one bit. We wouldn't give him the time of day."

"Of course not," Jaclyn emphasized. "He always talked over people like he was the smartest man in the room. The man tried too hard."

She held no lasting malice for her ex, and certainly wasn't going to talk about his faults in public. Even though he could've been the one who stole the pearls. "Parties just weren't his forte."

Kiki added, "I heard how he ripped the house right from under you—"

"Actually—" Ashtyn started.

"You should've hired Ike Garrett. He was a pitbull for my friend Margo's case! Got her everything and more. The house. The cars. Even the cottage in Maine, and that was in his family's name for generations."

"Yes," Jaclyn drawled, "It only took two and a half years, too."

"Margo would say it was worth it."

Jaclyn shooed her friend. "Whatever. Anyway Ashtyn, have your eye on anyone yet?"

"As if she wants to dive right in so soon after her divorce!" Kiki exclaimed. "It took me three years to get over my last marriage."

"Well, the girl's not getting any younger," her friend asserted.

Ashtyn gulped more sparkling wine. Did she need to be here for this conversation? Because it seemed the good friends were doing swell without her.

As though she hadn't already perused the room a dozen times, Jaclyn looked around them. "Too bad Savant is taken, right?"

"Oh I would never look at Logan like that—"

"Easy to say that now that he's not available." Jaclyn winked.

"Regardless, it's never crossed my mind." No matter how she said it, they wouldn't believe her.

"Oh please. You know if Logan had made a move, you would've been all over that. Any sane woman would," Kiki said. "Worth millions. Restaurants here and in New York. A mother in show business. If only I were twenty years younger, Jordana wouldn't have stood a chance." She laughed and flipped a hand down, her flower ring as big as a plum. "I'm just kidding."

No she wasn't.

Someone save me.

While Kiki and Jaclyn debated over who the latest bachelor was now that Logan was officially off the market, Ashtyn realized she'd have to save herself. Was there no one here she actually wanted to talk to? Excusing herself, she wandered around, then ventured outside for some air.

She sighed. The cool air soothed her neck.

A fingertip grazed the base of her spine, then there was heat, an electric current, making the little hairs at her nape stand up. "I'm surprised no one has taken you hostage, the way you look in that dress," said a deep, sexy voice behind her.

Joy swept through her. Pressing her lips together to suppress a girlish grin, she faced Neil. Polished and virile in his dark blue designer suit, hair run-through instead of combed, he took her breath away. Her heart fluttered. She wanted to wrap her arms around him and kiss him, but that would be the equivalent of throwing a baseball through the glass window to attract attention. "I love the way you give compliments."

He smiled, moving in to kiss her cheek. "Sorry I'm late."

Even her cheek tingled after his lips brushed it. "It's okay. Everyone has been asking me if I'm all right since the divorce, so in your absence I've had a tremendous supportive group of people around me."

"Sarcasm is sexy on you."

Her mouth twitched with a smile, the nervous lumps dissolved, replaced by a host of butterflies at his nearness. "I'm glad you're here."

A smile stretched his mouth. "Best thing I've heard all day."

"Did everything go okay with the corporate deal?" she asked as they ventured back inside.

"Of course. I'm the best."

She rolled her eyes. "Your modesty is endless."

"Sweet Ashtyn, when you're good at something, humility has no place except last place."

She chuckled.

Upon entering two men rushed toward Neil with grins and handshakes.

"Caenon! Was hoping you'd show," said one of the men.

He grinned. "You know me. All I do is give, give, give."

Observing his exchanges with people fascinated her. There was nothing like it. Men and women alike lit up in his presence and he accomplished such a thing without crass jokes or boasting about himself. Although, she thought staring at him while he told a story about his early days at the firm, he was a little too "on." For years she only saw *this* side of Neil and assumed that was all there was to him as a person. But he had several sides most wouldn't even know about.

A helpful, compassionate side.

With a private smile, she brought the glass to her lips.

Neil turned to her and spoke low in her ear. "I want you to count to one hundred, and when you're done, exclaim you forgot to feed your cat, and we'll leave."

"I don't have a cat," she whispered.

Out of the corner of his mouth, he replied, "Meow." They both laughed then, and he wrapped his arm around her waist, moving her in a circle to the music and making more ridiculous imitations of a feline.

And he has a silly side.

"Now I get it!" a male voice boomed behind them.

Ashtyn stiffened at the exclamation, and Neil turned his head.

Drunker than he had been a mere half hour ago, Charlie slashed them with a hard gaze, jacket askew.

"Pardon?" Neil asked, giving the man a quick assessment.

"Hey, how you doing? Charlie Richmond."

Warily, Neil shook his hand. "Neil Caenon."

"Ha! No. You're kidding."

"I never kid about my name."

Ashtyn's nerves were on high alert.

Charlie snickered. "Her husband mentioned you were trying to get in her pants. I can see that's allllready happened."

"*Ex*-husband," Ashtyn gritted through her teeth. "And who I spend my time with is none of his or *your* business."

"Oh so you—" Charlie made finger air quotes, "—don't have time for dating, huh?" He leaned in. "Lying slut."

She froze.

Fire shot out of Neil's eyes. He flattened his hand on Charlie's chest and smoothly pushed him back. "Apologize for that."

"What? No. Who do you think you are putting your hand on me?"

Fearing a scene, Ashtyn wrapped an arm around Neil's bicep. "Let's just go."

He was hard as iron, but he spoke lightly. "Not until he apologizes. He's way out of line."

"I don't want an apology."

She forced Neil to meet her gaze, and as he looked at her, his gaze finally cooled. "Okay. Let's go. The trash stinks around here."

"What? Fuck you!" called Charlie.

Neil turned and Charlie swung. Neil's head snapped to the side at the sloppy punch.

"Neil!" Ashtyn gasped, stunned, barely had time to react before Charlie aimed to punch him again, but Neil blocked it with his forearm, then kicked the man's knee with the heel of his shoe, and she heard a crunching sound. Charlie dropped in pain while a small crowd gathered around to see the commotion.

Satisfied the man was immobilized, he went to Ashtyn, grasping her hands. "You okay?"

"Yes," she replied shakily. "You're hurt." A small cut on the top of his cheek started to bleed.

He wiped it with the back of his hand. "It's not that bad."

While Charlie cursed on and on, security guards came over to drag him out, then pulled Neil aside to get the full story.

The guard mumbled something to his cohorts before facing Neil. "Mr. Caenon, although it's evident you didn't make the first move, we're going to have to ask you to leave."

One of the charity's coordinators rushed over and, after being apprised of what happened by one of the guests, he gaped at the guards. "They're kicking Caenon out? Absolutely not. Neil, of course you can stay. If you're not in too much pain that is." The man hissed, gesturing to the cut, and appeared more concerned of what would happen if he banished Neil than the scene caused by Charlie.

Neil tugged on the ends of his jacket sleeves, ever calm, cool, and collected as ever. "It's all right Maurice. I should go. You don't need a donator bleeding on your good cause unless its cash coming out of their pockets."

The coordinator bowed his head and stepped back, assuring the other guests the drama was over. Everyone stared at them, including Jaclyn and Kiki, murmuring to each other. Ashtyn's cheeks turned hot. She didn't even care. In fact, she was a little turned on Neil had defended her, but wished he hadn't gotten punched for it.

"Are you sure you don't want to press charges?" the guard asked Neil.

"He's not worth it."

"Okay. Well, all we can do at this point is escort him out."

Neil nodded, cupping the side of Ashtyn's face. "You sure you're all right?"

A little shaken by the abrupt violence, but knowing that would pass, she nodded. "We should get you to an ER."

"No, no. I'm okay. Really." He gave an assuring smile, fingers brushing under her chin. "I'm sure you want to get home—"

"With you. That is, if you feel like having company." She desperately wanted to be with him tonight.

He started to smile. "Are you good to drive?"

She hugged him, careful to avoid the wounded side of his face. "Yes. I'll meet you at the marina?"

He encircled his arms around her tightly before saying, "In case you beat me there, the extra key is under the mat on the upper deck. And the gate code is 01946. Got that? No climbing in my window like a common criminal."

She laughed, then repeated it to confirm. "I'll see you soon."

On the way to the marina, she drove to a pharmacy and purchased first aid items in case Neil didn't have any on hand at home. Then she stopped by a liquor store and picked up a bottle of his favorite whiskey. She beat him there, got in with the spare key, then set up a little nurses station at the dining table. When he walked in, the area around the cut was puffy, but it didn't seem to lessen his spirit at all.

Especially when he saw the whiskey. "Trying to get me drunk?"

"More or less," she shrugged, white towel in hand, "to help you with the pain. The wound needs tending to." She tapped the chair and, after he removed his jacket, he sat down as ordered, a little amused smile moving his mouth as he looked up at her.

With the Q-tip, she carefully wiped around the cut to get off the dried blood. She used soap, water, and the towel to clean the rest. "I can't believe this happened," she murmured.

Neil hissed when she accidentally brushed the cut, then sipped on his drink, nuzzling his nose on her breast. "Been a long time since anyone threw a punch at me. At least three days."

She chuckled, dabbing some ointment on it. "Nice move you had there debilitating him. He was limping out of the hotel."

"The way I see it, you can break your hand on someone's face, so better to try a good swift kick to the knee. Causes a ton of pain if you do it right. Any moron, big or small, will go down."

"Where did you learn that?"

"Some Patrick Swayze movie."

She laughed, shaking her head, affixing two butterfly bandages over his wound. "Are you sure you don't want a doctor looking at this?"

"Unless I'm hemorrhaging or suffering a gunshot wound, I don't go to hospitals. This is just a scratch. It'll heal."

"There. Done." She bent down and kissed his forehead. "Might leave a scar."

"That's okay. It'll give me more street cred."

She laughed as he pulled her down in his lap. Straddling him in the chair, she was instantly aroused in his arms, and when he kissed her, the whole room faded into watercolor around her. He tasted like hot whiskey and lust.

"Thanks, Nurse Ashtyn," he said, voice hoarse. "I'm afraid my health insurance won't cover you, so I'll have to pay you out-of-pocket. And I don't have cash." He began prying her dress off her shoulders, pressing kisses on her shoulder, and up her neck. "My body will be your compensation."

Flush against his hardness, she dropped her head back, threading her fingers in his thick hair. "Are you sure? Maybe you should lie down and rest."

"Fine idea. I'll lie down while you ride me slow," he said before licking up her throat, rubbing the pad of his thumb on her nipple. "Be gentle now."

Breath stolen, she quivered, wet, and wanting him. "Oh," she whispered, moaning as he dipped his mouth on her breast. "I'll do my best."

23

"YOU'RE WAY too happy so soon after a divorce," Emmy said as she and Ashtyn walked to the elevator bank.

Ashtyn chuckled, gripping her mocha. "Thanks a lot, Emmy. Would you rather I be depressed and mopey every day?"

"No, of course not! In fact, I'm impressed. You inspire me. My sister wouldn't leave the house for at least six months after her divorce and you've been going out every other night."

"It helps to stay busy."

"It helps to get laid," Emmy added brightly.

Ashtyn's cheeks bloomed red and she looked around. "Emmy."

"What? As if it isn't glaringly obvious you have a new man? Some rebound from nowhere? I keep waiting for you to tell me about him."

Emmy was just guessing. That was her sharp-pointed skill as a true gossip. She'd toss out some observation like it was fact and watch for the person's reaction. Ashtyn wasn't falling for it. No, she and Neil weren't a secret, but she didn't need to make a public announcement about it either. Even though she'd *love* to tell Emmy the reason for her mood had a lot to do with the handsome attorney. But any divulgence would lead to more questions and more unwelcome observations on Emmy's part.

"I just got a massage the other day," she deflected. "That must be it."

"Oh." Emmy stared at her. "When I get massages, they rarely make me glow like that. Maybe I should go to your masseuse instead."

Ashtyn pressed her lips together to keep from giggling. *You can't. He's booked.*

Back in the executive wing, Ashtyn sat down at her desk, unable to suppress her smile, thinking about Neil. About last night, and the night before. The man was insatiable. She'd stayed so late, she had to spend the night, and rode with him in his car to work. Since they planned to spend their Friday night together anyway and she'd already brought a weekend bag, it made sense to make the commute together.

They didn't talk during the drive, just listened to the radio, with him brushing her knee with his finger along the way and exciting her much too early in the day.

A ripple of awareness ran over her. Was he thinking about her too? They were a five-minute walk from each other every single day. Too easy for her to come up with an excuse to stop by his office. And even though he tried on several occasions to persuade her into a quickie during her lunch hour, she managed not to give in.

She just couldn't have sex with him then go back to work with Neil's musk all over her. They never were anything but polite and professional when he came by the office. He'd sit on the corner of her desk like he always did and they'd chitchat about their day. But she'd see the flamed promise in his eyes, the playful sexuality in his half-grin, even while he referred to something as banal as the weather.

One thing she could never stop herself from doing was laugh, because he did his hardest to see that she did. All those years she cut him off before he could even try, all those times she glared instead of smiled, and for what? Because she only knew the surface. A corporate lawyer who made rich people richer, who went in and out of women's beds on a weekly basis, who made light of everything. She'd had no idea that underneath infectious charm was a man with a vested interest in pro bono cases and was the kind of loyal friend anyone would be lucky to have.

The past few weeks had flown by between spending her days at work and her nights with Neil. With their varying schedules, sometimes she didn't get to see him until almost eleven o'clock at night, and told him she had to be in bed by midnight to get enough sleep to make it through her day. They jokingly referred to the sixty minutes between 11:00 pm and midnight as "rush hour", talking, then eating, then making love as quick and thoroughly as they could before her bedtime.

Catching a break in between her usual workday madness, she pulled out paperwork she needed scanned when the receptionist called. "There's someone here to see Mr. Savant. He doesn't have an appointment, but he says to tell him it's Danyer Makdesi."

This Danyer thinks pretty highly of himself. "Will do. I'll call you back in a moment." She switched to Logan's office, who surprisingly told her to let this gentleman through, even though he had a packed schedule. After relaying the message to the receptionist, she waited for the unscheduled guest.

He strolled through a minute later in a gray suit and yellow tie. Confident, but without a commanding air. More like someone who carried himself well than someone who demanded respect on sight. He was tall with a medium frame, and she guessed around the same age as Logan.

She smiled politely as she rose. "Good afternoon. Mr. Savant said to give him ten minutes and he'd be right with you. In the meantime, would you care for tea, coffee, or water?"

"No, thank you." He held out his hand. "Danyer Makdesi."

Hm. Most of Logan's guests didn't bother to shake an assistant's hand, preferring to mutter their names and order very specific beverages like tea with one squirt of lemon and three drops of cream or something equally particular. "I'm Ashtyn."

She shook his hand, which was large and warm. Lifting her gaze to his eyes, she realized how good-looking he was, not in a striking way, but with an exotic attractiveness. Brown hair and eyes, surrounded by full dark lashes. Although, his touch didn't shoot tingles down her spine like a sexy man with a nice smile usually did. Or maybe that was because she already had one of those in her life. "Please take a seat and make yourself comfortable."

Mr. Makdesi sat down on the chair, and she resumed finishing her email. She felt his eyes on her while she worked. Flicking him a glance, she asked, "Are you sure I can't get you anything?"

"I'm certain." He glanced at his watch.

Feeling as though he expected some conversation, she decided to put the pause on her paperwork. "Mr. Savant rarely allows unscheduled visits in the middle of the day. You must be special."

"And you're wondering what makes me so special."

She arched a brow. "Just a little."

"I used to let him stand on my shoulders so he could talk to a girl at her window back in the day."

A smile moved her mouth. "Ah, I see."

"I just moved back to San Francisco so I'm making the rounds to see old friends."

"In that case, welcome back. Where were you before this?"

"Dubai. Have you ever been?"

"No, but I would love to." She folded her hands and leaned forward. "I heard it's amazing."

"It is. Unfortunately I spent most of my days and nights working, but when I did go out to explore, I found it...a little too much. Excessive partying didn't interest me. Then again, I was mostly alone when I went out. Maybe my own company bores me."

She laughed softly, and noticed no wedding ring on his left hand, just a Rolex and a tan. A single millionaire, maybe even a billionaire, in the Bay?

She estimated he'd be taken in about two weeks. "Perhaps you work too much."

"Where have I heard that before?" he said drolly.

"No one lays in their deathbed wishing they'd worked more, Mr. Makdesi."

"Danyer, please. And I'll be too distracted working from my deathbed to worry about it."

Another short laugh escaped her. No wonder he and Logan were friends. They were a lot alike. Just when she was about to ask if he knew Neil as well, he pointed to the bowl on her desk.

"Are those sweet stripes candies?" he asked.

"They are. Would you like one?" At his grin, she swiveled in her chair, stood, and brought the bowl to him. He plucked one wrapped candy, and she held the bowl even closer to him, saying, "Nobody eats candy anymore. I insist you take another one for your pocket for later."

He chuckled, and took a second. "These are the best. A couple of chews and they melt in your mouth. Not like those caramel types that make you look like a camel while you're chewing. Or as hard to eat as one of those hard toffee candies. A long time ago, I was offered one before meeting a girl's parents, and like an idiot, I took it. There I was moving it from one cheek to another, making those annoying candy-on-teeth noises, saliva practically shooting from my lips. I was too mortified to spit it out. Needless to say, I didn't win them over right away."

She chuckled at the story.

Logan's door swung open. "Makdesi. Great of you to stop by," Logan said. They heartily shook hands and slapped one another's backs. "Come on in. Ashtyn, push my one-thirty to two-thirty?"

"Of course." She picked up the phone to alert the client of the change.

Danyer followed Logan in, glancing at her with a smile before closing the door.

The rest of her day consisted of several seemingly minor tasks that took up major chunks of time. The IT team sent out updates, which took a while to load, so she had to restart her computer and deal with the wireless printer issues after the update. Then the manager in their Dallas office had an emergency, and refused to speak to anyone but Logan, even though one of the managing directors could handle it.

Logan had asked her to find a luncheon place to accommodate a vegan, a loud talker, and a man with a drinking problem. Mainly, he needed an upscale establishment with lots of chatter, vegan options on the menu, and no bar. Not as easy as she thought it would be.

Thank God it was Friday.

A text from Neil popped up on her phone: *Drinks at Le Couer. 6pm.*

She smiled. *Perfect. You read my mind.*

If you read mine right now…

She bit her bottom lip. *Then I'd want to skip the drinks and go straight to your place?*

He wrote back: *Ha. That's my girl.*

Her heart skipped a beat. His girl. She liked that. Guess she was his for now. Eventually, either he or she would break it off when it stopped being fun. Stopped being hot. Stopped being simple. Then she'd have to get used to seeing him out flirting and seducing someone else.

Her stomach dropped suddenly.

What had she really gotten herself into?

A few hours later, she sat across from Mr. Right Now at the popular restaurant lounge Logan's mother half-owned. It was within walking distance from the parking garage and was one of the best spots for an after-work martini. The purple, black, fuchsia, and white décor with low lighting and sexy international music set the tone for salacious flirtation.

Neil kept her laughing with his witty rapport and interesting conversation, and she kept him squirming in his seat every time she brushed her foot up his pant leg. She'd ditched her heels a long time ago in favor of a little footsie.

He grinned, reaching under the table and brushing a hand over her knee. "What's gotten into you? Besides your second martini?"

She rested her hand in her chin and leaned in. "Too much for you to handle, Caenon?"

"Not even close. It's just you usually wait until we're at home to play."

"Oh?" Reaching back, she pulled the few Charlie pins from her hair, letting her hair loose. Every time she did that, Neil's eyes would heat and flame. "Are we going to order dinner?"

Neil clenched his jaw, fist closing and opening. "Do we have to?"

"I shouldn't keep drinking on an empty stomach," she informed him. She loved the fact he didn't admonish more than one drink in public. Cliff's influence on her actions was detaching more every day. "Good thing you're driving. I'd have to take a cab otherwise."

"You're coming home with me," he stated huskily. "Don't you forget it."

The server came by asking if they wanted another round.

"Actually," Neil said, "Can we get the ch—?"

"An order of the hummus, please," she cut in. She should really eat something for energy. By the feral look in Neil's gaze, she'd need it.

"Hummus isn't exactly a meal," he pointed out.

"Just a little bite. It's still early. You're used to eating late."

He studied her heatedly over the dim candlelight. "You know you're asking for it."

She feigned innocence. "Asking for what?"

Leaning in, he dropped a deep voice. "Asking for me to lose my patience in public, and do something to you that you know will make your prim side scream at the audacity." He ran his hand along her thigh. "Right now, I'd like to come around behind you, slip my hand in your blouse and caress your nipples. Because you like that. Then I'd draw your mouth into mine and kiss you so deep, we'd probably be asked to leave."

She gasped. "You wouldn't do those things here. In Ms. Savant's restaurant. She'd have you whipped."

"Are you daring me?"

"No!"

"And do you think I'd care?"

By the look on his face, no, he didn't.

The server brought the hummus and she belatedly wished she hadn't ordered it, but she also hated wasting food. "May I eat unmolested, please?" she asked Neil was still caressing her knee.

He smirked and sat back, raising his water glass to his mouth.

She took her time, dipping the carrot stick in the hummus, licking some, then biting it off. Quite aware she was torturing him, she lifted her lashes and slid her tongue along the piece before popping the whole thing in her mouth.

Neil snapped his fingers and waved the server over, placing his credit card in her hand before she could ask what he needed.

Ashtyn dropped her head back and softly laughed. His inability to wait thrilled her.

She'd barely sipped the rest of her martini before Neil came around and grasped her hand, pulling her out of her chair and out of the restaurant.

A drizzle of rain fell from the sky, misting her face. Neil pulled her with such urgency she scrambled to keep up, but grinned with every step. "Neil! I'm in heels."

He abruptly stopped and pressed her against the brick wall, blocking her in with his arms. When his firm lips met hers, she tasted rain, passion, and a flavor all his.

"You're getting wet," he pulled back, brushing her lips with his.

She gripped his jacket. "You have no idea."

Chuckling, he wrapped his arms around her waist and drew her in his secure warmth. "Now who's the one dropping the clever innuendo?" He dipped his head and began to kiss her.

An older gentleman hurried by, muttering for them to get a room. Even as Neil deepened the kiss, the stranger's remark reminded her public displays of affection—especially making out in the street—wasn't something she did. With Neil, she seemed to do a lot of things she didn't think she'd do. What about him made her behave with such wanton abandon? Smiling against his mouth, she broke away. "We should go. Though, I might make you pull over before we get to the marina."

He chuckled. "I like the way you think. Wait where it's dry. I'll get the car."

She watched him stride down the sidewalk with his usual bit of swagger, one hand in his pocket.

Suddenly freezing without him, she ducked under Le Coeur's awning, clutching her jacket tighter. A red Dodge Challenger zoomed by then slammed on its brakes in front of the restaurant.

She froze. She knew that car, even without seeing the vanity plate.

Le Coeur's valet came jogging toward them, opening the passenger side door first. Cliff got out and handed the young man the keys, and the woman climbed out, laughing.

Cliff was out on a date, and in about three seconds they would cross paths.

Smoothly, Ashtyn turned to her left, tucked her hair behind her ear, and went to stand beside a tall, neatly trimmed bush. Out of direct sight, she peeked through the branches.

Cliff came round the car, and his date hooked her arm in his. He smiled down at her, spoke something close to her ear, and she laughed.

Ashtyn cocked her head. Before they realized how incompatible they were, she and Cliff were a content couple, but they didn't laugh like that. Not enough at least. He looked happy…and strangely, she was happy *for* him. Not jealous at all. Maybe because she was never truly in love with Cliff and vice versa. They looked good next to each other, made sense on paper, but nowhere else. Whoever this woman was who walked into the restaurant with him made him smile in a way Ashtyn hadn't seen in years.

Well, good to luck to her. Perhaps *she* could be the woman Cliff tried so hard to mold Ashtyn to be.

And thank goodness she and Neil left or they might've run into them. Could've been awkward for all. Didn't matter. Clearly Cliff had moved on and so had she.

Moments later, Neil pulled up and opened the door for her, oblivious to why she'd chosen to stand by the bush and not under the protection of the awning.

"I was thinking," he said as he opened the passenger door, "of watching an eighties movie, ordering takeout so I can finally eat some place where I can molest you, snacking on kettle corn popcorn, and sharing a grape soda with two straws."

Her heart skipped a beat as she stepped off the curb and met his smiling gaze.

Of course he was utterly unaware of how his suggestion to include things she took pleasure in—just when her ex-husband reminded her of all the things he'd made her exclude—had just made everything very, very complicated.

24

ASHTYN OPENED her eyes the next morning, and it hit her. And hit her good.

She'd fallen in love with Neil.

Remnants of their night before were scattered around his bedroom: takeout boxes, kernels of popcorn, an empty can of grape soda, and the comforter that had slipped to the floor after they'd made love once the credits to *Risky Business* had rolled.

It was the perfect night. But now that she knew she was in love with him, it was the first day of the end of days with Neil Caenon.

With his warm chest beneath her cheek, one arm holding her tight against him, she suddenly couldn't breathe, stomach flittering with the knowledge that somewhere in between calling him that night from jail and yesterday she'd fallen in love. She turned to her other side, away from him, but Neil followed her with a short moan, sliding an arm around her waist, his face in her hair.

Ashtyn covered her mouth. *How could you?* a voice in her mind cried. *How could you fall for him?*

Shockingly, it wasn't that hard. With all he'd done for her, his tenderness and consideration, the mind-blowing sex, playfulness, and his unending charm, it was nearly impossible not to. So opposite to what she thought a man ought to be: serious, restrained, and cautious. Neil was proof a man could be sophisticated without being uptight, funny without being obnoxious.

But were her deep feelings real? Or had she simply fallen for the first man to give her attention since the dark days of her marriage?

Her heart sunk.

Yes.

That had to explain how quickly she'd fallen in such a short time.

He just happened to be in the right place at the right time, fulfilling that sexual yearning, touching her in places that hadn't been touched in years, and doing so with an expert lover's stroke. And as a startling result, her heart opened again.

She shakily smiled.

That wasn't necessarily a bad thing. Now she knew she wasn't a bitter divorcee who'd resent men forever. Right? If her feelings for Neil were true, then the palm reader was right, she did fall in love again. Maybe Neil was the man who would lead her to her future husband. A catalyst to healing her heart, so she would be ready for whomever she was meant to be with?

She closed her eyes. She didn't want another.

Neil stirred behind her, and a particularly hard part of him brushed her butt cheek.

"I know you're awake," he murmured, breathing in and grazing his nose along her shoulder, scooting closer. His hand glided over her stomach, hip, and up to cup her breast, gently pinching the nipple.

She moaned and arched.

Or maybe I just love the sex.

Best not to turn around and face him, she thought, afraid her emotions would reveal themselves with or without her consent. He'd told her the eyes gave themselves away and if anyone would notice when a woman had fallen for him, it would be the uncannily perceptive man in bed with her.

When his fingers sought her wet center, she let out a little cry of helplessness, molding her back to his front, parting her legs. She reached for his cock, but he gave a negative sound, took her wrist and pulled her over to face him.

Well, so much for hiding.

As soon as his mouth sought hers, she determined to keep her heart out of the lovemaking, and sell the sex kitten side of her as best she could.

It wouldn't be that difficult.

She climbed on top, wrapped her arms around his neck, and closed her eyes when he sat up and locked her to him.

Flush against his body, groaning while he awakened her to a fevered height of arousal with his lips, she sensually smiled. They caressed and kissed for a little while, taking their time. Once she came down on his hard shaft, all thoughts faded to black.

With his head of disheveled hair, heavy-lidded eyes, hungry kisses, and wonderful hands, he rocked her with quiet, intense thrusts, oblivious to her heart calling for his at the same time her voice called his name.

Afterward, they showered, and Neil made several suggestions of what to do with their Saturday. For all Ashtyn cared, they could sit on a bench and watch paint dry. Anything a man suggested for a good time sounded like the perfect day when the woman was in love.

"I have a few things to do for work," he said throwing on a plain white shirt that highlighted his tan skin and green eyes, "but after that, I'm all yours."

"Take your time." She grabbed her pale blue blouse and slipped her arms through, then donned a pair of white shorts. "I should check my email too. With Logan in Hong Kong, I usually have double the amount to respond to."

On her last button of her top, she froze when she heard a door open with feminine voices echoing through his first floor.

"Neil! We're here!" said one.

"Where are ya, big brother?" called the other.

She turned to him in question and Neil's head dropped back. "My sisters. I forgot they were going to be in town this weekend." He shook his head with a look of disbelief. "Completely forgot."

His sisters? Mentally unprepared for this surprise, she whispered, "What should we do?"

Neil shrugged with the nonchalance of a man who took unexpected moments in stride. "Go say hi." He raised his voice for his sisters to hear. "I'm here. Coming!" Then jogged down the steps.

Uh, okay. What was she supposed to do? Follow him? Stay up here and wait? She wasn't prepared to meet any family. Oh how she wished she could sneak out and get home, but that wasn't possible in his floating house. Even though his bedroom had an exit to the patio with a set of stairs that led off to the dock, there was a great chance she'd be seen through the windows.

Getting caught scurrying away would be worse than going to the first floor like a mature adult.

Animated voices mixed with rustles of bags and women's laughter.

The longer she stayed up here, the more agonizing the introductions would be.

Might as well get it over with. After rushing a brush through her hair, she gathered her things in her bag, and tried to affect a casual air, even though her heart wouldn't steady.

What would his sisters think of a woman emerging from their brother's bedroom? They probably would assume she was just another skirt he picked up.

As she descended, she listened to the amusing conversation between the three siblings.

"You forgot, didn't you?" asked one of the sisters with the husky voice.

Neil groaned. "I didn't forget, Teresa. I mixed up the dates."

"I reminded you at least six times," she exclaimed.

"Where's the plant I bought you?" asked the other sister.

He sighed. "It died, Loni."

"You only had to water it once a week. You *live* on water!"

"Don't worry, I gave it a proper funeral."

The questions continued, much to Ashtyn's amusement.

"What happened to your face?" Teresa strode toward him for a closer inspection.

He'd stopped using the bandages a couple weeks ago, and it was almost completely healed, but it still left a noticeable mark.

"It's just a cut," he explained nonchalantly.

"You were in a fight?" Loni asked with more incredulousness than concern.

"Yes, and I won."

Ashtyn stifled laughter, landing on the bottom step, and her movement caught all three pairs of eyes. A flush swept over her and she cleared her throat. "Good morning."

Neil, hands on hips, gave her a soft, apologetic but welcome-to-the-mayhem smile.

The sisters looked at each other, then at her.

To move past the awkward moment, she reached to shake one of the sister's hands. "Hi. I'm Ashtyn."

The brunette smiled and squeezed her hand. "Teresa."

Good looks ran in the family. This one had green eyes like Neil's, long dark hair set in a fishtail braid, and wore a maxi dress hugging her slim figure. No doubt she turned heads on the street.

The other sister gave her a quick once over before she shook Ashtyn's hand. "Loni." Though not as tall as Teresa, she had pretty, light brown, observant eyes, short hair, and plump, rosy cheeks. "Sorry. We didn't know

Neil had company." She not so discreetly sent her brother a wide-eyed look with pinched lips.

"Like I said, I forgot," he defended.

"Whatever. Anyway, good to meet you," Loni added with a friendly smile.

"Ashtyn," chimed in Teresa. "How do you know my brother?"

"Through a mutual friend. We've know each other for…four years now?"

"What?" Teresa laughed. "You didn't just meet last night?"

"Teresa!" her brother admonished.

Ashtyn laughed. She'd been right about their assumption. To clarify, she said, "I work for Neil's friend Logan Savant. That's how he and I got acquainted."

A twinkle lit Neil's eyes. *Acquainted, indeed,* his gaze said.

"You work for Logan? Omigod, I can't believe that dude actually got married," Teresa gushed.

"He got wise. His wife was so nice to us at the wedding," Loni said.

Teresa snapped her fingers. "That's where I've seen you! Gosh, there were so many people at that wedding, but I knew I recognized your face. You danced with Neil."

How did she not meet his sisters? Too busy playing wedding assistant, she supposed.

Teresa and Loni exchanged furtive glances.

How uncomfortable was it when people did that in front of you? What was exactly being unspoken between the sisters?

"I danced with everybody," he pointed out to save her the embarrassment of responding.

Ashtyn slid the bag's handle higher on her shoulder and edged toward the door. "Well, I should get going so you three can catch up. Very nice to meet you both."

Neil followed her. "I'll walk you out."

As he opened the door, Loni and Teresa huddled together, and Ashtyn pretended she didn't know they were obviously discussing her.

"Sorry for my poor memory skills," he told her in a quiet voice, tracing his knuckles down her arm. "You don't have to rush off. Stay for coffee."

Goosebumps followed the trailed he left. How could she say no to that voice and those eyes? Then again, enduring loaded looks from his sisters and opening the possibility of uncomfortable inquiries about her relationship with their brother kind of overrode his persuasive ways. "They came here to see you."

The sister's voices suddenly rang in unison. "You should stay!"

She and Neil turned their heads at the double exclamations.

Teresa pranced over, grabbed Ashtyn's hand, and pulled her back in. "Don't go on our account. Our visit isn't so special that we have a claim to him. We try to do this every couple months. Once Neil became a lawyer, he only comes home on holidays, so we demanded at least one day to harass him at our leisure. Here. Sit." She pressed down on Ashtyn's shoulders until she plopped down on a stool.

Neil grinned. Not only okay with this, but seemingly pleased. "Who wants coffee?"

Were Loni and Teresa insisting she stay so they could assess her good-enough scale? Because, really, they had no reason to if they knew their brother. By the time they approved or disapproved, he'd be gently pushing her out the proverbial door, she was sure.

During coffee, the tension in her eased, a mere spectator in the fast-talking candor between Teresa, Loni, and Neil. The Caenon sisters didn't spray her with a thousand personal questions, too busy filling Neil in on hometown gossip and updates on their personal lives.

Teresa worked for a photography studio, and in her spare time posted videos online of cute and simple hairstyles to accomplish at home. She currently had a whopping three-hundred-thousand subscribers and counting to her channel. Twenty-four, gorgeous, sweet natured, and outgoing, she basically had the world in the palm of her hand, but didn't have a stuck-up bone in her body. Her dating status remained "complicated" according to her, of which Neil and Loni rolled their eyes.

Loni, the middle sibling at thirty-two, was married with two children. Smart as a whip, she worked at the local bank, had once been on The Price is Right and won a dinette set, and wore a navy and white striped shirt with bright yellow capris. She had a contagious laugh, a jolly succession of giggles that made her eyes sparkle until one couldn't help but join in.

Watching the dynamic made Ashtyn ache for that close-knit familial institution. With her brother away overseas, her mother and stepfather in Lake Tahoe, and father in Florida, the only family she'd had close by was Cliff's, and now those associations were severed. The Turners always treated her like one of their own even before she and Cliff got married, especially during the holidays. She wondered how she would fill those occasions now. A sense of loneliness bloomed.

However, the sudden laughter of the high-spirited people in the room had her snapping out of her woeful train of thought. She smiled when Loni finished her story about accidentally using flour instead of powdered sugar in a recipe for the bake-off last week.

"I was soooo smug that my go-to recipe would destroy the competition, I didn't even taste it," she exclaimed. "Lesson learned. Always eat your masterpiece first." She pulled out a Tupperware container. "Speaking of, I brought you a cake."

"Cake?" Neil exclaimed. "I won't eat it. I told you not to bring that stuff here. I don't eat whole cakes by myself."

Loni tossed Ashtyn a wink. "You're not by yourself. Ashtyn is here. Ashtyn! You're in charge of making sure my bro doesn't throw out my hard work."

Her? In charge of Neil? Ha. "I'll do my best."

"You know what?" Teresa said, hopping on the counter. "We have four people. We could actually play Beersbee today. When was the last time we played?"

Loni exclaimed, "Yes!"

Clueless, Ashtyn had to ask. "What's Beersbee?"

"What? You've never heard of it? It's an amped-up version of Frisbee," Teresa explained, then kicked at her brother. "Still got the stuff in one of your storage seats?"

"I do," replied Neil. "What do you say, Ashtyn? Join us for a little friendly competition in the park?"

An hour at the park playing "Beersbee," Ashtyn learned two things: that Neil must've grown up with one fun family, and two, that she was a natural at this drinking game. Drinking! In the middle of the afternoon!

Nothing about her life now echoed her old. And she liked it.

They stuck two PVC poles in the ground, five feet apart, topped with rubber stoppers to balance the beer bottles on top of them, and the opposing team had the same set up about twenty feet across the way. The objective was to try to knock the opposing team's bottles off the poles using the Frisbee, all while grasping a beer in one hand. A bit silly, and definitely juvenile, but fun nonetheless.

She was on Neil's team, who kept a respectable distance throughout the day, not touching her once, which was fine since they were in front of his sisters who watched them like hawks. She assumed he didn't want to show affection with Loni and Teresa there analyzing their every move.

She gazed at Neil's profile while he teasingly taunted Teresa about her poor aim, and a sting formed in her throat. He didn't want his sisters to analyze their relationship as anything more than what it was, and therefore kept his distance. Of course, she understood if that was the reason. Of course she did.

That didn't mean it didn't hurt.

Teresa missed the bottle and Neil hollered in triumph, meeting Ashtyn's eyes with a grin. She clapped at Teresa's misfortune and scooped the Frisbee from the ground. Even though she shook with emotion, she flicked the Frisbee perfectly, and knocked down the final bottle.

Neil laughed. The sisters groaned, hands to their knees in defeat.

He came over. "That's game! Twenty-one points, girls. Losers buy the winners dinner!"

"You just made that up. Those weren't the stakes when we started," Teresa complained with a smile.

"Had I known that, I would've tried a lot harder!" Loni cried.

"You know that was the best you had, sis," Neil threw back.

He grabbed Ashtyn's hand, pulled her in, and gave her a quick, hard kiss. "Thanks for playing, gorgeous. You're the best."

The smile he gave made her heart skip a beat, and blew her assumption he wanted to avoid affection in front of his siblings out of the water.

They went to Loni's favorite karaoke pub for dinner. After their meals, Loni and Neil took off to play darts for a few minutes. The both of them were too competitive to let the Beersbee game be the final say.

Teresa sat across from her and pulled up some photos on her phone to show Ashtyn some of her latest hairstyles. The girl had amazing talent in transforming her hair, and all in under ten minutes. Ashtyn praised her on her gift and success, and promised to subscribe to her channel immediately. Teresa put away her phone.

"So. Who's Neil's latest project?" she asked before taking a sip of her diet soda.

Startled by the question, Ashtyn's brows drew together. "Project?"

Teresa nodded and shrugged at the same time. "He always has one. Makes him feel less like a sell-out for going corporate."

"Are you talking about his pro bono work?"

His sister shook her head. "No, no, more like someone he's taken under his wing. I figured you'd know. He's always helping out someone when they're down on their luck or going through tough times." She flipped her hair off her shoulder. "He's been doing it since junior high school. Got it from our Dad. One time, Neil brought a kid from school home and said 'Trent doesn't know how to swim. I'm going to teach him so he can get girls' and then proceeded to show little Trent how to dive in our pool. Or he'd show up late for dinner and say 'Marsha's dog is missing. We're gonna make flyers and look around the neighborhood.' Stuff like that. And he still does once in a while. But you know, in a cool, adult way now." She grinned in the direction of her brother. "He has a radar. When someone's lonely, vulnerable, or in a bind, he can't stand it, and will bend over backwards to help them." Teresa beamed, as though trying to make her brother more appealing in Ashtyn's eyes.

"Er, I…can't think of anyone he's been spending much time with." *Other than me*, she stopped herself from adding. Then mentally froze. *Wait a second.*

A lump formed in Ashtyn's throat as she realized…*she* was Neil's project.

Vulnerable. Lonely. She was all those things at some point. Sexually voracious was the only caveat separate from the others. It was probably a bonus. A sickening feeling came over her, one she attempted to squelch from showing on her face. "Maybe it's me," she questioned in a low voice.

"Oh, you're no project." His sister smiled and covered her hand, seemingly unaware of Ashtyn's anxiety. "Ash, don't worry. He doesn't take on more than he can handle. He'll always make time for you."

How sweet of Teresa to assure her, but Ashtyn didn't know why the young woman felt compelled to. She had no clue she and Neil were barely more than sex buddies.

Loni plopped next to her. "Neil cheats."

"Neil wins," he countered, hands on hips. "I missed a call while I was destroying Loni at darts. You girls okay while I step out? Promise not to be more than—seven minutes."

Loni set her cell phone on the table. "Timing you."

He turned around and strode out of the noisy pub.

Teresa barely waited for Neil to get ten feet away before she leaned in, saying to her sister, "I haven't seen him like this since Juliet."

"Me either," Loni responded, eyes wide. She raised her hand to the ceiling. "There's hope!"

Unable to help herself, Ashtyn asked, "Juliet?" The name rang a bell, but she couldn't pinpoint how…

"You don't know—?" Loni started to ask.

"Neil's first love," Teresa blurted.

Ashtyn recalled the one, very brief conversation when Neil mentioned he'd had someone special in his life. "I think he's mentioned her before. Not in name, though. I could be wrong. I got the impression she was the 'one who got away.' Something like that?" The one he almost married but didn't marry for some unshared reason.

The middle sister took on an uncomfortable look. "You could say that."

Teresa, however, seemed anxious to spill the beans. "Oh go on Loni, just tell her. She should know about Juliet."

Loni looked over to the front door, then folded her hands together on the table. "All right. Once upon a time, our big brother was a straight-A making, hilarious, chubby, practical joker. I'm sure you can believe the joker part. The chubby part, well, we all blame our mother's baking. He and Juliet were in the same high school class. The personified beauty queen. She was pretty, made the honor roll, was sickeningly nice to everyone, and Neil and every other boy loved her. Eventually, he ditched the extra weight, grew a foot, and gained a lot more confidence. As you can imagine."

Ashtyn smiled.

"A few summers pass, and he's in college. Runs into Juliet at the fair and she's all over my brother like white on rice. They became a couple pretty quick. Once he graduated, she moved in with him when he started attending Stanford, and then she got a loan to open a bakery. Even with his insane course load and her starting a small business, they managed to keep their relationship going. We thought for sure they'd get married. It was *that* serious."

Oh, God. Bakery. Juliet. Now that whole scene from that day finally made sense. When Neil had asked her to go with him to the grand re-opening, there'd been a sadness in his tone, even though he'd acted nonchalant. And when he'd looked at the photo with "In Loving Memory" above it, naked emotion had been in his eyes—however briefly—but Ashtyn had assumed he simply knew her or had been friends with her. Not once did she think he'd loved the young woman in the picture, but now it was glaringly obvious. How did she *miss* that? More importantly, why didn't he tell her about Juliet? "Yes. I know who she is," she said softly, almost to herself. "She died."

Teresa nodded sadly. "Car accident."

Loni shooed her sister to be quiet. "He's coming back."

When Neil strolled toward the table, and Ashtyn had the compulsion to throw her arms around him and tell him how sorry she was. She couldn't imagine how much pain he'd been through. Here she thought this charming player wasn't capable of loving just one woman, but he had, with all his heart, and she could never, ever compete with that. Didn't want to try. Ashtyn's stomach sank, imagining a young, energetic, totally-in-love Neil in a committed relationship with this vibrant Juliet, only to have tragedy strike. No wonder he wouldn't elaborate when she'd asked for details about almost getting married.

Another past conversation between her and Neil came to mind.

"What if you miss the woman of your dreams because you're too busy avoiding the real thing?" she'd asked.

"I had the real thing," he'd clipped. "That only comes along once."

On the drive home, she remained quiet and introspective back to Neil's houseboat. She sat in the backseat and insisted one of the sisters sit up front with their brother.

They stayed long enough to share a bottle of wine with them, then they called for a cab.

While Neil was on the phone with the taxi driver guiding him to the marina, Teresa pulled her aside. "We know he's a ladies man, but he doesn't look at you the way he looks at most women. You're special." The girl's expression asked a silent 'Right?' but Ashtyn couldn't assure her of something she knew wasn't true.

"He and I were friends before we got together. So he's probably more open around me than others."

She didn't appear terribly convinced. "Hm. Maybe." Teresa hugged her. "So glad we met you!" Then Loni gave her a similarly tight squeeze before Neil informed them the cab was waiting for them in the parking lot.

After embracing his sisters, he closed the door behind them, then turned and lifted her on the counter. "You might as well spend the night. You've been drinking."

"I could take a cab like your sisters did and pick up my car in the morning."

"Stop being rational. I forbid it." He grinned, planting his hands on either side of her thighs. "You must've made quite the impression. My sisters would've never asked you to spend the whole day with us otherwise."

"Maybe they were just being nice."

"Ha! You don't know them well enough."

She cocked her head, tracing her fingertips down the side of his face. *And you don't know what I feel.* Her touch ignited him, and while he started to undress her, Ashtyn almost stopped him. Her emotions were high, her heart ached, and she was so in love with Neil, she didn't think it wise for her to make love to him and make this any harder for herself.

"Ashtyn," he moaned. "God, I want you so much."

Oh how could deny him? Why stop this? She needed this. One more time. To feel him, be with him.

As he worshipped her body, planting kisses on her breasts, she threaded her hands in his hair. "Not here. Upstairs," she whispered.

He yanked off his shirt, eyes heavy with desire, then followed her up the short flight to his bedroom.

25

NEIL SPENT MOST of his waking hours talking to people. To clients, partners, social workers, street vendors. Whoever for whatever.

This morning, he didn't know what to say to Ashtyn. No doubt his sisters overwhelmed her a little—they did that to everybody—but she got along with them way more than he'd hoped for. Something he didn't even know he'd hoped for because their visit was, albeit on his calendar, unplanned. Although she seemed uneasy at first, she held herself with grace and politely tried to make an exit.

He'd thought, now that she was there, why not see how she handled his sisters?

Luckily, Loni and Teresa were too nosy to let her leave.

They'd had a blast at the park and the pub, but afterward, she seemed… different. He couldn't put a finger on what it was. Still couldn't. So he did what he usually did when confused, tried to make her feel better with sex, going the extra mile to make sure her pleasure went on and on. She'd clung to him, begged for more, and roused him a second time to make love again.

Then she got up and brought a slice of cake his sister made and put the frosting to use.

He thought he'd worn her out, but he'd been wrong. She kept surprising him, which he knew was important in any romantic relationship. And not once, in this time with Ashtyn, did he even itch for another. Could he be falling in love?

She came down the stairs, putting on an earring, and he stared at her.

No. You can't do this to me, Ashtyn Turner. I wasn't supposed to fall in love.

Beautiful, vivacious, intelligent, sensual…she had it all. What man wouldn't want all that to himself for a while? Before evaluating if his feelings for her truly went to such a level, he needed a sign from her. Nothing major. Just a hint she felt more than lust for him too.

"There's something I think we should discuss," he told her before she could say a word.

Her blue eyes snapped up to his.

"We've had some fun, haven't we?" he asked, studying her very closely.

She looked at him for a moment before answering with a soft nod. "We have."

"Obviously I didn't plan on introducing you to my family, but I'm glad you were here." He leaned a hip on his counter.

"They're great. You're lucky to have a close relationship with your siblings."

"I know. If my mother had come with them, it would've been a full-on family reunion. Unfortunately, you've missing meeting my father. He passed away when I was twenty-two."

"I didn't know that. I'm sorry to hear it."

"I think you would've liked him. We were a lot alike. Might've been too much to handle with the two of us in one room at the same time, though." He crossed his arms, a smile growing on his mouth. "You're, uh, not into that are you? Meeting the family? Making long term plans? Being...more than casual?" *This is a test. This is only a test.* One blink from her, one look of surprise, and he'd know she felt *something*. Even the tiniest seed of hope could bloom given a drop of water.

She brightened with potent relief, pressing a hand to her chest. "Oh! Oh, good. I'm so glad you brought it up. That was fun, and I adore Loni and Teresa, but I got the feeling they were hoping I was going to be your girlfriend. Bless their hearts, but yeah, we both know you're *not* into that, and neither am I."

Disappointment exploded in his stomach, but he played it off. Holy shit, he hadn't predicted this. Would've bet the ranch she felt their connection, too. Especially after the lovemaking last night while she stoked all his desires, clung to him, passionate and inhibited in his arms.

Frankly, he was shocked he'd been wrong and didn't know how to react. He strove for nonchalance, even though his heart pounded, his palms sweated. "I was just checking in case you might have thought...that I, you know, things were starting to feel serious." Fuck. He couldn't even speak coherently now.

"Don't worry. It didn't even cross my mind." She smiled.

She seems too relieved. "Good." The words came out of his mouth before he gave them any thought. "It's refreshing to be honest with a woman who doesn't secretly hope for me to settle down."

"I'd be the last woman to expect you to change, Neil. I've known you for too long."

Maybe this thing they had should come to an end then. What was point? *The hot sex is the point,* his inner voice drawled, but he disagreed. If she wanted someone she could only use for sex, then he was no longer the man for her. "So you'd be cool if we took a break?"

Say no, Ashtyn. Show me you wouldn't like that at all. But he couldn't read her. Not like he could everyone else.

She didn't so much as flinch. More relief spelled in her pretty face. "I was going to suggest the same thing. Think it's time we called a time-out."

In God's name why? Had she already gotten her fill of him? He had to know. "Bored with me already?"

"No," she replied. "I just think...it's time to move on."

They stood facing each other in silence for a while. Here he had one of the best weekends all year, and that, apparently, was his last. He and Ashtyn had hit the end of the road.

It hurt like hell. So he wanted her out as soon as possible so he could get over it.

"Well," he said, eager to end this immediately. "If you ever, you know, want me, call me. Unless I'm busy, I'm good for it."

Her cheeks stained. "Like a booty call?" She picked up her bag and purse.

"Sure."

She bit her bottom lip, blinking, as though she didn't know what to say to that. "I don't think that's a smart idea. Going back to each other for sex. Even when it's convenient."

He shrugged. And couldn't agree more. "I was just putting that out there. We *are* quite good at it."

She pressed her lips together, attempting to smother a knowing smile. "We are."

Every step he took to the door got heavier and heavier. *Fight for her, damn it.* But he'd never been in this situation before, didn't know how to fight. They had a great few weeks, which was about average for him anyway. Combined with their week hanging out while she was on vacation, and the two weeks aching for her, he'd spent almost two months with Ashtyn. Way more time with one woman than he ever should. He turned the knob with that affirmation and opened the door.

"Caenon, I'll miss you," she said. "This time, can we...be friends?"

Back to using his last name again? Despite himself, a slow grin spread his lips. He brushed her chin. "Of course." By God, he'd miss her, too. Hopefully, for a very short period.

He yearned to kiss her. Taste and feel those lips on his. It'd be a stupid move. Even one final kiss good-bye could weaken him, make him beg her to change her mind. That was how powerful she really was, and she didn't even know it. "Take care."

"Don't wait too long like you did last time. To come by and see us at SFG."

"I won't," he lied.

Ashtyn was gone. Really gone this time.

The next day, he brought up his laptop on the upper deck to get some work done, but had made zero progress, his thoughts insisting on sulking over his loss of Ashtyn in his life. Again.

The phone rang. He wanted to ignore it, but it was his sister, Teresa. "Since you never check your personal email, I knew I had to call to invite you to the surprise birthday party for Loni."

"Sure." He clicked his pen and scribbled on his desk calendar.

"Bring Ashtyn."

He closed his eyes. "Sorry, can't. We just ended things."

"What? Less than twenty-four hours later and she's already gotten the boot? You're an idiot."

He guffawed at her statement. "Pardon?"

"You dumped her, didn't you? Why? Because she was clearly in love with you?"

Transferring the phone from one ear to the other, he frowned. "What are you talking about?" he asked with more curtness than he meant to.

His sister heaved a sound of frustration, as if she had to explain it to a child. "She's in love with you. Don't act like you don't know it's true."

"I don't have to *act* because it's *not* true," he said. "Look, the break-up or whatever was mutual. She wasn't interested in a long-term thing and neither was I."

"Liar. How do you know she wasn't?"

"She was relieved when I asked her if she wanted to take a break. Kind of gave it away. Said she sensed you were hoping she'd become my girlfriend, which was the last thing she wanted to be. So it's partly your fault. Thanks for scaring her off."

"Seriously?" There was a long pause. "I swear, big brother, we never said anything about her being your girlfriend. We more or less assumed from the way you two interacted she already was. Though, now that I think about it, she did get weird when I asked her about your 'latest project' and she'd joked that maybe it was her."

"You did what?" he said, realizing how big of a hole he was sinking into. "What do you mean, my latest project?"

"Okay so maybe 'project' is the wrong word. You know, people you like to help when they're down. I'd asked if there was anyone like that in your life, and she seemed to think it was *her*, but I quickly told her she was mistaken."

He pinched the bridge of his nose. "I can't believe you would ask something like that."

"I didn't think it was a big deal."

He checked the leg of a chair. "Well it doesn't matter now."

"Er…there's one other thing I might have mentioned."

He opened his eyes. "Tell me."

"Don't yell at me afterward, okay?"

A promise he'd had to make since she was little. "I won't."

"I might've mentioned Juliet."

He sat in his chair, and inhaled deep, staring at a spot on the wall. "What exactly did you tell her?"

"Well, uh, I might've been trying to reassure you wouldn't break her heart, because you'd been in love before, and—"

"Jesus Christ, Theresa."

"Just because you curse me in a calm voice doesn't make it any less like yelling," she admonished.

The puzzle pieces were beginning to come together. Now he knew what frightened Ashtyn away. "What else?"

"That you hadn't been happy with one woman since and we thought it was hopeless. Until we saw you with Ashtyn."

He'd be angrier if what Theresa said wasn't true. But it was all true.

"Is this the beginning of the silent treatment?" Theresa asked sardonically.

"No. I was just thinking."

"Thinking about giving Ashtyn a call?"

"Sis, I have to go. I'll see you at the surprise party."

She groaned. "Fine. Love ya."

"Love you, too." He hung up, drumming his fingers on the desk.

His sister telling Ashtyn about Juliet was probably what scared Ashtyn away. It was a heavy thing to put on a woman who wanted to keep things "light," having relatives mention lost love and tragedy and asserting Ashtyn was the reason he was happy again. He couldn't blame her for being ready to move on. If the roles were reversed, he would've bowed out as well.

And had she truly been in love with him, she would've protested. She would've stayed.

Besides, he didn't deserve a second chance in love.

He'd had it and thrown it away, and there was no doubt he wouldn't do it again.

26

"DANYER MAKDESI is here," the receptionist told Ashtyn, who had thrown herself into work for the past two weeks.

Moments later, Danyer walked into the executive office with a gentle smile, coat slung over one arm. "Logan is out for the day, I'm afraid."

"That's fine, because I'm here to see you."

"Oh?" She stood, unhooking the Bluetooth from her ear, too exhausted to guess why he was there to see her. "What can I do for you?"

"It's what you can do with me. Dinner. This weekend. It's been a long time since I've gone out to eat for the sake of pleasure and not business."

She froze, caught off guard while he smiled at her, patiently waiting for her answer. A dozen exclamation points popped up in her mind. *Say no. Say yes. I can't. I should. He's nice. He's not Neil. Exactly.* She cleared her throat to quiet the head noise. "You're asking me out on a date?"

"I am. As soon as we met, I knew I'd want to see you again. I know it isn't very appropriate to ask you while you're working, but I wanted to do this in person, in case you had forgotten who I was."

A small smile tugged her mouth. "I'm flattered. Is it because I gave you candy?"

He chuckled. "One-hundred percent."

Danyer Makdesi was exactly the kind of man she should go out with. Some melancholy part of her whispered she wasn't ready, but she ignored it. "I'd love to."

His grin was wide. "Saturday. Seven o'clock? I'll pick you up."

A little old fashioned, but it wasn't as though he was a complete stranger. Any friend of Logan's could probably be trusted. Her heart caught at the thought of Neil. Why was she still hung up on him? "Perfect. I'll text you my address." He gave her his number and left.

"Why am I still obsessing over this?" Ashtyn asked Lila over the phone hours later at home. "Neil and I were done—for good this time—over two weeks ago."

She couldn't stop thinking about the last time she saw him. She'd been so relieved he'd been the one to bring up a split, she'd ignored the burn of despair in her chest. The burn that had refused to go away. She had to talk to somebody or go insane.

Lila, of course, was her first choice.

Her friend mused, "Maybe because it ended on such a weirdly mature note. When you break things off, you expect drama and tears and slamming doors, but he'd just chucked you under your chin and told you to take care."

"Neil's too cool for drama. Besides there was nothing to get upset about. Clearly we both wanted to call things off. Him especially."

"Tell me again why you freaked out after his sisters left?"

"Because…" She opened her mouth to finish, but stopped. Wait. What was her reason? "Oh! Because I was just a project remember? Everything his sister described was exactly how Neil has been treating me. Helping someone who is in need. Defending me against that jerk Charlie Richmond, setting me up to beat the hell out of a Challenger—"

"Ha! My favorite."

"Spending the weekend with me. Bailing me out of *jail!*" She continued wearing a hole in her living room, pacing and seeking a solution to end her madness.

"Now that you've listed everything, it does sound like he's a knight in shining armor. But you speculate he did these gestures because you're a project?"

"Yes! Because I'm vulnerable, and alone, and starting over. He felt sorry for me."

"In conclusion, that was all due to pity. Pity help. Pity party. Pity fuck?"

"Lila!"

"Ashtyn," she mocked. "Men are simple creatures. He's sounds great, but no man does all these things out of their charitable little hearts. He must've done these things for a reason and not just because he has a soft spot for the pitiful."

"Well, he *was* getting laid in between."

"That's how this works. Men do things to make you happy and in turn, you make them happy. Simple creatures."

Ashtyn chewed on that thought. "I don't know if I made him *happy* but we did have fun together."

"Lord, give me strength! Do I have to scream it over the phone? The man wanted to be with you, Ash. You're so smart, but this is really flying right over your head."

"Oh really? If he wanted to be with me why did he ask to take a break?"

"Beats me! I'm just a third party observer here. You two are doing a serious secret tango. He makes a move, you push. You make a move, he turns you away. That's the dance of love I guess."

"Love? Oh no. Now there you're wrong. I *thought* I was in love with him, but I'm pretty sure I was confusing lust with love."

"Did you? You don't think you could've genuinely fallen for this Disney prince? Weeks after you two part ways and you're still *whining* for him. Sounds a lot like love to me. If it was lust, you would've banged some guy from a bar by now."

"Can your uppity English in-laws hear you?" she teased, while her heart pounded. Was that her answer? She stopped pacing, and plopped on her living room sofa. "What if I did? Lila. What if I did really fall in love with him? I can't love him. He's totally unlovable. He goes through women like we go through lipgloss."

"He hasn't lately has he? I mean, when you two were together."

"Well, no, I guess not. He didn't have time. He was always hanging around me."

"See? *Wake up.* The writing's on the wall."

Neil? In love with her? Not possible. A man in love would've fought for her. Not suggested a break and let her walk out the door. "God knows what he's been up to since."

"Why don't you call him and ask?"

She flinched. "Uh, no. Not happening. Regardless of how I feel about Neil, we don't have a future. In any case, I have a date on Saturday. With someone who makes much more sense."

Lila gasped. "A date? I thought you weren't going to put yourself out there for a while."

"I'm not going to say no to a date just because I'm on the rebound. Danyer's nice."

"What's he like?"

"Smart. Successful. Very easy on the eyes."

"Those are your best adjectives? He sounds like Cliff. Snooze."

She sighed, staring in her fireplace, hoping this date would give her just the push to get over him. "Every man will be a snooze compared to Neil Caenon."

WALKING OUT of a deposition, Neil checked his voicemail.

A gruff, Southern-accented voice sounded on the message. "Caenon. It's Al. Call me."

Huh. Manager at one of the local pawn shops. Striding past Ingrid's desk, he told her not to let anyone disturb him until further notice. He returned the call as soon as he shut his door. "Al. How are you these days?"

"Can't complain. Listen, uh, I think I have something for you that might be of interest."

"Shoot."

"Guy came in this morning trying to sell off a pearl necklace."

Neil's heart skipped a beat. What were the chances they were Ashtyn's? "Go on."

"He knew what they were worth. The weasel wouldn't take my offer, and then I got to thinkin' they could be what you're lookin' for. They were antique, heavy, worth a minimum fifteen kay. Sound about right?"

"Yes." But he wouldn't get his hopes up.

"So I told 'im I knew a guy who'd probably pay double what I would and he got all excited and stuff. He'd only give his first name and a phone number though. I even wrote down a physical description for fun. I got it right here for ya."

"How much?"

"Eh, the usual."

He left the firm as soon as he could, stopped by the ATM, and headed to the pawnshop. Al had the information ready for him tucked in a book and Neil passed him an envelope of cash. On the way back, he made a few calls. His instinct told him this was what he'd been waiting for.

He drove out Ashtyn's old neighborhood, and walked to the neighbor's house. He rang the doorbell and a woman answered, kitchen towel in hand.

"Yes?"

"Good afternoon. Sorry to disturb you ma'am, may I speak to your husband Randy, please?"

"Sure. I'll get him. You are?"

"Neil Caenon. A friend of Ashtyn Turner's."

A man in his forties or so came to the door. "Can I help you?" He pulled the door shut.

"I've been hired by Ashtyn. She explained how when her belongings were put outside, you kept an eye on them for her."

He shrugged. "Sure. I mean, off and on. I'm not a security guard."

"She's missing some pretty significant pearls her grandmother gave her."

His face went sheet white. "Oh you're kidding. That's awful. No, no, that wasn't me though."

Guilty 100% percent. Neil's radar said so. "If you've pawned them, I want to know when and where before I press charges."

The man turned from white to crimson. "You have no proof!"

"Actually I do. I don't know if you're aware but the Turners have a camera set up by their garage. Cliff had it put there for Ashtyn's safety once he moved out." A bold-faced lie, but he was comfortable giving it.

Randy stepped down and looked over at the garage.

Of course there was no camera, but Neil knew he had the thief.

Neil kept his tone casual. "The evidence is pretty damning. Why else would I be here? Do you know what the penalty is for theft?"

Randy flicked him a glance, still staring at the garage, intent on seeing this camera for himself apparently. "It'd be a misdemeanor?"

"Correct...for merchandise under seven-thousand. However those pearls are worth over twenty-thousand. Minimum sentence is ten years."

The man went white. "Er, uh, what would happen if I gave them back? Would she still press charges?"

"Doubtful. But I can't guarantee it. I *can* guarantee she will once we hand over the camera evidence to the police." The important thing was to get the pearls back. Ashtyn could decide later what to do with her neighbor. "I'll wait while you go get them."

"How do I know this isn't some trick?" Randy asked, his voice shaky.

"If the police were involved, I wouldn't be here, and you could easily tell them you'd found the pearls and were safekeeping them for Ashtyn."

Ten long minutes later, Randy handed Neil a Walgreens bag. His wife probably had no idea what he'd done. Neil checked the bag. He'd have to have them appraised to make sure they were real, and not some fake substitute. But they looked and weighed heavy and he guessed they were indeed Ashtyn's precious pearls.

The man seemed almost happy to give them up. "Now get out of here."

Grinning from ear-to-ear, he strode back to his car, and checked his messages.

Ingrid left a voicemail about how Diana, Ritchie's mother, called and thanked him for the presents, which included a signed basketball by one of the Clipper's players, a jersey, and an invitation to take Ritchie and Carl to a game on Neil's dime. These were trivial gifts, and obviously meant to buy his way to their good graces, but hey, he was a lawyer, not a saint.

The next morning, sitting at his desk, Neil stared at the white box with the black ribbon he'd had made to carry her pearls. A Walgreens bag didn't cut it obviously.

The designer did a beautiful job, but his gaze wasn't fixated on it because it was attractive, but because it was his last link to Ashtyn. Of course he wanted to bring them to her, see the look on her face when she saw he'd recovered her necklace. Be her hero again.

Except using the pearls as an excuse to get her back was a desperate idea. She'd be happy and grateful, but it wouldn't change anything. Wouldn't change how she saw him. Wouldn't make him trustworthy boyfriend material. Besides, he wasn't even sure he could be the man she needed. Saying he was out of practice was an understatement.

He'd loved and been loved, but he'd taken it for granted. Instead of treating Juliet like she deserved, he'd focused on himself, and mocked her tears. Indeed, he'd achieved capturing the Homecoming queen, and once he had her, he didn't think he had to work for her love anymore. He drank, partied, gambled, and she always forgave him. By the time he got into law school and cleaned up his act, she was done with him. He loved her so much, but had wasted those years they had together, and just when she finally told him she'd had enough, she died.

He should've let her go long before that, but selfish as he was, he couldn't stand to lose.

Had he changed since then? Hard to say. Hard to self-evaluate yourself.

There was a knock on his door.

"Yeah?"

Mitch poked his head in. "You wanted to see me?"

"Come in. I have something important for you to do for me. In exchange, I'll take you for a drink at Tied Up."

He lit up at the offer. "No shit. Whatever it is, consider it done."

27

WHEN ASHTYN pulled up to her house, there was a young man sitting on her steps. He was wearing a suit and holding a white box.

Cautious, she got out of her car, hooking her purse on one arm. "Can I help you?"

The young man beamed her a big smile. "Ms. Turner, right?"

"Yes," she responded warily.

She meant to keep her distance, but he didn't seem to be aware of her guarded attitude—or was purposely ignoring it—as he strode straight toward her with an outstretched hand.

"Mitch." They shook hands and he kept direct eye contact. "Whoa. You're gorgeous."

Uh, yeah okay loverboy. "Sorry, Mitch, but who are you and what are you doing at my house?"

He thrust the box in her hands, grinning. "For you. Have a nice evening." With his thousand-watt smile, he went around her and walked away.

Huh? She swiveled on a heel, brows pinched together. What the heck was that?

When she got inside, she set the box on the counter and plucked the ribbon. The card inside simply read:

These belong to you.

Still puzzled, she lifted the tissue underneath and gasped in shock, hand flying to her chest. She took a step back, disbelieving her eyes.

It couldn't be them.

Heart thundering, she stepped toward them, transfixed. They glowed under her spotlighting, every flawless bead in place. She lifted the necklace and knew immediately they actually belonged to her. Tears flowed from her eyes.

How?

Who?

She dropped them in the box and scrambled to her door, flying it open and scurrying to the sidewalk. "Mitch?"

The guy was gone of course. Her only link to this amazing gift. Re-gift technically. She covered her mouth, smothering a giggle. Going back inside, she continued to stare at her pearls, elated beyond words.

The card gave nothing away. Neither did the box. Whoever sent them didn't want her to know.

She sat down, mind racing. If it was the thief, why would they return them? Remorse? And why would they bother using a fancy box and sending some twenty-something car salesman to deliver it?

It came anonymously for a reason. Had to be the thief.

Then again, how would they know her new address? A complete stranger off the street wouldn't know. Not very many did, unless they knew her personally. Then again, obtaining her home address wouldn't be too huge of a feat these days. All a person needed was $7 and access to the Internet for a background check.

Maybe she should be appreciative the pearls were back in her possession and let it go. After all, if it *was* the person who'd stolen them, did she really want to know who they were? If it by some chance turned out to be Cliff, was it worth finding out it'd been her ex all along? Although Neil had assured her it hadn't been, his liar radar might not be as awesome as he boasted.

Neil.

She closed her eyes and brushed a finger over the box's fine edge.

Could he all these weeks later still have found a way to recover them?

No. Impossible.

Right? He knew as much as she did. And there was no way if he *did* get these back for her somehow that he wouldn't take credit. That just wasn't Neil. He'd be the one on her stoop with that heart-stopping smile with the box in his hands. His ego would demand it.

She allowed the fantasy to form inside her imagination.

Neil at her door, those incredible green eyes smiling into hers, and him saying something like, "I have something for you you're going to thank me for. I'll take your body as compensation." Or something equally dirty and charming like that. Then he'd walk in, and she'd open the box, cry happy tears, and throw her arms around him. Their lips would meet. The passion would catch fire, and they'd move from her living room to her hall to her bedroom, undressing along the way. Naked and hungry for each other, they'd make love all night.

Her lips parted and a whimper escaped.

She *wished* it'd been Neil.

"CONGRATULATIONS."

Neil glanced over his shoulder from staring out his office window. "Thanks, Ingrid. Take the rest of the day off. You earned it."

She softly laughed. "It's six o'clock."

"Like I said." He tossed her a quick grin, but it disappeared when he faced the window again.

Usually after closing a million dollar deal he liked to celebrate. Not this time. Honestly, it wasn't him who'd won the settlement. It was the emotionally void, take-no-prisoners Neil Caenon who'd won. By now, that was practically on auto-pilot when it came to corporate litigation.

Winning the firm millions earned him a serious glance for senior partner, but it didn't make him feeling any goddamn better. Lonely and struggling to get past it. Pathetic, really. As promised, he took Mitch out for a drink after he'd delivered the pearls. The report had been brief. He'd given Ashtyn the box and bailed. Just imagining her reaction after opening it was enough. Knowing she had them again was enough.

A masculine clearing of a throat caught his attention.

"What is it?" Neil asked without turning to see who it was.

"Ingrid left. I'm announcing myself."

Neil glanced to see Logan in the doorway. "Hey. Come on in."

Caught off guard, Neil strove to disguise his mood, which partially lifted at the unexpected visit. Logan rarely just dropped by. "Here. Share a drink with me. I just closed on a multi-million dollar settlement." He moved toward his decanter set and poured two short glasses of vodka. Rather than sit across from Logan in his desk chair, he took the seat next to him, and handed over the glass. "It'll be at least another week before they think about firing me again."

Logan accepted it, watching him. "As if they ever would. Congrats."

"Thanks."

They raised their glasses. Logan came there for a reason and Neil couldn't guess what the hell for unless it was business related. "What's up?"

His friend stared at him as he brought the glass to his mouth. "You're both very good."

"Who? What are you talking about?" Neil smiled.

"You and Ashtyn. Impressively convincing. I knew you two had ended it, and I paid attention to see how it would affect you both. But it didn't. Ashtyn has been perfect at work and you're still the same old you. Nothing's changed."

Ignoring the burning in his stomach at the mention of her name, he raised a brow. "I told you there was nothing to worry about."

"And you were right. Which, oddly, now concerns me." A long pause settled between them, but Neil sensed Logan wasn't finished. Especially when his brows lowered and Logan huffed a dry laugh. "You moron."

That's the second time someone had called him stupid in the past month. "*I'm* a moron?"

"Yes. She's going out with Danyer Makdesi tomorrow tonight."

Danyer? Red-hot jealousy burned bright, and heat circled his collar, but he feigned indifference. "So what?" he said raspily.

"Do you care?"

He forced a chuckle, bringing the glass to his lips. More vodka. "I have zero interest in this topic. Danyer is a great guy. Perfect for her. In fact, I'm happy for them." He slowly loosened the tight fist he'd made. The thought of seeing them together, of Danyer making her laugh, romancing her, seducing her—

Throwing the crystal against the wall would feel so good right now.

Logan scrutinized him. "What happened, Neil? Between you and Ashtyn?"

"You already know. Why ask for details?" he drawled.

"Because you're both acting the same way as before, and that's not possible after how you acted while you were together. It was obvious you were in love. Much as you tried to play it off as a fling, it was anything but." He sat back. "I would've never noticed before Jordana came along, but now I have a real eye for it. When a woman loves a man, she can't hide it no matter what she does. And when you've known someone for as long as I've known you, you know the difference of what he looks like with a fling and what he looks like in love."

Neil snorted. "Yeah, okay, there must be a lull in business right now for *you* to whip out such fantasy bull. What's gotten into you?"

Logan crossed an ankle over a knee, swirling the liquid in the glass. "How come you haven't gone out with anyone since?"

"Didn't you just hear me five minutes ago? I've been busy working."

"Too busy for women? Come on, Caenon. Sell me another one."

Then he'd need more vodka. He rose from his seat to remedy that. "You're wasting your time. Why even bring this up?"

"Because I think she's the one for you." Logan stood and faced him. "Deny it all you want, but I know how you feel about her. How you've felt about her for years." He reached to set the glass down on the desk. "In my, uh, limited and admittedly cynical point of view, I thought when you looked at her, it was because you wanted to be between her legs."

"Don't talk about her legs."

Logan chuckled. "You couldn't stay away from her. Didn't matter that she was married or that she glared at you half the time. Or after I told you repeatedly to leave her alone. But you couldn't help it, and it wasn't until I knew what love was did I finally get it. You've always been in a little in love with her. Haven't you?"

Times, they have changed. He never thought he would ever have to endure this kind of conversation with Logan. Never. Proved how much influence his friend's relationship-now-marriage had really transformed him. If this new state of mind of Logan's was focusing on someone else's love life, Neil would drink to it. Instead, he drank to stall any response.

"Neil." Logan waited. "Don't bullshit."

Unable to stand the inquiry any longer, he gave up. "All right! Fuck. You got me. I love her." He held up his arms. "So I can barely breathe without her. So what? I don't want that kind of love in my life. I don't want to want a woman so badly I can't think straight. It sucks the life out of you. I'm a fucking mess and I hate it. But look at me. Handling it like a pro. I'm so damn good at it I even had you fooled for a while. And by the way, I love my life just the way it is."

Logan eyes crinkled, but he didn't smile. "I did too, but we're not robots. Everyone has a someone. Making her happy makes you happy. *She's* your someone."

"Being responsible for someone else's happiness long term isn't my thing. I'd screw it up."

"That's a given. I screw up all the time with Jordana, but she continues to love me anyway."

"Savant, I had that with Juliet and I blew it. You don't have the kind of baggage I do. The timing couldn't have been more perfect for you and Jordana. Fate brought her to you. You guys were meant for each other from the start, but Ashtyn and I aren't like that. This time last year she practically frosted the glass when I walked in the room. We had a month of fun and ended it on a surprisingly civil note. Not every story ends like yours."

But Logan wouldn't let up. "Have you told her how you feel?"

Neil sighed deep. "No. And I don't plan to."

"Look. You might still lose her if you tell her, but you *definitely* will if you don't."

Neil threw back more vodka, his voice coming out hoarse after he swallowed. He flinched as it burned his throat. "She's going on a date, Logan. She's moved on."

"Scared you'll lose her like you did Juliet?"

If he could be honest with anyone, it was Logan. Besides, his friend knew when lied. "Yes. All right? I can't go through that again."

"So you'd rather rip your heart out of your chest beforehand? The Neil I know is fearless. He'd get Ashtyn back and love her with everything he's got. I know because I've seen it before. Yes, once upon a time you were young and stupid, but you need to fucking forgive yourself for what happened with Juliet. Give up the blame and start over with Ashtyn." He walked to the doorway. "Have you thought what you're putting her through by denying you two a real shot? You're not just torturing yourself, Neil. You're torturing her, too."

He frowned, staring at the floor. "I think you've said enough."

"I won't say another word about this again. I hate repeating myself." With a crooked smile, Logan left.

Shit.

The glass clanked on the table loudly as he set it down with a little too much force.

Tucking his hands in his pockets, he went back to staring out his window, back to brooding.

He wasn't the brooding type; that was always Logan's thing.

So he was in love with her, and according to Logan, she was in love with him. The last time he saw her, she was quite convincing in looking the opposite of being in love. Then again, when it came to Ashtyn, his success rate in gauging her emotions was below zero. Maybe he should lay it all on the line and try to steal her heart.

Because if she loved him, and he was lost without her...

Then what the hell were they doing apart?

28

THE DATE with Danyer had been planned to perfection. Drinks at an upscale cocktail lounge, reservations for dinner at a five-star steakhouse, and box seats for the symphony. Who wouldn't be excited for an evening like that with a man like Danyer? While Ashtyn wasn't outright dreading it, her enthusiasm was definitely…lacking.

Nevertheless, she determined to enjoy herself. She wore a black lace dress with a nude underlay, her hair up, and at the last second, put on her pearls, when she heard her doorbell ring. Danyer picked her up right on time, sharp and debonair in his dark suit and silver tie.

Over drinks, they shared their respective fact sheets. Where they were from, went to school, what brought them to San Francisco. Danyer had led a full life, but the way he told her about himself came across rehearsed, as though he'd told every woman the exact same spiel a thousand times. She realized they were both being polite and enjoying each other's company, but there was no real spark. No palpable chemistry. He didn't look at her the way Neil had, and even though she swore to herself she wouldn't compare the two, she did anyway.

Perhaps some men weren't as bold about their attraction like others, but there was no banked desire in Danyer's eyes. There was no tingling at his nearness or thrill at his touch when his hand brushed hers in the car.

Neil had ruined her.

She *needed* the heat, the spontaneous reaction, the sexual tension she'd so often had to stifle around the lawyer. The kind that made her squirm, made her work to breathe.

Sitting across from Danyer, she was able to hold her poise effortlessly. That should be a good thing—a great thing—but to her, it meant she and Mr. Makdesi would never be more than friends.

Regret laced her stomach. Accepting this date was a desperate mistake.

While Danyer ordered a bottle of expensive red wine, she debated just how she was going to end this without him thinking she was a loony bitch.

"Is that fine with you, Ashtyn?" he asked. "Chardonnay?"

She caught herself and cleared her throat. "Yes. Sounds good."

Oblivious to the anguish inside her, Danyer murmured to the server, then handed back the wine list.

She swallowed her anxiety. "Danyer. There's something I should tell you—"

"Hold that thought." He reached in his pocket, pulled out his phone, and frowned at the display. "I have my cell set on priority calls only. It's my nephew. Do you mind…?"

"Of course not," she said with a smile of understanding, relieved for a few minutes to collect her thoughts.

"He tends to ramble before he gets to the point, so I might be a few minutes. Are you sure you're okay?"

"Yes!" She waved him off. "Please. I don't mind at all. Hurry before it goes to voicemail."

He smiled, then rose and strode away to take the call elsewhere.

The server swept over with a basket of breads and two wine glasses. She thanked him in a faraway tone, fiddling with her pearls. Fixing her gaze on a spot on the table, she grew uncharacteristically melancholy. She wasn't supposed to be here; Danyer deserved better…

Fingers brushed her shoulder and she gasped, lifting her gaze as Neil came around and smoothly slid in Danyer's seat, unbuttoning his jacket with one hand.

Her heart stopped for a moment before beginning to hammer a wild staccato. Their eyes locked and held for so long, it was if time stopped.

"You can't sit there," was the first thing that would come out of her mouth.

"You look beautiful," he said softly, shifting his gaze down for a second before meeting hers again. "You found your pearls."

"They found me." Her voice had barely been above a whisper. It *had* been Neil who'd recovered her necklace. She just knew it. "I…I'm on a date." She'd said it in a near-apologetic tone.

He gaze remained steady. "You sitting her alone is not a date."

Was this a coincidence or had he shown up here on purpose? Knowing how adept Neil was at retrieving information, she wouldn't be surprised if he'd tracked her down here. But why?

"He'll come back soon," she told him.

"I'll go. But not until I tell you something." He rested his forearm on the table, casual as a cat.

"Can it wait?"

"No."

She looked around, not seeing Danyer anywhere, and despite herself, was curious what he had to say that couldn't possibly wait. "What is it?"

His mouth quirked. "First of all, you were never a 'project' to me. What my sisters called my 'latest projects' when I was younger is what we adults call friends. So forgive Teresa for putting it in your head I was only with you out of pity. I spent all that time with you because I wanted to be close to you. That's all I've ever wanted."

The air had changed. He was making it hard to breathe. She almost welcomed the shortness of breath. "Neil," she said worriedly, "Danyer will be back any second—"

"I'm not done. Do you know why I live in the Bay?"

She shook her head, throat tight with emotion.

"Because I like it." He folded his hands together. "I also like the smell of a bonfire, a newly tailored suit, raisins on oatmeal, making billion dollars deals before noon, and playing basketball. But do you know what I love?"

"Besides yourself?" she quipped.

He chuckled, shaking his head. "I love your sassy little responses to my questions. I love how you never put up with my shit. That I don't have to make you laugh or show you off in order to see you smile. I love when you're in my arms pretending to sleep long after you're awake. How when we made love, you never held back."

Two quick breaths escaped before she could stop them, sensing what he was about to add to this list. "Neil—"

"I love you." He held her gaze for long seconds. "I've fallen in love with you, Ashtyn. And part of the reason why is because I love *us*. The man I always wanted to be comes out when you're near. You're the one I want, the woman I need. You see, we're good together because we don't have to try. Everything else in my life, I have to slave and please and obey. I still have to do those things with you, but the difference is, I love it." He shrugged, swallowing visibly, his voice husky as he repeated, "I love you."

Shocked wasn't quite the word that held her immobile. Tears burned at the back of her eyes at his admission. She didn't know how to respond, what to think. He loved her?

"I know it might be too late," he added softly. "I should've told you how I felt that day when you told you me you wanted to move on. I should've fought for you. I'm sorry…" He searched her gaze, waiting for a response. "Say something," he said in a voice tinged with plea.

If only she could. She licked her dry lips, heart pounding, neck hot. "You can't do this to me," she half-whispered.

His mouth half-lifted. "Funny. That's what I thought the second I realized I was falling for you."

She searched his gaze. "What do you expect me to do?"

"Come with me. If you feel like I do, then you'll come with me."

Of course that was what he wanted. He wouldn't wait for her or give her time. "I can't."

He lowered his gaze, defeated, clenching his jaw. She loved him so much in that moment. He'd poured his heart out, and thought he lost, ready to accept it because he assumed she didn't feel the same.

"Caenon," said Danyer, startling them both as he came from behind her, breaking the moment. "Here for dinner as well? I'm looking forward to our meeting next week."

Neil stood and shook Danyer's hand, replacing his expression with a congenial mask. "I just came by for a quick drink. Next week. Yes. Looking forward to it."

Danyer looked from Neil to Ashtyn. "You and Ms. Turner are acquainted I take it?"

"Yes. Gotta run unfortunately. Say hello to your mom for me," Neil said, slapping the man's arm with a grin. He stopped by her side, but she refused to meet his eyes. "Good-bye Ashtyn."

She turned her head and watched him walk out.

Danyer sat down, studying her for a moment before picking up the menu.

Why was it so hard to believe Neil was the love of her life? Because she used to dislike him? Because of his past? Because of her failed marriage? Using those as reasons wasn't altogether fair, but how could she trust her own judgment, let alone trust Neil?

She lifted her gaze to Danyer while he perused the menu.

Men like him were safe. She didn't know him very well at all, but he didn't seem like the type who would demand much from her. Wouldn't challenge her or inspire her either. Or bring her to an ecstasy that would make her weep. Even if he could do all those things, she didn't want to find out.

The past weeks she'd spent with Neil flashed like a mental slideshow. How he'd been there for her. The things he said, done for her. To her. With her. How unexpected and untimely, falling in love with the presumably unlovable attorney. She cherished their bond, too. Their relationship came easy, it was the unknown that was hard. But if she didn't go to him now, then he might let her go forever.

"Danyer."

Her date looked up, realization in his eyes. "You and Caenon have a history, don't you?"

"How did you know?"

"You just told me." He sat back. "And when I walked back in the room, I saw the way he looked at you before he noticed my presence."

She shook her head. "I'm so sorry. I said yes to going out with you and I shouldn't have. Staying would be a mistake, even though you're a wonderful man. Please don't think I was playing any game. I just…I thought I knew what I wanted. Actually, what I *didn't* want. I was wrong."

He gave her a sympathetic smile. "It's okay. I know when a woman is playing games and you're not one of those. You should go after him."

"Really?"

He chuckled. "Of course. I won't keep you hostage. Wouldn't be the first time I lost a girl to Neil Caenon, but it will be the last. I can see that."

She got up and went to kiss his cheek, hearing him murmur "good luck" when she turned away.

She made a beeline for the coat check and then rushed outside. She spotted Neil not far down the block, head down.

"Neil!"

He stopped and turned.

There was no sign of satisfaction on his face that she'd clearly ditched her date. No smugness or expression of triumph. The only thing she saw in his beautiful eyes was hope.

"It won't last," she blurted when she caught up, out of breath, her heart in her throat. "No matter how good your intentions are, nothing good lasts forever. I know. I tried."

He stuffed his hands in his pockets. "You haven't tried it with me."

She smiled, lips quivering. *So cocky.* And so right. "Are you sure it's me you want?"

"I already gave you an answer inside that restaurant. And now I want yours."

She gestured helplessly. "I think skipping out in the middle of a date and running after you in the street should say it all."

"It doesn't. If you can't say it, then you don't feel it." He turned to walk away.

"I love you," she called, and he stopped. "I do. I tried to deny it, and my love just got deeper." When he faced her, she took a step forward. "You make me feel alive again. I can be myself and you like it, encourage it. Beneath your designer suits and double innuendos, you have a heart bigger than *anyone* knows. I love how generous and kind you are when no one is looking. How whenever you're near, I know things are going to be okay. I'm so in love with you, Neil Caenon—"

He shoved his hands in her hair and kissed her. She parted her lips and clung to him as he deepened the kiss. He pressed kisses along her cheek, to her ear, drawing her against his body. "Say it again."

She smiled, then let out a sigh. "I love you."

He locked his arms around her waist, picked her up, and turned her around once, making her laugh.

Shaking his head, staring in her eyes, he said, "You know at some point you're going to regret telling me that. I guarantee there will be times I'm going to disappoint you, piss you off, and do things that will shock you."

She arched a brow. "Such as?"

"I'll work too much. For my corporate job and my pro bono cases. I'll get lost in them for days and forget to text you. I might forget we have tickets to a concert. I'll make inappropriate remarks at parties, and put people in their place when they deserve it. I'll touch you *constantly* to show every man in the room that you're mine."

She sighed, a smile moving her lips. "Don't you get it, Neil?" She wound her arms around his neck. "Those things will make me love you more. Except for the part about missing this future concert."

He chuckled, tracing his gaze over her features.

Caressing his nape, she had to upfront herself. "There will be times I'll lose trust, simply because it's been broken so many times, and you'll have to remind me not to compare you to Cliff. I'll go to the concert without you if I really want to go, but will expect flowers as an apology in the morning. I'll work long hours with Logan and won't put up with any 'him or me' ultimatums. Got it?"

He kissed her as an answer. Oh, he got it, all right.

Eventually they came up for air, and Ashtyn felt like she was floating on it. She linked her arm in his and lay her head on his shoulder as they walked toward the parking garage.

"I've probably lost a million dollar retainer interrupting your date," Neil said, a smile in his voice. "No doubt Makdesi is calling our rival law firm right this second."

She chuckled. "He wasn't that mad, actually."

"Ha! I'll never hear the end of it." He looked down at her. "I can't believe you went out on a date with him."

"I said yes without thinking. I wanted to get over you quickly. Besides, he's a catch. I'm sure he won't be lonely for long."

"You don't know Danyer."

"Oh?" She looked up to meet his gaze. "He's not like you? The quintessential ladies' man? Sure looks like one."

"I'll ignore that," he drawled, and she laughed again. "No, Danyer doesn't play the field. At least he hasn't since I've known him. He's way more discriminatory with who he spends time with. Calling him picky is an understatement."

"Oh? Then I'm flattered."

"Eh. You're not that special. He's got a thing for blondes." He kissed the top of her head.

She elbowed him in the ribs, then slipped her hand in his.

"About Juliet," he said, breaking the silence. He stopped and brushed strands away from her cheek. "You should know about my past with her."

She nodded, and they resumed their walk.

"She was my first serious crush. When I saw her in ninth grade, I had it bad," he began. "Then I grew up, went to college, and ran into her again when I went home to visit my family. I met her at the fair every day. I must've spent half my summer earnings buying her cotton candy, trying to impress her with those stupid games, and riding every damn ride she wanted."

"No wonder you hate fairs," she teased him.

"I don't hate them, but yeah, going to one always reminded me of her. But now, all I'll think about is you and me and that perfect day."

She smiled up at him.

"She finally agreed to go out with me after that. I was almost done with college by then, and getting more serious about my grades to get into a top tier law school. I got in to Stanford, she moved there with me, and things started to change. *We* changed. I ignored our relationship and focused all my attention on my studies, the parties, and gambling. I played poker to pay some of my tuition. Sometimes until one hour before I had to go to class."

"You're kidding. That's so risky." One day, she'd have to hear more about that.

"I know. I couldn't work full-time and go to law school at the same time, so I did what I did best. Poker is just reading people, and until you, I was pretty damn good at it. I loved Juliet, but I loved myself more, and she knew it. She and I put on cheerful faces for our friends and family, but it wasn't working out. When she brought up opening the bakery, I encouraged her more than anyone. I wanted her to have some happiness of her own, and I knew that wasn't coming from me. I helped her with the legal things, but after a while, we were becoming more roommates than lovers." He sighed. "Then one day she told me she wanted to see other people. I was upset, but I wasn't shocked." He visibly swallowed. "Less than a week later, she got in an accident and fell in a coma. We all prayed she'd wake up, but she didn't. Doctors declared her brain dead, and soon after her parents signed to have her taken off life support."

The weight of the story tugged at her compassion for Juliet's family. "Oh my God."

"Her parents needed my help. They had no idea we'd been broken up. They thought we were practically engaged. It was clear she hadn't told them, and I just couldn't add to their grief that we weren't anywhere near engagement. I thought it'd be heartless. Needless to say, I was a wreck for months. Angry with myself that I hadn't worked harder to make things work in those last days she was alive."

"You were young. How could you know? Think of all you've done to help her parents since then."

"Everyone wants to blame my age, but I wasn't *that* young, and it doesn't make up for how I treated Juliet."

"And if you'd been a better boyfriend? A perfect boyfriend? Would that have alleviated your grief any more, Neil?"

They walked half a block before he answered. "No."

"From what I hear, Juliet loved you, but it sounds like she was strong enough to put herself first when you didn't. Unfortunately, her life was cut way too short, Neil. I think a lot of your guilt comes from the injustice of that, too."

He stopped, brows lowering, and Ashtyn knew she'd struck a chord. No, she couldn't make the remorse go away, and didn't need to because that was *his* to process, just as her divorce was hers, but she could help him see things from a different view.

"I think you're right," he murmured. Turning to her, he lifted his gaze, and pressed a soft kiss on her lips, then tugged her hand to keep walking. "I'm glad my sisters told you about her, but why didn't ask me about her afterward?"

She considered her answer. "Well, to be frank, I didn't think I could compete with Juliet. I'd only realized I was in love with you that morning and—"

"What? That morning?" He squeezed her hand tight. "Why not tell me?"

"Come on, Neil. You didn't tell me either. I didn't trust it. And you were so cavalier about breaking up, I thought if I did tell you I was falling in love with you, then I'd just make it worse. When your sisters told me about Juliet, I thought…there's no way I can compete with that. Last year, when you'd accosted me in Logan's library, you'd said you'd had the woman of your dreams, and that you only thought she came along once."

He nodded. "I remember that. And I thought it was true. For so long, I thought love wouldn't come around a second time. That I was at my best as-is. Caring about myself, my family, my friends, my job. I was a complete man. Then I met you." They arrived at his car, and he set his hands at her waist, and gently pushed her up against it. "Ashtyn…a part of me has loved you since we met. I was drawn to you, and with you married to someone else, I thought fate was being cruel. Showing me a woman I would always want and never have. The way I see it, Cliff served his purpose by bringing you to me. You need to be loved by me," he said gently, skimming his fingertips down the side of her face. "And I definitely need to be loved by you."

So much love between them, but still so new, and overwhelming. She'd hold on as tight as she could, for as long as he did. She shrugged, emotion closing her voice. "I didn't know. I didn't know the next man I'd love was smiling at me and teasing me every week for the past four years."

"It's all right, baby, now we've got each other, and God willing, all the time we need. You can trust I'll screw up at times, but you can also trust how I feel."

She smoothed her hands up and down his chest. "It was you, wasn't it? The one who found my pearls."

His mouth curved, and he kissed her cheek. "Yes."

"I knew it! But then I thought if it *had* been you, then you would've brought them to me yourself." She shook her head, gazing at him in awe. "I didn't think you'd be able to give them back without taking credit."

"Finding them," he said as he floated his fingers along the pearls, "was what was most important, not taking credit."

She wrapped her arms around him and pulled him in. "Just when I think I know you so well, you do something to surprise me."

"Don't get me wrong gorgeous, the first thing I wanted to do was stand on your doorstep so I could see the look on your face. I imagined you'd be so grateful, we'd make love, and then you'd let me in your life again… what's so funny?" he asked at her giggle.

"That's exactly what I fantasized about, too."

He slowly grinned, brushing the hair from her cheek. "See? I think that's a good sign we're made for each other."

She kissed his lips. "I think it is." Searching his gaze, she asked, "Can you read me again?"

"Loving you doesn't make that any easier," he teased, feigning a serious analysis of her face. "Let's see…you're wildly in love with me. You can't wait to get to your place so you can tear off my clothes and make mad, passionate love to me on your sofa, floor, and kitchen counter." While she laughed, he added, "You're afraid I'm going to break your heart, but it's more likely you'll break mine, because you know you're a little too good for me—"

"Neil."

"You told me to read you. I see what I see."

Brushing her lips over his, she whispered, "What else do you see?"

"That I'm going to love you…as *hard* and *long* as you'll let me." He chuckled at his double entendre, and she lightly hit his shoulder, shaking her head.

"I hope that part of you *never* changes, Neil Caenon. Now, tell me how on earth you got my pearls back. I have to know."

Reaching in his pocket, he pressed the remote and unlocked the car. "Get in. I'll tell you all about it, but right now I want to get you home so I can get you in bed. I can talk all night in there, too. How's that sound?"

"Like I won't want to leave."

Smiling, he kissed her, and pressed his forehead to hers. "And I hope you never do."

Epilogue

Six months later...

ASHTYN COULD hear the fire of the tiki torches blowing against the night's wind outside their villa.

She and Neil were in the Caribbean on a ten-day vacation. It was early December, and to escape the drizzly cold of San Francisco, they headed to a more tropical locale to begin celebrating their first holiday season together.

They had both needed and earned it. Between the both of them working long hours, committing themselves to social events, Neil's volunteer-coaching, and her new appointment as head of a local charity, there was very little free time to laze about and be a couple, uninterrupted.

They were three days in to their getaway, and so far, they hadn't ventured beyond their overwater bungalow. After they had arrived, they slept in, made love, ordered food, made love again, went for a dip, took a nap, and repeated the same pattern for two more days. That was the itinerary so far. Ashtyn had jokingly pointed out they could've stayed home to accomplish naps and sex, and Neil swore they would go on an adventure, starting tomorrow.

Right now, they were content lying on their backs on the floor, grabbing grapes from a bowl between them. Both were naked but haphazardly wrapped in bed sheets. Neil read the brochure, and Ashtyn listened while he mentioned ambitious adventures like zip-lining and scuba diving, his enthusiasm rising in his voice with each suggestion.

He was her best friend and lover and she couldn't imagine life without him.

It'd been a whirlwind six months so far and she'd never had so much fun or been so in love. They had their arguments—usually over trifle things most couples argued about—but neither of them intended to let go. Their kind of love had a balance and honesty she'd never known before, and sometimes more excitement than she could handle, but she wouldn't have it any other way.

She looked over at Neil, beginning to smile at the thought.

Dragging his gaze from the brochure, he met hers. "There's nothing in here about swimming in the nude."

She chuckled, popping a grape in her mouth. "We have to get dressed sometime. One of these nights I want to dress up and go out to dinner instead of ordering in."

"You don't need an excuse to dress up," he told her flippantly. "We can pick coconuts off trees in a tux and a gown if you want to."

She giggled, imagining the scene.

"Hmm." He set his gaze back to the brochure. "Speaking of dressing up, guess what else they offer."

"Archery?"

His chuckle shook his chest. "No."

"Bingo?" she said with exaggerated exclaim. "I love bingo."

"No, sweetheart. Weddings. Everything from the marriage license to the champagne," he told her matter-of-factly.

Why would he mention that? Her heart tripped. "Is that so?" She kept her tone even.

"They do it all. Right here at the resort. You only have to be on the island three days before the actual wedding date."

Her heartbeat began to gallop at a high rate, disbelieving how the conversation had blindly flipped from zip-lining to possible vow-making. She bit her bottom lip. "Neil…"

He lowered the brochure. His green eyes searched hers as he softly asked, "What do you think? Marry me?"

Suddenly out of breath, Ashtyn sat up, holding the sheet to her chest.

That was unexpected.

Beyond unexpected, and therefore perhaps said in jest. But he wasn't kidding. By his tone and the look in his eyes, this was no joke. Indeed, she knew when he was kidding and when he was serious, and although the former happened far more than the latter, she didn't see any mirth behind his eyes.

Silence settled around them, the air heavy with her shock and his waiting for a response.

"I'm sorry," Neil said tenderly as he sat up. He pressed a kiss on her shoulder, nuzzling her skin with his nose. "That really wasn't how I wanted to ask."

"I can't believe you just did," she choked out. Just to be sure, she asked, "You're serious?"

"Of course I am." He guided her chin with his hand so she would look at him. "Ashtyn, I love you. So much. When I look at you, all I see is me loving you for the rest of my life. I want to make you mine."

"I *am* yours."

"Officially. I want the world to know I'm your husband. I want to introduce you as my wife." He smoothed a tendril from her cheek. "Tell me what you're thinking. You know I can't read you."

She sighed. "It's a little fast, isn't it? Not that long ago, you were the number one advocate for not getting married."

"That was until I fell in love with you."

Something inside her melted at that simple explanation. She searched his gaze. "How long have you been thinking about this?"

"Since July."

She gasped. "That long?" They were barely a couple in July.

"I knew it was too soon for you. I wanted to give you more time."

"But now you want me to make a decision on the spot and marry you tomorrow?"

He shrugged, undeterred by her incredulous tone. "Why not? We're here. It's just us. Let's elope."

It was utterly, romantically spontaneous and totally Neil. She loved him with all her heart and then some, but could she marry him? She'd thought she loved her ex-husband too when they got married. Look how that turned out five years later. And there had been nothing shocking or spontaneous about that union. "Neil...I just don't know." Climbing to her feet, she tucked the sheets under arms and walked toward the window looking out to the ocean.

He came up beside her, leaning a shoulder on the window frame. "Talk to me, Ashtyn."

One of the reasons she loved Neil was his insistence they remain frank with each other, when her ex would've walked away and let her think. Fiddling with the sheet, she finally raised her gaze to his. "Don't you think we should move in together before we jump in a big commitment? *The* commitment?"

In typical Neil fashion, he answered her with a simple, "Nope. I think we can skip all that."

This was so different than her first experience. She and her ex had planned everything out almost like a business plan. They dated thirteen months, then signed a lease to share an apartment. A year later, they went together to buy her ring, and a year after that, they were married. Then they bought the house, invested their money, and on and on. With Neil, she'd be jumping from girlfriend to wife with no small transitions in between. No discussion about where they would live or what their future goals would be as a married couple, nothing. Quite the leap.

Thing was, she actually already knew those things.

Now that she really thought about it, they'd talked about them on a constant basis for the past few months, she just realized. No in-depth or intense conversations, but little ones over dinner or in the car. Because his sly conversational skills were a true art form, he'd asked serious questions with such casualty, it didn't occur to her until now he'd been prepping for this "spontaneous" proposal for a while.

The night they got back together—the night she'd run out on Danyer—while she used his phone to search for something on Google, she'd found a "black book" category in his phone contacts, obviously created for all of the women in his life before her. She had joked he wasn't *that* in love with her if he still had it. Seconds later, he took the phone and deleted the category without flinching.

She'd assumed he'd asked if she liked children because he'd invited her to join him and his basketball kids for pizza, and didn't want her to be uncomfortable. Then he'd asked if she wanted any kids, and she'd told him some day she would. In turn he'd made a sweet remark about how beautiful she'd look pregnant.

The time Logan thought about taking her with him to Hong Kong for two months, she assumed Neil was just being silly when he'd said they should be engaged, so everyone would know she was taken while they were apart.

Had Neil been edging her toward this moment this entire time?

Bottom line was, she just wanted to be with him. Forever. That was it. The rest could work itself out. Right? Or was she just being gullible again? She gazed out the window, unable to believe she was considering marriage less than a year since her divorce.

"Are you worried about the logistics?" he asked, lacing his fingers in hers. "Look, you *own* me. We can live wherever you want. My place, your place, a new place. I don't care. Joint bank accounts, separate ones, doesn't matter to me."

Her mouth twitched. "I was just thinking the same thing."

"See? Come on, let's do it. I love you."

Turned out, Luna the palm reader was actually inaccurate; it didn't take much to persuade Ashtyn into marrying again. All Neil had to do was ask. "And I love you." She wrapped her arms around his neck and kissed him deeply. There was nothing else to think about. "But you've never been married, Neil. Don't you want the big ceremony with your sisters and your mom there? Your friends? With Logan as your best man?"

"Nah. I just want it to be us for this part. We can throw a big reception with all the speeches and fanfare when we get home." He searched her features. "Is that a yes?"

"Oh, yes."

"You're trembling, baby."

"I'm nervous. And suddenly, I can't wait." She laughed and tipped her head back. "I can't believe I'm going to be Mrs. Ashtyn Caenon."

He grinned, spreading his hands on her back. "Damn. I like the sound of that. Think you can handle having that last name?"

"I like to think I was meant to handle that last name."

With deep love in his eyes, he cupped her face. "I'll be good to you. It may take me a minute to figure out the husband thing, but I already know I blow your mind in the kitchen and in the bedroom, so I'm already ahead of the game."

"Oh you blow my mind, do you?"

"Isn't that why you scream my name every night?" He cocked his head.

"Does your ego have no limits?" she grinned.

"You'll just have to spend the rest of your life with me to find out," he drawled.

Yes, she thought as he started unraveling the sheet from her body, yes she would.

THE PRICELESS COLLECTION

DIAMONDS & DESIRE

PEARLS & PERSUASION

LOVERS BY CHRISTMAS

RUBIES & RAPTURE ~ *Coming 2016*

BE SCANDALOUS WITH ANGELITA ONLINE:

Website .... www.angelitagill.com

Facebook .... www.fb.com/angelita/authorofpassion

Twitter .... @Underawildsky

Email .... author@angelitagill.com

About the Author

Angelita has an obsession with romance stories and feeds it on the daily. She writes contemporary, paranormal, and fantasy romance, and loves to read historical. If she could travel back in time, she'd attend a ball in Regency England in a fabulously wicked red gown, dancing with the most handsome rogue in the room. This shameless romantic adores a good scandal, chocolate martinis, pin up couture, true crime documentaries, and ballet. To her, reading romance is and should be a sensational escape, with visceral emotion, a dash of drama, and the coveted Happily Ever After. She loves to hear from readers and vows to keep on writing…even if there's a zombie apocalypse.

Made in the USA
Middletown, DE
21 August 2016